Ralph N. Wornum, Charles Lock Eastlake

Descriptive and Historical Catalogue of the Pictures in The National Gallery

SALZWASSER VERLAG

Ralph N. Wornum, Charles Lock Eastlake

Descriptive and Historical Catalogue of the Pictures in The National Gallery

Reprint of the original, first published in 1863.

1st Edition 2022 | ISBN: 978-3-37500-635-8

Verlag (Publisher): Salzwasser Verlag GmbH, Zeilweg 44, 60439 Frankfurt, Deutschland
Vertretungsberechtigt (Authorized to represent): E. Roepke, Zeilweg 44, 60439 Frankfurt, Deutschland
Druck (Print): Books on Demand GmbH, In de Tarpen 42, 22848 Norderstedt, Deutschland

DESCRIPTIVE AND HISTORICAL

CATALOGUE

OF THE

PICTURES

IN

THE NATIONAL GALLERY:

WITH

Biographical Notices of the Painters.

FOREIGN SCHOOLS.

BY

RALPH N. WORNUM.

REVISED BY SIR CHARLES LOCK EASTLAKE, P.R.A.

By Authority.

THIRTY-SEVENTH EDITION.

LONDON:

1865.

NOTICE.

In using this catalogue in the Gallery, reference should be made from the painter's name on the frame of the picture to the corresponding name at the head of the page in the catalogue, where the order is alphabetical. When more than one designation occurs, as for example, Sebastiano del Piombo, the name to be looked for in the catalogue may be found by referring to the number in the Index list, page 8, corresponding with the number of the picture. The same list may be consulted, if the name of the master on the picture-frame should not be easily legible.

The plan of the catalogue is historical, as well as descriptive. Biographical notices of the several painters precede, in most cases, the descriptions of their works: the history, as far as known, of each picture is also given; together with its dimensions, the material on which it is executed, and other details which may sometimes serve to identify it. Among the sources of information which have reference to the history of the art, the opinions of eminent critics on the merits of particular masters, and of remarkable works, have not been overlooked.

A certain degree of historical knowledge, as regards both the art itself and its criticism, is perhaps indispensable for the due appreciation of some works; the merit of which, depending on the time and circumstances of their production, is in a great measure relative. The information thus offered, without superseding individual predilections, may sometimes assist in the formation of a correct judgment, which is the basis of a correct taste.

The present catalogue is thus designed, not merely as a book of reference for visitors in the Gallery, but also as a guide to the history of painting, as represented by the examples in the collection: it may be used likewise, so far as it extends, as a Biographical Dictionary of Painters. The first edition, printed in 1846, was published in the beginning of 1847. To this edition are now first added the painters' monograms and signatures, engraved in wood, from copies in fac-simile made by me in October 1862. I have omitted some few, which are too obscure for reliable reproduction; most of them are of the size of the originals, the very large only have been reduced.

The Gallery is open to the public on Mondays, Tuesdays, Wednesdays, and Saturdays; and on Thursdays and Fridays to students only. It is open from *Ten* to *Five* from October until April 30, inclusive; and from *Ten* to *Six* from April until the middle of September. It is wholly closed during the month of October.

The Vernon Collection and other pictures of the British School are for the present exhibited at South Kensington. Of these a separate catalogue is published, which comprises also an account of the Turner Collection now exhibited in the Gallery, Trafalgar Square.

THE

NATIONAL GALLERY.

THE British National Gallery of Pictures was founded in 1824, during the administration of the Earl of Liverpool, by the purchase of the collection of the late John Julius Angerstein, Esq., which thus formed the nucleus of the present national collection.

The establishment of a National Gallery had long been desired, and His Majesty George IV. is said to have been the first * to suggest the propriety of purchasing the Angerstein collection. Sir George Beaumont, also, and the late Lord Dover, then the Hon. George Agar Ellis, took an active part towards the accomplishment of this object. Lord Dover first brought the subject before Parliament in 1823; † and Sir George Beaumont was so desirous to see a National Gallery established, that he offered to give his own pictures to the nation as soon as the Government should allot a proper place for their reception.

The Angerstein collection, consisting of thirty-eight pictures, ‡ was accordingly secured to the nation, and a grant of Parliament of 60,000*l.*, proposed by Government, was voted April 2, 1824, to defray the charge of purchase and the expense incidental to the preservation and public exhibition of the collection for that year—57,000*l.* for the pictures, and 3,000*l.* for the incidental expenses.§

* Hansard, *Parliamentary Debates*, speech of Sir C. Long, April 2, 1824.

† Hansard, *Parliamentary Debates*, July 1, 1823; Cunningham, *Lives of the most Eminent British Painters, &c.*; Sir George Beaumont, vol. vi.

‡ The entire collection was not included in the Government purchase; a few pictures were excepted. See the *Catalogue of the Pictures of J. J. Angerstein, Esq., with Historical and Biographical Notices*, by John Young, fol. 1823, which contains etchings of all the pictures.

§ Hansard, *Parliamentary Debates*, April 2, 1824; and the *Report from the Select Committee on National Monuments and Works of Art, with the Minutes of Evidence and Appendix*, 1841. Appendix.

A National Gallery was thus established. It was opened to the public, in the house of Mr. Angerstein, in Pall Mall, May 10, 1824. In 1826 the collection was increased by the munificent donation to the Trustees of the British Museum for the National Gallery, of sixteen pictures from Sir George Beaumont, as well as by further purchases on the part of the Government. In 1831 it was enriched by the valuable collection (consisting of thirty-five pictures) which was bequeathed to the Trustees of the British Museum, to be placed in the same building with the Angerstein pictures, by the Rev. William Holwell Carr;* and from that time to this, works have been constantly added to it, by donation, by bequest, and by Government purchase.

The principal donations and bequests, besides those already mentioned, are: six pictures presented in 1836 by William IV.; fifteen bequeathed, in 1838, by Lord Farnborough; eleven bequeathed, in 1846, by Richard Simmons, Esq.; eight bequeathed, in 1854, by Lord Colborne; twenty bequeathed, in 1859, by Jacob Bell, Esq.; and six presented at different times by the Governors of the British Institution. The "Corn Field," by John Constable, R.A., "Serena rescued by Sir Calepine," by William Hilton, R.A., and "Jerusalem," by Thomas Seddon, were purchased, by subscription, by the respective friends of the painters, from their executors, and presented by them to the National Gallery.

Of the 424 pictures which now constitute the national collection, exclusive of the Vernon and Turner pictures, 203 have been presented or bequeathed,† the remaining 221 have been purchased by Government, by grants of Parliament: the number of pictures in the National Gallery, including all the works of the British School, is now 686.‡

---

* The Farnborough bequest was also made to the Trustees of the British Museum for the National Gallery.

† Complete lists of the pictures purchased, as well as of donations and bequests, are given at the end of the Catalogue. The pictures of the British School are separately catalogued, and are at present exhibited at South Kensington.

‡ Of these, 88 are for the present removed from the walls owing to want of space. It may not be uninteresting to the reader to compare the number of pictures in the National Gallery, with the number, according to the published catalogues, in the several principal national collections in Europe. In Rome, in the gallery of the Vatican, there are only 87 pictures; in that of the Capitol there are 225; at the academy of Bologna there are about 280; the Brera of Milan has 503; at Turin there are 569; at Venice 668; at Naples, there are 700, exclusive of the ancient paintings from Pompeii and

The building in which the Collection—Foreign Schools—is at present deposited was erected at the national expense, expressly for the purpose, after a design by William Wilkins, R.A., architect. It was commenced in 1832, and was opened to the public April 9, 1838.*

Herculaneum; in the Städel Institution, at Frankfort, there are about 380; in the Berlin Gallery, recently established, there are about 1,350 pictures; in the Pinacothek, at Munich, there are about 1,270; in the gallery of the Belvedere, at Vienna, there are upwards of 1,300; in the Imperial Gallery of Florence (Degl' Uffizj), there are upwards of 1,200, and about 500 in the Pitti Palace. At Amsterdam, there are 386; at the Hague, in the Museum, there are 304. The collection of Antwerp contains 584 pictures; and at Brussels there are upwards of 400. There are upwards of 1,800 in the Louvre, 543 of which are Italian; in the Museo of the Prado, at Madrid, there are 1,833; and the celebrated gallery of Dresden contains about 2,000 pictures, exclusive of the pastel collection. At Versailles, there are about 3,300 works of art, chiefly paintings, and almost exclusively illustrative of French history. The Borghese Gallery at Rome, which is the best private collection in Europe, contains 526 pictures. In the Grosvenor Gallery there are 157; in the collection of the Duke of Sutherland, 328; in the Bridgewater Gallery, belonging to the Earl of Ellesmere, there are 318; and in that of Burghley House, Northamptonshire, belonging to the Marquis of Exeter, there are upwards of 600 pictures.

* The number of visitors to the National Gallery has, with one or two exceptions, annually increased from the date of its opening up to the present time. It has already been visited in a single year by upwards of 1,000,000 persons.—*See* the National Gallery *Reports*.

INDEX

TO THE NAMES OF THE MASTERS OF THE PICTURES IN THE NATIONAL GALLERY, FOREIGN SCHOOLS.

ARRANGED ACCORDING TO THE NUMBERS OF THE PICTURES.

THE SCHOOLS OF PAINTING.

THE word "school" has various significations with writers on art: in its general and widest sense it denotes all the painters of a given country, without special reference to time or sub-divisions of style; as, the Italian School. In a more restricted sense, it refers to the characteristic style which may distinguish the painters of a particular locality or period; as, the Bolognese School. In its most limited sense, it signifies the distinctive style of a particular master; as, the School of Raphael: whence it is also applied to the scholars or imitators of an individual, who are said to be *of the school* of such master.

In the following table, the word is used in its wider senses. With regard to the chronology there observed, it must be apparent that it is impossible to fix with precision the commencement of any school. There are isolated facts of very remote dates, connected with the history of painting in many countries; but such facts cannot be assumed to indicate the existence of a class of painters having a more or less common and definite style. It is only when such a class exists that a school can be said to be established; and when there is evidence of the practice of painting in a more limited degree, yet tending to such development, the school may be said to have commenced.

Tabular View of the Schools of Painting, as represented by the Pictures in the National Gallery.

TUSCAN OR FLORENTINE SCHOOL.

Commencement in the thirteenth century, in Florence, in Pisa, and in Siena.* Distinguished chiefly for form.

* The Sienese school may be considered to have a character of its own, but as it is represented, as yet, in the National Gallery, by unimportant specimens only, it is for the present comprehended in the Florentine school.

Thirteenth Century.

Margaritone D'Arezzo, 1236—1313. Cimabue, 1240, *living* 1302. Duccio di Buoninsegna, *painted* 1282—1339.

Fourteenth Century.

Segna di Buonaventura, *painted* 1305—1319.
Giotto, 1276—1336. Taddeo Gaddi, 1300—1366.
Andrea Orcagna, 1315—1376.
Jacopo di Casentino, *about* 1310—1390.
Spinello Aretino, *about* 1330, *living* 1408.

Fifteenth Century.

Fra Giovanni Angelico, 1387—1455. Paolo Uccello, 1396—1479. Masaccio, 1402—1428-9. Fra Filippo Lippi, 1412—1469. Benozzo Gozzoli, 1424, *living* 1485. Antonio Pollajuolo, 1430—1498. Domenico Ghirlandajo, 1449—1498. Cosimo Rosselli, 1439—1506. Sandro Botticelli, 1447—1515. Leonardo Da Vinci, 1452—1519. Filippino Lippi, 1460—1505. Lorenzo di Credi, 1459—1537.

Sixteenth Century.

Albertinelli, 1475—1520. Michelangelo, 1475—1564. Baldassare Peruzzi, 1481—1536. Andrea del Sarto, 1488—1530. Jacopo Pacchiarotto, 1474—1540. Jacopo da Pontormo, 1493—1558. Angelo Bronzino, 1502—1572. Salviati, 1510—1563.

Seventeenth Century.

Cristoforo Allori, 1577—1621.

UMBRIAN SCHOOL.

Commencement in the thirteenth century, in Assisi, Perugia, Gubbio, and other cities of Umbria. Distinguished for colour and sentiment.

Fifteenth Century.

Lorenzo di San Severino, *painted* 1416—
Pietro della Francesca, *about* 1415—1494.
Niccolo Alunno, *painted* from 1458 to 1499.
Pietro Perugino, 1446—1524.

Sixteenth Century.

Lo Spagna, *painted* 1503—1530.

SCHOOL OF THE ROMAGNA.

Marco Palmezzano, *about* 1456—1537.

ROMAN SCHOOL.

Established in the sixteenth century. Distinguished for form and expression.

Sixteenth Century.

Raphael, 1483—1520.
Giulio Romano, 1492—1546. Barocci, 1528—1612.

Seventeenth Century.

Michelangelo da Caravaggio, 1569—1609.*
Il Sassoferrato, 1605—1685. Carlo Maratti, 1625—1713.

Eighteenth Century.

Paolo Pannini, 1691—1764.

VENETIAN SCHOOL.

Commencement in the thirteenth century. Distinguished chiefly for colour.

Fifteenth Century.

Antonello da Messina, *about* 1414—1496.
Giovanni Bellini, 1426—1516.
Carlo Crivelli, *painted* 1468—1493.
Bartolommeo Vivarini, *painted* 1459—1498.
Marco Basaiti, *painted* 1470—1520.
Giambattista Cima, *painted* 1489—1517.

Sixteenth Century.

Giorgione, 1477—1511. Titian, 1477—1576.
Bissolo, *painted* 1500—1528.
Romanino, about 1480—1560.
Pordenone, 1483—1539.
Sebastiano del Piombo, 1485—1547.
Bartolommeo Veneziano, *painted* 1505—1530.
Girolamo dai Libri, 1472—1555.†
Girolamo da Santacroce, *painted* 1520—1548.
Il Moretto, about 1490—1560.
Paris Bordone, 1500—1571.
Girolamo da Treviso, 1497—1544.
Jacopo Bassano, 1510—1592. Tintoretto, 1512—1594.
Paolo Veronese, 1528—1588. Battista Zelotti, 1532—92.

* According to the sense, before explained, in which the word school is here used, it must be apparent that individual painters may sometimes have but slender claims to the characteristic attributes of those chiefly constituting the school.

† Strictly of the school of Verona.

Seventeenth Century.

Padovanino, 1590—1650.

Eighteenth Century.

Canaletto, 1697—1768. Guardi, 1712—1793.

SCHOOL OF PADUA.

Established in the fifteenth century.

Fifteenth Century.

Andrea Mantegna, 1431—1506.
Gregorio Schiavone, *painted* 1470.
Francesco Mantegna, *living* 1517.

BOLOGNESE SCHOOL.

Commencement in the fourteenth century. Distinguished, in its later and chief period, for execution, or general technical excellence.

Fifteenth Century.

Marco Zoppo, *painted* 1471—98. Francia, about 1450—1518. Lorenzo Costa, 1460—1535.

Sixteenth Century.

Lodovico Carracci, 1555—1619.
Agostino Carracci, 1558—1601. Annibale Carracci, 1560—1609.

Seventeenth Century.

Domenichino, 1581—1641. Guido, 1575—1642.
Guercino, 1592—1666. Pier Francesco Mola, 1612—1668.*

FERRARESE SCHOOL.

Established in the fifteenth century.

Fifteenth Century.

Cosimo Tura, *living* 1481.

* For a concise history and account of the above Italian schools of painting, see the articles "Bolognese," "Roman," "Tuscan," and "Venetian" Schools of Painting, in the *Penny Cyclopædia*.

Sixteenth Century.

Mazzolini da Ferrara, 1481—1530.
Garofalo, 1481—1559. Ercole da Ferrara, 1462—1531.
Dosso Dossi, 1480—1560.

PARMESE (LOMBARD) SCHOOL.

Commencement in the fifteenth century. The Parmese is one of several subdivisions* of the Lombard School, which is distinguished chiefly for chiaroscuro.†

Sixteenth Century.

Correggio, 1494—1534. Parmigiano, 1503—1540.

CREMONESE (LOMBARD) SCHOOL.

Established in the fifteenth century.

Fifteenth Century.

Francesco Tacconi, *painted* 1464—1490.

MILANESE (LOMBARD) SCHOOL.

Established in the fifteenth century.

Ambrogio Borgognone, *painted* 1490—1522.

NEAPOLITAN SCHOOL.

Commencement in the fifteenth century.

Seventeenth Century.

Spagnoletto, 1588—1656.
Salvator Rosa, 1615—1673.

GREEK OR BYZANTINE SCHOOL.

Established in the fifth century. Distinguished for its strict adherence to traditionary forms and practice.

---

* Lanzi, in his *History of Painting in Italy*, treats of five several schools of Lombardy—the Mantuan, the Modenese, the Parmese, the Cremonese, and the Milanese.—*Storia Pittorica dell' Italia*, vol. iv.

† Chiaroscuro (literally *light-dark*) means the mutual relation of bright and obscure masses; it is therefore not limited to light and shade, but comprehends also light and dark colours.

Seventeenth Century.

Emmanuel the Priest, *living* 1660.

FLEMISH SCHOOL.

Commencement in the fourteenth century.

Fifteenth Century.

Jan Van Eyck, about 1390—1440.
G. Vander Meire, *painted* about 1450.
Roger Vander Weyden, the elder, 1400–64.
Memling, *deceased*, 1495.
Roger Vander Weyden, the younger, 1450—1529.
Quintin Matsys, 1460—1530–1.
Jan de Mabuse, 1470—1532.

Sixteenth Century.

Bernard Van Orley, 1470—1541.
Lambert Lombard, 1506—1560.
Antony Moro, 1525—1581.

Seventeenth Century.

Rubens, 1577—1640. Vandyck, 1599—1641.
Teniers, 1610—1694 Huysman, 1656—1696.

Nineteenth Century.

J. L. Dyckmans, 1811—

DUTCH SCHOOL.

Commencement in the fifteenth century.

Sixteenth Century.

Jacob Cornelissen, 1480—1560.

Seventeenth Century.

C. Poelenburg, 1586—1666.
T. De Keyser, between 1595 and 1660.
Rembrandt, 1608—1669.
Both, 1610—1656. Cuyp, 1605—1683.
Gerard Dow, 1613 or 1598—1680. Vander Helst, 1613—1670.
Ferdinand Bol, 1611—81.

A. Vander Neer, about 1613—1691.
Nicholas Berchem, 1624—1683. Nicolas Maas, 1632—1693.
M. Hondecoeter, 1636—1695.
W. Vandevelde, 1633—1707.
Jacob Ruysdael, *about* 1625—1681.
Hobbema, *living*, 1669. Jan Weenix, 1644—1719.
Schalcken, 1643—1706. Huchtenburg, 1646—1733.
L. Bakhuizen, 1631—1709. Vander Plaas, 1647—1704.

GERMAN SCHOOL.

Established in the fifteenth century.

Fourteenth Century.

William of Cologne, *died*, 1378.

Fifteenth Century.

The Meister Von Liesborn, *painted* about 1445—1465.
Martin Schoen, 1420—1488.

Sixteenth Century.

Albrecht Dürer, 1471—1528.
Lucas Cranach, 1472—1553.

Seventeenth Century.

J. Rottenhammer, 1564—1623.

Eighteenth Century.

C. W. E. Dietrich, 1712—1774.

SPANISH SCHOOL.

Commencement in the fourteenth century.

Seventeenth Century.

Velazquez de Silva, 1599—1660.
Esteban Murillo, 1618—1682. Zurbaran 1598—1662.

FRENCH SCHOOL.

Commencement in the fifteenth century.

Sixteenth Century.

Francois Clouet, 1510—1574.

Seventeenth Century.

N. Poussin, 1594—1665. Claude Lorrain, 1600—1682.
G. Poussin, 1613—1675.
Sebastien Bourdon, 1616—1671.

Eighteenth Century.

Nicolas Lancret, 1690—1743.
Claude Joseph Vernet, 1714—1789.
Jean Baptiste Greuze, 1725—1805.

CATALOGUE.

ALBERTINELLI.

Mariotto Albertinelli, a pupil of Cosimo Rosselli, became the intimate friend and assistant of Fra Bartolommeo; he was born at Florence about the year 1475. When Fra Bartolommeo, under the influence of Savonarola, gave up painting and took to a monastic life, Albertinelli completed some of his unfinished pictures, and acquired much of the style of Il Frate, especially his taste for *tone* or chiaroscuro. Albertinelli was of an impatient character, and being offended with the criticisms which were passed on his works, for a time gave up painting, says Vasari, and turned publican. He died at Florence about 1520, having shortened his life by dissipation.*

No. **645.** The Virgin and Child, seated; entire small figures.

On wood, 6 in. *h.* by 4 in. *w.*
Purchased from M. Edmond Beaucousin at Paris, in 1860.

ALLORI.

Cristoforo Allori, the son of Alessandro, was born at Florence in 1577, and was sometimes called Bronzino, after his great uncle. He left his father to study under Gregorio Pagani, one of the reformers of the Florentine school, and a good colourist. Cristoforo had a dislike to the anatomical school of Michelangelo, to which his father belonged. He was fastidious in his execution, and exceedingly elaborate; his style was well suited to portraits, in which he was excellent; he was also a skilful landscape painter, and he is said to have made some copies, with slight alterations in the back-grounds, of Correggio's Magdalen, which have passed as duplicates by Correggio. His pictures are not numerous; among his masterpieces is the

* Vasari, *Vite de' Pittori, &c.*

"Judith with the Head of Holophernes," in the Pitti Palace, in which the Judith is said to have been painted from his own mistress, and the head of Holophernes from himself; the picture was in the Louvre in 1814, and was engraved by Gandolfi for the "Musée Napoléon." Cristoforo died at Florence in 1621.*

No. **21.** PORTRAIT OF A LADY, in a white bodice with red sleeves, and a head-dress richly ornamented with gold: the red sleeves are relieved by a green curtain, which constitutes the back-ground.

Engraved by J. Jenkins, for Jones's *National Gallery.* On panel, 1 ft. 11 in. *h.* by 1 ft. 6¾ in. *w.*

From the collection of the Duke of San Vitale, at Parma, whence it was procured by the Rev. W. H. Carr, who bequeathed it, in 1831, to the National Gallery.

ALUNNO.

NICCOLO ALUNNO (Nicolaus Alumnus) of Foligno, painted from 1458 to 1499. There are several pictures bearing the signature "Nicolai Fulginatis opus," but as there was apparently another Niccolo of Foligno called Deliberatore living at the same time, it is not always possible to distinguish their works with certainty. Niccolo was one of the principal Umbrian painters of his time; the pictures attributed to him are in *tempera,* (he did not paint in oil,) and are bright and pure in colour: he painted directly from nature, then an unusual practice, and the few works that remain have great merit for their period. There are still some remnants of the Pietà in the Cathedral of Assisi, in which were the weeping angels admired by Vasari in the life of Pinturicchio. One of his best remaining pictures is a Madonna and child with a choir of angels, in the gallery of the Brera at Milan, and engraved in Rosini's History of Italian Painting with the date 1465: another is still in San Niccolo di Foligno, the predella of which is in the Louvre at Paris. Rumohr attributes all pictures signed "Nicolai Fulginatis opus," or similar signature, to Alunno; who is further, by Mariotti, assumed to have been the master of Pietro Perugino.

---

* Baldinucci, *Notizie de' Professori del Disegno, &c.*; Lanzi, *Storia Pittorica, &c.*; Fiorillo, *Geschichte der Malerei in Toscana,* Vol. I.

Pinturicchio and Andrea di Luigi are also supposed to have been the scholars of Niccolo Alunno.*

No. 247. "ECCE HOMO." Christ crowned with thorns; the hands crossed on his breast: bust on a blue ground. In the glory around the head are the letters—YHS. XPS. NAZ.—Jesus Christ of Nazareth: and on the outer edge of the ground, the words of the Vulgate from Paul's Epistle to the Philippians. IN NOMINE JĒU OMNE GENU FLECT.: CELESTIUM TERRESTRIUM ET INFENO.:—In nomine Jesu omne genu flectatur, cœlestium, terrestrium, et infernorum.†

In tempera on wood, 8½ in *h.* by 8½ in. *w.* Purchased in 1854 at the sale of M. Joly De Bammeville's Collection.

ANGELICO, FRA GIOVANNI.

FRA GIOVANNI DA FIESOLE, commonly called from his great piety, L'ANGELICO, and Il Beato Angelico,‡ was born near the Castello di Vicchio, in the Mugello, in 1387: his family name was Guido. He joined the Order of the Predicants at Fiesole in 1407, and began his career in art, as an illuminator of manuscripts.

Fra Giovanni left Fiesole in 1409, in the pontificate of Alexander V., and practised as a fresco painter for several years at Cortona, where several of his best pictures are still preserved. In 1418 he returned to Fiesole, where he resided until 1436, when he was invited to Florence to decorate the new Convent of St. Mark, then assigned to the Predicants as their abode. For this convent Fra Giovanni executed his most important works, which occupied him about nine years. His brother, Fra Benedetto, is said to have assisted him in some portions.

In 1445 he was invited to Rome by Pope Eugenio IV., who employed him in the Vatican, where he also painted a chapel for that pope's successor, Nicolas V. While engaged for Nicolas V., he was invited to Orvieto to paint the

---

* Mariotti, *Letiere Pittoriche Perugine*, &c. 8vo. Perugia, 1788. Rumohr, *Italienische Forschungen*, 3 vols., 8vo., Berlin, 1827–31.

† "At the name of Jesus every knee should bow, of things in heaven, and things in earth, and things under the earth." *Phil.* ii. 10. See note, p. 68, on the title, "Ecce Homo."

‡ The beatification of a deceased person eminent for piety is a solemn distinction conferred by the church, and is second only to canonization.

chapel of the Madonna di San Brizio, in the cathedral, which he undertook, and commenced in 1447, but left it incomplete. He did not return to Orvieto after the autumn of that year. The chapel was completed many years afterwards by Luca Signorelli.

Fra Giovanni returned to Rome in September 1447, and remained there until his death in 1455. He was buried in the Church of Santa Maria Sopra Minerva; and the following inscription was placed on his tomb.

HIC JACET VEN. PICTOR FR. IO. DE FLOR. ORD. P. MCCCCLV.*

Fra Giovanni Angelico, says Vasari, was a man of such fervent piety, that he never commenced painting without prayer. He is still well represented in the Convent of St. Mark, at Florence, and the Florentine academy possesses a fine collection of his smaller works. Engravings also from his paintings are numerous.

No. **582.** THE ADORATION OF THE MAGI; OR, THE WISE MEN'S OFFERING.

"Now when Jesus was born in Bethlehem of Judea, there came wise men from the East." "And when they were come into the house they saw the young child with Mary his mother, and fell down and worshipped him: and when they had opened their treasures, they presented unto him gifts; gold, and frankincense, and myrrh."—*Matthew* ii. 1, 11.

A rocky landscape with a small building on the spectator's right, near which the Virgin is seated holding the child on er knees. Composition of many small figures.

In tempera, on wood, 7½ in. *h.* by 1 ft. 6½ in. *w.*
Formerly in the Collection of Professor Rosini, at Pisa. Purchased from the Lombardi-Baldi Collection, at Florence, in 1857.

No. **663.** CHRIST with the Banner of the Resurrection in his left hand, in the midst of a choir of Angels, some blowing trumpets, others playing various musical instruments. On the two sides are kneeling a great crowd of the Blessed:—the Patriarchs; the Prophets; the Madonna; the Apostles; and the saints and martyrs of both sexes: at the extreme ends are the "Blessed" or Beati of the

* Vasari, *Vite de' Pittori, &c.* Ed. Le Monnier, Flor. 1846, et seq. Marchese, *Memorie dei più insigni Pittori, &c. Domenicani.* Florence, 1845; and *San Marco Convento dei Padri Predicatori in Firenze, illustrato e inciso principalmente nei dipinti del B. Giovanni Angelico, &c.* Folio, Flor., 1852.

Order of the Dominicans, in their black robes. Altogether two hundred and sixty-six figures or portions of figures; many with their names attached; "so beautiful," says Vasari, "that they appear to be truly beings of Paradise."*

In tempera, on wood, in five compartments—each 12½ in. *h.* by 8½ in. 2 ft. 1 in. *w.* the sides respectively, and 2 ft. 4½ in *w.* the centre picture.

Formerly the Predella of an altar-piece in San Domenico at Fiesole, and sold by the monks about 50 years since to Signor Valentini, the Prussian Consul at Rome. Purchased from his nephew, Signor Gioacchino Valentini, at Rome, in 1860.†

BAKHUIZEN.

LUDOLF BAKHUIZEN was born at Emden, Dec. 18, 1631. His father was a government secretary at Emden, and Ludolf acted as his clerk until 1650, when he was placed with a merchant at Amsterdam, to learn commercial business. While thus engaged, Bakhuizen commenced making drawings of ships from nature, for which he soon found willing purchasers. He eventually studied painting under Albert van Everdingen, and he received also some instruction in the style which he had chosen from the marine-painter Hendrik Dubbels.

Bakhuizen's favourite subjects were wrecks and stormy seas, which he frequently sketched from nature in an open boat, at the great peril of himself and the boatmen. He engraved a few pieces: there are some etchings of the Y,‡ and other marine views, executed by him when old. He made also many constructive drawings of ships for the Czar Peter the Great, who took lessons of the painter, and frequently visited his painting-room. Among his other avocations, Bakhuizen also gave lessons in writing, in which he had introduced a new and approved method. He died at Amsterdam, in 1709. Ludolf Bakhuizen, called the younger, a battle-painter, was the nephew of the subject of this notice.§

* Vasari, Ed. Le Monnier, vol. iv. p. 29.

† Rumohr in his *Italienische Forschungen*, ii. 253–4, notices the admirable state of preservation, and the beautiful surface of these *tempera* pictures.

‡ That part of the Zuider Zee on which Amsterdam is situated.

§ Houbraken, *Groote Schouburg der Nederlantsche Kunstschilders, &c.* Amsterdam, 1718-21. Immerzeel, *De Levens en Werken der Hollandsche en Vlaamsche Kunstschilders*, &c. Amsterdam, 1842–3.

No. **204.** Dutch Shipping. A Dutch ship of war, firing a salute; with fishing-boats, and other vessels, in a fresh breeze, off the Dutch coast.

On canvas, 3 ft. 4$\frac{3}{4}$ in. *h.* by 4 ft. 6$\frac{3}{4}$ in. *w.*

Bequeathed to the National Gallery, in 1846, by Mr. Richard Simmons.

Signed and dated—

No. **223.** Dutch Shipping. A frigate, with a yacht saluting, a boat, and many small vessels; in a fresh breeze, off the Dutch coast.

On canvas, 2 ft. 5$\frac{1}{2}$ in. *h.* by 3 ft. 5$\frac{1}{2}$ in. *w.*

Bequeathed to the National Gallery by Mr. Charles L. Bredel, in 1851.

BARO'CCI.*

Federigo Barocci, called also Baroccio, was born at Urbino, in the Papal State, in 1528. His father Ambrogio Barocci, a sculptor, originally of a Milanese family, gave him his first instruction in design; he was afterwards placed with the distinguished painter Battista Franco, who spent some time at Urbino in the service of the Duke Guidubaldo II. After the departure of Franco, Barocci also left Urbino, and accompanied his uncle Bartolomeo Genga, the duke's architect, who taught him perspective, to Pesaro, then under the dominion of the Dukes of Urbino; his uncle procured him permission to copy some pictures by Titian in the ducal gallery there.

In 1548, in his twentieth year, Barocci visited Rome, and remained there a few years, devoting his time chiefly to the study of the works of Raphael.

After his return to Urbino, he painted several pictures which gained him great reputation.

In 1560, he returned to Rome, and was employed in

* The mark here inserted against the second vowel is not an accent, but merely a guide to the emphasis in pronunciation of the name, as on all other occasions where it so occurs in this catalogue. It may not be superfluous to add, for the benefit of the reader unacquainted with Italian pronunciation, that in all Italian words *c* before *e* or *i* is pronounced *ch*, and *i* as the letter *e* in English, as ci-*che*; *ch* on the contrary in Italian is pronounced as *k*, and *e* as *a* in English, as che-*ka*.

the following year by Pius IV., with Federigo Zuccaro, in the Vatican. While engaged in this work he was nearly poisoned, by some rival, as supposed. Though the attempt failed, it wholly incapacitated Barocci for painting for four years, and afflicted him for the remainder of his life, fifty-two years, with a disease of the stomach which rendered it impossible for him to work for more than two hours in the day. From the period of this misfortune, with the exception of three years passed at Perugia, and during which he paid a short visit to Florence, Barocci spent the remainder of his long life at Urbino, where he died of apoplexy on the last day of September, 1612, aged 84: he was buried there in the church of San Francesco, with all the ceremony due to his great merits and reputation.

Barocci painted almost exclusively religious subjects; he executed several large and excellent altar-pieces, some of which he etched himself—as the Pardon of San Francesco d'Assisi, at Urbino, in 1581; and The Annunciation, at Loreto, a few years later; two of his masterpieces.

Barocci is generally said to have founded his style upon the works of Raphael and Correggio: his works have considerable resemblance to those of Correggio in delicacy of light and shade. In colouring he was peculiar; Mengs * has observed, that his works are deficient in yellow tints. Bellori has also pointed out the defects of his colouring, remarking that he used too much vermilion and too much ultra-marine.† Reynolds observes that he "falls under the criticism that was made on an ancient painter, 'that his figures looked as if they fed upon roses.'"‡ His style had considerable influence upon the painters of his time, both at Rome and Florence. Of all his followers, the most distinguished was Lodovico Cardi, commonly called Cigoli, who, partly through the example of Barocci's works, became a reformer of the then degenerate Florentine school.

No. **29.** A "HOLY FAMILY," known as "La Madonna del Gatto," from the circumstance of a cat being introduced

---

* Mengs, *Hinterlassne Werke*, vol. i. p. 252.

† Bellori, *Vite de' Pittori, Scultori, ed Architetti moderni, &c.* Rome, 1672. Baldinucci, *Notizie de' Professori del Disegno da Cimabue in qua.* Florence, 1681-88.

‡ Sir J. Reynolds, *Notes on Du Fresnoy's Art of Painting*, note lv.

into the picture. Though the subject is ostensibly holy, it is here treated merely as an ordinary domestic scene. The little St. John, leaning with his left arm upon the lap of the Virgin, is playfully teasing a cat, by holding up a little bird beyond its reach. The Madonna is pointing with her right hand to the cat, as if to direct the attention of her infant son, who has just turned from the breast, to the incident. Behind is Joseph, who, with his left hand resting upon a table, is leaning forward, and appears to be equally engrossed by the trivial circumstance.

Engraved by C. Cort, in 1577; and by A. Cardon, and others. On canvas, 3 ft. 9 in. *h.* by 3 ft. *w.*

A "Madonna del Gatto" is noticed by Bellori, and he appears to allude to this picture, though he calls the little bird a swallow, and mentions that it is tied with a piece of string, which is not evident at present, and the bird is a goldfinch. Bellori terms the composition a *scherzo* (a playful piece), and adds that it was painted for the Count Antonio Brancaleoni. The picture above described was long in the Cesarei Palace at Perugia, whence it was procured by Mr. Irvine for Mr. Buchanan in 1805, of whom it was purchased by the Rev. W. H. Carr, who bequeathed it, in 1831, to the National Gallery. There are several old copies of it.

BASAI'TI.

Marco Basaiti, a Venetian painter, was born in Friuli according to some writers, of Greek parents. He was the contemporary, and in some respects the rival, of Giovanni Bellini; the circumstances of his life are unknown. His pictures, several of which are preserved, are signed M. Baxit, Marcus Baxaiti, and Marcus Basaiti. He painted from about 1470 until 1520: Moschini mentions a picture with the latter date. An altar-piece, representing the "Calling of St. Peter and St. Andrew," painted in 1511, formerly in the Certosa, and now in the Academy of the Fine Arts at Venice, was once considered his masterpiece; but another specimen in the same gallery—"Christ in the Garden with his Disciples"—is now justly preferred to it. Basaiti's works, when well preserved, are brilliant in colour, and display great ability in the general management of the accessories, especially in the landscape back-grounds, which, according to Zanetti, he contrived to unite with his figures more skilfully than his contemporaries. As one of the early Venetian oil-painters he may be regarded as having successfully adopted the del acy and brilliancy of the Flemish masters of the fifteenth century.*

No. **281.** St. Jerome Reading. The saint is seated, reading a folio volume which rests upon his knee. A small figure in a rocky landscape, with a distant view of a fortified town.

On wood, 18¼ in. *h.* by 13 in. *w.*
Purchased from M. Marcovich, in Venice, in 1855.

No. **599.** The Infant Christ asleep on the Lap of the Virgin, who is seated on the ground in a meadow and adoring the child. Behind are some goats and cattle pasturing; in the back-ground is a convent on a hill, with mountains in the distance. On the left is an eagle perched on a dead or leafless tree, watching a contest between a stork and a snake at the foot of the tree.

On wood, 2 ft. 2 in. *h.* by 2 ft. 9 in. *w.*
Purchased in Florence from Signor Achille Farina in 1858.

BASSA'NO, JA'COPO.

Jacopo da Ponte, commonly called Il Bassano, or Jacopo da Bassano, from his native place, in the Venetian State, was born in 1510. His father Francesco da Ponte, who was a painter of the school of the Bellini, was his first instructor in letters and in the arts; he studied afterwards under Bonifazio at Venice After a short stay in Venice, which he spent chiefly in copying the drawings of Parmigiano, and the pictures of Bonifazio and of Titian, Jacopo returned, in consequence of the death of his father, to Bassano, where he established himself for the remainder of his life, visiting neighbouring places only as his engagements required. He died at Bassano, Feb. 13, 1592.†

The works of Bassano are conspicuous for Venetian excellence of colour, and for masterly chiaroscuro; and some of his best pictures are not unworthy of Titian. In a few years, however, he forsook what may be termed the grand style, for one more in unison with untutored apprehensions,

---

* Zanetti, *Della Pittura Veneziana*, p. 73. Moschini, *Guida per la Città di Venezia*, vol. 1. *p.* 11.

† Ridolfi, *Le Maraviglie dell' Arte, ovvero le Vite degli illustri Pittori Veneti, e dello Stato.* Venice, 1648; Verci, *Notizie intorno alla Vita e alle Opere de Pittori, Scultori, ed Intagliatori della città di Bassano.* Venice, 1775; Lanzi, *Storia Pittorica dell' Italia.* Florence, 1822.

and characterised by the introduction of all sorts of familiar objects, whatever may be the subject of the picture. He was perhaps the earliest Italian *genre**-painter. Even when he painted religious subjects from the Old or New Testament, which he frequently did, he treated them as familiar scenes of his own time. He excelled in landscape and animals, particularly the latter, in which he took great delight, introducing them on all occasions when admissible with, or even without, propriety. His works are very numerous in the Venetian State, and they are not uncommon in picture-galleries generally: his masterpieces are considered the Nativity, at San Giuseppe, and the Baptism of Santa Lucilla, at Santa Maria delle Grazie, in Bassano. Portraits by Jacopo Bassano are comparatively rare. Of his four sons—Francesco, Giambattista, Leandro and Girolamo, all of whom he brought up as painters, Francesco, the eldest, was the most distinguished.

No. **173.** PORTRAIT OF A GENTLEMAN, standing, dressed in a black robe trimmed with fur; his right hand rests on a table placed before an open window, and on which is a silver vase containing a sprig of myrtle; in his left hand he holds a black cap. Three-quarter length.

On canvas, 3 ft. 11 in. *h.* by 3 ft. 2 in. *w.*
Presented, in 1839, by Mr. Henry Gally Knight.

No. **228.** CHRIST DRIVING THE MONEY CHANGERS OUT OF THE TEMPLE. A crowded composition of men and animals, representing the expulsion of "all them that sold and bought"—money-changers, dealers in cattle, sheep,

---

* *Genre* is a term borrowed from the French, for which we have no equivalent in English. As it is a term of frequent occurrence in works which treat of painting, an explanation of it may not be out of place here. Strictly speaking a *peintre de genre*, or *genre*-painter, signifies a painter of any particular class of subject; and, according to some explanations, any painter except an historical painter—but this is a meaning too vague for any critical purpose. Common usage has now limited the signification of the term *genre-painting* to a less elevated class of painting. The full expression is apparently *peintre du genre bas*, painter of a low class of subjects, which occasionally occurs (Millin, *Dictionnaire des Beaux-Arts*, vol. iii. p. 160). It does not however follow that a *genre-picture* is low in its subject; yet, it must be a picture of some familiar object, or ordinary custom or incident; and every such picture which does not belong to any other recognised class of paintings, as history, portrait, animal, landscape, marine, fruit and flower, or still-life, but which may nevertheless be something of all, is a *genre-picture*.

The Dutch have hitherto been the great *genre*-painters; indeed, their pictorial fame is so closely associated with this class of painting, that *genre* and *the Dutch style* are nearly synonymous.

goats, birds, &c.—from the interior of the "Temple," a spacious building, of ordinary Italian architecture. Small figures on a dark ground.

On canvas, 5 ft. 3 in. *h.* by 8 ft. 9 in. *w.*

Brought to England by Mr. A. Wilson in 1806. Presented, in 1853, by Mr. P. L. Hinds.

No. **277.** THE GOOD SAMARITAN, in a crimson dress, raising the wounded Jew to place him on his mule; by his side is a silver flask; two dogs are in the foreground; the Leviteis seen in prayer behind.

On canvas, 3 ft. 4¼ in. *h.* by 2 ft. 7½ in. *w.*

Formerly in the Pisani Palace, Venice; subsequently in the collection of Sir Joshua Reynolds, who is said to have kept it always in his studio. Purchased for the National Gallery, at the sale of Mr. Rogers's pictures, in 1856.

BELLI'NI, GIOVA'NNI.

GIOVANNI BELLINI, the most distinguished of the *quattrocentisti*, or painters of the fifteenth century, at Venice, was born in that city about 1426. He was the son and pupil of Jacopo, and the younger brother of Gentile, Bellini, both distinguished painters in their time, but inferior to Giovanni. Ridolfi observes, that the style of Giovanni was an aggregate of all that was beautiful in painting in his time; and Lanzi remarks, that had his outline been less hard, he would have been a just representative of even the modern or *cinquecento* style—that of the great masters of the sixteenth century. His style is individual, and rather full than meagre in form; it is positive in colour, and is distinguished for much detail of costume and ornament. His works, which are still very numerous, though probably many have perished, range in their dates from 1464 to 1516. The celebrated pictures described by Vasari, which he painted with his brother Gentile and with Luigi Vivarini, in the Sala del Gran Consiglio, in the ducal palace of Venice, were destroyed by fire in 1577. They were, however, replaced by others painted by the great Venetian masters of the sixteenth century.

Giovanni Bellini's earlier works were executed in *tempera;* but upon seeing some of the oil pictures of Antonello da Messina, who settled in Venice about 1470, he perceived the great advantage of the new method, and, according to a story told by Ridolfi, he disguised himself as a Venetian cavaliere, sat to Antonello for his portrait, and by watching the painter's proceedings during the sittings, contrived to discover his secret.* Bellini's best works are in oil, and consist chiefly of Madonnas and portraits. The last picture painted by *Joannes Bellinus*, as he wrote his name, is the Madonna of Santa Giustina at Padua, mentioned by Brandolese and others, which bears the date 1516. Ridolfi erroneously states that his last picture was the Bacchanalian piece, painted in 1514 for Alfonso I. of Ferrara, long preserved subsequently in the Aldobrandini Villa at Rome, and now in the collection of the Duke of Northumberland. Giovanni died without finishing it, and it was completed by Titian, who painted the landscape back-ground to it. Giovanni Bellini died at the advanced age of 90, November 29, 1516.† Albert Dürer, who was in Venice in 1506, describes him in a letter to Pirkheimer, though very old, as the best of all the Venetian painters. Giorgione and Titian were two of his many eminent scholars.‡

No. **189.** BUST PORTRAIT OF THE DOGE LEONARDO LOREDANO, IN HIS STATE ROBES. He died in 1521, having filled the office of Doge from 1500. Joannes Bellinus is written on an unfolded scrip of paper, or cartellino :

---

* It must have been after 1473 that Giovanni practised the new method; for according to Zanetti, the first oil picture known to have been executed in Venice by a Venetian master was painted in that year, by Bartolommeo Vivarini, for the church of SS. Giovanni e Paolo. It does not appear that Antonello executed many pictures in Venice during his first visit there on his return from Flanders, about 1445; and Domenico Veneziano, to whom he communicated his secret about 1451, was soon invited to Florence, where he was afterwards employed. Lanzi (vol. i.) appears to think that Domenico painted several pictures in Venice after his acquaintance with Antonello. Had this been the case, or had Antonello made known his secret at once to others besides Domenico (as Vasari in one place seems to say), oil painting must have been practised in Venice much earlier than 1473. The first oil pictures known to have been executed in Italy by Italian artists, in consequence of Antonello's communication, were those (now no longer existing) by Domenico Veneziano and Andrea del Castagno on the walls of the Portinari chapel in Santa Maria Nuova, at Florence. The execution of those works must have taken a considerable time, the middle period of which may have been about 1460.

† Cadorin, *Dello Amore ai Veneziani di Tiziano Vecellio*, Venice, 1833.

‡ Vasari, *Vite*, &c., and Schorn's translation—*Leben der ausgezeichnetsten Maler*, &c., Notes; Ridolfi, *Le Maraviglie dell' Arte*, &c.; Zanetti, *Della Pittura Veneziana, e delle opere pubbliche de' Veneziani Maestri*, Venice, 1771; Lanzi, *Storia Pittorica dell' Italia*; Von Murr, *Journal der Kunstgeschichte*, vol. x. p. 7.

On wood, 2 ft. *h.* by 1 ft. 5½ in. *w.*

This picture was formerly in the Grimani Palace at Venice, whence it was brought to England by the late Lord Cawdor. It passed subsequently into the possession of Mr. Beckford, from whom it was purchased for the National Gallery, in 1844.

No. **280.** MADONNA AND CHILD. The Virgin with the Child on her knee. In her left hand she holds an apple, on which the right hand of the Child rests; her right hand supports the Child. Behind is suspended a green curtain with a red border. Landscape back-ground. Inscribed on an unfolded scrip of paper, on a coloured marble screen below, JOANNES BELLINUS, P.

On wood, 2 ft. 11¾ in. *h.* by 2 ft. 1¼ in. *w.* Engraved by L. Boscolo. Purchased from the Baron Galvagna, in Venice, in 1855.

OF THE SCHOOL OF GIOVANNI BELLINI.

No. **234.** A WARRIOR ADORING THE INFANT CHRIST. On the left is the Virgin seated, with the Infant Christ on her knees; St. Joseph leans on a low wall behind. In the centre of the picture a knight in armour, with a turban on his head, is represented kneeling on a carpet in the act of adoring the divine infant: in the back ground to the right, behind a parapet wall, is a servant holding the horse of the Knight, in the distance a hilly landscape, with a church and probably a convent. Six figures, small life-size.

On canvas, 5 ft. 1 in. *h.* by 8 ft. 7 in. *w.*

Formerly in the collection of Mr. Samuel Woodburn, by whom, as well as by many others, it was attributed to Giorgione. Connoisseurs are agreed that it is, at all events, of the School of Bellini, and it is therefore for the present, so classed. It was purchased for the National Gallery at the sale of Mr. Woodburn's collection in 1853.

BERCHEM.

NICOLAS BERGHEM, or rather BERCHEM as the Dutch write it, was born at Haarlem in 1624; where he also died, Feb. 18, 1683. He had many masters, among whom were his father Pieter Klaasze, Jan Van Goyen, J. B. Weenix, and Jan Wils, whose daughter he married. Bercham painted in several styles—portrait, figure (large and small), battles, and landscape with cattle and small figures, in which last class he is chiefly distinguished. His pictures are remarkable for their composition, their careful finish, and at the same time freedom of handling; and for their warm tone of colour and brilliant lighting. He is supposed by some, from the nature of his scenes, to have studied in Italy. At the height of his reputation, in 1665, Berchem sold his labour, from early morning until four in the after, noon, for 10 florins a day: his wife is said to have suffered him to keep very little money; he appears to have been prone to spend it too freely on Italian drawings. At the sale of his effects after his death his pictures produced 12,000 florins, and his sketches 800. Berchem also etched; there are in all 56 plates attributed to him, chiefly of animals, and which are very scarce. Berchem was a nickname or surname that originated with himself: it is variously accounted for.*

No. **240.** Crossing the Ford, a hilly scene with clumps of trees; figures and cattle, sheep, &c. crossing a stream in the fore-ground: sunset.

On wood, $11\frac{3}{4}$ in. *h.* by 1 ft. $5\frac{1}{2}$ in. *w.*
Bequeathed to the National Gallery by Lord Colborne, in 1854.
Signed—

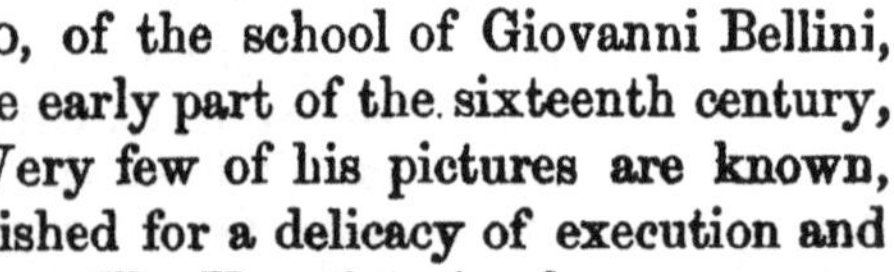

BISSO'LO.

Francesco Bisso'lo, of the school of Giovanni Bellini, painted at Venice in the early part of the sixteenth century, about 1500—1528. Very few of his pictures are known, but these are distinguished for a delicacy of execution and a fine feeling for colour. The Venetian Academy possesses

* Houbraken, *Groote Schouburg der Nederlantsche Konstschilders*, &c., 3 vols., 8vo., Amsterdam, 1719. Van Eynden and Vander Willigen, *Geschiedenis der Vaderlandsche Schilderkunst, sedert de helft der XVIII. eeuw*, 4 vols., 8vo., Amsterdam, 1842. Immerzeel, *De Levens en Werken der Hollandsche en Vlaamsche Kunstschilders*, &c., 3 vols., 8vo., Amsterdam, 1842-3. Bartsch, *Peintre-Graveur*, 21 vols., 8vo., Vienna and Leipzig, 1803-21, vol. v.

a fine picture of "Christ exchanging the crown of thorns of St. Catherine of Siena for a crown of gold;" it is signed *Franciscus Bissolo*, and was formerly in the church of San Pietro Martire at Murano. In San Floriano, near Castel-Franco, is a picture by him, signed and dated MDXXVIII.*

No. **631.** PORTRAIT OF A LADY, with blond hair confined in a net, and in a rich dress of embroidered Byzantine stuff. Bust.

On wood, 14½ in. *h.* by 12 in. *w.*
Purchased from M. Edmond Beaucousin, at Paris, in 1860.

BOL.

FERDINAND BOL was born at Dort in 1611, and became the pupil of Rembrandt at Amsterdam, where he acquired the rights of a burgess on the 24th of January 1652. He is distinguished chiefly as a portrait painter, and his pictures are remarkable for a prevailing yellow tone. He died rich at Amsterdam, in 1681.† He generally signed *Bol* or *Bol fecit*, the B being composed of an F and a B combined.

No. **679.** THE PORTRAIT OF AN ASTRONOMER? half-length, seated before a table, on which are an open book and two globes. Signed, and dated 1652.

On canvas, 4 ft. 1½ in. *h.* by 4 ft. 4½ in. *w.*
Presented in 1862 by Miss E. A. Benett.
Signed—

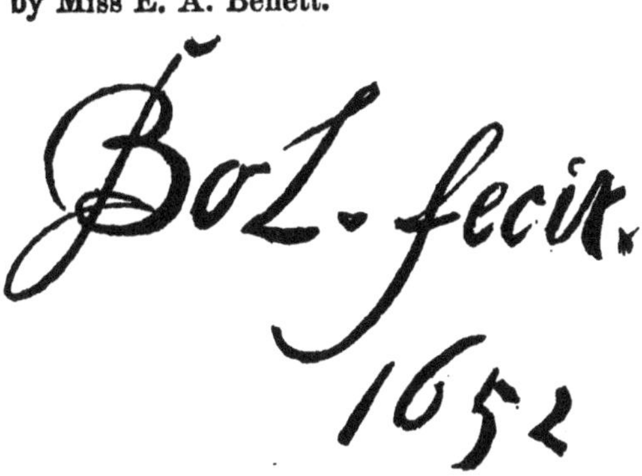

---

* Zanetti, *Della Pittura Veneziana, &c.*; Moschini, *Guida di Venezia.* In some accounts Bissolo's Christian name is given as Pier Francesco.

† Houbraken, *Groote Schouburg*, &c. Scheltema, *Rembrand. Redevoering*, &c. p. 69; French Translation of Bürger, p. 53.

BORDONE.

Paris Bordone, *Cavaliere*, of a noble family of Treviso, was born in 1500, and learnt painting for a short while in the school of Titian at Venice. He became an imitator of Giorgione, and obtained great distinction for his female portraits, and about 1538 was invited by Francis I. to France, where he painted many of the ladies of the French court; and he had the art, says Ridolfi, of making such works appear more like fancy pictures than portraits. Bordone painted also historical pictures as well as portraits; his masterpiece is the large picture in the Venetian Academy, of "The Fisherman presenting the Ring of St. Mark to the Doge." He died at Venice on the 19th of January, 1571, and was buried in the church of San Marziale.

No. **637.** Daphnis and Chloe, a Greek shepherd and shepherdess, seated on a bank among some trees; Chloe, who holds the pipes of Daphnis in her hand, is about to be crowned by Cupid with a wreath of myrtle. From the Greek of Longus.

On canvas, 4 ft. 5½ in. *h.* by 3 ft. 11 in. *w.*
Purchased from M. Edmond Beaucousin, at Paris, in 1860.

No. **674**. Portrait of a Lady, of the Brignole family of Genoa; she has yellow hair, is dressed in a crimson gown with a low body and long sleeves, and has on a pearl necklace; her right hand rests on her side, in her left she holds a chain; in the back-ground is seen a portion of a hospital at Genoa. Inscribed ÆTATIS. SUÆ. ANN. XVIIII.; and lower down Paris . B. O. Front view, half length life size.

On canvas, 3 ft. 5½ in. *h.* by 2 ft. 9 in. *w.*
Purchased from the Duca di Cardinale, at Naples, in 1861.

PARIS · B ·
· O ·

BORGOGNONE.

Ambrogio Borgognone, called also Ambrogio da Fossano, from his birthplace in Piedmont, was born probably about 1455. He was distinguished as architect and painter, and was employed on the façade of the Certosa or Carthusian convent near Pavia very early in his career, but scarcely before 1475.* The earliest known date on any of his paintings is 1490: he appears to have been engaged many years at Pavia, from about 1475 to 1493.

Lanzi, and others, have assumed Ambrogio da Fossano, the architect, and Ambrogio Borgognone, the painter, to have been distinct persons, but existing signatures on pictures show that they are designations of the same artist: the altarpiece of the "Crucifixion," in the Certosa of Pavia, by this painter, is signed *Ambrosius Fosanus, pinxit* 1490, *May* 14; a picture of the "Baptism of Christ," in the sacristy of the church of Melegnano, is signed *Ambrogio da Fosano Brgognone;* and an "Assumption of the Virgin," in the Brera at Milan, is signed and dated *Ambrosio Bgogoj,* 1522. In the Berlin Gallery is a "Madonna and Child enthroned," which was formerly in the Solly collection, signed *Ambrosii Bergognoni, op.*

Borgognone's works, scarce out of the Milanese, are in fresco and in tempera; they are very refined in their forms, and delicate and pallid in their colouring. There is no satisfactory account of him by any early writer; Lomazzo merely mentions him as a Milanese painter worthy of being celebrated, though he executed several considerable works at Milan, some of which are still preserved, as in San Simpliciano, Sant' Ambrosio, San Satiro, Sant' Agostino, and other churches.†

No. **298.** The Marriage of St. Catherine of Alexandria. The Virgin is taking the hand of and presenting St. Catherine of Siena to the Infant Christ, who, standing on his mother's knee, holds a ring in each hand. While placing one ring on the finger of St. Catherine of Alexandria, standing on his right, he extends the other towards St. Catherine of Siena, habited as a nun, on his left. The virgin is seated between the two saints, enthroned under a marble canopy of rich cinquecento architecture. Four figures small life-size.

In tempera, on wood, 6 ft. 7 in. *h.* by 4 ft. 3 in. *w.*

Originally in the chapel of Rebecchino, near Pavia, and formerly under the rule of the Certosa: purchased out of that chapel from Signor Carlo Taddeo of Pavia, in 1857.

---

* Malaspina, *Guida di Pavia*, 1819, p. 113, says about 1473, but considering that Borgognone was painting in 1522, this date, which is not fixed by documents, appears to be too early.

† Lomazzo, *Trattato della Pittura*, &c., ed. 1844, vol. iii. p. 297; Torre, *Il Ritratto di Milano*, 1714, pp. 48, 173; Pirovano, *Milano Nuovamente descritta*, &c., 1824; Rio, *Leonard de Vinci et son Ecole*, 1855, ch. 3.

BOTH.

JAN or JOHN BOTH was born at Utrecht about 1610. He and his younger brother Andries, or Andrew, both learnt the first rudiments of their art under their father, a painter on glass, who placed them afterwards with Abraham Bloemart. The two brothers visited France and Italy together, and spent some time in Rome. Jan was an excellent landscape painter, and Andries embellished his landscapes with figures and cattle, which his brother had little skill in painting. Andries Both fell into a canal at Venice, and was drowned, in 1650; Jan returned to Utrecht, and died there in 1656.*

No. **71.** LANDSCAPE, A PARTY OF MULETEERS, WITH LADEN MULES: MORNING. Mountain scenery; a dark picturesque rocky fore-ground, with a lake in the middle-ground, and blue mountains in the distance, contrasting forcibly with the fore-ground.

Engraved by W. Byrne; and by J. C. Bentley, for Jones's *National Gallery*. On canvas, 3 ft. 9 in. *h.* by 5 ft. 3 in. *w.* Signed, *J. Both, f.*

Presented to the nation, in 1826, by Sir George Beaumont.

No. **209.** LANDSCAPE, WITH FIGURES. A rocky and woody landscape, with figures by Cornelis Poelenburg,† representing the Judgment of Paris.

On canvas, 3 ft. 3 in. *h.* by 4 ft. 3½ in. *w.* Signed, *J. Both.*

Bequeathed to the National Gallery, in 1846, by Mr. Richard Simmons.

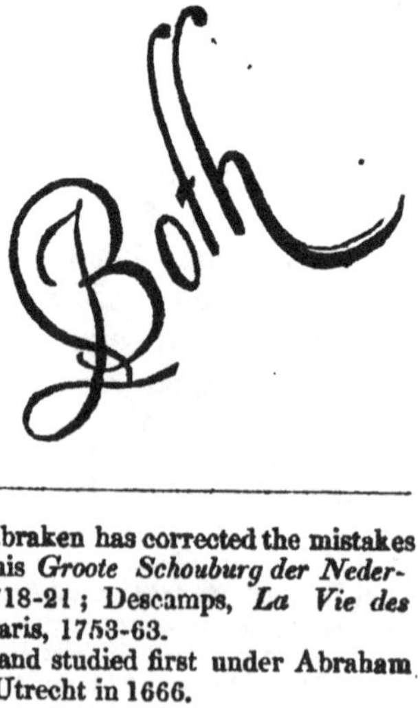

---

* Sandrart, *Teutsche Academie*, 1675. Houbraken has corrected the mistakes of some writers respecting these painters, in his *Groote Schouburg der Nederlantsche Konstschilders*, &c., Amsterdam, 1718-21; Descamps, *La Vie des Peintres Flamands, Allemands et Hollandois*, Paris, 1753-63.

† Poelenburg was born at Utrecht in 1586, and studied first under Abraham Bloemart, and afterwards in Italy. He died at Utrecht in 1666.

BOTTICELLI.

SANDRO or ALESSANDRO FILIPEPI, commonly called BOTTICELLI, after his first master, who was a jeweller, was born at Florence in 1447. He studied painting under Fra Filippo Lippi, and became one of the most celebrated painters of the fifteenth century, though all his works are characterized by that hardness of manner common to most of the painters of this time, and known among the Italians by the term *quattrocentismo*. He was one of those employed at Rome about 1480–84, to decorate the Vatican Chapel, then recently completed by Pope Sixtus IV., and which was afterwards known by the name of the "Sistine Chapel." Botticelli's competitors on this occasion were Cosimo Rosselli, Domenico Ghirlandajo, Luca Signorelli, and Pietro Perugino. The three frescoes of Botticelli, illustrating the life of Moses and the temptation of Christ, are still in a good state of preservation.

The pictures of this painter, in tempera, and nearly all on wood, are generally distinguished for the appropriate expression and the fine drawing of the faces. Many of his best works are still preserved in the public galleries of Florence.

He died poor at Florence in 1515, and was buried in the church of Ognissanti.*

No. **226.** THE VIRGIN AND CHILD, ST. JOHN THE BAPTIST AND ANGELS. The Virgin is seated in a garden, with the Child on her knees; two Angels are holding a crown over her head. St. John, kneeling by her side, is adoring the Divine Infant. Five figures, small life-size.

In tempera, on wood, circular; 3 ft. 8½ in. in diameter.

Formerly in the possession of the Polli family, at Florence, where it was purchased for the National Collection of Mr. J. H. Brown, in 1855.

No. **275.** THE VIRGIN AND CHILD, ST. JOHN THE BAPTIST AND AN ANGEL. The Virgin richly dressed in gold brocades, is holding the Child to her bosom. St. John and the Angel are standing one on each side, a little behind the Virgin, in the act of adoring the Divine Infant. Half-figures, small life-size.

In tempera, on wood; circular, 2 ft. 9 in. in diameter.

---

* Vasari, *Vite de' Pittori, &c.* Ed. Flor. 1846 *et seq.*

This picture appears to have originally belonged to the celebrated architect Giuliano da San Gallo; his name, in the manner and orthography of the 16th century, is written on the back—M. Giuliano da San Ghallo.* In the last century it was the property of the Abate Carlo Bianconi, Secretary of the Academy of the Arts at Milan, who died in 1802; when the picture passed into the possession of Professor Gio. Giuseppe Bianconi of Bologna, from whom it was purchased for the National Collection in October 1855. It is mentioned in Bassani's *Guida per Bologna*, 1816, as a work of Ghirlandajo.

BOURDON.

SEBASTIEN BOURDON was born at Montpellier in 1616. He was instructed by his father, and exhibited great ability at a very early age; he painted a ceiling in fresco in a château near Bordeaux, in his fourteenth year. He studied afterwards at Paris, and subsequently three years at Rome; and obtained great reputation, in 1643, by his celebrated picture of the Crucifixion of St. Peter, which was originally placed in the Cathedral of Notre Dame, at Paris, but is now in the Louvre. Bourdon was a Protestant, and being anxious to avoid the troubles of the civil wars of the time, he went in 1652 to Sweden, where he was appointed by Christina her principal painter. On the abdication of Christina he returned to France, and in 1663 again settled in Paris, where he executed many works in different styles, history, landscape, and *genre*, by which he added greatly to his reputation. He was one of the original twelve *anciens* of the old academy of painting established at Paris in 1648: he died rector of the academy May 8, 1671.

The landscapes of Bourdon somewhat resemble those of Salvator Rosa, and have a wild melancholy character. In his historical works colour and effect appear to have engrossed more of his attention than form; his less finished works, says D'Argenville, are his best. Bourdon has also executed many masterly etchings, the most celebrated of which are the "Seven Acts of Mercy."†

* Vasari, *Vite, &c.*, notices San Gallo as a possessor of works of Art in two instances; in the life of the brothers San Gallo, and (in the first edition) in the life of Masaccio.

† D'Argenville, *Abrégé de la Vie des plus fameux Peintres*, Paris, 1745-52; Gault de Saint-Germain, *Les Trois Siècles de la Peinture en France*, Paris, 1808. Robert Dumesnil, *Le Peintre-Graveur Français*, vol. i, 1835, describes forty-four etchings by Bourdon.

No. 64. The Return of the Ark from Captivity.

The Philistines "took two milch kine, and tied them to the cart..., and they laid the ark of the Lord upon the cart, and the coffer with the mice of gold, and the images of their emerods. And the kine took the straight way to the way of Beth-shemesh, and went along the highway, lowing as they went, and turned not aside to the right hand, or to the left; and the lords of the Philistines went after them unto the border of Beth-shemesh. And they of Beth-shemesh were reaping their wheat harvest in the valley: and they lifted up their eyes, and saw the ark, and rejoiced to see it. And the cart came into the field of Joshua, a Beth-shemite, and stood there, where there was a great stone."—1 *Samuel*, vi. 10-14.

A dark rocky landscape, intersected by a large river: in the middle-ground is the "great stone of Abel," and by the side of it is the city Beth-shemesh. The ark is represented in the fore-ground as having crossed the river; the car having stopped near the "great stone": the five lords of the Philistines are on the bridge over which the ark has passed: the Beth-shemites are rejoicing, and returning thanks for its restoration.

Engraved by J. C. Varrall, for Jones's *National Gallery*. On canvas, 3 ft. 5 in. *h*. by 4 ft. 5 in. *w*.

This picture was long in the possession of Sir Joshua Reynolds, and was much admired by him. He instanced it, and a picture of "Jacob's Dream" by Salvator Rosa, as happy examples of the poetical style of landscape, in his discourse on the character of Gainsborough to the students of the Royal Academy in 1788. It was bequeathed by Sir Joshua to Sir George Beaumont, by whom it was presented to the nation in 1826.

BRONZI'NO, ANGELO.

Angelo Bronzi'no was born at Monticelli, in the neighbourhood of Florence, in 1502. Having acquired the rudiments of his art from an obscure painter, he became the scholar, first of Raffaellino del Garbo, and subsequently of Jacopo da Pontormo, some of whose works, left unfinished, Bronzino completed. He executed several works, in fresco and in oil, in the public buildings of Florence and its vicinity; but is now, though not a good colorist, most appreciated as a portrait painter, in which capacity he was much employed by the Grand Duke Cosmo I. Many of Bronzino's portraits of the Medici family are still preserved at Florence. Of his more important works now remaining, the picture of "Limbo," or "The Descent of Christ into Hell," in the Gallery of the Uffizj at Florence, is the most celebrated. He was a devoted admirer of Michelangelo, and was also the intimate friend of Vasari. Bronzino died at Florence, towards the close of the year 1572, aged sixty-nine. He was both poet and painter, and was a member of the Florentine academy.*

No. **650.** Portrait of a Lady, in the rich costume of he sixteenth century, holding up her hand before her; she s dressed in a gold-quilted white satin bodice, with a blue velvet gown, the body and sleeves of which are embroidered with gold; on her neck is a pearl necklace supporting a cross. Three-quarter length, life-size.

On canvas, 3 ft. 8 in. *h.* by 2 ft. 7 in. *w.*

No. **651.** Venus, Cupid, Folly, and Time. An Allegory. Venus with the apple of Discord in her hand is reclining on a piece of blue drapery on the ground, and turning her head to kiss Cupid, kneeling behind her; Folly unconsciously treading on a thorn is preparing to throw a handful of roses at them; behind is Time unveiling Envy and other evils; a Harpy offering a piece of honeycomb in one hand is holding her sting behind her in the other. In one lower corner are some doves, in the other human masks. Seven figures, life-size.

On wood, 4ft. 9 in. *h.* by 3 ft. 9½ in. *w.*

Both purchased from M. Edmond Beaucousin at Paris, in 1860. The latter was originally painted for Francis I. of France†: it was subsequently in the collection at Althorp.

CANALETTO.

Antonio Canal, commonly called Canaletto, was born in Venice, in 1697. His father, Bernardo Canal, was a scene-painter, and Antonio practised the same art for several years: he, however, gave it up while still young, and went to Rome, where he devoted the whole of his time to the study of architectural views and ancient ruins. He was accompanied while at Rome by his nephew and pupil, Bernardo Bellotto, who painted similar pictures to those of his uncle, and is known by the same name; whence the works of the two are often confounded together. After his

* See Vasari, *Vite, &c.*, among the notices of the Academicians; and Borghini, *Il Riposo*, vol. iii. p. 79. Borghini mentions that some of Bronzino's burlesque pieces were published with the works of Berni in 1723, at Naples, but with Florence on the title page.

† See Vasari, *Vite*, &c. Ed. Le Monnier, vol. xiii. p. 164, where he describes it as a picture of singular beauty, *quadro di singolare bellezza*.

return to Venice, Canaletto painted pictures of that city, one of the most remarkable of which is a view on the Grand Canal, in which he has substituted a design by Palladio for the Rialto instead of the actual scene; he took also other liberties with the disposition of the buildings. Tiepolo occasionally painted the figures in his pictures. In 1746 he came to England, and remained here two years. Walpole possessed an interior of King's College Chapel, Cambridge, by him. His nephew was in the same year made a member of the Academy of Dresden, where he was known by the title of Count Bellotto. He painted many pictures there: twenty-five of them are still preserved under the name of Canaletto, in a distinct collection at Dresden. He died at Prague in 1780. Canaletto, the uncle, died at Venice in 1768, aged 71.* Many of his works have been engraved, especially his Venetian views, of which there are three sets, one by himself, another by Vicentino, and a third by Fletcher and Boitard.

The two Canaletti painted so much alike that it is very difficult to distinguish their works. Bellotto being long the pupil of his uncle, completely acquired his manner of execution. Canaletto's style is architectural portraiture, distinct in forms, individual in colour, and effective in light and shade; it displays so much or so little of contrivance, that, as Lanzi has remarked, the common observer perceives nature, and the artist art in his works. He used the camera lucida, which, says Lanzi, he was the first to apply to its proper use, to the linear perspective only; aerial effects he commonly painted from nature.

No. **127.** A VIEW IN VENICE. In the fore-ground are the sheds and yard of a stone mason; in the middle distance are a quay and a portion of the grand canal, with gondolas upon it; beyond these are various buildings, the most conspicuous is a tall campanile, next to which are the old buildings of the Scuola della Carità erected in 1349, now much altered, and known as the Accademia delle Belle Arti.

---

* Zanetti, *Della Pittura Veneziana*, &c.; Lanzi, *Storia Pittorica*, &c.; Matthäy, *Beschreibung der neu errichteten Sammlung Vaterländischer Prospecte von Alexander Thiele und Canaletto*, Dresden, 1834.

Engraved by H. Le Keux, in the series of prints published for the '*Associated Engravers;*' and by E. Challis, for Jones's *National Gallery.* On canvas, 4 ft. *h.* by 5 ft. 4 in. *w.*

Presented to the nation, in 1826, by Sir George Beaumont, Bart.

No. **163.** A VIEW ON THE GRAND CANAL, VENICE. The church, which is a principal feature in this picture, was built in the early part of the last century, (1718-38,) from the designs of Giovanni Scalfarotto; it is dedicated to Saints Simon and Jude, Apostles, and is known by the name of San Simeone Piccolo.

On canvas, 4 ft. 1 in. *h.* by 6 ft. 8½ in. *w.*

Bequeathed to the National Gallery, in 1838, by Lord Farnborough.

CARAVA'GGIO, M. DA.

MICHELANGELO MERI'GI was born at Caravaggio in the Milanese, in 1569, and on this account is generally known as Michelangelo da Caravaggio. His father was a mason.

He maintained himself for about five years painting portraits at Milan; he then went to Venice. From Venice he proceeded to Rome; but there, owing to his poverty, he could not procure the requisite materials to produce a picture; he therefore entered the service of the Cavaliere Cesare d'Arpino, who employed him in painting fruit and flowers and other ornamental parts of his own works. Caravaggio at length produced the celebrated picture of "Il Giuoco di Carte," or the Card-players, which was purchased by the Cardinal del Monte. He also painted about this time several oil pictures for the Contarelli Chapel, in the Church of San Luigi de' Francesi. His first altarpiece in this chapel, "St. Matthew writing the Gospel," was removed by the priests as too vulgar for such a subject: Caravaggio painted a second, which gave satisfaction, and the first was purchased by the Marchese Vincenzio Giustiniani. His masterpiece at Rome is "The Pietà," or Deposition of Christ, formerly in the Chiesa Nuova de' Padri dell' Oratorio, or Santa Maria in Vallicella, now in the gallery of the Vatican; a copy was substituted in the church for the original, and there is a mosaic of it in the Chapel of the Sacrament in St. Peter's.

Caravaggio was now fully established; but his disposition was violent and his habits peculiar. He was playing at tennis with an acquaintance, and he became so violent in a dispute that he killed his companion. He immediately fled to Naples, whence, after executing a few pictures, he proceeded to Malta, where he obtained the favour of the Grand-master Vignacourt, who sat to Caravaggio for two portraits, and made him a knight of the Cross of Malta. Here again his temper was his enemy, he quarrelled with one of the knights, and was cast into prison; he contrived, however, to escape, and fled to Syracuse. He afterwards visited Messina and Palermo: having executed a few pictures in those cities, he returned to Naples, where, after a little time, he hired a felucca and set out for Rome, having by means of his friends at length procured the pope's pardon for the offence which caused his flight from that city. On his way, however, he fell in with a Spanish coast-guard, who arrested him, mistaking him for another person, and when he was at length liberated he found that the people of the felucca had gone off with all his property. He wandered despondingly along the coast until he came to Porto Ercole, where, partly from his disappointment and partly from the extreme heat of the weather, he was seized with a fever and died in a few days, in 1609, aged only forty.*

The followers of Caravaggio have been called *naturalists:* their style, which was founded on a literal imitation of the model, was thus opposed to that more *ideal* view of nature which is founded on selection. He had a host of imitators among the younger painters of the age; even Guido and Domenichino were not exempt from the influence. Guercino in part adopted his style, but Bartolomeo Manfredi, Spagnoletto, Carlo Saracino, Valentin, and Gerard Honthorst (Gherardo della Notte) became his decided imitators.

No. 172. CHRIST AND THE TWO DISCIPLES AT EMMAUS.

As he sat at meat with them,—"He took bread and blessed it, and brake and gave to them. And their eyes were opened, and they knew him."—*Luke* xxiv. 30, 31.

A composition of four half-length figures. Christ breaking bread is seated between the two disciples at a table, on which is spread an Italian meal; the fourth figure behind is the cook or host. Ramdohr, in his account of the pic-

---

* Bellori, *Vite de' Pittori, Scultori, ed Architetti Moderni*, &c., Rome, 1672.

tures and statues in Rome in 1784, notices the masterly manner in which the accessory objects in this picture are executed.*

On canvas, 4 ft. 7 in. *h.* by 6 ft. 5½ in. *w.*

Bellori mentions three pictures of this subject, which were painted by Caravaggio, all slightly different. The first, containing five figures, was painted at Rome, for the Marchese Patrizj; the second was painted likewise at Rome, for the Cardinal Scipione Borghese; and the third at Zagarolo, near Palestrina, after Caravaggio's flight from Rome, for the Duke Marzio Colonna. The picture in this collection is the second mentioned; it constituted part of the Borghese Gallery at Rome, until the great dispersion of pictures which took place in Italy in consequence of the French occupation of that country. It came eventually into the possession of Lord Vernon, who presented it, in 1839, to the National Gallery.

CARRA'CCI, AGOSTI'NO.

AGOSTINO CARRACCI was born at Bologna of an old family of that place, in 1558.† His father Antonio was a tailor. He was placed first with a jeweller, then, by the advice of his cousin Lodovico, with Prospero Fontana, the master of Lodovico, and afterwards with Domenico Tibaldi and Cornelius Cort, under whom he advanced greatly in engraving an art with which he was always more occupied than with painting. He studied also some time at Parma and at Venice, and after his return to Bologna, in 1589, was the most active teacher in the celebrated school of the Carracci, then first established there. When Annibale was engaged on his frescoes in the Farnese Palace at Rome, Agostino joined him, and, for a time, assisted him: he executed the Triumph of Galatea, and the Cephalus and Aurora of that series. According to Malvasia, he was not only the painter but the designer of those compositions, and their success appears to have caused the separation of the two brothers; it was

* Ramdohr, *Ueber Malerei und Bildhauerarbeit in Rom, für Liebhader des Schönen in der Kunst.* Second Edition. Leipzig, 1798.

† Agostino's age and the date of his death are thus inscribed on a monumental tablet in the cathedral of Parma:—"OB. V. ID. MART. M.DCI. ÆT. SUÆ. AN. XLIII.," Bellori, who gives the whole inscription, writes by mistake 1602. His transcript, which professes to be faithful to the marble tablet, is inaccurate in other respects. If the dates in that monumental record are to be regarded as infallible, the year of Agostino's birth, ostensibly quoted by Malvasia from the baptismal register at Bologna, August 16, 1557, must be a misprint for August 16, 1558. Lanzi, Giordani, and others have followed Malvasia in this particular. Bellori, *Le Vite de' Pittori*, &c., Roma, 1672, p. 113.; Malvasia, *Felsina Pittrice*, Bologna, 1678, p. 455.

reported that the engraver (for as such Agostino was chiefly known) had surpassed the painter in the Farnese. This is said to have excited the jealousy of Annibale; differences arose between them, and Agostino left Rome for Parma, where he entered the service of the Duke Ranuccio, brother of the Cardinal Odoardo Farnese; after painting a few pictures, he died there on the 11th of March, 1601, in his forty-third year only. He was buried in the Cathedral of Parma; his funeral was, however, celebrated with great pomp at Bologna, by the artists of that school, and a description of it was published by Vittorio Benacci, in 1603.*

Agostino was painter, engraver, poet, and musician, and well versed in the arts and sciences generally. He was also fond of the society of the great, and this disposition was, according to Malvasia, the principal cause of his separation from Annibale while engaged in the Farnese Gallery; the immediate ground of offence being a caricature of their father and mother engaged in their tailor's work, which Annibale put into the hands of Agostino while surrounded by some of his distinguished acquaintances.

Agostino is allowed to have been the most learned of the Carracci, in the principles of art; he is said by Malvasia to have been at all times more correct than Annibale, and sometimes more correct than Lodovico. His masterpiece is the communion of St. Jerome, formerly in the church of the Certosa, now in the gallery of the Academy at Bologna; it is said to be the only picture on which he wrote his name.† He left an unfinished engraving of it, which was completed by Francesco Brizzio. Agostino's prints are very numerous; one of the earliest, largest, and best of them is the "Crucifixion," painted by Tintoretto for the Scuola of San Rocco in Venice. That engraving, completed in Venice in 1589, received the highest encomiums from Tintoretto himself. The print after the St. Jerome of Vanni is also one of Agostino's earliest and best works.‡

---

* Reprinted, without the cuts, in the *Felsina Pittrice* of Malvasia.

† Giordani, *Catalogo dei Quadri nella Pinacoteca della Pontificia Accademia di Belle Arti in Bologna*, 1835.

‡ See, besides the works of Bellori and Malvasia already quoted, the following works on engravings:—Gandellini, *Notizie Istoriche degl' Intagliatori*, Siena, 1771, reprinted in 1808; Heineken, *Dictionnaire des Artistes dont nous avons des Estampes; avec une notice détaillée de leurs ouvrages gravés*, 4 vols. 8vo. to DIZ. only, Leipzig, 1768-90; Bartsch, *Le Peintre-Graveur*, Vienna, 1803-21.

No. **147.** Cephalus and Aurora. Cephalus, while on a hunting expedition on Mount Hymettus, is forcibly carried off by Aurora, who was enamoured of him. The aged Tithonus, her husband, is represented in the foreground sleeping.* Figures larger than life.

A cartoon, 13 ft. 4 in. *w.* by 6 ft. 8 in. *h.*

No. **148.** Galatea. The sea-nymph Galatea is borne on the ocean by Glaucus, or some other marine deity, preceded by a Triton blowing his horn, and surrounded by Nereïdes and Cupids on dolphins. Some of the Cupids, bearing torches and bow and arrow, are sporting in the air; one of them, as if stunned by the noise made by the marine horn of the Triton, holds his hands to his ears.

A cartoon, 13 ft. 7½ in. *w.* by 6 ft. 8½ in. *h.*

These cartoons, which formed part of the celebrated collection of drawings belonging to Sir Thomas Lawrence, are the original designs made by Agostino Carracci, for the frescoes of the two principal lateral compartments of the vault of the Carracci Gallery, in the Farnese Palace at Rome. This Gallery has been engraved in whole and in part, several times. The first set of prints executed from it was by Carlo Cesio, published at Rome in 1657, in thirty sheets, and with the descriptions of Bellori, *Galleria nel Palazzo Farnese in Roma*, &c. It was subsequently engraved by Pietro Aquila, *Galeriæ Farnesianæ Icones*, &c., and by others. In the explanations accompanying Cesio's prints,† the principal figure is named Galatea or Venus, but in the life of Annibale Carracci, published fifteen years later, Bellori describes the subject definitely as the Triumph of Galatea. Both cartoons were presented to the National Gallery, in 1837, by the Earl of Ellesmere, by whom they were purchased from Messrs. Woodburn.

CARRA'CCI, ANNI'BALE.

Annibale Carracci, the younger brother of Agostino, was born at Bologna in 1560. His father intended to bring him up to his own business, and employed him in his shop; but his decided ability and taste for painting, led him, with the aid of his cousin Lodovico Carracci, to adopt that art as his profession; and Lodovico, who was five years his senior, was his first and only master in the art. In 1580 he visited Parma, and studied the works of Correggio there for about

* Ovid, *Met.* vii. 701.

† *Argomento della Galleria Farnese dipinta da Annibale Carracci, disegnata ed intagliata da Carlo Cesio. Nel quale spiegansi et riduconsi allegoricamente alla moralità, le Favole Poetiche in essa rappresentate.* It is reprinted by Malvasia in his *Felsina Pittrice*.

three years. It seems that he was joined at Parma by his brother Agostino, who, however, left Annibale to go to Venice, where they again met, and dwelt a considerable time. Agostino did not return to Bologna until 1589; Annibale returned somewhat earlier. The three Carracci opened their academy in 1589. After executing, together with Lodovico and Agostino, several public and private works in Bologna, Annibale was invited, about 1600, to Rome, by the Cardinal Odoardo Farnese, who, says Bellori, received and treated him as a gentleman—granting the usual table allowance of a courtier, for himself and two attendants, and a monthly salary. He was assisted in the frescoes of the Farnese Palace, as already stated, by his brother Agostino, who arrived shortly after Annibale at Rome, by Lanfranco, and by Domenichino, then a very young man. The whole works of the Farnese must have been completed before or about 1604; for, according to a letter of Annibale's intimate friend, Monsignore Agucchi, in whose arms he died, he painted scarcely anything (*quasi niente*) during the last five years of his life. He died July 15th, 1609, and was buried near Raphael, in the Pantheon. Malvasia says that Annibale was assisted also by Lodovico in the Farnese; but, as Lodovico was only a fortnight in Rome, from May 31st to June 13th, 1602, he could scarcely have afforded any great assistance beyond his advice. The altar-piece and frescoes of the chapel of San Diego, in the church of San Giacomo degli Spagnuoli, were probably also completed in 1604; they were all designed by Annibale, but he painted the altar-piece only; the frescoes were executed by Albani.* Annibale Carracci engraved a few plates.

The Farnese gallery was preferred by Poussin to all the works in Rome after those of Raphael. It is superior in form to those executed previously by the Carracci, but is inferior in colour to the works of the Sala of the Signori

---

* Annibale contracted to paint these works for 2,000 scudi, 1,000 of which he gave to Albani, though it was his wish that Albani should receive 1,800, reserving only 200 for himself, which, he maintained, was as much as his designs were worth. Albani, however, would not accept more than the half. The account of the remuneration which Annibale received for the Farnese gallery is unsatisfactory. He is said to have been paid only 500 scudi, through the interference of Don Juan de Castro, a courtier of the cardinal's. Baglione, however (*Vite de' Pittori*, &c. Rome, 1642), mentions this sum as a *present* (*regalo*), and, therefore, as over and above his salary (10 scudi a month), which it doubtless was.

Magnani at Bologna. Annibale's portrait, by himself, from the Orleans gallery, is in the collection of the Earl of Carlisle, at Castle Howard, where there are also several other excellent pictures by him, from the same gallery.*

No. **9.** CHRIST APPEARING TO SIMON PETER AFTER HIS RESURRECTION. St. Peter, according to a legend of the Roman church, when flying from Rome to avoid persecution, was surprised on the Appian Way by a vision of Christ bearing his cross; and on asking "Lord, whither goest thou?" was answered, "To Rome, to be crucified again." Feeling thus rebuked for his own pusillanimity, he returned to the city, and was shortly afterwards crucified, about the year 64 or 65, during the reign of the Emperor Nero.† The keys are attached to the girdle of St. Peter. Small full-length figures.

Engraved by G. Chasteau; in a large size by G. T. Doo, R.A., for the series of prints published for the *Associated Engravers;* and, small, by J. W. Shaw, in Jones's *National Gallery,* &c. On wood, 2 ft. 6 in. *h.* by 1 ft. 9 in. *w.*.

A picture of this subject, which was often treated by the early Italian painters, is generally described under its Latin title as a "*Domine, quo vadis?*" the words of the question of St. Peter to the Lord. Before the French Revolution, this picture was in the apartments of Prince Aldobrandini in the Borghese Palace at Rome, and is described by Ramdohr in his account of the Paintings and Sculptures of Rome, in 1784.‡ It was brought to England by Mr. Day in 1800, and passed subsequently into the possession of Lord Northwick and of Mr. Hamlet, and was purchased from the latter for the National Gallery in 1826.

No. **25.** ST. JOHN IN THE WILDERNESS.

"And the child grew, and waxed strong in spirit, and was in the deserts till the day of his showing unto Israel."—*Luke* i. 80.

A rocky picturesque landscape; St. John is reclining upon a skin, and holds in his left hand the standard of the Lamb, the symbol of his mission; while, with his right he is catching water in a cup from a stream which flows from the rocks. Whole figure, less than life size.

---

* The Orleans collection was brought to England in 1792, and was disposed of by private and public sales, in 1798, 1799. and 1800. The principal works contained in it are engraved in *La Galerie du Palais Royal,* Paris, 2 vols. fol. 1786. See the list of the Italian and French pictures in Mr. Buchanan's *Memoirs of Painting, &c.*; and in Passavant's *Kunstreise durch England,* &c. Dr. Waagen also has given a nearly complete catalogue of the collection in his *Kuntswerke und Künstler in England,* vol. i. Appendix B.

† Eusebius, *Hist. Eccles.*, l. ii. c. 25.

‡ Von Ramdohr, *Ueber Malerei und Bildhauerarbeit in Rom,* &c.

Engraved by Le Cerf in the *Galerie du Palais Royal*; also in Young's *Catalogue of the Angerstein Collection*; and in Jones's *National Gallery*. On canvas, 5 ft. 5 in. *h.* by 3 ft. 1 in. *w.*

Formerly in the Orleans collection, from which it passed, in 1799, into the possession of Mr. Angerstein, from whose son it was purchased for the nation, in 1824.

No. **56.** LANDSCAPE, WITH FIGURES. A lake or river scene, with much foliage, and mountains in the distance. On the water are parties of pleasure; in the fore-ground are an angler and another figure conversing.

Engraved by H. Wallis, for Jones's *National Gallery*. On canvas, 3 ft. 1½ in. *h.* by 4 ft. 4½ in. *w.*

Formerly in the collection of Prince Cellamare, at Naples, whence it came into the possession of the Rev. W. H. Carr, who bequeathed it, in 1831, to the National Gallery.

No. **63.** LANDSCAPE, WITH FIGURES. A rocky and woody landscape, with mountains in the distance, and a party of figures on foot and on horseback; supposed to represent Prince Giustiniani and attendants returning from the chase: in the middle distance, to the right, is a villa situated upon a rocky eminence.

Engraved in Jones's *National Gallery*. On canvas, 3 ft. 5 in. *h.* by 4 ft. 5 in. *w.*

Formerly in the Giustiniani Palace at Rome, whence it was procured by the Rev. W. H. Carr, who bequeathed it, in 1831, to to the National Gallery.

No. **88.** ERMINIA TAKES REFUGE WITH THE SHEPHERDS. From the story of Erminia, in Tasso's *Jerusalem Delivered.*

Erminia, daughter of the King of Antioch, having disguised herself in the armour of the heroic Clorinda, leaves Jerusalem, and attempts to gain the tent of the wounded Tancred, but being discovered by some Christian soldiers, she is pursued, and escapes with difficulty, eventually taking refuge among some shepherds. The picture represents that part of the story when Erminia, startled by the sound of pastoral music from the first repose which she had taken after her flight, rises, and attracted by the rustic strains, discovers an old shepherd, whilst tending his flock, busy making curd-baskets, and listening the while to the music of three children:—

> "Risorge, e là s'indrizza a passi lenti,
> E vede un uom canuto all' ombre amene
> Tesser fiscelle alla sua greggia accanto,
> Ed ascoltar di tre fanciulli il canto."
>
> *La Gerusalemme*, c. vii. st. 6.

Engraved in Young's *Catalogue of the Angerstein Collection*, and by G. Presbury, for Jones's *National Gallery*. On canvas, 4 ft. 10 in. *h.* by 7 ft. *w.*

This picture was formerly in the Camuccini Collection at Rome, from which it was purchased by Mr. Irvine in 1804 as a work by Annibale Carracci, but while in the possession of Mr. Angerstein, it was attributed to Domenichino; upon the removal, however, of the collection into the present building, it was again assigned to Annibale Carracci. As Annibale occasionally employed Domenichino to execute some of his designs, both masters may have had a share in the painting of this picture.* It was purchased with the other works of the Angerstein collection in 1824.

No. **93.** SILENUS GATHERING GRAPES. Two fauns are raising Silenus on a skin to enable him to pluck some grapes from a vine above his head: on each side is a stripling boy or young faun climbing the supports of the vine with a similar object. The autumnal colour of the leaves is assisted with gold leaf.

Engraved by W. Bromley, for the series of prints published for the *Associated Engravers;* and, on a small scale, for Jones's *National Gallery.* On wood, 1 ft. 9½ in. *h.* by 2 ft. 11 in. *w.*

No. **94.** PAN TEACHING APOLLO TO PLAY ON THE PIPES. Such is the title Lanzi gives to this picture. Ramdohr describes it as BACCHUS PLAYING TO SILENUS. Both figures are musicians, for the pipes of Silenus are hanging on the stem of a tree behind him; and a double flute is suspended to the tree by the side of the younger musician, who has the pipes in his hands, and appears to be watching the effects of his notes upon his companion.†

Engraved by D. Cunego for Hamilton's *Schola Italica;* and by J. Rolls, for Jones's *National Gallery.* On wood, 1 ft. 2 in. *h.* by 2 ft. 8 in. *w.*

These two pictures, purchased at Rome by Mr. Irvine for Mr. Buchanan in 1804, used to hang in the Lancellotti Palace there, together with the "Lot" and the "Susannah" of Guido, in this collection. No. 94 is described both by Ramdohr and Lanzi as a painting *a colla*, or in distemper, but it is now saturated with oil. Ramdohr says, that the "Silenus" decorated the top of a harpsichord, and he supposed that the "Apollo" or "Bacchus" decorated the front of the same instrument. Lanzi speaks highly of the second picture,‡ which formed part of the Angerstein collection, and was purchased by Parliament in 1824. The "Silenus" was in the collection of the Rev. W. H. Carr, and was added to the National Gallery, with the rest of that gentleman's bequest, in 1831.

---

* Passeri, *Vite de' Pittori*, &c. p. 12.

† Pan is represented by Greek writers as having the legs of a goat, and horns. Compare Lucian's *Dialogues of the Gods*, xxii., and Lord Bacon's exposition of the fable of Pan. *Works*, vol. i.

‡ Ramdohr, *Ueber Malerei und Bildhauerarbeit in Rom*, &c. (1784), vol. iii. p. 75; Lanzi, *Storia Pittorica dell' Italia*, vol. v. p. 76. The Marchese Melchiorri, in his *Guida Metodica di Roma* of 1836, apparently copying earlier accounts, speaks of the Silenus as still in the Lancellotti Palace.

No. 198. THE TEMPTATION OF ST. ANTHONY IN THE DESERT. The Saint, tempted on each side by demons, is reclining on his back, and appears engrossed at the moment by a vision above of the Saviour supported by angels. At his feet is a crouching lion.

Engraved by G. Audran and by B. Farjat. On copper, 1 ft. 7½ in. *h.* by 1 ft. 1½ in. *w.*

This picture was formerly in the Borghese Gallery at Rome, where it was much admired by Mengs, who said of it, that with Italian composition and drawing, it combined the execution of the Netherlands school.* It was some time in the collection of Lord Radstock, and was purchased for the nation in 1846 of the Earl of Dartmouth.

CARRA'CCI, LODOVI'CO.

LODOVICO CARRACCI, the founder of the eclectic school of Bologna, was born at Bologna, April 21st, 1555. He was placed with Prospero Fontana; and while in his school his apprehension appeared to be so slow, that like Domenichino afterwards he was called by his companions the ox, *il bue*. He afterwards entered the school of Passignano at Florence, and studied the works of Correggio and Parmigiano at Parma, those of Giulio Romano at Mantua, and those of Titian at Venice. The works of these and other masters afforded the elements of the eclectic style of the Carracci, as expressed in the well-known sonnet of Agostino.†

The school of the Carracci was opened in 1589, and carried on by the cousins conjointly up to 1600, from which time it was conducted by Lodovico alone, until his death (December 13th, 1619), which is said to have been considerably hastened by some errors in the fresco of the Annunciation, in the Cathedral of Bologna, his last work. The frescoes of the Convent of San Michele in Bosco, from the life of St. Benedict, commenced in 1602, after Lodovico's

* Ramdohr, *Ueber Mahlerei und Bildhauerarbeit in Rom*, &c. vol. i. p. 294.

† "Let him who wishes to be a good painter acquire the design of Rome, Venetian action, and Venetian management of shade, the dignified colour of Lombardy; the terrible manner of Michelangelo, Titian's truth and nature, the sovereign purity of Correggio's style, and the just symmetry of a Raphael; the decorum and well-grounded study of Tibaldi, the invention of the learned Primaticcio, and a *little* of Parmigiano's grace; but, without so much study and toil, let him only apply himself to imitate the works which our Niccolino has left us here." The last sentence, which is a mere compliment, refers to Niccolo del Abate. This sonnet sufficiently explains the principles of the electic school, and, at the same time, shows their mere technical tendency.

short visit to Rome, and which were generally considered his masterpieces, have long since perished, though the designs are preserved in the prints of G. M. Giovannini, *Il claustro di San Michele in Bosco di Bologna*, &c., published in 1694, with descriptions by Malvasia. There are thirteen pictures by Lodovico Carracci in the gallery of the Academy at Bologna, including some of his most celebrated worksin oil.*

In the opinion of Sir Joshua Reynolds, no painter knew how to harmonize the treatment of a picture with its subject better than Lodovico Carracci. "Style in painting," says Sir Joshua, "is the same as in writing, a power over materials, whether words or colours, by which conceptions or sentiments are conveyed. And in this Lodovico Carracci, I mean in his best works, appears to me to approach the nearest to perfection. His unaffected breadth of light and shadow, the simplicity of colouring, which, holding its proper rank, does not draw aside the least part of the attention from the subject, and the solemn effect of that twilight which seems diffused over his pictures, appear to me to correspond with grave and dignified subjects better than the more artificial brilliancy of sunshine which enlightens the pictures of Titian."†

The scholars of the Carracci produced a change in all the schools of Italy; but the qualities of their works, in contradistinction to those of the great masters of the preceding century, are strictly technical or material. They remained as much below the great masters of Rome and Florence in expression, composition, and character, as they surpassed them in general execution. The most distinguished masters of this school were Domenichino, Guido, Albani, and Lanfranco.

No. **28.** SUSANNAH AND THE TWO ELDERS, in the Garden of Joachim, at Babylon. Susannah, an entire figure, is kneeling in the fore-ground, and is holding back her garment from the rough touch of one of the elders.—*Apocryphal Book of Susannah.*

Engraved by J. H. Watt for the ***Associated Engravers***; also by A. L. Romanet in the ***Galerie du Palais Royal***; in Young's

---

* Malvasia, *Felsina Pittrice*; Lanzi, *Storia Pittorica, &c.* Belvisi, *Elogio Storico del Pittore Lodovico Caracci*, 8vo. Bologna, 1825. Giordani, *Catalogo dei Quadri nella Pinacoteca di Bologna.*

† Discourse II.

Catalogue of the Angerstein Collection; and in Jones's *National Gallery.* On canvas, 4 ft. 8 in. *h.* by 3 ft. 7 in. *w.*

Formerly in the Orleans collection, from which it passed in 1799 into the possession of Mr. Angerstein, from whose heir it was purchased for the nation, in 1824.

CASENTINO, JACOPO DI.

JACOPO LANDINI, of Prato Vecchio, in the Casentino, where he was born about 1310, was a pupil of Taddeo Gaddi, and painted in a very similar style. He was an established painter at Florence in 1350, when he assisted in the formation of the Florentine Academy of St. Luke; he was enrolled one of the Company of Painters in 1351. He was also an architect.

Jacopo was distinguished chiefly as a fresco painter;* he executed many frescoes in various places in Tuscany, some of which are highly spoken of by Vasari; but few traces of them now remain. He was the master of Spinello Aretino, who when young assisted him in some of the many works he executed in Arezzo. Jacopo di Casentino died at an advanced age, in his native place, towards the close of the fourteenth century, about 1390. Vasari states that he attained the age of eighty.†

No. **580.** ST. JOHN THE EVANGELIST, LIFTED UP INTO HEAVEN; with various saints, and other scenes from the life of the Evangelist. In the centre is St. John lifted up by the Lord among the patriarchs and apostles of the church;‡ on the left are, Saints Bernard, Scholastica, Benedict, and John the Baptist; on the right, Saints Peter, Romualdo, Catherine, and Jerome.§ Immediately over the centre picture, is Christ risen from the Dead, the gates of hell cast down on one side, and on the other the donor

* The term fresco is used by Vasari and others, in describing the wall paintings of the early Italian masters, but the method of *buon fresco* was not in use till the close of the 14th century. *See note p. 106.*

† Vasari, *Vite de' Pittori, &c.* Ed. Le Monnier, Flor. 1846, et seq.

‡ "Post hæc juxta altare foveam quadratam fieri jussit et terram extra ecclesiam jactari. In quam beatus Evangelista descendens expansis manibus gratias Deo egit, et orationem devotissimam fudit. Qua finita tanta lux super eum emicuit quod a nemine videri potuit. Recedenteque lumine, fovea reperta est Manna repleta." &c. See the *Golden Legend.* St. John Evan. p. 27; and Peter de Natalibus, *Catalogus Sanctorum,* ii. 7.

§ In the open book held by St. Jerome is written *Penitenciam agere, est perpetrata mala peragere, et peragendo non perpetrare:* to do penance is to work out sins, and in working them out to sin no more.

and his family presented to him by St. John the Evangelist and St. John the Baptist; over the left picture is the archangel Michael, and over the right, the archangel Raphael with Tobias. In the three upper pictures are represented, in the middle the Trinity, and the Virgin and the Angel of the Annunciation, at the sides.

In the predella below, are St. John the Evangelist, distributing alms, and baptizing catechumens; the vision in the Island of Patmos, in which four angels are binding four beasts, and the woman pursued by the serpent is flying into the wilderness; St. John liberated from the cauldron of boiling oil, in which he was placed by the orders of the Emperor Domitian; and at the extreme ends, St. Apollonia,* and St. Verdiana.

In the pilasters—on the left, are Saint Francis, St. Cosmas, and another saint above; on the right, St. Margaret, St. Damianus, and St. Nicholas of Bari. In all, twenty-two pictures.

In tempera, on wood. Principal pictures, centre 4 ft. *h.* by 2 ft. 1 in. *w.*, sides 3 ft. 9 in. *h.* by 2 ft. *w.*; *cuspidi*, or upper pictures, centre 1 ft. 4½ in. *h.* by 11 in. *w.*, sides 1 ft. 4½ in. *h.* by 10 in. *w.*; predella pictures 1 ft. *h.*, centre 1 ft. 10½ in. *w.*, sides 1 ft. 9½ in. *w.* Outside measure of the altar piece, 9 ft. 5 in. *h.* by 8 ft. 5 in. *w.* In its original frame, restored.

Formerly in the church of San Giovanni Evangelista, at Prato Vecchio, in the Casentino. Purchased at Florence, from the Lombardi-Baldi collection, in 1857.

CIMA DA CONEGLIANO.

Giambattista Cima da Conegliano was the contemporary, and one of the principal rivals, of Giovanni Bellini at Venice, but while equally as brilliant in colouring, he was more skilful, more vigorous, and more various in his drawing and composition than Bellini. The editors of the "Le Monnier" Vasari term Giambattista Cima the Masaccio of the Venetian school. He was born at Conegliano, near Treviso, but his exact time is uncertain. His pictures bear dates from 1489 to 1517. He signed his name Joannes Baptista and Joannes Baptista Coneglianensis. He was, according to some accounts, the scholar of Giovanni

* Inscribed St. Apollonia, but the emblem, a female breast held by a pair of pincers, is generally that of St. Agatha. The common emblem of St. Apollonia is the tooth held in a pair of pincers.

Bellini.* The Castello di Conegliano, Cima's native place is often represented in the back-grounds of his pictures, tho' landscapes of which he treated with unusual skill for the period. His son, Carlo Cima, imitated his works, genuine examples of which are rare out of Venice.

No. **300.** The INFANT CHRIST STANDING ON THE KNEES OF THE VIRGIN, who is sitting on a marble seat, and holding the child with her right hand, while she supports one of his feet with her left. A hilly landscape, with a town in the back-ground. Inscribed JOANNES BAPTISTA, P. in the lower corner to the spectator's right.

IOANNESBAPTISTA P

On wood, 2 ft. 3 in. *h.* by 1 ft. 10½ in. *w.*
Purchased from M. Roussel in Paris, in 1858.

No. **634.** MADONNA, WITH THE INFANT CHRIST STANDING ON HER KNEES, who holds a goldfinch in his hand; a hilly landscape, with the view of a town in the background. Signed JOANES. BAPTISTA. CONEGLA^S. P.

IOANES·BAPTISTA·CONEGLA^S ·P

On wood, 1 ft. 8½ in. *h.* by 1 ft. 5 in. *w.*
Purchased at Paris, from the collection of M. Edmond Beaucousin, in 1860. Formerly at Powerscourt Castle, where it was known as the Madonna del Cardellino; subsequently in the collection of Mr. William Coningham, M.P.

CIMABUE.

GIOVANNI GUALTIERI, or CIMABUE, regarded by Vasari as the father of modern painting, was born at Florence in 1240. Though not the first of the Italians to forsake the conventional habits of the Byzantine School, he was the most successful of the painters of the thirteenth century in combining the study of nature with the traditionary art of his time. His reputed master was Giunta of Pisa, a crucifix by whom, painted in 1236, is still preserved in Santa Maria Degli Angeli at Assisi.† Whether, as Vasari

---

* Vasari, Ed. Le Monnier, vol. vi. pp. 100 and 118; Zanetti, *Pittura Veneziana*, 1771, p. 60.

† Traced in Ramboux's Outlines from old Christian Paintings in Italy, *Umrisse zur Veranschaulichung alt Christlicher Kunst in Italien*, vom Jahre 1200 bis 1600, &c., folio.

states, Cimabue executed any of the frescoes in the upper church of San Francesco at Assisi, is doubtful.

Two well-authenticated pictures by him are—the Madonna with Angels, in the Academy at Florence, (formerly in the church of the SS. Trinita,) and the colossal Madonna still in the Rucellai chapel, in the church of Santa Maria Novella at Florence. The last named is not only the best of the remaining works ascribed to him, but, compared with contemporary and even some later productions, has merits sufficient to entitle him to the distinguished place which Vasari assigns to him. The tradition, preserved by the biographer, that the Rucellai Madonna was carried in a procession with great festivity from the painter's house to the church, is supposed to have been embellished as regards some of the incidents; but there seems no reason to doubt that such a work, intended for a religious purpose should, at the time, have excited general enthusiasm.

Cimabue's additional claim to distinction is that of having discovered and trained the superior abilities of Giotto.

In 1302 it appears that he was occupied on a mosaic in the Duomo at Pisa, and as the work was left unfinished, that date may, with probability, be assigned as the year of his death.*

No. **565.** THE MADONNA AND CHILD ENTHRONED, ANGELS ADORING. The Virgin is seated, and holds the child sitting on her left knee: on each side, behind the throne, are three angels in adoration. Half-figures, larger than life.

In tempera, on wood, with a gable top, 6 ft. 3 in. *h.* by 5 ft. 6 in. *w.*

This picture is described by Vasari as having been attached to a pilaster in the choir in the church of Santa Croce at Florence. It was still in its place in 1591;† but in 1677 it had been deposited elsewhere in the convent of Santa Croce, in consequence of alterations in the church;‡ it remained in the convent until it came into the possession of the Signori Lombardi and Baldi, from whose collection, at Florence, it was purchased for the National Gallery in 1857.

---

* Vasari, *Vite*, &c. Ed. Le Monnier, Flor. 1846, *et seq.*

† Bocchi, *Le Bellezze della Città di Fiorenza*, p. 153.

‡ Cinelli, *Le Bellezze della Città di Firenze, &c., ampliate ed accresciute.* Flor. 1677, p. 316.

CLAUDE.

Claude Gele'e or Gille'e, called Claude de Lorraine, or le Lorrain, and also Claude Lorrain, was born in Lorraine, at Château de Chamagne, near Charmes, department des Vosges, in the year 1600. His parents were very poor, and as Claude showed no disposition to learn to read or write he was placed with a baker and pastry-cook. The cooks of Lorraine were celebrated in the time of Claude's youth, and according to his friend and biographer, Sandrart, Claude travelled to Rome in the company of some of these cooks, like them, to seek employment there. He found it with Agostino Tassi, and the circumstance of his master being a painter appears to have first inspired Claude with a fondness for art. Tassi was a good landscape-painter (he had been the pupil of Paul Bril), and with this painter Claude engaged himself as an ordinary domestic servant. He both prepared his master's meals and ground his colours for him; but he acquired at the same time the rudiments of his art.*

How long Claude was engaged in this menial capacity is uncertain, but probably some years after his repeated efforts in art. Tassi's principal works were those of the Lancellotti and Quirinal palaces, executed during the pontificate of Paul V. (1605-21), and it must have been during their progress that

* Sandrart, from whose *Teutsche Academie*, &c., or *Accademia Todesca*, the above account is taken, was the intimate companion of Claude, and his work was published during Claude's lifetime (1675); it is therefore most probably correct, or at least must be of more authority than the account in the posthumous volume of Baldinucci, who lived at Florence, and was probably not even acquainted with Claude. This subject is noticed here, as Baldinucci (*Notizie dei Professori del Disegno*, &c.) is represented in the *Biographie Universelle*, and elsewhere, as contradicting Sandrart's account of Claude's origin. Baldinucci does not contradict Sandrart; he merely gives a different account of Claude's journey to Rome. He states that Claude, after the death of his parents, who died when he was twelve years of age, joined an elder brother in Alsace, who was a wood-engraver, and subsequently accompanied a lace-merchant, his relation, to Rome. This may have taken place after Claude had been some years with the pastry-cook with whom he was placed by his parents, according to Sandrart. But Claude's history was too remarkable for Sandrart not to have heard it from his own mouth during their repeated intercourse and sketching excursions together when in Rome (*Lebenslauf Joachims von Sandrart*, &c., p. 12, and in the second volume of the *Academia Todesca* p. 332). In the Latin translation of Sandrart, which was published in 1684, nine years after the original work, there is a mis-print in the text of *pictori* for *pistori*, by which Sandrart is made to say that Claude's master was a *painter* of pies instead of a baker of pies (*pictori cuidam artocreatum*); the same mistake occurs in the marginal note, and in the *index*, and a few recent writers have been led into error by it. The misprint, however, is quite evident merely from the context.

Claude was Tassi's servant. In the pontificate of Urban VIII. (1623-44), he was already known at Rome as a great landscape-painter. The intervening pontificate of Gregory XV., therefore, was about the period that he was struggling for the obscure independence noticed by Sandrart, and he appears at this time to have visited his native country. He visited also Venice and Naples, and in the latter place he is said to have received some instruction from a landscape-painter of the name of Gottfried Vals. Sandrart first taught Claude to paint from nature. In 1630 he appeared as an engraver: of the several etchings ascribed to him, about one-half bear dates from 1630 to 1663,* the rest are without dates. His earliest pictures of note may have been painted from about 1630, the best, fifteen or twenty years later. He was in the habit of preserving sketches of his pictures in a portfolio or book, which he called *Libro di Verità*, or Book of Truth; and on the backs of some of these drawings are written the dates of the completion of the pictures, and the names of the purchasers. This remarkable collection of drawings is now in the possession of the Duke of Devonshire.†

Claude was extremely slow and careful in his execution. Sandrart says that he often painted for a week or a fortnight on one part of a picture, without showing any progress. He always had a great difficulty in painting or drawing the human figure or animals, though he drew much from the life, and attended the Academy of Rome many years. He generally procured the assistance of F. Lauri, J. Courtois, A. Both, and others, in executing this part of his pictures.

Claude's chief excellence is in aërial perspective, and in the management of light generally. He died at Rome in

---

* Robert Dumesnil, in *Le Peintre-Graveur Français*, describes forty-two etchings by Claude, and gives fac-similes of eighteen of his signatures, no two of which are alike. He wrote his christian name generally in the Italian form—Claudio, and sometimes in the Latin form—Claudius. His surname is written in a variety of ways; Gillee seems to be the most constant.

† It was engraved by Richard Earlom, for John Boydell, under the following title:—"*Liber Veritatis; or, a Collection of Two Hundred Prints after the original designs of Claude le Lorrain, in the Collection of his Grace the Duke of Devonshire*, London, 1777." Copied by Ludovico Caracciolo, Roma, 1815. Caracciolo, in a Life of Claude prefixed to his work, pretends to correct previous writers by referring to the (misprinted) Latin passage in Sandrart above quoted.

1682, and was buried in the church of La Trinità de' Monti. The two Poussins and Salvator Rosa were contemporary with him at Rome.* There is a good collection of Claude's drawings in the British Museum.

No. 2. Pastoral Landscape, with Figures, illustrating the reconciliation of Cephalus and Procris. The principal feature of this picture is a large cluster of trees in the centre; at the left is a stream, with cattle wading through it; a bridge through which the stream flows and forms a small cascade, and a castellated height behind it, constitute the back-ground on this side; on the other is a distant view of a champaign country, bordered by mountains. To the right, Cephalus is receiving from Procris the presents of Diana, the hound Lelaps, and the fatal dart with which she was subsequently killed.

Engraved by R. Earlom, in the *Liber Veritatis*, No. 91; by J. Browne, for Boydell, in 1779; by J. Pye, for the series of prints published for the *Associated Engravers;* and small, in Jones's *National Gallery*. On canvas, 3 ft. 4 in. *h*. by 4 ft. 5 in. *w*.

Painted, according to the date upon it, in 1645, for some person residing in Paris. It was brought to England by Mr. Delahante, and formed subsequently part of the Angerstein Gallery, and was purchased, with that collection, in 1824. Signed—

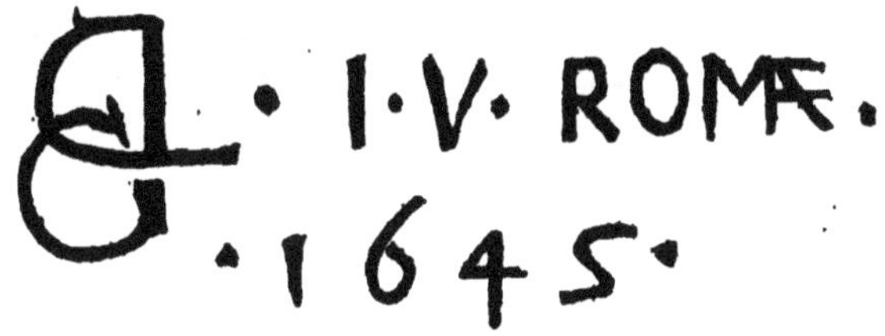

No. 3. A Seaport at Sunset. A composition On the left are masses of Italian architecture in perspective; on the extreme right a few ships are lying at anchor: in the fore-ground are several figures, variously occupied. Towards the middle of the picture, the declining sun is already nearly level with the horizon.

Engraved in the *Liber Veritatis*, No. 28; in Jones's *National Gallery;* and by E. Goodall, for the series of prints published

---

* Sandrart, *L'Accademia Todesca*; or, *Teutsche Academie der edlen Bau- Bild- und Malerey-Künste*, 4 vols. folio, Nürnberg, 1675-79; Pascoli, *Vite de' Pittori, Scultori, ed Architetti Moderni*, Rome, 1736; D'Argenville, *Abrégé de la Vie des plus fameux Peintres*, Paris, 1745.

for the *Associated Engravers.* On canvas, 3 ft. 3 in. *h.* by 4 ft. 3 in. *w.*

This picture is dated 1644: it was painted for the Cardinal de' Medici. It was imported into this country by Mr. Delahante, and formed part of the Angerstein collection, with which it was purchased for the nation in 1824. Signed—

CLAVDIO. G.I.V. ROMÆ 1644

No. **6.** LANDSCAPE, WITH FIGURES, supposed to represent David at the Cave of Adullam. Also called Sinon brought before Priam.

"And David longed, and said, Oh, that one would give me drink of the water of Beth-lehem, which is by the gate!

"And the three mighty men brake through the host of the Philistines, and drew water out of the well of Beth-lehem, that was by the gate, and took it and brought it to David."—II. *Samuel,* xxiii. 16.

On the right, behind the principal figures, is a broken rocky height, thinly covered with small trees and bushes; opposite this, towards the left, is a very prominent group of trees, constituting with its fore-ground the principal dark mass of the picture, and giving distance to the woody castellated eminence in the middle-ground behind. Immediately before the trees two warriors are hastening to join the assemblage around David. The distance is an extensive and varied country. Several groups of small figures are interspersed about the picture. Signed CLAUDIO GILLEE I.V. ROMÆ, 1658.

Engraved in the *Liber Veritatis,* No. 145; and by J. C. Varrall, for Jones's *National Gallery.* On canvas, 3 ft. 9 in. *h.* by 6 ft. 2½ in.

This picture, called the Chigi Claude, was painted in 1658 for Agostino Chigi, and was, up to the time of the French revolution, in the Chigi Palace at Rome, from which it passed into the possession of Mr. Sloane, an English banker there; after his death it was sent by his family to England. It came subsequently into the possession of the Rev. W. H. Carr, who bequeathed it in 1831 to the National Gallery.

No. **12.** LANDSCAPE, WITH FIGURES, representing the marriage festival of Isaac and Rebecca. A broad river, with a picturesque water-mill on the left hand, and a more distant bridge leading to a town on the opposite side, constitute the centre of the picture: the scene is bounded by mountains. On each side are lofty spreading trees, and behind those on the left is seen a waterfall: in the fore-ground is a bridge of a single arch, with cattle drinking from the stream which flows under it; to the right are the figures celebrating the marriage festival of Isaac and Rebecca, according to the inscription on the picture itself—"*Mariage d'Isaac avec Rebecca.*"

MARIAGE · DI SAC AVEC REBECA

·CLAVDIO·GIL·

·I·N·V· ROMA 1648·

Engraved in the *Liber Veritatis*, No. 113; by J. Mason, in 1748; by E. Goodall, for the series of prints published for the *Associated Engravers;* and small, in Jones's *National Gallery*. On canvas, 4 ft. 11 in. *h.* by 6 ft. 7 in. *w.*

This picture, which, with the following, was painted in 1648, for the Duke de Bouillon, at Paris, is a repetition, with considerable variations in the details, of the celebrated Doria or Panfili Claude, known as "*Il Molino*," or Claude's Mill, and is of the same dimensions. There is a print of the Doria picture, by F. Vivares, engraved in 1766, and another by F. W. Gmelin, engraved in 1804. The picture above described was subsequently in the Angerstein collection, with which it was purchased in 1824.*

No. **14.** Seaport, with Figures, representing the embarkation of the Queen of Sheba, on the occasion of her visit to Solomon. The time appears to be the early morning, as the sun is represented only a little above the horizon; on the left, in the fore-ground, and occupying the whole height of the picture, is a Corinthian ruin, behind which is seen some shipping; on the right, extending back towards the centre of the picture, is a pile of Italian architecture, partly relieved by foliage: the queen and her attendants are descending a broad flight of steps on this side, to enter a boat, which is waiting to receive them. A ship is lying at anchor near the entrance of the port. Several figures to the right, and a boat in the centre, occupy part of the fore-ground. The words *La Reine de Saba va trover Salomon*, nearly obliterated, are written in the right corner of the picture.

LA· REINE·DE· SABA VA·

TROVER· SALOMON·

* Some connoisseurs have pronounced this picture a *copy* of the Doria Claude, but a comparison of the above-mentioned prints will show that there are considerable variations in all parts of the two pictures. The figures are very different.

Engraved in the *Liber Veritatis*, No. 114; by J. C. Varrall, for Jones's *National Gallery;* and by J. Pye. On canvas, 4 ft. 11 in. *h.* by 6 ft. 7 in. *w.*

This picture is known as the Bouillon Claude, from the Duke de Bouillon, with whose name it is inscribed in the left corner, and for whom it was painted, together with No. 12, in 1648. Both pictures remained in the possession of the Bouillon family until the French revolution, when they were brought to England, and were bought by Mr. Angerstein, with whose collection they were purchased for the nation, in 1824. The inscription referred to is—

CLAVDE GIL· ·IV· FAICT· POVR·SON·ALTESSE·LE·DVC·DE·
·BVILLON·AROMA· 1648·

No. **19.** Landscape, with Figures, representing the story of Narcissus and Echo. This picture is almost equally divided into two principal masses: dark shady foliage, occupying the whole left, is separated from the bright sky of the rest of the picture by a castellated eminence and more distant foliage in the middle-ground. The distance to the right represents a bay of the sea, with a small town on either side, and is bounded by mountains. There is also a small cluster of trees to the right of the picture. The fore-ground is occupied by a transparent shady pool, on the farther side of which Narcissus is admiring his image in the water; above him, to the left, are two nymphs, almost hidden by the trees, watching him. The nymph, lying at the extreme left on this side of the pool, is apparently the disconsolate Echo, pining for the love of Narcissus.

Engraved in the *Liber Veritatis*, No. 77; by F. Vivares, in 1743; and by W. B. Cooke, in Jones's *National Gallery*. On canvas, 3 ft. 1 in. *h.* by 3 ft. 11 in. *w.* There is an obscure inscription in the left corner.

According to the *Liber Veritatis*, this picture was painted for England in 1644. It was formerly in the possession of Mr. P. Delmé, from whose collection it was purchased by Sir George Beaumont, who presented it, with other pictures, in 1826, to the National Gallery.

No. **30.** Seaport, with the Embarkation of St. Ursula. The water in this picture is a small basin or harbour; on the left side is a perspective view of a rich pile of architecture, on the other are harbour works and foliage, and the ships about to conduct St. Ursula and her followers on their pilgrimage. The saint, with a long train of virgins, is descending a flight of steps to the boats, which are ready to convey them on board the ships. In the fore-ground are various figures busily occupied, some with merchandise, others with their boats. "The effect of the breeze upon the water and upon the trees, and the freshness of the morning atmosphere, in this picture," says Mr. Ottley,* "are expressed with a closeness of imitation bordering on illusion."†

Engraved in the *Liber Veritatis*, No. 54; also by Dominique Barriere, at Rome, in 1665; by J. Fitler, in 1787; by H. Le Keux, for the series of prints published for the *Associated Engravers*; and small, in Jones's *National Gallery*. On canvas, 3 ft. 8 in. *h.* by 4 ft. 11 in. *w.* Signed, but the signature is not legible.

This picture was painted for Cardinal Barberini, in 1646, and remained in the possession of the Barberini family until 1760, when it was purchased by Mr. Lock, of Norbury Park. It formed subsequently part of the Angerstein Gallery, and was purchased with the other works of that collection, in 1824.

No. 55. Landscape, with Figures, representing the death of Procris. The scene is in a forest; the sun is still high. In the middle-ground, among the trees, may be discerned a town on the border of a small lake; a deer is also very prominently introduced descending a hill which leads towards the lake. In the fore-ground Procris lies pierced by the fatal arrow from the hand of her husband Cephalus, who, followed by his hound, is hastening to her assistance.

Engraved in the *Liber Veritatis*, No. 100; of the full size, by J. Browne; and small, in Jones's *National Gallery*. On canvas, 1 ft. 8 in. *h.* by 1 ft. 7 in. *w.*

Presented to the nation in 1826 by Sir George Beaumont, Bart.

No. 58. Landscape, with Goatherd and Goats; sometimes called a study of trees. A large open cluster of trees constitutes nearly the whole picture: in the foreground is a goatherd, playing the pipes while tending his goats.

Engraved by G. A. Chocarne for Jones's *National Gallery*. On canvas, 1 ft. 8½ in. *h.* by 1 ft. 4 in. *w.*

Presented to the nation in 1826 by Sir George Beaumont, Bart.

---

* *Descriptive Catalogue of the Pictures in the National Gallery*, &c. London, 1832.

† The pilgrimage of St. Ursula and her attendant virgins is the subject of the beautiful paintings by Memling, on the celebrated Shrine or Châsse de St. Ursule, preserved in the Hospital of St. John, at Bruges. St. Ursula, according to the legend, was an English princess; she and her followers suffered martyrdom at Cologne, in the third century. In some accounts the number of virgins is not specified, in others 11,000 are mentioned, but the figures XI.M.V. might be explained as Undecim Martyrum Virginum, eleven martyr virgins, with much more probability than as Undecim Millia Virginum, eleven thousand virgins. See *Notice des Tableaux de l'Hôpital Civil de S. Jean à Bruges*, 1842; also Baron Keversberg, *Ursule, Princesse britannique, d'après la Légende, et les Peintures d'Hemling*; and the Article Memling, in the Supplement to the *Penny Cyclopædia*.

No. **61.** Landscape, with Figures, supposed to represent either the Annunciation or the Angel appearing to Hagar. The figures are in the fore-ground to the left; on each side of the picture is foliage, that to the right covering a great portion of the picture. The middle-ground is occupied by a broad winding river, over which a single arch conducts to a high rock, occupying the centre of the middle distance, and which is surmounted by a castle or town. The view is bounded by low mountains.

Engraved in the *Liber Veritatis* No. 106; by J. Pye, for the series of prints published for the *Associated Engravers*; and by J. C. Varrall, in Jones's *National Gallery*. On canvas, 1 ft. 8 in. *h.* by 1 ft. 5 in. *w.*

Presented to the nation in 1826 by Sir George Beaumont, Bart., with whom, however, this picture was so great a favourite, that he requested permission to have it returned to him for his life-time; it was restored to the National Gallery, upon Sir George's death, by his widow, Lady Beaumont, in 1828.

CLOUET.

François Clouet, born in France, probably at Tours, about 1510, was the son of Jean Clouet, a Fleming settled in France, commonly called Jeannet, and his wife, Jeanne Boucault, a native of Tours: Jeannet was painter and *varlet de chambre ordinaire* to Francis I. as early as 1518, but as he had never been naturalized, when he died, in 1541, his property was forfeited to the king. This property was restored to François Clouet, his heir, who had then the same rank as his father, in the month of November of 1541. François was the fourth painter of this family; his grandfather Jean had also settled in France, at Tours, and an uncle (a brother of John) was painter to Margaret and Henry of Navarre, at a salary of 200 francs the year. They appear to have been all employed and distinguished as portrait painters. François was still living January 1st, 1571, but was already dead in 1574.*

No. **662.** A Man's Portrait, in the costume of the sixteenth century. Small figure, bust. Dated 1543.

On wood, 12 in. *h.* by 9 in. *w.*

Purchased from M. Edmond Beaucousin, at Paris, in 1860.

* Le Cte De Laborde, *La Renaissance des Arts à la Cour de France.*—Peinture, 1850–5.

CORNELISSEN.

JACOB CORNELISSEN, or CORNELISZ, was born at East Zaandam, in North Holland, about 1475—1480, and died, very old, at Amsterdam, about 1555—1560; he was still painting in 1553. Van Mander speaks of him as a great painter, and mentions some altar-pieces by him: he was the master of Jan Schoorel, and he had a son Dirk, who was likewise a good painter, especially of portraits; he died in 1567. Jacob Cornelissen was also an engraver. There are still some prints preserved by him, the "Life of Christ" and others, dated 1517 and 1518.*

No. **657.** PORTRAITS OF A DUTCH GENTLEMAN AND LADY, kneeling, with their patron saints, Peter and Paul, standing behind them. Small full-length figures.

On wood, each panel 2 ft. 8 in. *h.* by 10½ in. *w.*

Formerly the doors of a small altar-piece. Purchased from M. Edmond Beaucousin, at Paris, in 1860.

CORREGGIO.

ANTONIO ALLEGRI, commonly called CORREGGIO from his birth-place, a small town now constituting part of the duchy of Modena, was born probably in the winter of 1493-4; the exact date is not known. His father, Pellegrino Allegri, was a merchant in good circumstances. The whole youth of Antonio is involved in obscurity; but he is supposed to have been first instructed in painting by Antonio Bartolotti, a painter of Correggio. He executed several good pictures in his native place. In 1519 we find him a master of established reputation at Parma. The celebrated cupola of San Giovanni was commenced in the following year; and two years later, 1522, he contracted for the great works of the dome of the cathedral of that place. The works of these two churches are painted in fresco. In the church of San Giovanni he has represented the Ascension of Christ; and in the cathedral, the Assumption of the Virgin, the apostles being witnesses of both events.†

---

* Van Mander, *Het Leven der Schilders*, &c., vol. i. ed. 1764.

† Engraved by G. B. Vanni. A new series of admirable prints from these and from the frescoes of San Giovanni were in the course of being engraved by the late Cav. Toschi; it is to be hoped that the undertaking will be continued by his numerous and able scholars.

The frescoes of the cathedral were left unfinished by Correggio. He contracted to paint the whole dome and choir for 1000 ducats,* but he did not complete even the dome; it was finished by his pupil, Giorgio Gandini. He died of a fever at Correggio, on March the 5th, 1534, in his forty-first year, being survived by his father, his wife, his son Pomponio, and one of three daughters.

Correggio was married, in 1520, to Girolama Merlini, a young lady of Mantua, with whom he received a considerable dowry. She is supposed to have been the original of the Madonna in the Holy Family, known as *La Zingarella*.† Correggio's great reputation rests chiefly upon the frescoes mentioned above, but he is the master likewise of many of the most celebrated productions of oil-painting extant; and some of these were painted at Correggio before his visit to Parma in 1519, when he was then only in his twenty-sixth year; as the St. George and the St. Sebastian, now two of the principal ornaments of the magnificent gallery of Dresden. The celebrated pictures of the "Notte," and the "Magdalen Reading," are also in that collection.

Correggio's frescoes, and even some of his oil pictures, are remarkable for violent, but skilful foreshortenings. His proverbial *grace*—apparent, not only in his undulating forms and soft transitions, but in the action and expression of his figures,—is a distinctive characteristic of his works; and he is still unrivalled in a certain harmony which results from delicate gradations of light and shade.

The pictures of Correggio were so exclusively conspicuous for these qualities before the rise of the modern school of Bologna, that the first sight of some of his works forced Annibale Carracci, in a letter to his cousin Lodovico, to declare that in comparison with them the St. Cecilia of Raphael appeared to be wooden. He says, in a letter to his cousin, dated Parma, April 18th, 1580, "Tibaldi, Niccolino,

---

* This and other circumstances, shown by documents published by Pungileoni in his Memoir of Correggio, prove that the common report, circulated by Vasari about Correggio's poverty, is more than doubtful. He appears on all occasions to have been well paid for his works. One thousand ducats are equal to about five hundred pounds sterling, and must, at that period, have been equivalent to the value of at least three or four thousand pounds at the present day.

† Pungileoni, *Memorie Istoriche di Antonio Allegri detto il Correggio*, Parma, 1817-21; *Sketches of the Lives of Correggio and Parmigiano*. London, 1823.

I would almost say Raphael himself, are not to be compared [with Correggio].—The St. Jerome, the St. Catherine, the Madonna della Scodella, I would rather have any one of them than the 'Saint Cecilia.' How much grander, and at the same time more delicate is St. Jerome, than that St. Paul,* which at first appeared to me to be a miracle; but now I feel as if it were made of wood, it is so hard!"†

No. **7.** Group of Heads. Ten various views of heads, representing apparently part of a choir of angels. These are marked as being "*after* Correggio."

Engraved in Jones's *National Gallery*. On canvas, 5 ft. *h.* by 3 ft. 6 in. *w.*

This picture and its companion, No. 37, were formerly in the possession of Christina, Queen of Sweden: they subsequently passed into the Orleans collection, with which they were brought to this country, and were purchased by Mr. Angerstein. They were probably taken to Sweden as part of the plunder of Prague, when that city was captured by the Swedes under Count Königsmark, July 15, 1648, and the pictures collected by the Emperor Rudolph II. were carried to Stockholm. Among these pictures were several by Correggio, which had been presented to the Emperor by Federigo Gonzaga, Duke of Mantua, for whom they had been originally painted.‡

No. **10.** Mercury instructing Cupid in the presence of Venus. Mercury, dressed only in his winged cap (Petasus) and sandals (Talaria), is seated on the ground, and is endeavouring to teach Cupid his letters, of which, according to a Greek myth, he was the inventor. The little god, standing by his side, appears to be paying due attention to his lesson. Venus, here represented as winged, has taken temporary charge of Cupid's bow, which she holds in her left hand, and appears to be entertained with the novel spectacle. The back-ground of dark foliage contrasts finely with the well-rounded nude of the figures. Entire figures nearly of the natural size.

Engraved on a large scale by Arnold de Jode, in 1667, and in small, in 1786, by Le Villain, for the *Galerie du Palais Royal*,

---

* The figure of Paul in the picture of St. Cecilia.

† Malvasia, *Felsina Pittrice*, vol. i. p. 365. The St. Jerome is now in the Gallery of the Academy of Parma. There are prints of it by Ag. Carracci, C. Cort, and Sir R. Strange. Annibale was only twenty years of age when he wrote this letter; he would probably not have used such expressions after his acquaintance with the works of Raphael in Rome. They, however, explain the tendency of the rising school of Bologna; it was sensuous and technical.

‡ Winckelmann, *Werke*, vol. i. p. 70.

in which there was a duplicate of this composition. On canvas, 5 ft. 1 in. *h.* by 3 ft. *w.*

This picture, one of Correggio's masterpieces, was formerly in the possession of Charles I., who purchased it of the Duke of Mantua with the rest of that prince's collection in 1630. It was bought, after the dispersion of the King's effects (it brought 800*l.* at the sale), by the Duke of Alva : it was subsequently the property of the Prince of Peace, in whose collection it was at the time of the occupation of Madrid by the French, when in 1808 it fell into the possession of Murat, afterwards King of Naples, and it was thus, after a lapse of two centuries, restored to Italy. Its next possessor was the Marquis of Londonderry, who obtained it, together with the "Ecce Homo," No. 15 in this collection, of the ex-Queen of Naples, at Vienna; and both pictures were purchased from the Marquis of Londonderry, in 1834, for the National Gallery.

No. **15.** CHRIST PRESENTED BY PILATE TO THE PEOPLE, called the "ECCE HOMO."

"Then came Jesus forth, wearing the crown of thorns, and the purple robe. And *Pilate* saith unto them, Behold the man!"*—*John* xix. 5.

The greater part of the picture is occupied by the figure of our Saviour, behind whom, to the left, is Pilate, pointing with his right hand to Christ, and uttering the words which constitute the title of the subject. On the right is seen the head of a Roman soldier, and in the fore-ground, to the left, the Virgin Mary is represented in a swoon, supported in the arms of St. John. Half-length figures, of the natural size.

Engraved in 1587 by Agostino Carracci, of which print there are several copies; more recently by P. Bettelini, and by G. T. Doo, R.A.; and in small, in Jones's *National Gallery.* On wood, 3 ft. 2½ in. *h.* by 2 ft. 7½ in. *w.*

This picture, formerly in the possession of the Counts Prati of Parma, was subsequently long in the Colonna Palace in Rome, and it was, according to Ramdohr† the best picture by Correggio in that city (in 1784). It is noticed also by Mengs, who supposed it to be one of the painter's earlier works.‡ It was purchased of the Colonna family by Sir Simon Clarke, who, being unable to remove it from Italy, sold it to Murat, then King of Naples, and, as already mentioned, it was purchased, with No. 10, from the Marquis of Londonderry, in 1834.

No. **23.** THE HOLY FAMILY. The infant Saviour is seated on the lap of the Virgin. In the back-ground is St. Joseph occupied as a carpenter planing a board. In the

---

* Et dicit eis: Ecce Homo! in the words of the Latin Vulgate, whence the common title of "Ecce Homo" to a picture of this subject.

† *Ueber Malerei und Bildhauerarbeit in Rom,* &c., vol. ii. p. 85.

‡ *Hinterlassne Werke,* vol. iii. p. 157.

fore-ground, to the left, is a small toilet-basket whence this picture is known on the continent as "La Vierge au Panier." "This picture," says Mengs, "shows that Correggio was the greatest master of aërial perspective of his time."*

Engraved by Diana Ghisi in 1577; by F. F. Aquila in 1691; and recently by G. Faccioli; by G. T. Doo, R.A., for the *Associated Engravers;* and in Jones's *National Gallery.* On wood, 1 ft. 1½ in. *h.* by 10 in. *w.*

Formerly in the royal collection at Madrid, from which it passed, by the gift of Charles IV., to Emanuel Godoy, Prince of Peace. After falling into various hands during the French invasion of Spain, it was brought to England by Mr. Buchanan in 1813, and was purchased in 1825, for the National Gallery.

No. **37.** GROUP OF HEADS AND FIGURES. Nine various views of heads and figures, constituting probably a part of the same composition as its companion piece, No. 7, described at page 81. In the lower part of the picture, to the left, is the head of a lamb.

On canvas, 5 ft. 1 in. *h.* by 3 ft. 6 in. *w.*

No. **76.** CHRIST'S AGONY IN THE GARDEN.

"And he was withdrawn from them about a stone's cast, and kneeled down and prayed, saying, Father, if thou be willing, remove this cup from me; nevertheless not my will, but thine, be done.

"And there appeared an angel unto him from heaven, strengthening him." —*Luke* xxii. 41–43.

The effect of light in this picture is peculiar. The time is in the night, and our Saviour is lighted directly from heaven, while the angel is illuminated by the light reflected from the Lord.† The angel points with his right hand to a cross and crown of thorns lying upon the ground, as emblems of the approaching consummation of the passion of Christ; with the left he points to heaven, intimating the will of the Father. In the background, to the right, the three disciples are seen asleep, and beyond them is the Jewish crowd, led on by Judas.

Engraved by B. Corti in 1640; by Volpato; by S. Cousins; and others. On wood, 1 ft. 2 in. *h.* by 1 ft. 4 in. *w.*

This picture is a repetition or copy of the original, now in the possession of his Grace the Duke of Wellington, which is said to have been painted by Correggio for an apothecary to whom he was indebted four scudi; it was sold shortly afterwards for 500 scudi.‡ It was subsequently in the royal collection at Madrid, and was presented by Ferdinand VII. to the Duke of Wellington. The picture in this gallery formed part of the Angerstein collection, with which it was purchased for the National Gallery in 1824.

---

* *Werke*, vol. iii. p. 156.

† See Mengs, *Werke*, iii. 156.

‡ Gandellini, *Notizie, &c., degl' Intagliatori*, article—Corti, B.

COSTA.

LORENZO COSTA was born at Ferrara in 1460, where he is supposed to have been the pupil of Francesco Cossa; and he is said, by Vasari, to have studied painting with Benozzo Gozzoli, in Florence. He afterwards became the friend and assistant of Francia, in Bologna. Costa resided in Bologna many years, and subsequently settled in Mantua, where he entered the service of Francesco Gonzaga, from whom he received an estate, and an annual pension from 1510 until his death. He died of a fever in his house in the *Contrada Unicorno,* at Mantua, on the 5th of March, 1535.*

Costa was an imitator of Perugino and of Francia, and was fond of introducing landscapes as the back-grounds of his pictures. His principal works remaining are at Bologna—the frescoes of the Bentivoglio Chapel, in San Giacomo Maggiore, painted in 1488; and the St. Sebastian, in San Petronio, painted in 1492. Costa left two sons, painters, Ippolito and Girolamo. Lorenzo Costa, the younger, was the son of Girolamo; he died in 1583, aged 46.†

No. **629.** THE MADONNA AND CHILD ENTHRONED WITH ANGELS: on the spectator's left, St. John the Baptist and St. Peter; on the right, St. John the Evangelist and St. Philip. Small figures.

Transferred from wood to canvas,‡ in five compartments, centre picture 5 ft. 5½ in. *h.* by 2 ft. 5 in. *w.* Side pictures 1 ft. 9½ in. and 3 ft. 7 in. *h.* by 1 ft. 10½ in. *w.* Signed—

LAVRENTIVS · COSTA · F · 1505 ·

This picture was formerly over the principal altar of the Oratorio delle Grazie, at Faenza (now a post house). In 1780 it formed part of the Hercolani collection in Bologna,§ from which

---

* This is ascertained from an entry in the Necrologio, or Register of Deaths of Mantua, published in the *Memorie* of Gualandi, Serie iii. p. 8, 1842. But as the Italians at that time commenced the year with the 25th of March, the correct year is 1536.

† Baruffaldi, *Vite de' Pittori, &c., Ferraresi*; Gualandi, *Memorie Originali*, &c. Serie iii.; Vasari, *Vite*, &c., Ed. Le Monnier, vol. iv.; Laderchi, *Pittura Ferrarese*, p. 39, 1856.

‡ It is painted on fine linen, *renso*, which was attached to wood; this *renso* is now lined with canvas in the place of the original *tavola*; it was transferred at Antwerp in 1848.

§ It is described in the Hercolani Catalogue by Calvi, *Versi e Prose*, &c. Bologna, 1780, p. 10, as the best of Costa's pictures on wood (in Tavola); Calvi terms it *uno stupore*. This picture is noticed also as an admirable example of the master, by Rio, in his life of Leonardo Da Vinci, *Art Chretienne*, vol. ii.

it passed, in 1837, into the possession of Mr. Wigram, at Rome. In 1848 it became the property of M. Van Cuyck, who sold it in the following year to M. Reiset, from whom it was purchased for the National Gallery in 1859.

CRANACH.

LUCAS SUNDER, commonly called LUCAS CRANACH, from his birthplace, was born in 1472 at Cronach, near Bamberg, in Bavaria. In 1495 he was appointed court painter to the Elector of Saxony, and then took up his residence in the Electoral palace of Frederick the Wise at Wittemberg; Cranach had accompanied that prince on his pilgrimage to the Holy Land two years previously. He served three Saxon Electors in the capacity of court painter, and he was so much attached to John Frederick, the Magnanimous, that when that prince was taken prisoner by the Emperor Charles V. after the battle of Mühlberg in 1547, Cranach preferred sharing with him his five years' captivity at Innsbruck to accompanying the Emperor to the Netherlands.

They returned to Wittemberg in 1552, when Cranach retired to Weimar, where he died on the 16th of October in the following year, aged 80.

Cranach lived at an eventful period; his principal works were painted between 1506 and 1540; he was the intimate friend of Luther and painted his portrait several times; he is said to have brought about the marriage of Luther and Catherine Bora, of which he was one of the witnesses. Cranach was twice burgomaster of Wittemberg. After his death a medal was struck to his honour, with his portrait on one side, and on the other the arms granted to him by the Elector Frederick the Wise in 1508, consisting in a crowned winged serpent on a gold ground. This crest was the ordinary mark Cranach used on his pictures and prints. He was not only a painter, but also an engraver in copper and wood, and an illuminator of manuscripts. His biographer, Heller, enumerates, as his accredited works, upwards of 800 prints, chiefly woodcuts.*

* *Lucas Cranach's Leben und Werke.* 2nd ed. Nürnberg, 1854. See also *Lucas Cranach des Aelteren Leben und Werke*, by Christian Schuchardt. 2 vols. small 8vo. Leipsig, 1851.

No. **291.** Portrait of a Young Lady in a red dress with slashed and puffed sleeves, gold chain, and necklace; her gloves slashed for rings. Small figure, half-length.

On wood, 14 in. *h.* by 10 in. *w.*

The painter's mark, the crowned serpent or dragon, is seen in the lower corner to the spectator's left. Purchased at the sale at Alton Towers in 1857.

CREDI.

Lorenzo di Credi was born at Florence in 1459, and was the fellow pupil of Leonardo da Vinci and Pietro Perugino, in the School of Verrocchio. He owes his celebrity to his works in painting; it appears, however, that he was not unskilled in sculpture also, since his master, Verrocchio, expressed a desire in his will (in 1488) that Lorenzo might be employed to finish the colossal equestrian statue of Bartolommeo Colleoni at Venice, which Verrocchio had left incomplete.

Lorenzo is distinguished for the careful execution and elaborate finish of his works. The "Adoration of the Shepherds," formerly in Santa Chiara at Florence, now in the Academy there, is an admirable example of his style. The "Madonna and Child, with Saints Julian and Nicolas," noticed by Vasari as his masterpiece, is now in the Louvre. He died at Florence, on the 12th of January, 1537.*

No. **593.** The Virgin and Child, seated under a portico in a garden; the Virgin holding the Child to her breast.

On wood, 2 ft. 3½ in. *h.* by 1 ft. 7½ in. *w.*

Formerly in the possession of the Cavaliere Mancini of Florence. Purchased at Florence from the Lombardi-Baldi Collection, in 1857.

No. **648.** The Virgin adoring the Infant Christ. The child is resting on a pillow on the ground; the Virgin is kneeling before him in adoration. Landscape background, with a ruin, and the angel appearing to the shepherds in the distance.

* Vasari, *Vite de' Pittori, &c.*, Ed. Le Monnier, vol. viii.; Gaye, *Carteggio Inedito d'Artisti*, vol. i.

On wood, 2 ft. 10 in. *h.* by 1 ft. 11½ in. *w.*

Formerly in the Northwick collection, at Thirlstane House, Cheltenham. Purchased from M. Edmond Beaucousin, at Paris, in 1860.

CRIVELLI.

Carlo Crivelli, *Cavaliere,* was born at Venice in the early part of the fifteenth century, and is said to have studied under Jacobello del Fiore, who was still painting as late as 1436, when, however, Crivelli was most probably only a boy.

Though of a Venetian family, Crivelli appears to have lived and worked chiefly at Ascoli and its neighbourhood; his pictures are invariably signed *Carolus Crivellus Venetus,* but he rarely added the date; the earliest year yet known is 1468, which is inscribed on an altar-piece in the church of San Silvestro at Massa, between Macerata and Fermo; the latest is 1493, found on a picture in the Oggioni collection at Milan—Carolus Crivellus Venetus Miles pinxit M.CCCC.LXXXXIII. *Miles* is a title he added to his signature in 1490, when he was ennobled (knighted) by Ferdinand II. of Naples. Crivelli was a good colourist, but one of the hardest in his forms of the *quattrocento* painters; he is also distinguished for his introduction of fruit and flowers in the accessaries of his compositions. He painted only in *tempera.**

No. **602.** The Dead Christ, a Pietà. Two infant angels supporting the body of Christ, seated on the edge of the tomb. Half-figure.

In tempera, on wood, 2 ft. 4½ in. *h.* by 1 ft. 10 in. *w.*

Part of an altar-piece, formerly in the church of the Frati Conventuali Riformati at Monte Fiore, near Fermo. Purchased in Rome, from Cavaliere Vallati in 1859. Signed—

CAROLVS · CRIVELLVS · VENETVS · PINSIT

No. **668.** The Beato Ferretti,† kneeling in a rocky landscape, in adoration; a vision of the Virgin and Child,

---

* Ridolfi, *Le Maraviglie, &c.*; Orsini, *Guida D'Ascoli,* Perugia, 1790; Carboni, *Memorie intorno i Letterati e gli Artisti Ascolani,* Ascoli, 1830, p. 119; Ricci, *Memorie Storiche delle Arti, &c. della Marca di Ancona,* Macerata, 1834, vol. i. p. 228.

† The present Pontiff, Pius IX., *Giovanni Maria Mastai Ferretti,* is of the family of the Beato Ferretti.

surrounded by the *Mandorla* or *Vesica* glory, is seen above; on the ground before him is an open book. The background to the right is a village street, and in the foreground to the left are two ducks on a piece of water, near which are lying a pair of clogs; in the upper part of the picture is a festoon of fruit.

On wood, in tempera, 4 ft. 7½ in. *h.* by 2 ft. 10½ in. *w.*
Purchased from Mr. Alexander Barker in 1861. Signed—

OPVS·KAROLI·CRIVELLI
·VENETI·

CUYP.

Albert Cuyp was born at Dort in 1605. The date of his death is not known, but he was still living in the beginning of 1683. He was taught painting by his father, Jacob Gerritz Cuyp, but his true instructor was nature. Cuyp was by trade a brewer, and it is perhaps partly owing to this circumstance that he was so much underrated as a painter during his lifetime, and indeed for many years after his death. Though known chiefly as a landscape-painter, he executed also some good portraits. The management of light was Cuyp's great power, and he has been called the Dutch Claude. Though among the best of cattle-painters, his highest excellence is his treatment of atmospheres, whether that of the misty morning, of the glowing noon, or of the golden evening. He painted likewise birds, fish, fruit, flowers, still life, and executed also a few etchings.*

No. **53.** Landscape, with Cattle and Figures; Evening. A man dressed in a red coat, seated on a gray horse, conversing with a female standing near him, and pointing to the opposite side of the picture, is a very prominent feature in this composition; some cattle and sheep add to the beauty of the group. The figures are finely relieved by foliage, and a sloping hill behind, which is made to retire by the branches of a wide-spreading tree

---

* Houbraken, *Groote Schouburg der Nederlandsche Konstschilders*, &c.; Van Eynden and Vander Willigen, *Geschiedenis der Vaderlandsche Schilderkunst*, i. 382; Immerzeel, *De Levens en Werken Hollandsche en Vlaamsche Kunstschilders*, &c., Amsterdam, 1842.

overhanging this part of the picture. On the opposite side is a picturesque sheet of water, at the further bank of which three horsemen are refreshing their steeds: the distance is bounded by low hills; two dogs, a goat, and the stump of a tree occupy the fore-ground on this side. A sunny atmosphere pervades the whole picture.

Engraved by J. C. Bently, for Jones's *National Gallery;* and by E. Goodall, for the series of prints published by the *Associated Engravers.* On canvas, 4 ft. 4 in. *h.* by 6 ft. 6 in. *w.* Signed—

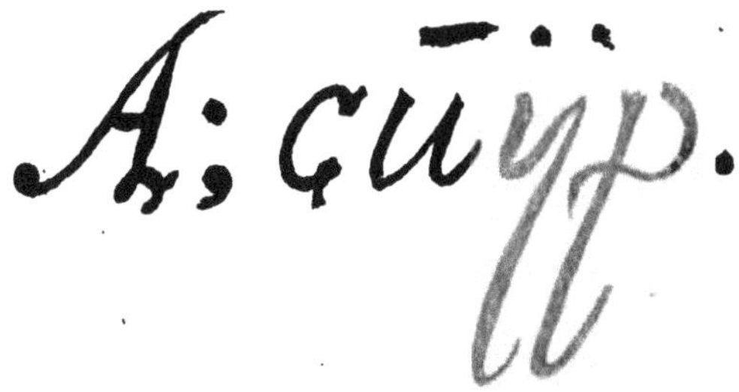

Formerly in the collection of Sir Lawrence Dundas, and subsequently in that of Mr. Angerstein, with which it was purchased by Parliament in 1824.

DIETRICH.

JOHANN WILHELM ERNST DIETRICH was born at Weimar in 1712, where his father, Johan Georg Dietrich, was court-painter. After acquiring the rudiments of his art from his father, he was sent to Dresden to pursue his studies under the celebrated landscape-painter Alexander Thiele. Dietrich was of such precocious talent, that he was appointed, when only in his eighteenth year, court-painter to Augustus II. King of Poland and Elector of Saxony. In 1741 he received a similar appointment from Augustus III., who, in 1743, sent him to Rome, in order that he might become acquainted with the great productions of Italian art.

In 1746 he was appointed keeper of the celebrated Dresden gallery of pictures; he was likewise one of the professors of the Academy of the Arts at Dresden, and director of the school of painting attached to the porcelain manufactory of Meissen. He died at Dresden, April 24, 1774.

Dietrich painted almost all subjects, and was remarkable for the facility and fidelity with which he imitated any style or any manner. His pictures are very numerous, and there are likewise many etchings by his hand.*

No. **205.** The Itinerant Musicians. An old man playing the fiddle, and a boy accompanying him on the bagpipes, are standing under a doorway, and entertaining a small rustic audience; some rich foliage in the back-ground.

Etched by Dietrich himself; admirably engraved by J. G. Wille in 1764; also by J. F. Bause and others. On wood, 1 ft. 5¼ in. *h.* by 1 ft. 1 in. *w.* Signed and dated—

Dietricy fecit. 1,745.

Bequeathed to the National Gallery in 1846 by Mr. Richard Simmons.

DOMENICHI'NO.

Dome'nico Zampie'ri, commonly called Domenichino, was born at Bologna in 1581. Having studied some time in the school of Denis Calvart, he entered that of the Carracci. He was invited in the beginning of the seventeenth century by Albani, to Rome, where he lived for some time in his friend's house, and he soon earned a reputation equal to that of any of his competitors for fame. He acquired great honour for a fresco of the "Flagellation of St. Andrew," painted opposite to a fresco by Guido, representing the same saint going to martyrdom, in the church of San Gregorio at Rome. It was at first a question which was the superior production, but Domenichino appears to have finally secured the general voice on his side. When Annibale Carracci was asked his opinion of the two works, he answered, "That Guido appeared to be the master, and Domenichino the scholar, but that the scholar was more able than the master."

The most celebrated picture by Domenichino is "The Communion of St. Jerome in the Church at Bethlehem," painted about 1614, now in the Vatican, hanging opposite to the picture of "The Transfiguration," by Raphael. The "Martyrdom

---

* Meusel, *Miscellaneen Artistischen Inhalts*, Erfurt, 1779; Heineken, *Neue Nachrichten von Künstlern und Kunstsachen*, Dresden, 1786; and his *Dictionnaire des Artistes dont nous avons des Estampes*, vol. iv. Dietrich is said, about 1733, after his visit to Italy, to have written his name Dietricy.

of St. Sebastian," formerly in the chapel of that saint in St. Peter's, is likewise one of this painter's masterpieces; it is now in the church of Santa Maria degli Angeli, and a mosaic has been substituted for it in St. Peter's.

The "Communion of St. Jerome,"* considered by Sacchi and Poussin the best altar-piece in Rome, with the single exception of Raphael's "Transfiguration," was painted by Domenichino for *fifty scudi*, about *ten guineas*. He adopted in this picture, says Bellori, Agostino Carracci's treatment of the same subject. Domenichino was engaged from 1630 chiefly in the Cappella del Tesoro at Naples; but the works there were not completed: he was much persecuted by his rivals both at Rome and at Naples, and especially by the notorious triumvirate† known as the "Cabal of Naples." He died at Naples, April 15, 1641, not without suspicion of having been poisoned by the agents of this Cabal. Domenichino is generally accounted the ablest of all the scholars of the Carracci: he excelled in design, in composition, and in expression.‡

No. **48.** LANDSCAPE, WITH FIGURES, representing the story of Tobias and the angel, from the apocryphal book of 'Tobit.' Tobias, directed by the angel, is drawing out of the water the fish that had attacked him. The landscape is intended to represent a view on the banks of the Tigris.—*Tobit* vi. 4, 5.

Engraved in Jones's *National Gallery*. On copper, 1 ft. 5½ in. *h.* by 1 ft. 1¼ in. *w.*

Formerly in the Colonna Palace at Rome. Bequeathed to the National Gallery by the Rev. W. H. Carr, in 1831.

No. **75.** LANDSCAPE, WITH FIGURES, representing the story of St. George and the Dragon.§ The saint, mounted on

---

* Engraved by Cesare Testa, J. Frey, B. Farjat, and A. Tardieu.

† Belisario Corenzio, Guiseppe Ribera (Spagnoletto), and Giambattista Carracciolo. See Dominici, *Vite de' Pittori, &c.*, and Lanzi.

‡ Bellori, *Vite de' Pittori, &c.*; Passeri, *Vite de' Pittori, &c.*

§ This was a dragon which dwelt in the time of Diocletian, in a marsh near the city of Lysia, in the province of Lybia, and was appeased only by two sheep daily; when all the sheep were exhausted, human victims were offered to him, their fate being decided by lot. At length it came to the lot of the King's daughter to be given to the dragon, and after much useless resistance, the King finally delivered her, clad in her royal robes, to the people, who exposed her to the dragon and looked on from the walls. St. George passing at the time, and learning from the lady the cause of her distress, immediately resolved to become her champion. Accordingly, when the monster made his appearance, St. George mounted his steed, and couching his lance, attacked him vigorously, and having given him a fatal wound, he dismounted and cut off the dragon's head with his sword. See the account, from Peter de Natalibus, in Lord Lindsay's *Sketches of the History of Christian Art*, vol. i.

his charger, is on the point of spearing the dragon; the princess is running from the spot. The landscape, to which the figures are merely accessory, is a picturesque country; on the right is the view of a fortified town, before which is a sheet of water. The inhabitants are watching the result of the combat from the walls.

Engraved by A. W. Graham in Jones's *National Gallery*. On wood, 1 ft. 8½ in. *h.* by 2 ft. 1 in. *w.*

Formerly in the Collection of Prince Lucien Bonaparte. Bequeathed to the National Gallery, in 1831, by the Rev. W. H. Carr.

No. **77.** THE STONING OF ST. STEPHEN.

"Then they cried out with a loud voice, and stopped their ears, and ran upon him with one accord, and cast him out of the city, and stoned him; and the witnesses laid down their clothes at a young man's feet, whose name was Saul."—*Acts* vii. 57, 58.

The scene is taking place immediately outside the walls, which occupy a large portion of the picture; above them are seen the upper parts of some buildings, and a few figures are distributed on the ramparts, witnessing the tragedy enacting beneath. Seven small figures.[1]

Engraved in Jones's *National Gallery*. On canvas, 2 ft. 1 in. *h.* by 1 ft. 7 in. *w.*

Formerly in the Collection of Prince Lucien Bonaparte. Bequeathed to the National Gallery, in 1831, by the Rev. W. H. Carr.

No. **85.** ST. JEROME AND THE ANGEL. The saint is represented seated in a cave, occupied in the study of his books and manuscripts; his attendant lion is crouching at his feet; the apparition of the angel seems to imply the special mission of St. Jerome as the interpreter of the Scriptures: his version of the Old and New Testaments into Latin is the first translation that was made into that language; it is known as the Vulgate of the Roman church. St. Jerome died about the year 420, at an advanced age, in the monastery of Bethlehem, near Jerusalem. The red robe, and the Cardinal's hat, placed against a skull, upon the piece of rock which serves him as a table, indicate his rank as a Cardinal of the Church.

Engraved in Jones's *National Gallery*. On canvas, 1 ft. 8 in. *h.* by 1 ft. 3½ in. *w.*

Formerly in the Aldobrandini Collection at Rome. Imported into this country by Mr. Day. Bequeathed to the National Gallery, in 1831, by the Rev. W. H. Carr.

DOSSI.

DOSSO DOSSI was born about 1480, at Ferrara, or at Dosso, near Cento; his father was in the service of the Duke Ercole I., of Ferrara. Dosso and his brother, Giambattista, who generally worked together, were pupils of Lorenzo Costa; they studied also some years at Rome and Venice. Dosso excelled in figures, and especially portraits; Giambattista was excellent in landscape. Dosso died about 1560, having survived his brother some years. Giambattista had an attack of apoplexy, Nov. 1st, 1545, but he survived, without working, until 1549. Both are mentioned by Ariosto (Canto XXXIII. St. 2).

> "E quei che furo à nostri di, e son ora
> Leonardo, Andrea Mantegna e Gian Bellino,
> Duo Dossi, e quel che a par sculpe e colora
> Michel più che mortale angel divino."

Several of Dosso's frescoes are still preserved in the Castello di Ferrara: his master-pieces are said to be the "Madonna and Child enthroned, with various Saints," in the Gallery at Ferrara, formerly in the Church of Sant' Andrea there; and the "Four Doctors of the Church, with San Bernardino," in the Dresden Gallery.*

No. **640.** THE ADORATION OF THE MAGI. A hilly landscape, with trees in the background, the star of the Epiphany above. One of the kings appears to be attacked by a robber.

On wood, arched at the top, 17 in. *h.* by 12¼ in. *w.*
Purchased from M. Edmond Beaucousin, at Paris, in 1860.

DOW.

GERARD DOW or rather DOU, one of the most celebrated of the Dutch *genre*-painters, was born at Leyden, in 1613 or 1598.† His father was a glazier, and Gerard was at first brought up to be a painter on glass, but afterwards entered the school of Rembrandt at Amsterdam, and remained with that painter three years. He attained wonderful mastery in delicate execution; his works are remarkable at once for high finish and for lightness of handling. He died at Leyden, in 1680, not, however, before he had reaped ample fruits from his great reputation. An amateur of the name of Spiering paid the

---

* Baruffaldi, *Vite de' Pittori Ferraresi*, &c. Laderchi, *Pittura Ferrarese*.

† This appears to be the correct date from the signature on the picture of the "Femme Hydropique" in the Louvre "1663 G. DOV. OVT 65 JAER" showing the painter's name to be Dou; the same form of the capital U is used in the word *out* OVT, old or aged.

painter annually, a thousand florins, alone a good income, for the mere privilege of having the first offer of his pictures,* which have steadily increased in value up to the present time. Schalcken, Mieris, and Metsu, were pupils of Gerard Dow.

No. **192.** THE PAINTER'S OWN PORTRAIT. He holds a pipe in his hand. Signed G. DOV, that is DOU.

On wood; an oval, 7½ in. *h.* by 5¾ in. *w.* Signed—

GDOV. f.

Formerly in the Collection of M. Paignon Dijonval, at Paris. Purchased for the National Gallery, at the sale of Mr. J. Harman's Collection, in 1844.

DUCCIO.

DUCCIO DI BUONINSEGNA of Siena was born about 1260; the earliest accounts of him are from 1282,† the latest are said to extend down to 1339.‡ He is the first of the Sienese painters who forsook the Byzantine manner and strove to imitate nature. His earliest works were illuminations of manuscripts, but already in 1285 Duccio must have been a painter of reputation, as in that year he entered into a contract at Florence to paint, for 150 florins, an altar-piece for the chapel of the Virgin, in the church of Santa Maria Novella. His masterpiece, however, the high altar-piece of the Cathedral of Siena, which is still in existence, was painted many years later. It occupied him between the 9th of October 1308, and the 9th of June 1310, when it was carried with great pomp to the cathedral.§ Duccio executed it for the small pay of sixteen soldi or eight pence the working day, paid to him in monthly instalments of ten *lire* or francs; but he was at no expense for the materials, which, owing to the quantity

* Houbraken, *Groote Schouburg, &c.*; Immerzeel, *Levens en Werken der Hollandsche Kunstschilders, &c.*

† Della Valle, *Lettere Senesi*, p. 277.

‡ Vasari, *Vite dei Pittori, &c.* Ed. Le Monnier, Flor. 1846, *et seq.*

§ Milanesi, *Documenti per la Storia dell' Arte Senese*, vol. i. p. 169.

of gold and ultramarine used, raised the cost of the altar-piece altogether to upwards of 3,000 gold florins.*

Duccio is mentioned by Vasari as the artist of the *Sgraffiti* or Chiaroscuri of the pavement in the Cathedral at Siena, but Rumohr has shown that those designs were not commenced until a century after the death of Duccio.†

No. **566.** THE MADONNA AND CHILD WITH ANGELS; and DAVID with six Prophets above. ST. DOMINIC and ST. CATHERINE of Alexandria, on the doors. A Triptych.

In tempera, on wood, 2 ft. *h.* by 2 ft. 7 in. *w.*
Formerly in a gallery at Pisa. Purchased at Florence from the Lombardi-Baldi Collection in 1857.

DÜRER.

ALBERT OR ALBRECHT DÜRER was born at Nuremberg, May 20, 1471. His father was a Hungarian goldsmith, who had settled in that city in 1455, and had married Barbara the daughter of the Nuremberg goldsmith, Jerome Haller. Albert was the third of eighteen children by this marriage, three only however attained to maturity; his mother survived till 1514. Though brought up to be a goldsmith, he, at an early age, adopted painting as his profession, and was first apprenticed in 1486, with Martin Schoen or Hüpsh (Schongauer), at Colmar, but as this master died shortly afterwards, he became the scholar of Michael Wolgemuth, a painter of Nuremberg, with whom he remained three years; he then travelled for four years. These seven years were Albert's *Lehr-* and *Wander-jahre.*‡

* Tura del Grasso, the writer of an old Sienese Chronicle, says, "fu la più bella tavola che mai si vedesse et facesse et chostò più di tremila fiorini d'oro." It was similar in plan to the altar-piece by Jacopo di Casentino in this Collection; consisting of centre, upper pictures, pilasters, and predella. The centre was double or painted on both sides, front and back: on the front was represented the Virgin and Child enthroned, with Angels; on the back, the Life of Christ in many small pictures. It is still in the Cathedral at Siena, but was removed from the high altar in 1506, and the principal picture has been separated into two; the front and the back being distinct pictures: they were executed at different times, and according to separate contracts, which are still preserved. The Life of Christ being in thirty-eight stories, for which Duccio was to receive two and a half gold florins each.—Milanesi, *Documenti, &c.*, vol. i. p. 178.

† Rumohr, *Italienische Forschungen*, ii. p. 33.

‡ It has been stated, on his own authority, by German writers, that Albert never saw Martin Schoen, as the latter died before Albert's arrival at Colmar; but a document quoted by Passavant in the Kunstblatt for 1846, p. 168, shows

Albert Dürer distinguished himself equally as painter and as engraver on copper and on wood; as an engraver he was, perhaps, superior to all men of his time in the practical execution of his work; in painting also, apparently a secondary study with him, his execution was extremely elaborate, but at the same time very hard, and his forms are inelegant; he had, however, great powers of invention.

On Feb. 2, 1494, he married Agnes Frey, the pretty daughter of a Nuremberg singer and player on the harp, and with her he received a dowry of 200 florins; but for which, says an old writer quoted by Arend, he had afterwards at least 2,000 unhappy days. She is said to have been imperious, avaricious, and fretful, constantly urging him to work, to make provision for her after his death.

In January 1506, Dürer visited the north of Italy: in Venice he painted a picture of the Martyrdom of St. Bartholomew, or, according to some, the Coronation of the Virgin; and he remarks in a letter to his friend Pirkheimer: "The Venetian painters abuse my style, and say that it is not after the antique, and therefore that it is not good—*Noch schelten sy es und sagen, es sey nit antigisch art, dozu sey es nit gut;*" but they praised his beautiful colouring. He admired the works of Giovanni Bellini, who was then very old, and speaks of him as the best Venetian painter. Albert outlived the taste of his earlier years, under the influence of which he had sometimes painted in a crude and florid manner. He himself confessed to Melancthon that he did not admire his own early pictures as at first, and that they often made him sigh when he looked upon them.*

He was well pleased with his visit to Venice; he executed several pictures there, and writes to his friend Pirkheimer with satisfaction, that there he was a gentleman, while at home he was but a parasite. Afterwards, in 1525, writing to the town council of Nuremberg, he complained that during the thirty years he had worked in that city he had not received 500 florins of Nuremberg money, that his commissions were from princes and strangers, and that he spent strange money in the town,—while he might have

that Martin died in 1488, two years later than was commonly reported, so that there must have been some other reason than Martin's death for Albert's not becoming his apprentice. Albert visited Colmar in his *wanderjahre* in 1492.

* Epistolæ D. Erasmi Roter. Et Ph. Melanchthonis, &c., folio, London, 1642; quoted by Füssli, *Allgemeines Künstler Lexicon.*

remained at Venice with an annual grant of 200 ducats from the Signory, and that he had received a similar offer of 300 florins and free lodging from Antwerp, all of which he had declined out of love to his native place. The Emperor Maximilian appointed him court-painter, and the same dignity was continued to him in 1520 by Charles V.; the emolument was, however, only 100 florins a year.

Albert was certainly the most distinguished artist of his time north of the Alps, and in 1515 an interesting exchange of drawings took place between him and Raphael. One of the great Roman painter's drawings is still preserved at Vienna in the collection of the Archduke Charles; it represents two figures drawn in red chalk from the life, and on the paper is written by Albert: "1515, Raphael of Urbino, who has been so highly esteemed by the Pope, drew these naked figures, and sent them to Albrecht Dürer in Nuremberg, to show him his hand."

In Whitsun-week, 1520, he set out with his wife and her maid for a visit to the Netherlands, where he remained during a considerable portion of 1521. His diary of this journey is preserved, and contains many interesting details.* He was chiefly occupied in visits, and negotiating the sale of his prints; he also drew several pencil portraits, for which he appears to have been commonly paid a florin, or twenty pence English; but two or three pence a day were the ordinary wages even of a skilled workman at that time in the north of Europe: the price was therefore not a contemptible one.

Dürer's pictures are not numerous, though there are some works of note in most of the German galleries, as at Munich, Vienna, Prague, and Nuremberg. The most celebrated perhaps of his paintings are the two panels in the Munich gallery, containing respectively St. John and St. Peter, St. Paul and St. Mark, painted in 1526, and presented by Albert to the council of Nuremberg. In portrait he was often very successful; his most celebrated picture of

* It is remarkable that Arend, Albert's townsman, and the author of the earliest monograph on Dürer, should have asserted that he made this journey to escape from his wife. In the very first sentence of the Diary he mentions that she accompanied him, and he notices her frequently afterwards. See *Reise-journal Albrecht Dürers, von seiner Niederländischen Reise, 1520 und 1521. E. Bibliotheca Ebneriana.* In Von Murr's *Journal zur Kunstgeschichte*, vol. vii. Nürnberg, 1779; and also in the *Reliquien von Albrecht Dürer*, Nürnberg, 1828.

this class is that of Jerome Holtzschuer* at Nuremberg, also painted in 1526; there are likewise good portraits of Frederick der Weise, Melanchthon, Erasmus, and his own intimate friend Pirkheimer. His series of woodcuts have, however, a more extended European reputation; namely, the "Apocalypse," sixteen cuts, 1498; the "Life of the Virgin," twenty cuts, 1511; and about the same time the "History of Christ's Passion," twelve large cuts. The last is known as the "Grosse Passion." There is another series in thirty-seven small cuts, known as the "Kleine Passion." Of his copper-plate engravings, which are exquisitely finished, may be mentioned,—"St. Hubert," "St. Jerome," "Adam and Eve," the "Christian Knight," "Melancholy," and "Fortune." All his works are generally marked with the same monogram, a large A with a small D in the middle of it, below the bar of the A.

Albert was also sculptor as well as painter and engraver, and, according to the inscription on his tomb, without a rival in either art—*Artium lumen, sol artificum; pictor, chalcographus, sculptor, sine exemplo.* He was the author of several works, on *Human Proportion*, on *Geometry, &c.*, on *Fortification;* and was unquestionably a man of remarkable attainments; even Melanchthon had said, that painting was the least of his accomplishments.

This celebrated German artist died at Nuremberg, April 6, 1528, leaving to his wife, notwithstanding his general poverty, a little fortune of 6,000 florins. He had joined the Reformers under Luther, but he appears to have died, according to Pirkheimer, a member of the Roman church.†

No. **245.** Bust Portrait of a Senator. An old man with a grey beard, in a purple robe with a fur collar, and a cap on his head, and on his neck a chain and order decoration; a plain blue back-ground, with the date 1514, and the painter's usual monogram, a D within an A.

---

* Engraved by Fr. Wagner.

† Sandrart, *Accademia Todesca*, &c. Arend, *Das Gedechtniss der ehren eines derer vollkomnesten Künstler seiner und aller nachfolgenden Zeiten, Albrecht Dürers*, &c., 12mo., Gosslar. 1728. Von Murr, *Journal zur Kunstgeschichte*, vols. vii. and x. containing the letters of Dürer and Pirkheimer, 12mo., Nürnberg, 1779–81. Heller, *Das Leben und die Werke Albrecht Dürers*, 8vo., Leipzig, 1831, vol. ii., the works only. Von Rettberg, *Nürnberg's Kunstleben in seinen Denkmalen dargestellt*, 8vo., Stuttgart, 1854.

On wood, 1 ft. 11½ in. *h.* by 1 ft. 7 in *w.*

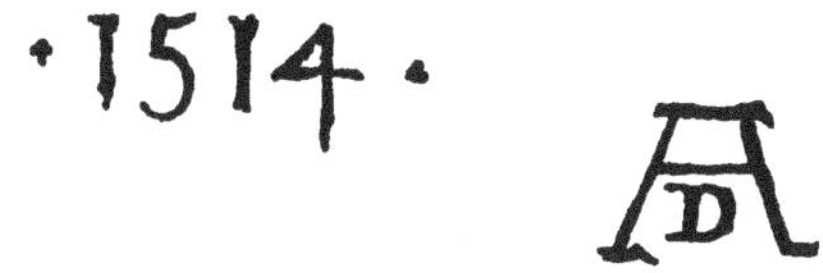

Purchased for the National Gallery, in 1854, at the sale of M. Joly De Bammeville's collection.

DYCKMANS.

JOSEPH LAURENS DYCKMANS was born at Antwerp in 1811, and is still living.

No. **600.** THE BLIND BEGGAR. A blind old man is standing in the sunshine by a church door; before him, holding out her hand, is a young girl asking alms of the passers by; and coming out from the church is an old lady feeling in her pocket for a sou: some other figures are seen in the porch, at their devotions before a crucifix. Small three-quarter figures. Modern Flemish school.

On wood, 1 ft. 7½ in. *h.* by 1 ft. 6 in. *w.* Engraved by W. H. Simmons.

Painted at Antwerp. Signed *J. Dyckmans*, 1853. Bequeathed by Miss Jane Clarke in 1859.*

EMMANUEL.

EMMANUEL, a Greek priest and painter. He signs himself in the example of his work in this collection *Emmanouel, priest of Tzane.* Lanzi refers to a picture, dated 1660, by Emmanuel, a priest, who lived at Venice, in the 17th century, and who is apparently the same painter.†

* Exhibited for the present at South Kensington.

† The period of a Byzantine picture cannot always be ascertained from its style, as the Greek Christian Art is purely conventional, and has been practised without material alteration from about the tenth century to the present time. This singular constancy in the practice of an art is thoroughly explained in the *Guide or Manual of Painting,* Ἑρμηνεία της ζωγραφικῆς, printed by M. Didron, from a MS. of the eleventh century, procured by him from Mount Athos, and published at Paris in 1845, under the title, *Manuel d'Iconographie Chretienne, Grecque et Latine, avec une Introduction et des notes. Traduit du MS. Byzantin,* "*Le Guide de la Peinture,*" *par le Dr. Paul Durand.*

There is also a German translation by Dr. Schäfer. *Das Handbuch der Malerei vom Berge Athos,* &c., 8vo., Trier, 1855. In this remarkable guide are given, not only the subjects to be represented, and their orthodox treatment, but even the costume, age, and lineaments of the characters introduced; and it is as indispensable to the Greek painter as his palette and brushes.

No. **594.** SAINTS COSMAS AND DAMIANUS, receiving the Divine blessing, according to the Greek rite.* The Lord surrounded by the *Vesica Piscis* or *Ichthus*,† is represented above. Inscribed O' A' Κοσμας, O' A' Δαμιανο:, and signed χείρ 'Εμμανουηλ 'ιερεως του τζάνε.—The hand of Emmanuel, priest of Tzane.‡

In tempera, on wood, 2 ft. 2 in. *h.* by 1 ft. 9 in. *w.*

Formerly in the possession of Sig. Nardi, of Florence. Purchased in Florence from the Lombardi-Baldi Collection, in 1857.

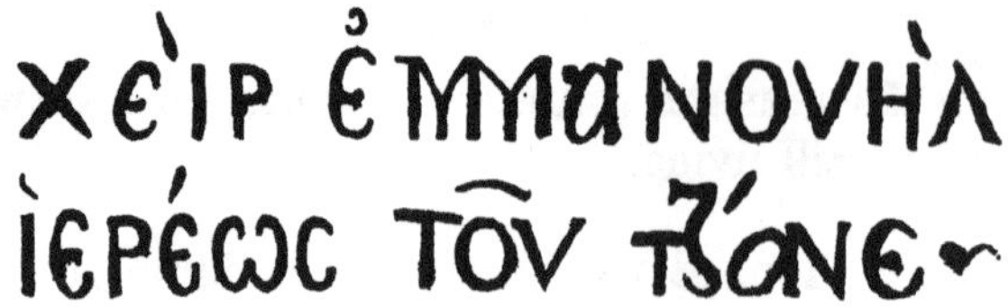

ER'COLE DA FERRA'RA.

ERCOLE GRANDI, commonly called Ercole da Ferrara, was born in Ferrara, about 1462. He was, according to Vasari, the pupil of Lorenzo Costa, at Bologna, where he chiefly resided and executed his best works. Costa and Ercole were contemporaries and friends; but it is more probable that Francesco Cossa was his master. He died at Ferrara, in 1531. His pictures are very rare; § his greatest works, the frescoes of the Garganelli Chapel in San Pietro in Bologna, were destroyed with the Chapel in 1605. There are a few specimens in the Costabili Gallery of Ferrara.

No. **73.** THE CONVERSION OF SAINT PAUL. Confused groups of men and horses, with the Saviour in the clouds, and a view of Jerusalem in the back-ground.

Engraved in Jones's *National Gallery*. On wood, 1 ft. 11 in. *h.* by 2 ft. 3 in. *w.*

Formerly in the Aldobrandini Collection at Rome. Bequeathed to the National Gallery, in 1831, by the Rev. W. H. Carr.

* In the Greek mode of blessing the hand attempts to form the monogram of Christ IC. XC, or the first and last letters of the name of Christ, 'ΙησοῦC ΧριστόC; the first finger is straight, the second slightly curved, the thumb holding down the third, forming the X, and the fourth slightly curved. See the Greek "Guide," German translation, p. 418.

† See page 133, note, for the explanation of the *Ichthus*.

‡ The Saints Cosmas and Damianus, martyrs of the fourth century, are called from their practising medicine gratuitously, δι ἅγιοι ἀνάργυροι—*the holy money despisers*. They are represented always together and in three different modes, in Greek art—one mode being peculiar to two saints of Rome, July 1st, another to two of Asia (Minor?), November 1st, and a third to two of Arabia, October 7th. The saints of this picture are the Roman pair. See the German translation of the Greek "Guide" before mentioned, p. 320.

§ Baruffaldi, *Le Vite de' Piu Insigni Pittori e Scultori Ferraresi*, Ferrara, 1846-8; Vasari, Ed. Le Monnier vol. iv.; Laderchi, *Pittura Ferrarese*, 1856.

VAN EYCK.

JAN OR JEAN VAN EYCK was born probably at Alden Eyck, near Maas Eyck, on the Maas, about 1390, the exact date being doubtful. His elder brother, Hubert, was born, according to Van Mander, in 1366: this leaves a long interval between the births of the two brothers, though longer intervals occasionally occur, especially in cases of first and second marriages. There is sufficient historical evidence to show that John was many years younger than Hubert: in their portraits in the Gallery of Berlin, on one of the wings originally belonging to the altar-piece of the Adoration of the Lamb, in St. Bavon's, at Ghent, Hubert looks at least old enough to have been John's father; and according to Markus Van Vaernewyck, in his 'History of Belgium,' published in 1565, John Van Eyck was still young when he died. Making due allowance for the diversity of opinions as to when a man ceases to be young, it may be assumed that he was not much more than fifty at his death; and as it is now established that he died on the 9th of July, 1440,* he may have been born shortly before 1390, but hardly later. His brother Hubert died September 18, 1426. The third brother Lambert survived John some years. Of a sister, Marguerite, little is known.

The Van Eycks resided chiefly at Ghent and Bruges, where they founded a great school. Both Hubert and John were granted the freedom of the profession by the Corporation of Painters of Ghent, in the year 1421.† They are particularly distinguished as the inventors (or improvers) of *Oil Painting;* general repute gives the credit of this discovery to John, but from all the circumstances, Hubert appears to have a better claim to the invention. The whole of the upper part of the interior of the "Adoration of the Lamb," their master-

---

* See the documents published by W. H. James Weale in his *Notes sur Jean Van Eyck*, &c., Londres, Barthès and Lowell, 1861; rectifying some mistakes in the Abbé Carton's work, *Les Trois Frères Van Eyck, &c.*, Bruges, 1848. The following publications (anterior to the discovery of facts now established) may be consulted for other particulars, Dr. Waagen, *Kunstblatt*, 1859, No. 25. De Bast, *Messager des Sciences et des Arts*, Gand, 1824. The *Kunstblatt*, 1826, No. 78, &c. Passavant, *Kunstreise durch England und Belgien*, Frankfort, A.M. 1833. Rathgeber, *Annalen der Niederländischen Malerei, &c.*, Gotha, 1842. Michiels. *Peintres Brugeois*, 1846. The Author's *Epochs of Painting*, 1859, ch. xxiii.; and Eastlake's *Materials for a History of Oil Painting*, 1847.

† Busscher, *Notice sur L'Ancienne Corporation des Peintres et Sculpteurs à Gand.* Brussels, 1853.

piece, except perhaps the wing containing the "Singing Angels," was painted by Hubert, who was thus evidently complete master of the method; and at the date at which Van Mander fixes the discovery, 1410, Hubert was already forty-four years of age, while John was still but a youth.

This celebrated picture, painted for Judocus Vyd, was finished by John in 1432, six years after the death of his brother, and in the inscription on the work the chief merit is given to Hubert, who is called the greatest in art, while John is styled the second.* The external pictures representing the Annunciation, St. John the Baptist, St. John the Evangelist, and the donors, are by John.

Vasari's general statement that John Van Eyck was the inventor of *oil painting* or literally *varnish* painting, was formerly much impugned, as it was known that the mere immixture of oil with colours was practised in Germany and elsewhere long before the time of Van Eyck. Vasari, however, in his Life of Agnolo Gaddi, intimates that oil painting, though sometimes adopted by the earlier masters, was not employed by them for figures, but for decorative purposes only.†

No. **186.** PORTRAITS OF JEAN ARNOLFINI AND JEANNE DE CHENANY HIS WIFE‡, standing in the middle of an apartment with their hands joined. In the back-ground are a bed, a mirror, and a window partly open; the objects in the room, and even beyond that portion of it represented in the picture,—for a door and two additional figures may

---

* The inscription is as follows, the last line containing what is termed a chronogram, the Roman capitals making together, according to their value as numerals, the date 1432, on the sixth of May of which year the picture was fixed in its place:—

Pictor Hubertus e Eyck, major quo nemo repertus
Incepit; pondusque Johannes arte secundus
Frater perfecit, Judoci Vyd prece fretus
VersV seXta MaI Vos CoLLoCat aCta tUeri.

The two central divisions of this picture are all that now remain in the church at Ghent. The eight wings, with the exception of the figures of Adam and Eve, are in the Gallery of Berlin. The figures of Adam and Eve (the latter not the most fortunate of the upper series, though extolled by Albert Dürer) were, in 1860, placed in the Gallery at Brussels. The alterpiece is engraved in outline in Passavant's *Kunstreise*, &c., in Crowe and Cavalcaselle's *Early Flemish Painters*, London, 1857, and in Waagen's *Handbuch der Deutschen and Niderländischen Malerschulen*. Stuttgart, 1862. It was copied by Michael Coxie for Philip II. of Spain, in 1559; it occupied him two years, and he received 4,000 florins for his labour.

† Compare the Life of Antonello da Messina in this Catalogue.

‡ Weale, *Notes*, &c. p. 27.

be distinguished,—are distinctly reflected in the mirror. A branch brass chandelier hangs from the ceiling, with a candle still burning in it; in the fore-ground is a small poodle. In the frame of the mirror are ten minute circular compartments, in which are painted subjects relating to the Passion of Christ; immediately above the mirror is written "Johannes de Eyck fuit hic," with the date 1434 below.*

On wood, 2 ft. 9 in. *h.* by 2 ft. ½ in. *w.*

This picture belonged in 1516 to Margaret of Austria, to whom it was presented by Don Diego de Guevara; it was also in her possession in 1524: the picture originally had shutters on the outside of which the arms of Don Diego were painted.† Afterwards, according to Van Mander, it passed into the possession of a barber-surgeon at Bruges, who presented it to the then Regent of the Netherlands, Mary, the sister of Charles V., and Queen Dowager of Hungary. This princess valued the picture so highly, that she granted the barber-surgeon in return, a pension, or office worth 100 florins per annum.‡ The picture belonged to her in 1556; it is even included in the list of valuables which she carried with her to Spain. Its subsequent history, however, shows that it either did not go to Spain or returned again to Flanders: there it must have passed into obscure hands; it was discovered by Major-Gen. Hay, in the apartments to which he was taken, in 1815, at Brussels, to recover from wounds he had received in the battle of Waterloo.§ He purchased the picture after his recovery, and disposed of it to the British Government in 1842, when it was placed in the National Gallery.

No. **222.** A MAN'S PORTRAIT, in a cloak and fur collar, with a red handkerchief twisted round the head as a turban. In small.

* The researches of Mr. Weale having proved beyond all question who the personages represented in this picture were, there can no longer be any ambiguity in the meaning of the words "fuit hic." Why the presence of the painter should be so recorded, must be left to conjecture.

† Weale, *Notes*, &c., p. 27.

‡ Van Mander, *Het Schilder Boeck*, 1618, p. 126.

§ C. I. Nieuwenhuys, *Description de la Galerie des Tableaux de S. M. Le Roi des Pays-Bas*, Bruxelles, 1843, p. 4, note. Kugler's *Hand-book*, &c., revised by Waagen, London, Murray, 1860, vol. i. p. 70.

• ALS • IXH • XAN •

IOHES • DE • EYCK • ME • FECIT • ANO • MCCCC • 33 • 21 • OCTOBRIS •

TYM. ωΘΕΟΣ

LEAL SOUVENIR

Actu ano dni · 1432 · 10 · die · octobris · a ioh de Eyck ·

On wood, 10¼ in. *h.* by 7½ in. *w.*

This picture was apparently, from the inscription on the back,—"Ex Collectione Arundeliana," formerly in the Arundel Collection: it was lately in that of Viscount Midleton, at Pepper-harrow. It was painted, according to an inscription on the lower part of the frame, Oct. 21, 1433.* Purchased for the National Gallery, from Mr. H. Farrer, in 1851.

No. **290.** A MAN'S PORTRAIT, in a dark red dress with a green head-covering, the ends of which hang down on the sides; in his hand he holds a paper with writing upon it. The lower part of the picture represents a stone parapet, on which is inscribed in Greek characters what appears to be meant for Τίμόθεος, Timothy; below is written LEAL SOUVENIR, and under this the painter's signature as follows:—*Factū año. Dm̃. 1432. 10. die Octobris. a Joh. de Eyck.*

On wood, 13¼ in. *h.* by 7½ in. *w.*

Purchased from Herr Carl Ross at Munich in 1857.†

PIETRO DELLA FRANCESCA.

PIETRO, called DELLA FRANCESCA after his mother,‡ and also Pietro Borghese, was born at Borgo San Sepolcro

* The original inscription, given in fac simile opposite, is Joh'es + de + Eyck + me + fecit + anno + MCCCC + 33 + 21 Octobris. On the upper part of the frame are the three words ALS IXH XAN (als ich kan), signifying, as well as I can,—which appear from several examples still extant to have been often written by Van Eyck on the frames of his pictures; they are the first words of an old Flemish proverb,—As I can, but not as I will.—See l'Abbé C. Carton, *Les trois Frères Van Eyck*. p. 73, Bruges, 1848.

† The brothers Van Eyck appear to have resided in Ghent while they were employed on the altar-piece of St. Bavon. After the death of Hubert, John Van Eyck remained in that city till May 1432, when the work was completed. In August of the same year (as is proved by a document) he had returned to Bruges. A picture by him in the possession of Mr. Weld Blundell, of Ince Hall near Liverpool, is supposed to have been the first work painted by the master after his return: it has the date 1432, with the addition *Brugis*. The portrait above described, dated October 1432, ranks next or possibly before it in chronological order. Weale, *Notes*, &c., p. 9, note. In the *Kunstblatt*, October 19, 1854, there is a careful description of this picture by Dr. E. Förster. More than one copy of the portrait exists, whence it may be inferred that the personage represented was of some note.

‡ Vasari, *Vite*, &c. explains this by informing us that Pietro was born after the death of his father. The name of the latter is supposed to have been Benedetto. The mention of "Pietro di Benedetto dal Borgho a San Sepolchro," which occurs in a document hereafter to be noticed, is the plausible ground for this conclusion, but a similar expression sometimes implies a different relation, such for example, as that of master and scholar. It is not to be overlooked that Fra Luca Pacioli, the contemporary and scholar of Pietro, invariably calls him Pietro de' Franceschi and Petrus de Franciscis. The present descendants of the painter are called Marini-Franceschi.

about 1415.* He received at first a scientific education which appears to have influenced his subsequent tendencies in art. At the age of fifteen he turned his attention to painting, and ultimately became one of the most distinguished of the Umbrian masters.

His earliest productions are no longer to be traced. In 1439 he assisted Domenico Venziano in some wall paintings in the church of Santa Maria Nuova in Florence.† In 1450, and probably for some time previously, he was occupied with the same master at Loreto‡, and in 1451, independently, at Rimini, where a fresco by him with that date still exists. His maturer works in his native city of Borgo San Sepolcro, appear to have been executed during a period comprehending the year 1460.§ Among those works, a fresco of the Resurrection, still preserved in good state in the Palazzo de' Conservatori, is justly extolled by Vasari. Pietro was subsequently in Urbino: the portraits of Federigo da Montefeltro and Battista Sforza, now in the Gallery of the Uffizj in Florence, must have been painted after 1460, in which year the marriage of those personages took place. The age of the lady in that picture

---

* The annotators of the Le Monnier edition of Vasari, (vol. iv., p. 13.) place the birth of Pietro della Francesca in the "first years" of the fifteenth century. Hitherto no evidence has come to light which can suffice to establish a precise date, but various circumstances seem to render it necessary to assume a period later than 1410. E. Harzen, in an essay in the *Archiv für den zeichnenden Künste*, Leipzig, 1856, after concluding that Vasari's statements must, by inference, place Pietro's birth in 1398, selects 1426 as a more convenient date. For this considerable alteration there seems to be no sufficient reason; indeed, according to the assumption Pietro must have been a recognised painter at the age of thirteen. A document in the archives of Santa Maria Nuova in Florence, quoted by Harzen, shows that in 1439 Pietro was employed, apparently as the assistant of Domenico Veneziano, when that master was painting in the chapel of Saint Egidio in the church referred to. It is in this record that Pietro is called "di Benedetto." The birth of Domenico Veneziano is placed by the annotators of Vasari after 1410; and Pietro, as the scholar, can hardly be supposed to be the elder of the two. Compare the life of Antonello da Messina in this Catalogue.

† See the preceding note.

‡ Compare Vasari's life of Domenico Veneziano with that of Pietro della Francesca. The ceiling of the sacristy at Loreto, though not completed by them, gained Domenico, as the principal painter, considerable reputation, whence it may be inferred that the work must have occupied some time. The resemblance between the two remaining works of Domenico Veneziano in Florence (especially in the character of the Madonnas' heads), and the style of Pietro della Francesca, has been noticed by many observers, and may perhaps be accounted for by the circumstances above detailed.

§ A fresco of San Lodovico, ascribed to Pietro, in a hall of the Tribunale in Borgo San Sepolcro, has the date 1460. Dragomanoi, *Vita di Pietro della Francesca*, Firenze, 1835, p. 22.

indicates a later period as its date*; and the presence of Pietro in Urbino in 1469, when he appears to have been the guest of Giovanni Santi,† may possibly coincide with the time when that work and another, still preserved in the sacristy of the Duomo at Urbino,‡ were executed. The period when he was employed by Duke Borso of Ferrara in the palace of Schifanoia in that city, and the date of his visit to Rome, when he painted for Pope Nicholas V. two frescoes in the Vatican, which were afterwards destroyed to make room for the works of Raphael, cannot be precisely defined.§ His frescoes relating to the history of the Cross, in the church of San Francesco at Arezzo, are also of uncertain date, although the magnitude of the series supposes a residence of some years.‖ The partial or total blindness

---

* Battista Sforza was only thirteen at the time of her marriage, she died at the age of twenty-five in 1472. Dennistoun, *Memoirs of the Dukes of Urbino*, London, 1851, vol. i., pp. 86, 114, 204. At p. 207 will be found an accurate engraving of the portraits.

† Passavant, *Raphael d'Urbin*, Paris, 1860, tome 1, p. 392; Pungileoni, *Elogio Storico di Giovanni Santi*, Urbino, 1822, pp. 12, 75. In the extract from a document dated April 8, 1469, with an account of disbursements for Pietro by Giovanni Santi, it appears that the former was to have painted an altarpiece for the Confraternity of Corpus Domini; Pungileoni adds that the picture was, for some unknown reason, not executed; thus the painter's visit to Urbino in 1469 would have had no apparent result unless we suppose that the portraits and the small picture in the Duomo were painted about that time.

‡ The subject of the last-named picture is partly allegorical. On the left of the spectator, in the middle distance under a portico, is represented the Flagellation of Christ. In the foreground, on the other side, stand three personages of distinction; the motto "convenerunt in unum" is inscribed near them. Passavant (*Raphael*, &c., i, p. 389) concludes that they represent three princes or leaders who were hostile to Federigo. The picture bears the inscription OPUS PETRI DE BURGO SCI SEPULCHRI.

§ Borso succeeded to the sovereignty of Ferrara in 1453. In 1469 an alteration in the Schifanoia palace is supposed to have involved the partial destruction of Pietro's frescoes which it seems were on the walls of the lower story. The two dates include the period of his residence in Ferrara. See Laderchi, *Sopra i dipinti del Palazzo di Schifanoia*, Bologna, 1840. The years 1447, 1455, the limits of the pontificate of Nicholas V., define the period within which Pietro's Roman labours must be placed. In the life of Raphael, Vasari speaks but of one fresco in the Vatican by Pietro; in the life of Pietro himself, he alludes to two, and informs us that they occupied the places where Raphael's frescoes of the Deliverance of Peter and the Mass of Bolsena now are.

‖ Luca Pacioli, in his "Divina Proporzione," speaking generally of Pietro's works in painting, adds "especially in the city of Arezzo." According to Vasari, the order of Pietro's principal works, as defined by that of the places where he successively resided would be Urbino, Ferrara, Rome, Borgo San Sepolcro, Loreto, Arezzo. The inconsistency of this, in point of chronology is apparent, more especially as the biographer supposes Pietro to have been employed in Urbino by Duke Guidobaldo, who succeeded his father Federigo in 1482 at the age of ten. It is, however, not impossible that the aged artist may have painted for Guidobaldo; the date of Pietro's blindness being uncertain.

with which this painter was afflicted, as Vasari states, in his "old age,"* is quite reconcileable with the ascertained or probable dates of the works above-mentioned as compared with the assumed year of his birth. Pietro was, beyond doubt, still living in 1494;† the year of his death is as yet unknown.

Among his scholars Vasari names Pietro Perugino and Luca Signorelli. Luca Pacioli was his pupil in geometry and in scientific investigations generally.‡

The mathematical studies of this remarkable painter, which appear to have been occasionally prosecuted during his life, and to which his latter like his early years were exclusively devoted, led him to give his attention to some branches of art, such as the effects of perspective and light, which were imperfectly practised when he began his career, and in these respects he undoubtedly contributed to prepare the way for the more accomplished masters who succeeded him.§

No. **585.** PORTRAIT, SUPPOSED TO BE THAT OF ISOTTA DA RIMINI, fourth wife of Sigismondo Malatesta.‖ Head in profile.

In tempera, on wood, 1 ft. 4½ in *h.* by 11½ in *w.*

As Pietro painted the portrait of Sigismondo Malatesta in 1451, this portrait of his wife may have been executed in the same year.

---

* Elsewhere the biographer says that Pietro became blind in his sixtieth year. This, as various writers have shown, is hardly consistent with his own narrative taken in connexion with the known dates of some of the master's works.

† See Luca Pacioli *Summa de Arithmetica*, published in 1494, p. 68. The passage is quoted in the Le Monnier Vasari, vol. iv. p. 24, note 1.

‡ In a M.S. catalogue of pictures, which is preserved in private hands in Urbino, a portrait is mentioned as the work of Luca del Borgo. This may have been Luca Pacioli (called by Vasari, Luca del Borgo) who, as the scholar of Pietro della Francesca, probably acquired some knowledge of painting as well as much of scientific subjects. He became a Franciscan monk in 1487. On the question of his supposed plagiarism of Pietro's writings, an accusation rashly brought against him by Vasari, see the authorities quoted by Dragomanni, *Vita,* &c., p. 19; Gaye, *Kunstblatt*, 1836, No. 69; and the Essay before referred to, by Harzen. Bossi, *Del Cenacolo di Leonardo da Vinci*, 1810, p. 17, states that he himself was in possession of an original MS. on perspective by Pietro della Francesca.

§ A drawing by Pietro for one of the frescoes at Arezzo (once in the Lawrence collection) in which the angel descends by night to Constantine, is so powerful and original in its light and shade, that it was published by Ottley as the work of Giorgione. Compare Vasari's description of the fresco.

‖ Dennistoun, *Memoirs of the Dukes of Urbino*, vol. i., pp. 181, 185 note.

It was formerly in the possession of the Marchese Carlo Guicciardini of Florence. Purchased at Florence from the Lombardi-Baldi collection in 1857.

No. 665. THE BAPTISM OF CHRIST, in the River Jordan.

"And it came to pass in those days, that Jesus came from Nazareth of Galilee, and was baptized of John in Jordan. And straightway coming out of the water, he saw the heavens opened, and the Spirit like a dove descending upon him."—*Mark* i., 9-10.

Christ is standing in the river, under the shade of a pomegranate tree, receiving the water on his head from the cup of John; the dove is descending upon him. On the spectator's left are three angels witnessing the ceremony; other figures are on the banks of the river, in the background. Composition of six principal figures.

In tempera, on wood, 5 ft. 5½ in. *h.* by 3 ft. 9½ in. *w.*

Formerly the principal altar-piece of the Priory of St. John the Baptist at Borgo San Sepolcro. When the priory was suppressed in 1807 the picture was removed to the sacristy of the Cathedral, where it formed the centre portion of an altar decoration, the remainder of which was by another hand. It was bought by Mr. J. C. Robinson for Mr. Uzielli, at whose sale it was purchased for the National Collection in 1861.*

FRANCIA.

FRANCE'SCO RAIBOLI'NI, commonly called FRANCIA, was born at Bologna about the year 1450: his father, Marco di Giacomo Raibolini, was a carpenter. He assumed the name of Francia from his master, the goldsmith to whom he was apprenticed; he was originally a goldsmith, and die and niello engraver, in which profession he was very eminent. He must, however, have attained also some distinction as a painter before the year 1490, as he was then employed on several important works, both in oil and in fresco, especially for the Bentivogli family. He frequently signed his pictures *Aurifex*, jeweller; and on his jewellery he inscribed himself *Pictor*, painter.

Francia died, according to a document discovered by J. A. Calvi, on the 6th of January, 1517.† This date agrees

* Dragomanni, *Vita di Pietro della Francesca*, &c., Florence. 1835.

† The date as in the document in question is 1517, the old custom of beginning the ecclesiastical and legal year on the 25th of March was never established at Bologna. This custom prevailed very generally in Europe, not excepting England, at that time and until 1752. Much confusion occasionally

with the time assigned for his death by Vasari, though the circumstance to which that writer imputes the cause of his death may be doubted. Vasari states, that Francia died of grief, at seeing himself so much surpassed in painting by his young friend Raphael, who had consigned to the Bolognese painter his picture of St. Cecilia, painted for the church of San Giovanni in Monte, requesting him to repair any damage that might have happened to it, or to correct it if necessary, and to superintend the placing of it in the church.

Though Francia appears to have died soon after the arrival of the St. Cecilia at Bologna, there is hardly a necessity for accounting for the coincidence in any extraordinary way, as he was then nearly seventy years of age.

Francia is the greatest painter of the earlier school of Bologna; his works are considered the most perfect specimens extant of that intermediate style of painting which the Italians term the *antico-moderno*, and which immediately preceded the more complete development of the art, which distinguished the great masters of the sixteenth century; the latter is known as the *cinquecento* style, in contradistinction to the *quattrocento*, or the *antico-moderno*.*

No. **179.** The Virgin with the Infant Christ, and St. Anne enthroned, surrounded by Saints. Before the throne in the front is the little St. John with the standard of the Lamb, pointing to the infant Saviour above; on the left are St. Sebastian and St. Paul; on the right, St. Cawrence and St. Romualdo. The picture is marked—Francia Aurifex Bononiensis P. Full-length figures, nearly of the natural size.

On wood, 6 ft. 6½ in. *h.* by 6 ft. *w.*

FRANCIA · AVRIFEX-BONONIĒSIS · P.

---

resulted: in the year 1667 there were two Easters, the first on the 25th of April, and the second on the 22d of March following. Similar confusion occurred in the dates of State documents. See Granger's *Biographical History of England*, Preface. Vasari, to avoid mistake, has given the date according to both systems, in his notice of the death of Michelangelo.—See *L'Art de Vérifier les Dates.*

* Vasari; Malvasia; Lanzi; and Calvi, *Memorie della Vita e delle Opere di Francesco Raibolini detto il Francia*, Bologna, 1812; see also Passavant, *Rafael von Urbino*, &c.

No. **180.** THE VIRGIN AND TWO ANGELS WEEPING OVER THE DEAD BODY OF CHRIST. A Pietà; formerly the lunette of the picture described above.

On wood, 3 ft. 2 in. *h.* by 6 ft. *w.*

These two pictures constituted formerly one altar-piece, and were originally placed in the Buonvisi chapel in the church of San Fridiano at Lucca, for which they were painted. They were subsequently purchased by the Duke of Lucca, and were placed in the palace. They were finally brought to England with the rest of the Duke of Lucca's Collection in 1840, and became the property of Mr. E. G. Flight, from whom they were purchased for the National Gallery in 1841. There is an old copy or repetition of No. 180 in the Gallery of Berlin.

No. **638.** THE VIRGIN AND CHILD, WITH TWO SAINTS. The child standing on a stone parapet is supported by his mother behind him; his hand is in the attitude of benediction. On each side is a Saint; the child entire, the others half figures. Landscape back-ground.

On wood, 2 ft. 8in. *h.* by 2 ft. 1½ in. *w.*

Purchased from M. Edmond Beaucousin, at Paris, in 1860.

GADDI, TADDEO.

TADDEO, the son of Gaddo GADDI, was born at Florence, according to Vasari, in the year 1300. He was the godson and pupil of Giotto, with whom he lived twenty-four years; and he became the most eminent of that painter's numerous scholars. He enlarged somewhat upon the style of Giotto, though he preserved its general character; but he surpassed his master, says Vasari, in colour, and, in some of his works, even in expression. Taddeo, however, adhered strictly to the prevailing symmetrical disposition of the figures which, in altar-pieces at least, characterizes the compositions of the early Italian masters.

He executed many works at Florence, both in fresco and in *tempera*, but few are now preserved. The best of those that remain are the frescoes of the Giugni (formerly Baroncelli) chapel, in the church of Santa Croce at Florence.* But his most extensive works were the frescoes of the Cappella degli Spagnuoli, in the church of Santa Maria Novella, now much decayed.

* They are engraved by Count Lasinio in his *Affreschi Celebri del* xiv. *e* xv. *Secolo*, Firenze, 1841.

Taddeo was equally distinguished as painter and as architect; he built the present Ponte Vecchio, and also the Ponte della Trinità, which was destroyed by a flood in 1557: he also constructed the famous Campanile of Florence, from the design of Giotto.

The date of Taddeo's death is not known; but he was still living in 1366, as shown by Rumohr, from a document respecting a commission undertaken by him on the 20th of August of that year, connected with the building of the present cathedral of Florence.*

Taddeo Gaddi amassed considerable wealth, and was the founder of the distinguished Florentine family of the name. He left two sons, Giovanni and Agnolo, who both followed the arts, but the former died young: Agnolo became an eminent painter, who was the master of Cennino Cennini.

No. **215.** VARIOUS SAINTS: apparently St. Ambrose, St. Stephen, St. Francis, St. Paul, St. Catherine? St. John the Baptist, St. Matthew, and St. Benedict?

On wood, 5 ft. 11 in. *h.* by 3 ft. 4½ in. *w.*

No. **216.** VARIOUS SAINTS. St. Gregory, St. Philip? St. Lawrence, St. Thomas? St. Dominick? St. John, St. Peter, and St. Romualdo.

On wood, 5 ft. 10 in. *h.* by 3 ft. 4½ in. *w.*

These pictures, painted in *tempera*, appear, from the corresponding symmetrical disposition of the figures, to have formed the wings of an altar-piece. They were presented to the National Gallery, in 1848, by Mr. W. Coningham, by whom they were purchased at Rome; one was formerly in the collection of Cardinal Fesch, the other had been taken from Florence to Rome on speculation.

No. **579.** THE BAPTISM OF CHRIST IN THE RIVER JORDAN.

"And straightway coming up out of the water, he saw the heavens opened, and the spirit like a dove descending upon him: and there came a voice from Heaven, saying, Thou art my beloved Son in whom I am well pleased.—*Mark* i. 10-11."

In the centre picture is St. John baptising Christ; above which subject is an angel; on the spectator's left is St. Peter, on the right St. Paul. In the *cuspidi* or upper pictures above, is, in the centre, the Almighty; on the left, the

---

* Arch. dell' op. del Duomo di Fir., 1363-1396, fo. 71 Rumohr, *Italienisech Forschungen*, ii. p. 82.

Virgin; on the right, Isaiah holding a scroll containing the words *Ecce virgo concipiet.*

In the predella pictures,—the angel announcing the birth of St. John the Baptist to Zaccharias; the birth of St. John; his death; the feast of Herod; Herodias receiving the head of the Saint from her daughter; and at the extreme ends, St. Benedict, and St. Romualdo; in all, eleven pictures.

Altar-piece in tempera, on wood, 11 ft. *h.* by 6 ft. 7 in. *w.* Of the principal pictures, the centre 5 ft 3½ in. *h.* by 2 ft. 6 in. *w.*, the sides 4 ft. ½ in. *h.* by 1 ft. 2½ in. *w.*; of the upper pictures, the centre 2 ft. 1 in. *h.* by 10 in. *w.*, the sides, 1 ft. 11 in. *h.* by 10 in. *w.*; the predella pictures, 1 ft. 1 in. *h.* by 2 ft. 3 in. *w.*

According to an inscription, now partly obliterated, on the principal picture, this work was painted for Filippo Neroni, in 1337. Formerly in the Abbey del Sasso di Camaldoli, in the Casentino. Purchased at Florence from the Lombardi-Baldi collection in 1857.

GARO'FALO.

BENVENU'TO TISIO, commonly called GARO'FALO, from the monogram (the Gilliflower) with which he marked his pictures, was born in the Ferrarese in 1481. He had many masters. He was at first the pupil of Domenico Panetti, at Ferrara, and studied afterwards under his uncle, Niccolo Soriani at Cremona. In 1500 he visited Rome, and remained there fifteen months with Giovanni Baldini; he studied subsequently under Lorenzo Costa at Mantua, and was finally, in 1508, engaged by Raphael at Rome, to assist him in the frescoes of the Vatican.

Garofalo had remained some years with Raphael in Rome, when his family affairs called him to Ferrara, whither he went, with the intention, however, of returning to Rome as soon as his occupations might permit; but circumstances detained him in Ferrara, and he never afterwards quitted it. He was employed by Alphonso I., with the two Dossi, at Belriguardo and elsewhere. He died at Ferrara in 1559, having become quite blind a few years previously.

Garofalo is the chief of the Ferrarese painters. His small easel pictures are universally admired. In these works he was a close imitator of Raphael's style, a Raphael in miniature; and these small pictures are sometimes attributed to his great master.

Several of his frescoes are still extant at Ferrara, the

principal of which, painted about 1519–24, are in the church of San Francesco; among them is the Slaughter of the Innocents. Other frescoes by Garofalo are still preserved in the Palazzo del Magistrato at Ferrara.*

No. **81.** THE VISION OF ST. AUGUSTIN. Augustinus, one of the four "Doctors" of the church, and bishop of Hippo, in Africa,† relates, that while engaged on a work on the Trinity, he had a vision in which he saw a child endeavouring with a ladle to empty the ocean into a hole which he had made in the sand; and upon the saint pointing out the futility of his labour, the child retorted by observing how much more futile must be his efforts to explain that which it had pleased the Deity to make an inscrutable mystery. The picture illustrates the moment of the dialogue; St. Catherine is represented behind the saint, and in the clouds above is a vision of the Holy Family attended by a choir of angels: the back-ground is a varied rocky landscape, with a view of the sea.

Engraved by P. W. Tomkins; and by J. Rolls in Jones's *National Gallery*. On wood, 2 ft. 1½ in. *h.* by 2 ft. 8 in. *w.*

Formerly in the Corsini palace at Rome; subsequently in the Ottley collection: bequeathed to the National Gallery in 1831, by the Rev. W. H. Carr.

No. **170.** THE HOLY FAMILY, WITH ELIZABETH AND THE YOUNG ST. JOHN, and two other saints: above is a vision of God the Father surrounded by a choir of angels.

On canvas, 2 ft. 6½ in. *h.* by 1 ft. 11½ in. *w.*

Formerly in the collection of Mr. Beckford, from whom it was purchased for the National Gallery, in 1839.

No. **642.** CHRIST'S AGONY IN THE GARDEN. Above is an angel bearing the cup and cross; the three apostles are asleep in the fore-ground: a crowd with torches is approaching from behind. *Luke* XXII., 41–43. (See No. 76.)

On canvas, from wood, 19 in. *h.* by 14 in. *w.*

Purchased at Paris, from M. Edmond Beaucousin, in 1860.

No. **671.** THE MADONNA AND CHILD ENTHRONED, under a canopy; on their left are standing Saints Francis and Anthony; on their right, Saint Guglielmo in armour, with his right hand resting on a shield, and St. Clara holding

---

* Vasari, *Vite de' Pittori*, &c.; Lanzi, *Storia Pittorica*, &c.

† He was born at Tagasta, in Africa, in the year 354, and died at Hippo in 430.—*Acta Sanctorum*, vol. vi., Aug. 28.

a crucifix. The back-ground represents an architectural interior. Figures small life-size.

On wood arched at the top, 7 ft. 11 in. *h.* by 6 ft. 10½ in. *w.* Engraved by G. Domenichini.

Originally the principal altar-piece of the church of San Guglielmo at Ferrara, but from which it was removed in 1832, when the convent was suppressed, to the cathedral, and thence to the residence of the archbishop. Purchased from the Count Antonio Mazza in 1861.*

GHIRLANDAJO.

DOMENICO BIGORDI, commonly called GHIRLANDAJO, was born at Florence in 1449. His father, Tommaso Bigordi, a goldsmith, had acquired the name of Il Ghirlandajo, from his celebrity for the manufacture of children's garlands. Domenico was brought up as a jeweller and goldsmith; but became at an early age also one of the most distinguished painters of his time. He surpassed all his Florentine contemporaries in the precision of his drawing and the delicacy of his execution. When little more than thirty, about 1480–84, he was invited by Sixtus IV. to Rome, to assist in the decoration of the Sistine Chapel. In 1488 he received Michelangelo, then in his fourteenth year, as an apprentice for three years.

The principal works of Domenico Ghirlandajo, both in fresco and in tempera, are to be seen at Florence, as the series of frescoes in the Sássetti Chapel, in the Church of the Trinità, consisting of scenes from the life of St. Francis, completed in December 1485; and those of the Choir of Santa Maria Novella, finished in 1490. The first series contains portraits of Lorenzo de' Medici and other eminent Florentines; and in the last series, in that portion illustrating the life of the Virgin,† is the celebrated portrait of Ginevra de' Benci, a young Florentine lady distinguished for her beauty. The altar-piece of the Sassetti Chapel, in tempera, representing the "Nativity," is now in the Gallery of the Academy.‡ Another important tempera picture,

* Baruffaldi, *Vite*, &c., vol. i. p. 362; Laderchi, *Pittura Ferrarese*, &c., p. 91. A copy of this picture by Alessandro Candi of Ferrara is now in the church of San Giuseppe a' Cappucini in Bologna.

† Engraved by Carlo Lasinio. The "Death of St. Francis," one of this series, is considered by Rumohr the painter's masterpiece.

‡ Engraved in the *Galleria delle Belle Arti di Firenze*, 1845. Domenico has introduced his own portrait among the shepherds in this picture.

attributed to this master, is the round panel in the Uffizj, representing the "Adoration of the Kings;" it is dated 1487.*

Ghirlandajo worked also in mosaic; the latest of his known productions is an "Annunciation," executed in this method, over one of the doors of the Cathedral at Florence, the completion of which was interrupted by the death of Lorenzo de' Medici, in 1492. Ghirlandajo was already dead in 1498, and as he was born in 1449, he did not exceed the comparatively early age of 48.† He was the father of Ridolfo Ghirlandajo; David and Benedetto were his brothers.

No. **296.** THE VIRGIN ADORING THE INFANT CHRIST, with an Angel standing on each side of her. The Virgin, very richly dressed, is seated with her hands raised together, as if in prayer, and is regarding the child who is lying upon her knees, and holding a raspberry to its lips. Landscape back-ground. Half figures, nearly life-size.‡

In tempera, on wood, 3 ft. 2 in. *h.* by 2 ft. 3¼ in. *w.*

Originally in the possession of the Contugi family, of Volterra. Purchased at Florence from M. L. Hombert, in 1857.

GIORGIONE.

GIORGIO BARBARELLI, commonly called, from his large and handsome stature, GIORGIONE, was born of parents in good circumstances, in the neighbourhood of Castelfranco, in 1477. He was the fellow-pupil of Titian with Giovanni Bellini at Venice, and early distinguished himself for his beautiful colouring, and his effective treatment of light and shade. He was further distinguished for a general objective truth of representation, which he acquired by his practice of referring

---

* Engraved in Rosini's *Storia della Pittura*, &c., and in the "*Reale Galleria degli Uffizj.*" This picture is by some connoisseurs supposed to be a work by Botticelli.

† Gaye, *Carteggio Inedito*, &c. Vasari, Ed. Le Monnier, vol. v.

‡ Vasari's statement that Antonio Pollaiuolo acquired the art of painting from his brother Piero should, perhaps, be understood to relate to oil-painting. The biographer speaks of no works by Antonio in tempera; yet it is probable that he, like other masters of the time, began with that method in which, indeed, a greater finish was considered attainable. In consequence of the silence of Vasari, the tempera pictures of Antonio Pollaiuolo can only be discovered by their style. Several are now believed to exist under other names, and among them, not impossibly, may hereafter be classed the picture above described.

to nature on all occasions. After having visited his native place, where he painted some pictures, Giorgione returned to Venice, and by way of exhibiting a specimen of his ability, he decorated the front of his house with subjects in fresco: he was, in consequence, employed on other works of the kind. Like many artists of the period, he was also in the habit of painting panels for various articles of ornamental furniture; for these he generally chose his subjects from Ovid, enriching them with appropriate landscape back-grounds. Giorgione's frescoes have perished, and few even of his oil pictures are now in existence. The works by which he is at present most generally known are his portraits, in some of which he is still unsurpassed. Du Fresnoy observes of Giorgione's pictures of this class, "He dressed his figures wonderfully well: and it may be truly said, that, but for him, Titian would never have attained that perfection which was the consequence of the rivalship and jealousy which prevailed between them."*

This great painter died in 1511, before the completion of his thirty-fourth year. Some of the greatest masters of the Venetian and neighbouring schools were the scholars or imitators of Giorgione:—Sebastiano del Piombo, Giovanni da Udine, Francesco Torbido, and others.†

No. **41.** THE DEATH OF PETER MARTYR OF MARTIRE. St. Peter the Dominican, a native of Verona, was an active agent of the Inquisition in the thirteenth century; and having, as such, made many enemies, he was at length assassinated by one of these, named Cavina, at the entrance of a wood on the road from Milan to Como. He was attended by a single brother of his order, who is seen attacked by another assassin in the middle-ground to the right.

Engraved in Jones's *National Gallery*. On canvas, 3 ft. 4½ in. *h.* by 4 ft. 9½ in. *w.*

Formerly in the possession of Christina, queen of Sweden, and subsequently in the Orleans collection. Bequeathed to the National Gallery, in 1831, by the Rev. W. H. Carr.

(*See* No. **234**, BELLINI, SCHOOL OF.)

---

* Du Fresnoy's *Sentiments*, printed with Sir Joshua Reynolds's Notes on his Poem.

† Vasari, *Vite de' Pittori, &c.*; Ridolfi, *Le Maraviglie dell' Arte, &c.*

No. **269.** A KNIGHT IN ARMOUR. A small figure completely armed with the exception of the head; in his left hand he holds his lance. A dark background.

On wood, 1 ft. 3½ in. *h.* by 10¾ in. *w.*

This appears to be a study for the figure of San Liberale in the altar-piece by Giorgione at Castel Franco. The only difference is, that in the altar-piece the warrior wears his helmet, while in this picture he is bare-headed. From a MS. memorandum on the back of the picture, it appears that Mariette had also noticed the resemblance of this figure to the warrior in the Castel Franco altar-piece, which, he observes, was said to represent Gaston de Foix. Formerly in the collection of Benjamin West, P.R.A. Bequeathed to the National Gallery by Mr. Samuel Rogers, in 1855.

GIOTTO.

GIOTTO, or MAGISTER JOCTUS, called also Giotto di Bondone, from his father's name, was born in 1276, in the commune of Vespignano in the Val del Mugello, fifteen miles north-east of Florence; his occupation as a boy was to tend sheep.

About the year 1286 the celebrated painter Cimabue, being in that neighbourhood, surprised the young Giotto, while keeping his father's sheep, in the act of sketching one of his flock upon a stone. Astonished at the ability of the effort, he took the boy, with the father's consent, back with him to Florence and instructed him in the art of painting.

Few of Giotto's works remain; his earliest were executed in the Badia or Abbey of Florence. The fresco of the Last Supper in the refectory* of the church of Santa Croce at Florence, is now admitted to be the work of a later hand, and probably by his scholar Taddeo Gaddi. But a Coronation of the Virgin by Giotto, in the Baroncelli chapel in the same church, and some smaller works removed from thence to the academy, with a large Crucifix in the church of Santa Maria Novella, are still preserved.

Giotto also decorated the walls of the chapel of St. John the Baptist, in the church of Santa Maria del Carmine, at Florence; the chapel was destroyed by fire in 1771. Portions of the paintings, such, for instance, as the two half figures below mentioned, were, however, saved.

* Now (1856) a carpet manufactory.

At the close of the 13th century, Giotto appears to have been in the service of Pope Boniface the 8th, for whom, in 1298,* he executed the mosaic of the Disciples in the Storm known as the "Navicella" of Giotto, which, much altered and modernized, is now in the portico of St. Peter's at Rome.

Early in the 14th century he executed extensive works in the church of San Francesco at Assisi. In 1306, we find him engaged at Padua, where he painted a comprehensive series of subjects from the Life of the Virgin and the Passion of Christ, with other representations, in the Scrovegni chapel in the church of the Madonna dell'Arena. The greater part of these still exist.†

From Padua Giotto proceeded to Avignon, whence he returned to Florence in 1316; and from this time he appears to have devoted his attention to architecture and sculpture as much as to painting. In 1322 he visited Lucca, and in 1327 painted a chapel for King Robert in the Castel Nuovo at Naples, which has been destroyed. He died at Florence in 1336, and was buried with great pomp in the cathedral.‡

Giotto was a great innovator in the practice of art. He wholly forsook the traditionary remains of the Byzantine style, and studied nature. Some of the best specimens of decorative art, partaking of the same vigour which characterizes this period, are also attributed to him. The Campanile of Florence was carried out, after the design of Giotto, by his scholar Taddeo Gaddi, who lived twenty-four years with him and completed his unfinished works.§

---

* See Baldinucci. *Notizie dei Professori del Disegno. Decenn.* IV., *sec.* 1.

† These wall-paintings are now being engraved and published by the *Arundel Society*. Dante visited Giotto while engaged on these works; the poet mentions the painter in the following terms in his *Purgatory*:—

> "In painting Cimabue once believed
> He held the field: now Giotto has the cry,
> So that he dims the reputation of the first."
>
> Pollock's Dante, Purgatorio, Canto XI.

‡ Vasari, *Vite, &c.*, Ed. Le Monnier, Florence, 1846, *et seq.*

§ There is a saying, "rounder than the O of Giotto." This, according to Vasari, has reference to a mechanical feat performed by the painter before he went to Rome. Pope Boniface, wishing to decorate St. Peter's, sent an envoy to Florence and Siena for artists of whose ability he required specimens. Giotto sent a circle, drawn without the aid of compasses, with a brush, in red colour. This, it is said, appeared in the eyes of His Holiness more wonderful, than any other specimens of skill; but it is probable that he was guided by the safer evidence of Giotto's fame.

No. **276.** Two Apostles, one with the hands clasped; half figures, under life size; a fragment.

Engraved by Thomas Patch in 1772.* Painted in *secco*,† on plaster; 19½ in. square.

This is a fragment from one of the wall paintings formerly in the chapel of San Giovanni Battista, in the church of Santa Maria del Carmine, at Florence. The subject of the composition to which these figures belong was the burial of St. John the Baptist. This and two portions from other paintings of the series, now in the institution at Liverpool, were saved from the fire which destroyed this chapel in 1771, and became the property of Mr. Thomas Patch, the engraver. They were brought to England by Mr. Townley. This fragment was subsequently in the collection of the Right Hon. C. Greville, from whom it passed into the possession of Mr. Rogers, and at the sale of his pictures in 1856 was purchased for the National Gallery. Some other fragments are preserved in the Cappella dell' Ammannati, in the Campo Santo at Pisa. From some chronological evidences referred to by Patch, it appears that the wall paintings in question must have been painted within the last five years of Giotto's life, and not, as Vasari states, at an earlier period.

School of Giotto.

No. **568.** The Coronation of the Virgin.—The Virgin is inclining her head to receive the crown from the hands of Christ: four angels are kneeling below, in front of the throne, two of them hold golden vessels in their hands. The principal figures are small life-size.

In tempera, on wood, 5 ft. 11 in. *h.* by 3 ft. 1 in *w.*

Painted about 1330. Formerly in the Convent of the Minori Osservanti of San Miniato, near Florence. Purchased at Florence from the Lombardi-Baldi collection in 1857.

GO'ZZOLI.

Benozzo Go'zzoli was born at Florence in 1424; he was the son of Lese di Sandro, and the scholar of Fra Angelico

---

* Selections from the works of the Florentine painters Masaccio, Fra Bartolommeo, and Giotto, Part III., pl. 7. Florence, 1770, 1772.

† For a description of the method called *secco*, or *fresco secco*, as opposed to *buon fresco*, see Eastlake's "Materials for a History of Oil Painting," 1847, p. 142. Secco is thus described by Theophilus:—"When figures or other objects are drawn on a dry wall the surface should be first saturated with water till it is quite moist. While the wall is in this state the colours are to be applied, all the tints being mixed with lime, and drying as the wall dries, in order that they may adhere." *Div. Art. Schedula*, *l.* 1, *c.* 15. *Buon fresco* cannot be executed on a large surface without joinings in the plaster. *Secco* may be executed without joinings, but the colours have not the brilliancy of fresco. The earliest example of *buon fresco* is supposed to be a work by Pietro D'Orvieto, painted in 1390, in the Campo Santo at Pisa.

da Fiesole, whom he assisted in some works in the Cathedral of Orvieto. His style, for some time, nearly resembled that of his master; but in his later works, as in the Campo Santo at Pisa, his own natural talent displayed itself, which was as decidedly *objective* as Fra Angelico's was *subjective.* His known works extend over a period of thirty-eight years, from 1447 to 1485, after which date we have no accounts of him.

His last are his greatest works,—the extensive series of frescoes in the Campo Santo, commenced in 1469, representing twenty-four scenes from the Old Testament, from the time of Noah to the visit of the Queen of Sheba to Solomon. These frescoes he contracted to paint, three a year, for the moderate remuneration of 66 lire or about ten ducats each; at that time, however, worth perhaps about £100 of our present money. Benozzo displays the most varied resources in these works, in the rich landscape backgrounds, in the architectural accessories, and in the introduction of all kinds of birds and animals, especially dogs. The Drunkenness of Noah, the Marriage of Rebecca, and Moses in the Wilderness, are perhaps the best of all the Campo Santo frescoes.* The works of Masaccio in the Brancacci Chapel seem to have been his models in the style of his figures, which are often graceful and natural, though inferior in dignity to the earlier works of the Brancacci Chapel. Benozzo evidently delighted in the beauty of the material world; his landscapes are more varied and circumstantial than any previous representations of their class, and his scenes are filled with charming and natural incidents. The painter gave so much satisfaction to the authorities during the progress of these frescoes, that they presented him in 1478 with a tomb, that his body might repose amidst the glorious achievements of his life; and the commemorating inscription led to the error that Benozzo died in that year:—*Hic tumulus est Benotii Florentini, qui proxime has pinxit historias. Hunc sibi Pisanorum donavit humanitas.* MCCCCLXXVIII.

The tomb was a personal gift to the painter in that year.†

* See the engravings in Count Lasinio's *Pitture a fresco del Campo Santo di Pisa*, large oblong folio, Florence, 1812.

† Vasari, *Vite de' Pittori, &c.*, ed. Florence, 1846, et seq.; Rumohr, *Italienische Forschungen*; Gaye, *Carteggio Inedito d' Artisti.*

No. **283.** THE VIRGIN AND CHILD, ENTHRONED. Behind the throne, above the screen forming the background, are five angels with extended wings. On the right of the Virgin are St. John the Baptist, and St. Zenobius dressed in an embroidered chasuble; on the left St. Peter and St. Dominic; in front St. Jerome and St. Francis kneeling; all the saints with their names inscribed. Two small birds, goldfinches, are represented on the step of the throne. Composition of thirteen figures, small life size.*

In tempera, on wood, 5 ft. 2½ in. *h.* by 5 ft. 7½ in. *w.*

The original contract for this picture, dated 23d Oct. 1461, is still preserved; it was published in Florence in 1855.† The figure of the Virgin is in this contract specially directed to be made similar in mode, form, and ornaments to the Virgin Enthroned, in the picture over the high altar of San Marco, Florence, by Fra Giovanni da Fiesole, and now in the Academy there. It is also directed, "that the said Benozzo shall at his own cost prepare with *gesso*, and diligently gild the said panel throughout, both as regards figures and ornaments; and that no other painter shall be allowed to take part in the execution of the said picture, neither in the Predella‡ nor in any portion of the same." Then follows the description of the picture.

The painter engages to complete the work within a year from the date of the contract.

This picture was originally the altar piece of the Compagnia di San Marco, Florence. It is mentioned by Vasari, 1550; and is noticed by Richa § in 1757, as being in the refectory of the Spedale del Melani or de' Pellegrini, in Florence. It became eventually the property of the Rinuccini family, and was purchased in Florence for the National Gallery, from the agent of the heirs of the Rinuccini estate, in 1855.

No. **591.** THE RAPE OF HELEN. A rocky landscape with an inlet of the sea; on the spectator's right is a small temple in which is seen a gilt statue of one of the Greek deities. From this temple, Helen the beautiful wife of Menelaus, king of Lacedæmon, and the ladies of her court, are being carried off to a ship, by the Trojan Paris and his companions.

The panel on which this painting is executed may not improbably have formed the cover or end of some box or *cassettone*, such as were used for wedding gifts. Composition of many small figures in the costume of the fifteenth century.

---

* On the hem of the Virgin's mantle is written, AVE REGINA CELORUM, MATER ANGELORUM. SANCTA ES QUA MUNDO LUX EST ORTA."

† *Alcuni documenti artistici non mai stampati, &c.* Florence, Le Monnier, 1855, p. 12.

‡ This portion of the altar piece, more particularly described in the contract afterwards, has disappeared.

§ *Notizie Istoriche delle Chiese Fiorentine*, &c., vol. v. p. 335.

In tempera, on an octagonal panel, 1 ft. 7½ in *h.* by 2 ft. *w.*

Formerly in the possession of the Marchese Albergotti, of Arezzo. Purchased at Florence, in 1857, from the Lombardi-Baldi collection, in the catalogue of which it was called "The Rape of the Venetian Brides."

GREUZE.

JEAN BAPTISTE GREUZE was born at Tournus, near Mâcon, in Burgundy 21st August 1725. He was at first the pupil of Grandon or Gromdon, at Lyons; he studied afterwards in the academy at Paris, and at Rome. He was elected an *agrée* or associate of the French Academy of Painting in 1755; but, as he was placed in the class of *genre* painters, when he was elected a member in 1769, he considered it a degradation, and retired altogether from the academy. He died in very poor circumstances March 21, 1805.

Greuze was a portrait and *genre* painter; he executed only one historical picture—Severus reprimanding his son Caracalla, which is now in the Louvre. His favourite subjects were illustrations of the affections or domestic duties, their observance or violation. He is unique in the French school, and is sometimes termed the Lachausée of Painting, and sometimes, but very inappropriately, the French Hogarth. Among his most celebrated pieces are—The Village Bride (*L'Accordée de Village*); The Broken Pitcher (*La Cruche Cassée*); The Little Girl with the Dog (*La Petite Fille au Chien*), and others: the two former are in the Louvre, and the last is considered by some the painter's best picture: there is a print of it by Ch. Porporati. Greuze etched a few plates.*

No. 206. THE HEAD OF A GIRL.

On wood, 1 ft. 6 in. *h.* by 1 ft. 3 in. *w.*

Bequeathed to the National Gallery, in 1846, by Mr. Richard Simmons.

---

* Gault de Saint-Germain, *Les trois Siècles de la Peinture en France*, 1808; Villot, *Notice des Tableaux exposés dans les Galeries du Louvre*, 1861; Baudicour, *Le Peintre-Graveur Français continué*, 1859.

GUARDI.

Francesco Guardi, born in Venice in 1712, was the scholar and imitator of Canaletto, but remained far behind him in the accuracy of his architectural details, and was careless and sketchy in the execution of his figures; his works are, however, rich and forcible in their colouring. He died at Venice in 1793.

No. **210.** View of the Church, Campanile, and Piazza, of San Marco, at Venice. The building of the church was commenced in the tenth and finished in the eleventh century; the campanile, which was commenced in the ninth, was not completed until the fourteenth century.

On canvas, 2 ft. 4 in. *h.* by 3 ft. 11½ in. *w.*

Bequeathed to the National Gallery, in 1846, by Mr. Richard Simmons.

GUERCI'NO.

Giova'nni Francesco Barbie'ri, *Cavaliere*, commonly called, from his squinting, Guercino, was born of very humble parents at Cento, near Bologna, Feb. 2. 1592; his father carried supplies of wood and faggots to the towns, and Guercino used to take care of his cart. He was self-taught: and after studying some time at Bologna and Venice, he repaired in the time of Paul V. to Rome; he there made the acquaintance of Michelangelo da Caravaggio,* and became a decided imitator of his style; but, in consequence of the impetuous temper of that painter, soon avoided his society. Having executed several honourable commissions at Rome, he returned to his native place after the death of his patron, Gregory XV. (Ludovisi), in 1623.

Guercino remained at Cento for a space of twenty years, when, after the death of Guido in 1642, he removed to Bologna, where he died in very affluent circumstances in 1666.† He is one of the principal masters of the class called *Tenebrosi;* but in his later works, or those which he painted after he settled in Bologna, in which he appears

---

* See the notice of Caravaggio in this Catalogue.

† Passeri, *Vite de' Pittori*, &c.; Malvasia, *Felsina Pittrice.* A Life of Guercino was published by J. A. Calvi at Bologna in 1808. *Notizia della Vita, &c., di Gio. Francesco Barbieri.*

to have endeavoured to approximate the style of Guido, he forsook the vigorous handling and treatment of his earlier pictures, and fell into an insipid manner. His masterpiece is the great picture of Santa Petronilla,* in the Capitol of Rome. It was painted for one of the chapels of St Peter's, where there is now a mosaic of it: the body of the saint is being deposited in the vault prepared for it in the Via Ardeatina outside the walls of Rome: above is a vision of the Saviour, with angels, receiving the soul of the saint.

No. 22. ANGELS WEEPING OVER THE DEAD BODY OF CHRIST. The head and shoulders are supported against a stone; the figure is slightly foreshortened: two angels kneeling complete the composition.

Engraved by J. Cheesman; by P. W. Tomkins; and by S. Freeman in Jones's *National Gallery*. On copper, 1 ft. 2½ in. *h.* by 1 ft. 5½ in. *w.*

Formerly in the Borghese Gallery at Rome. Ramdohr, in his account of that collection (1784), notices this picture as one of the productions of Guercino's best time.† It was bequeathed to the National Gallery, in 1831, by the Rev. W. H. Carr.

GUIDO.

GUIDO RENI, commonly called GUIDO, was born at Calvenzano, near Bologna Nov. 4, 1575. His father was a musician, and Guido was himself intended for the same calling; but evincing at an early age a decided taste for painting, he was placed in the school of Denis Calvart, whence he removed, about the year 1595, to that of the Carracci, and became one of their most distinguished pupils. In the beginning of the seventeenth century he, with Albani, followed Annibale Carracci to Rome, where he attracted universal notice, and he obtained great distinction there in the pontificate of Paul V. (Borghese). After a residence of about twenty years in Rome, including a short visit to Naples, Guido returned to, and settled in, Bologna. He left Rome abruptly, during the pontificate of Urban VIII., in consequence of an offensive reprimand which he received from the Cardinal Spinola. Guido had been commissioned to paint one of the altar-

* Santa Petronilla, or Perina, was the reputed daughter of St. Peter the apostle. Guercino's picture has been engraved by Frey and by Dorigny.

† *Malerei und Bildhauerarbeit in Rom*, &c.

pieces of St. Peter's, and had received 400 scudi in advance; but having allowed a few years to pass without even commencing the picture, he was rather harshly reminded by Cardinal Spinola of the money that he had received, for which he had done nothing. Guido immediately restored the 400 scudi, and in a few days left Rome: all attempts to induce him to return were vain. He from this time settled in Bologna, where he lived in great splendour, and established a celebrated school.* He died at Bologna, August 18, 1642, and was buried with great pomp in the church of San Domenico. Notwithstanding the princely income of which Guido was in receipt for many years, he died in debt: his embarrassed circumstances are attributed to his habit of gaming, and a profuse and indiscriminate liberality. It was during the latter unhappy period of his career, according to his well-informed biographer, Malvasia, that he sold his time at a stipulated sum per hour, to certain dealers, one of whom tasked the painter so rigidly, as to stand by him, with watch in hand, while he worked. Thus were produced numbers of heads and half figures which, though executed with the facility of a master, had little else to recommend them. Malvasia relates that such works were sometimes begun and finished in three hours, and even in less time. †

Guido painted in various styles; his earlier works were painted much in the forcible style of Caravaggio. This style he laid aside during his residence in Rome for one more graceful but of an *ornamental* character, of which the Aurora,‡ of the Rospigliosi Palace, is an excellent example; it is by some considered his masterpiece. Latterly he was engrossed by a species of *ideal*, of form rather than of character, of which the Niobe appears to have been a standard example with him: he was absorbed by this ideality, and at the same time he adopted a very slight mode of painting, and a cold silvery tone of colour. Of his numerous scholars, Simone Cantarini, called Il Pesarese, is

---

* Passeri mentions the following as Guido's charges when he settled in Bologna: for an entire figure, 100 scudi, about twenty guineas; for a half-length, 50 scudi; and for a simple head, 25 scudi, or five guineas. He raised them afterwards to five times the amount.

† *Felsina Pittrice*, tom. ii. p. 46.

‡ Engraved by Frey and Morghen.

the most distinguished: there is an admirable head of Guido, by this painter, in the Gallery of Bologna.

Guido painted very few portraits; his pictures are chiefly scriptural or mythological: of these there are between two and three hundred in the various collections of Europe. Many etchings are attributed to this celebrated painter.*

No. **11.** ST. JEROME kneeling before a crucifix, and beating his breast with a stone. Large half-length figure.

Engraved by B. Coriolano; by D. Cunego, for Gavin Hamilton's *Schola Italica Picturæ, &c.*; by W. Sharp; by Schiavonetti; and by J. Fussell, in Jones's *National Gallery*. On canvas, 3 ft. 10½ in. *h.* by 3 ft. *w.*

Formerly in the possession of Gavin Hamilton. Bequeathed to the National Gallery, in 1831, by the Rev. W. H. Carr.

No. **177.** THE MAGDALEN. Half-length, of the natural size.

Engraved by J. Bouillard, in the *Galerie du Palais Royal*; and by W. Sharp. This subject was often repeated by Guido, with but slight variations; and the prints after these pictures are very numerous. On canvas, 2 ft. 7 in. *h.* by 2 ft. 3 in. *w.*

Formerly in the Orleans Gallery. Purchased by Parliament for the National Gallery, at the sale of Sir Simon Clarke's pictures, in 1840.

No. **191.** THE YOUTHFUL CHRIST EMBRACING ST. JOHN. Two heads.

Engraved by J. B. Cecchi. On canvas, 2 ft. 3 in. *h.* by 1 ft. 7 in. *w.*

Formerly in the Camuccini Collection at Rome; it was bought by Mr. Irvine for Mr. Buchanan in 1805, and purchased for the National Gallery, at the sale of Mr. J. Harman's pictures, in 1844.

No. **193.** LOT AND HIS DAUGHTERS LEAVING SODOM.

"And Lot went up out of Zoar, and dwelt in the mountain, and his two daughters with him."—*Gen.* xix. 30.

Three half-length figures of the natural size.

Engraved by D. Cunego for the *Schola Italica, &c.* On canvas, 3 ft. 9½ in. *h.* by 4 ft. 10½ in. *w.*

No. **196.** SUSANNAH ASSAULTED BY THE TWO ELDERS, in the garden of her husband Joachim, at Babylon.—*Apocryphal Book of Susannah.*

Three half-length figures of the natural size.

Engraved by Corn. Visscher; and by P. Beljambe for the *Galerie du Palais Royal.* On canvas, 3 ft. 10 in. *h.* by 4 ft. 11½ in. *w.*

---

* Passeri, *Vite de' Pittori, &c.*; Malvasia, *Felsina Pittrice*; Lanzi, *Storia Pittorica, &c.*; Landon, *Vies et Œuvres des Peintres, &c.*; Bartsch, *Le Peintre-Graveur.*

These two pictures, probably painted as companions, were, until the French Revolution, in the Lancellotti Palace at Rome: they are both described by Ramdohr, in his account of the pictures of Rome in 1784.* They were brought to England by Mr. Irvine for Mr. Champernowne, passed subsequently into the possession of Mr. Penrice of Norfolk, and were finally purchased for the National Gallery; the "Lot," in 1844, and the "Susannah" in the following year. There was a duplicate of the "Susannah" in the Orleans Gallery. There are several repetitions of it.

No. **214.** THE CORONATION OF THE VIRGIN. The Virgin Mary, with a glory of stars around her head, and attended by cherubim, is borne upwards by angels; a heavenly choir surrounds her, some singing, others performing on various musical instruments. The heavens above are opened, and two cherubim descend from the midst of the divine glory, bearing the crown of the Virgin, the emblem of her glorification. The whole composition is symmetrically arranged.

On copper, 2 ft. 1¾ in. *h.* by 1 ft. 6¾ in. *w.*

This picture appears to be an early work of the master, and was painted probably before his visit to Rome. It was formerly in the Royal Collection at Madrid, and subsequently in the possession of Sir Thomas Lawrence, from whom it was purchased by the late William Wells, Esq., who bequeathed it, in 1847, to the National Gallery.

No. **271.** The "ECCE HOMO." The head of Christ crowned with thorns.

"And Pilate saith unto them, Behold the man!"—*John* xix. 5.

Engraved by William Sharp, with the inscription, "Behold and see if there be any sorrow like unto my sorrow." An oval, on wood. 1 ft. 9½ in. *h.* by 1 ft. 4 in. *w.*

Formerly in the collection of Benjamin West, P.R.A. Bequeathed to the National Gallery by Mr. Samuel Rogers, in 1855.

HOBBEMA.

The circumstances of the life of MEINDERT or MINDERHOUT HOBBEMA are almost wholly unknown; it is not even known whether he was a painter by profession or an amateur only; some accounts assume him to have been the scholar of Jacob Ruysdael, and others his master. The city of Haarlem, the town of Koeverden, and the village of Middelharins, in Holland, are each said to have been his birth-place; and he is reported to have lived some time in

* *Malerei und Bildhauerarbeit in Rom, &c.*, iii. 74.

Amsterdam.* The earliest date on his works in 1650; the year 1663 is inscribed on two of his finest pictures, one in the possession of Lord Hatherton, and the other in the collection of Mr. Holford, in Hyde Park. The latest acknowledged date is 1669, but a fine work by the master in the collection of Sir Robert Peel is said to be inscribed with the year 1689.†

The landscapes of Hobbema consist generally of simple wooded scenes, often sunny, with an occasional pool of water or a mill; the figures in them are inserted sometimes by himself and sometimes by Berchem, A. Vandevelde, or Lingelbach, and others. The majority of his works are in this country; they were little known or little appreciated in Holland till about a century after his death; they are now more generally valued, perhaps, than the works of any other landscape painter, and realize very large prices at auctions.

No. **685.** LANDSCAPE, SHOWERY WEATHER. Rain and sunshine are both represented, and everything seems wet; but the chief feature of the picture is a cluster of large trees in the centre, slightly moved by the wind; on the one side is a shaded pool, with a man angling on the bank; on the other is a road-side cottage with a woman looking out at a doorway; on the road in front of it are a few figures. Signed—

On wood, 1 ft. 11¾ in. *h.* by 2 ft. 9⅛ in. *w.*

Formerly in the collection of Count Perregaux; imported into England by Mr. Farrer; purchased from Mr. G. H. Phillips in 1862.

---

* See Van Eynden en Vander Willigen, *Geschiedenis der Vaderlandsche Schilderkunst*, &c., 4 vols., 8vo., 1816-1842. These writers give, in their supplement or fourth volume, p. 101, a statement that Meindert Hobbema was the son of a Serjeant Willem Hobbema, of the company of Captain Solema, in garrison at Koeverden, and that he was baptized at Koeverden on the 6th of August 1654, when he was grown up therefore. They also notice a drawing attributed to him, bearing the date 1647.

† See Smith, *Catalogue Raisonnée, &c.* Of the 142 pictures attributed to Hobbema in this work, 16 only are dated, and of these five had the same year —1663.

HONDECOETER.

Melchior de Hondecoeter, one of the most distinguished of the Dutch painters of birds and animals, foreign and domestic, was born at Utrecht in 1636. He was first instructed by his father, Gysbert de Hondecoeter, and after his death in 1653, by his uncle, J. B. Weenix. Melchior died at Utrecht, April 3, 1695.*

No. **202.** Domestic Poultry; a beautiful brood of young chickens in the fore-ground. The cock was Hondecoeter's favourite bird, which he is said to have taught to stand to him in a fixed position as a model.

On canvas, 2 ft. 10 in. *h.* by 3 ft. 8 in. *w.*
Bequeathed to the National Gallery by Richard Simmons, Esq., in 1846.

HUCHTENBURG.

Johan van Huchtenburg, or Hugtenburg, a distinguished Dutch battle-painter, was born at Haarlem in 1646. He went to Rome in 1667, to join his brother Jacob, a landscape-painter, upon whose death, in 1669, he removed to Paris, and there studied a short time under Vander Meulen. He returned to Holland in 1670, and died at Amsterdam in 1733, but he resided chiefly at the Hague.

Huchtenburg was commissioned, in 1708, or the following year, by Prince Eugene, to paint pictures of the recent victories which that prince, the Prince of Orange, and the Duke of Marlborough had obtained over the French. There are etchings of these battles by Huchtenburg himself: † there are also many other etchings by the hand of this painter, some after Vander Meulen.‡

No. **211.** A Battle; in the fore-ground a cavalry fight, with a town burning in the distance.

On wood, 1 ft. 4¾ in. *h.* by 1 ft. 11 in. *w.*
Brought to England by Mr. Bryan in 1801. Bequeathed to the National Gallery by Mr. Richard Simmons, in 1846.

---

* Houbraken, *Groote Schouburg der Kunstschilders*, &c.; Immerzeel, *Levens en Werken*, &c.

† In the *Beschrijving der Veldslagen van Prins Eugenius van Savoije, den Prins van Oranje, en den Hertog van Marlborough.* 's Hage, 1727.

‡ Van Gool, *Nieuwe Schouburg der Kunstschilders*, &c.; Bartsch, *Peintre-Graveur.*

DE KEYSER.

THEODORE DE KEYSER, son of the sculptor and architect Hendrick de Keyser, was born about 1595, probably at Amsterdam. He is distinguished as a portrait-painter, both in large and small, but especially in his full-length portraits of a small size: his execution is very exact and elaborate. There are several capital pictures by De Keyser in the museums of Amsterdam and the Hague. He died at Amsterdam about the year 1660.*

No. **212.** A MERCHANT WITH HIS CLERK; a portrait. The "merchant," dressed in riding costume, is seated at a table in a private apartment which bespeaks affluence in the owner: the back-ground is a costly piece of tapestry. On the table are a plan, books, a guitar, and other objects.

The "clerk" is standing with his hat in his hand behind the chair of the seated figure, to whom he is respectfully handing a packet. Small, full-length figures.

On wood, 3 ft. ½ in. *h.* by 2 ft. 3¼ in. *w.* Signed, on the mantel-piece, with the painter's monogram composed of T. D. K., and dated 1627.

 AN. 1627.

Bequeathed to the National Gallery by Mr. Richard Simmons, in 1846.

LANCRET.

NICOLAS LANCRET was born at Paris 22d Jan. 1690. He was the pupil of Pierre d'Ulin, but he adopted Watteau as his model. He soon distinguished himself in this style, and became the rival of his model: he was elected a member of the French Academy of Painting in 1719, as a painter of *Fêtes Galantes.* He died at Paris 14th Sept. 1743.

The pictures of Lancret have not the facility of those of Watteau, but they are more finished.†

Nos. **101-4.** THE FOUR AGES OF MAN.

* Van Eynden en Vander Willigen, *Geschiedenis der Vaderlandsche Schilderkunst, &c.*, 1842.

† D'Argenville, *Abrégé de la Vie des plus Fameux Peintres*, &c.; Villot, *Notice des Tableaux, &c., du Louvre*, 1861.

No. **101.** INFANCY. Groups of gaily-dressed children, at play, under a stately arcade or portico.

No. **102.** YOUTH. An assemblage of young people of both sexes, who appear to be contemplating the adornment of the person: a group of seven figures in a garden pavilion.

No. **103.** MANHOOD. A party of pleasure, some reclining upon the green-sward: two archers are shooting at the popinjay. A composition of ten figures: the arrangement of the grouping indicates the age of courtship.

No. **104.** AGE. An old woman spinning, with another asleep in a chair by her side: of the male portion of the group, one old man is caressing a dog, another is making advances to a young girl. Composition of six figures.

Engraved by Desplaces; and by L'Armessin, fils. On canvas 1 ft. 1 in. *h.* by 1 ft. 5½ in. *w.* each picture.

They are mentioned by D'Argenville among the principal works of Lancret. Bequeathed to the National Gallery, in 1837, by Lieut. Col. Ollney.

DAI LIBRI.

GIROLAMO DAI LIBRI was born at Verona in 1472. His only known surname of Dai Libri he inherited from the occupation of his father, who was an illuminator of manuscripts, and known as Francesco Dai Libri. In the church of San Giorgio Maggiore, at Verona, is a picture by Girolamo, painted in 1526, signed HIERONYMUS A LIBRIS. Girolamo was one of the most distinguished masters of his time at Verona, both as a painter of altar-pieces and as a miniature painter and illuminator of books for church service. But though he lived long in the sixteenth century he always painted more in the taste of the fifteenth. He died at Verona July 2d, 1555. Several of his principal works are still preserved at Verona. He left a son, Francesco dai Libri the younger, who was also a distinguished illuminator. Girolamo was the instructor of Giulio Clovio in miniature painting.*

No. **285.** MADONNA AND CHILD, the Virgin seated with the child in her arms, and holding an apple in her hand. Behind is a red curtain on a rod, extending half

* Vasari, *Vite, &c.*, Ed. Le Monnier, Florence, 1846 *et seq.* vol. ix. p. 210.

across the picture: a town upon a rock in the distance. Figures half the scale of life.

On wood, 2 ft. *h.* by 1 ft. 5 in. *w.*

Purchased from Baron Galvagna in Venice in 1855. This picture, while in the Galvagna Collection, was attributed to Pellegrino da San Daniele. A comparison, however, of this specimen with the works of Girolamo dai Libri has led to the conclusion that it may be more fitly ascribed to that master.

THE MEISTER VON LIESBORN.

The Meister von Liesborn (Master of Liesborn) is the designation given by the Germans to an unknown painter of Westphalia who executed some considerable works, about the year 1465, for the Benedictine Abbey of Liesborn, near Münster: he is the chief or *caposcuola* of the Westphalian school of German painting, and one of the principal German artists of the fifteenth century. The school is evidently allied to that of the Van Eycks, and to the school of Cologne.

The principal work of this master was the Crucifixion, formerly the high altar-piece of the second convent church of Liesborn; it was sold and cut in pieces in 1807, when the convent was suspended, and Napoleon established the modern kingdom of Westphalia. Some of the pieces were afterwards lost, others were obtained by different collectors, and some portions which were acquired by Herr Krüger of Minden have now found a place in this gallery.

This altar-piece was a picture in several compartments, of which the centre represented Christ on the cross, and four angels receiving the blood from the hands, side, and feet in golden vessels; by the side of the cross, on a field of flowers, were standing St. John, St. Scholastica, St. Benedict, St. Cosmas, St. Damianus, and the Virgin Mary. On either side were represented, in four compartments,—the Annunciation, the Nativity, the Adoration of the Kings, and the Presentation in the Temple; the Resurrection, the Ascension, the Descent of the Holy Ghost, and the Last Judgment. Of these compartments there are in the Gallery now only the upper portions of the six saints. These pictures are painted on canvas primed with chalk, and stretched on wood, and are executed partly in tempera and partly in oil colours.*

No. **260.** THREE SAINTS.—St. John the Evangelist, St. Scholastica, and St. Benedict. Busts, small-life size, gold ground.

No. **261.** THREE SAINTS.—St. Cosmas and St. Damianus, martyrs, and the Virgin Mary; the martyrs holding vessels of ointment. Busts, small-life size, gold ground.

Companion pieces, in tempera and in oil, on canvas stretched on wood, 1 ft. 10 in. *h.* by 2 ft. 4 in. *w.*

These two pictures are corresponding portions of the centre compartment of the high altar-piece of the Liesborn convent, consecrated in 1465; representing the upper portions of the saints standing on either side of the cross. Purchased by Government, with the other pictures by the same master, of Herr Krüger, of Minden, in 1854.

FRA FILIPPO LIPPI.

FILIPPO LIPPI, or FRA FILIPPO, as he is called, to distinguish him more clearly from his son Filippino Lippi, died in 1469, about the age of fifty-seven. The date of his death is proved by documents,† that of his birth is uncertain. His life is a romance. Born in Florence, probably in 1412, he lost his parents in childhood, and being left in indigence, was placed by an aunt in the Carmelite convent, where, at the age of eight, he began his noviciate as a brother of the order. His aptitude for drawing soon manifesting itself, the prior afforded him the means of following what seemed to be his favourite occupation, and at an early age he painted some figures in fresco in the precincts of the church and convent. Of those first productions nothing now remains; they were finally destroyed by fire with the building in 1771.‡

---

* Passavant, *Kunstreise durch England und Belgien*, 8vo., Frankfurt, 1833; *Kunstblatt*, No. 90, 1843, No. 6, 1847; the latter number containing a comprehensive notice of the Westphalian school by Dr. E. Förster. See also *Verzeichniss der Gemaelde-Sammlung des Geheimen Regierungs-Rathes Krüger zu Minden*, 8vo., ph., Minden, 1848.

† Vasari, *Vite, &c.*, Ed. Le Monnier, 1846, *et seq.* vol. iv., p. 128, note.

‡ Vasari may be quite correct in affirming that Filippo Lippi derived his first inspirations from Masaccio. The biographer states that the former painted in *terra verde*, in the cloisters of the convent, "The Confirmation of the Rules of the Carmelites," next to the "Consecration of the Church," by Masaccio. As the portrait of Lorenzo Ridolfi was introduced into the last-named painting "at the time when Lorenzo was ambassador to Venice," that is, in 1425, the picture must have been painted in that year. The "Confirmation of the Rules" above-mentioned was probably one of Filippo's earliest works.

Fra Filippo left the convent about 1430, and during an excursion at sea near Ancona, he and his companions were taken by some Moorish pirates and carried as slaves to Barbary. After eighteen months captivity in fetters, Fra Filippo found opportunity to draw a whole length portrait of his master, with charcoal, on a white wall. This display of a skill so unknown in those regions excited general wonder and procured the painter's release from chains; and upon his subsequently executing some coloured works for his Moorish patron he was set at liberty. Whether he visited Naples immediately on his return to Italy, or afterwards, is uncertain. He left a picture in Naples, and in 1438 was occupied on one of his best works for the sacristy of Santo Spirito, in Florence.

In Prato, before undertaking the celebrated frescoes of the choir of the cathedral, he painted various pictures. While occupied on an altar-piece, representing the nativity, for the nuns of Santa Margherita, he became enamoured of Lucrezia Buti, then residing in the convent, either intended for a nun or as a ward of the nuns. He requested to be allowed to introduce her portrait in the picture, as the Madonna.* Eventually he carried her off from the convent in 1458, and by this desperate act exposed himself to endless troubles. His frescoes in Prato were begun in 1456, and after many interruptions were completed about 1464. His latest works were the frescoes in the choir of the cathedral at Spoleto. He died there, as was supposed by poison, October the 8th, 1469. The unfinished frescoes in Spoleto were completed by his scholar and assistant Fra Diamante, in 1470.†

No. **248.** THE VISION OF ST. BERNARD. The Saint, dressed in white, is represented writing his homilies at a desk placed on a table formed of the solid rock. On the

---

* The picture, in an injured state, is now in the Louvre. Vasari states that Fra Filippo threw aside the habit of a monk at the age of seventeen; but the painter, in two of his letters, the latest of which is dated 1457, signs himself "Frate." In the altar-piece of Sant' Ambrogio, now in the Gallery *delle Belle Arti* in Florence, his portrait has the friar's tonsure; and in the record of his death, preserved in the annals of the Carmelite Convent in Florence, he is named "Fr. Philippus."

† *Delle Pitture di Fra Filippo Lippi nel coro della Cattedrale di Prato*, by the Canonico Baldanzi, Prato, 1836; *Della chiesa Cattedrale di Prato, Descrizione corredata di notizie Storiche, &c., Prato* 1846; Vasari, *Vite, &c.*; Baldinucci, *Notizie, &c.*; and Gaye, *Carteggio Inedito d'Artisti.*

desk is some paper and a leathern ink bottle; by his side are some books. The Virgin, surrounded by angels, appears before him.*

In tempera, on a hexagonal panel, the upper corners of a square being cut away, 3 ft. 2 in. *h.* by 3 ft. 5½ in. *w.*

Vasari states that Fra Filippo painted two pictures to be placed over doors in the *Palazzo della Signoria* at Florence. The subject of one was the Annunciation; of the other a St. Bernard. The date of the latter picture is fixed by a record quoted by Baldinucci from the register of the *Provveditori di Camera,* whence it appears that on the 16th of May, 1447, Fra Filippo received 40 *lire,* "for having painted the figure of the Virgin and of St. Bernard, to be placed before [above] the door of the cancelleria of the *Palazzo de' Signori.*"† Purchased at M. De Bammeville's sale in 1854. In the catalogue of that sale this picture was attributed to Masaccio.

No. **586.** THE MADONNA AND CHILD ENTHRONED, SURROUNDED BY ANGELS AND SAINTS. The Virgin is seated, with the infant Christ standing on her knee. Two angels are at the foot of the throne playing on musical instruments, one on the lute, the other on the violin. On each side, in separate compartments, are standing two saints, a monk and a bishop on the left, St. Bartholomew and a nun on the right.‡ Figures nearly life size.

In tempera, on wood, the centre picture 5 ft. 4 in. *h.* by 2 ft. 4 in. *w.*; the two side pictures 4 ft. 8 in. *h.* by 1 ft. 10½ in. *w.*

---

* "St. Bernard was remarkable for his devotion to the Blessed Virgin: one of his most celebrated works, the *Missus est,* was composed in her honour as Mother of the Redeemer; and in eighty sermons or texts from the Song of Solomon, he set forth her divine perfection. . . . Accordingly, the Blessed Virgin regarded her votary with peculiar favour. His health was extremely feeble; and once, when he was employed in writing his homilies, and was so ill that he could scarcely hold the pen, she graciously appeared to him, and comforted and restored him by her divine presence."—Mrs. Jameson, *Legends of the Monastic Orders,* p. 152.

† Baldinucci, vol. v., p. 353. As the painter received 1200 *lire* for the altar-piece of Sant Ambrogio before mentioned, it may be inferred that 40 *lire* was the price of one and not of both the works noticed by Vasari. The picture in question is about the width of a door, and the peculiar form of its upper portion is explained by its adaptation to the architecture. Fra Filippo appears to have frequently painted subjects relating to St. Bernard. The picture of the Death of the Saint is still preserved in the Cathedral at Prato. In the church *Delle Murate* at Florence, now suppressed, he painted incidents from the lives of St. Benedict and St. Bernard. At Arezzo he painted the altarpiece for the Chapel of St. Bernard; the same Saint is introduced in one of the specimens in the Berlin Gallery, and to these instances is to be added the picture above described.

‡ It is difficult to come to a decision respecting the three saints here not named; they may be St. Dominic, St. Zenobius, and St. Scholastica, or as the picture was originally painted for an Augustine convent, St. Nicholas of Tolentino, St. Augustine, and St. Monica. St. Bartholomew is introduced apparently on account of the name of the donor, Gherardo di Bartolommeo Barbadori.

This is supposed to be the picture painted in or before 1438, when Fra Filippo was 25 years old, for Gherardo di Bartolommeo Barbadori, to be placed in the church of Santo Spirito, at Florence. Formerly in the convent of Santo Spirito, where it was placed, when removed from the sacristy, in the latter part of the last century. It was subsequently in the possession of the Primicerio Crociani, of Montepulciano, from whom it was obtained by the late proprietors. Purchased in Florence from the Lombardi-Baldi collection in 1857.*

No. **589.** THE VIRGIN MARY SEATED, AN ANGEL PRESENTING THE INFANT CHRIST TO HER. Under an arch is seen a distant view of a lake. Three figures small life size.

In tempera, on wood, 2 ft. 4 in. *h.* by 1 ft. 7½ in. *w.*

Formerly in the possession of Sig. Zambrini of Imola. Purchased at Florence from the Lombardi-Baldi collection in 1857.

No. **666.** THE ANNUNCIATION. The Virgin Mary is seated in a richly furnished chamber, and in a garden opposite to her, on the spectator's left, is the angel Gabriel, announcing the birth of Christ.

"The Holy Ghost shall come upon thee, and the power of the Highest shall overshadow thee, therefore also that holy thing which shall be born of thee shall be called the Son of God."—*Luke*, i. 35.

In the centre of the picture a dove, proceeding in a ray of glories from a hand above, is approaching Mary. Small entire figures.

On wood, in tempera, a lunette, 2 ft. 2 in. *h.* by 4 ft. 11½ in. *w.*

This and the following picture, No. 667, were painted for Cosmo de' Medici. This is marked with the *crest* of Cosmo, three feathers tied together in a ring. The pictures were both procured from the Riccardi (Medici) Palace at Florence by the brothers Metzger, about 15 years ago.†

Presented to the National Gallery by Sir Charles Lock Eastlake, P.R.A., in 1861.

No. **667.** ST. JOHN THE BAPTIST WITH SIX OTHER SAINTS; on his right are Saints Francis, Lawrence, and Cosmas; on his left, Saints Damianus, Anthony, and Peter Martire: all seated on a marble bench in a garden. Small entire figures.

---

* Vasari, *Vite, &c.*, Ed. Le Monnier, vol. iv. p. 119, note 4. The annotators of Vasari here quoted, in affirming the identity of this work with the Barbadori altar-piece, deny the similar pretensions of a characteristic specimen of Fra Filippo now in the gallery of the Louvre. Notwithstanding the high authority of the critics referred to, it may reasonably be questioned not only whether the picture above described is the identical work referred to, but even whether it is to any great extent by the hand of the master. The probability is that the Madonna and Child are partly by Fra Filippo, and that the angels below, as well as the side figures, are by Alessio Baldovinetti.

† Vasari, *Vite, &c.*, Ed. Le Monnier, vol. iv., p. 118.

On wood, in tempera, a lunette, 2 ft. 2 in *h.* by 4 ft. 11½ in *w.* Companion picture to No. 666, described above. Purchased from Mr. Alexander Barker, in 1861.

FILIPPINO LIPPI.

FILIPPO, commonly called FILIPPINO LIPPI, the son of Fra Filippo and Lucrezia Buti, was born at Florence in 1460. In consequence of the death of his father when Filippino was still a child, he became the scholar of Sandro Botticelli. He soon acquired celebrity, and was employed about 1485 to complete the frescoes of the Brancacci Chapel in the Church del Carmine in Florence, which had been left unfinished by Masolino da Panicale and Masaccio.* His works in this chapel exhibit great dramatic power in composition, and prove Filippino to have been one of the best masters of his time. His pictures are also distinguished for their rich architecture, their costume, and their ornamental accessories. He subsequently painted some frescoes in the Strozzi Chapel, in the Church of Santa Maria Novella at Florence.

In 1492 Filippino visited Rome, and executed some frescoes there for the Cardinal Caraffa, in the Church of Santa Maria Sopra Minerva. He also left some works at Prato. Filippino died, and was buried at Florence on the 13th of April 1505, aged only forty-five. He signed his name Philippinus Florentinus, Philippinus de Lippis, and also Filippus de Lipis.†

No. **293.** THE VIRGIN AND CHILD; ST. JEROME AND ST. DOMINIC ADORING THE INFANT CHRIST. The Virgin is seated in a landscape, with the infant at her breast; the two saints are kneeling one on each side of the Virgin, St. Jerome on her right, St. Dominic on her left. Below, in a predella, are represented the dead Christ, supported by Joseph of Arimathea, with half figures of St. Francis and the Magdalen in separate compartments on each side The

* The works of Filippino in the Brancacci Chapel are :—"The Restoring a Youth to Life," part of which was painted by Masaccio ; the "Crucifixion of St. Peter," "St. Peter and St. Paul before Nero or the Proconsul," "St. Peter liberated from Prison ;" and according to some "St. Paul visiting St. Peter in Prison," in which is the figure of St. Paul that was adopted by Raphael in his cartoon of "Paul preaching at Athens."—See Kugler, *Handbook of Painting*, Italian Schools ; Rumohr, *Italienische Forschungen* ; Gaye, *Carteggio Inedito d' Artisti*; and Vasari, *Vite, &c.*, Ed. Le Monnier, note, vol. iii. p. 190.

† Vasari, *Vite, &c.*, Ed. Le Monnier, vol. v., p. 242.

arms of the Rucellai family are painted at the extreme ends.

In tempera, on wood, 6 ft. 9 in. *h.* by 6 ft. 1 in. *w.* The predella 8 in. *h.* by 7 ft. 9 in. *w.*

We learn from Vasari that this picture was originally painted for the Rucellai Chapel in the church of San Pancrazio at Florence;* after the suppression of this church it was removed to the Palazzo Rucellai, where it remained until it was purchased of the Cavaliere Giuseppe Rucellai, in 1857, for the National Gallery.

No. **592.** THE ADORATION OF THE MAGI; OR, THE WISE MEN'S OFFERING.—*Matthew* ii. 1, 11. The holy family is in front of a ruined building on the spectator's right, and the magi are prostrating themselves before the divine Infant; on the left is an immense retinue of followers, reaching to the extreme limits of the picture on that side. A rocky back-ground. Small figures.

In tempera, on wood, 1 ft. 8 in. *h.* by 4 ft. 7 in. *w.*

Formerly in the possession of the Marchese Ippolito Orlandini of Florence. Purchased at Florence from the Lombardi-Baldi collection in 1857.

No. **598.** ST. FRANCIS IN GLORY, with the *stigmata;* standing, holding in his arms and contemplating a small crucifix; above on each side five angels playing musical instruments. Inscribed below—HUNC SEQUANTUR, HUIC JUNGANTUR, QUI EX EGYPTO EXEUNT, IN QUO NOBIS CLARA LUCE VEXILLA REGIS PRODEUNT, and dated A.D. MCCCCXCII.† Gold back-ground.

In tempera, on wood, 19½ in. *h.* by 12½ in. *w.*

Formerly in the collection of the Marchese Giovanni Costabili, at Ferrara, from which it was purchased for the National Gallery in 1858.

LOMBARD.

LAMBERT or LAMPRECHT LOMBARD, commonly called Lambert Lombardus, was born at Liége, of humble parents,

* *Vite dei Pittori, &c.,* Ed. Le Monnier, vol. v., p. 245.

† "Let those who depart out of Egypt follow him, and be united to him, in whom the standards of the king come forth, for us, in clear light." This is, with a slight variation, one of the eight strophes of a hymn to St. Francis, which will be found in a "Breviarium secundum ritum Romanum Venetiis impressum arte et impensis Andree de Torresanis de Asula MCCCCXCV.," &c.

Hunc sequantur,
Huic jungantur,
Qui ex Ægypto exeunt,
In quo duce
Clara luce
Vexilla Regis prodeunt.

in 1506, and was the scholar of Jan de Mabuse and Arnold Beer. He married when very young, and travelled in Germany and France, and visited Italy in the suite of the English cardinal Pole, when he became acquainted with Vasari, who speaks highly of his general attainments, calling him, among other things, "an excellent architect."

In Italy, though Lambert resided there for a very short time, he entirely acquired the Italian style of design. At the death of his patron, Cardinal Erhard de la Marck, Bishop of Liége, in 1538, he was compelled to return home, —where his example, however, says Van Mander, greatly advanced the school of his native place. Hubert Golzius and Frans Floris were both scholars of Lambert Lombard. He died poor, at Liége, in 1560: he was three times married and had children by each wife, which imposed burdens upon him that the art-patronage of Liége did not enable him to support. He is reported to have died in the Hospital of Mont Cornillon.

The pictures of this master are scarce; they are generally remarkable for the correctness of their drawing, and they are executed in a manner somewhat peculiar to himself: the drawing is in the first instance elaborately and delicately defined, and the colours and shadows are only very slightly scumbled over the light ground. In 1565 a life of Lambert Lombard was published by Dominicus Lampsonius, one of his scholars.* Lambert's drawings are numerous, in chalk and with the pen; he also etched some plates; he was the best antiquary of his time and district.

No. **266.** The Deposition from the Cross. St. John and the Virgin are supporting the dead body of Christ; above is the Holy Spirit in the form of the dove. Three figures half length, life size.

On wood, in oil, 3 ft. 6 in. *h.* by 2 ft. 3 in *w.* Purchased with the collection of Herr Krüger of Minden, in 1854.

---

* Lamberti Lombardi apud Eburones Pictoris celeberrimi Vita, 8vo., Brugen Hubert Golzius, 1565. Rathgeber, *Annalen der Niederländischen Malerei, &c.* folio, Gotha, 1843. Van Mander, *Het Schilder Boek.* Michiels, *Histoire de la Peinture Flamande et Hollandaise*, vol. iii., 8vo., Brussels, 1846. Though we have so early a life of Lombard by one of his own scholars, there are few facts supported by documents; the dates both of his birth and death are found only on engraved portraits of him. The works of Rathgeber and Michiels contain lists of his pictures.

MAAS.

NICOLAS MAAS or MAES,* a distinguished Dutch portrait and *genre* painter, was born at Dort, in 1632. He was the pupil of Rembrandt. In 1678 he settled at Amsterdam, where he died in 1693. He etched a few plates.†

No. **153.** THE CRADLE. A little girl is rocking a child to sleep in a cradle. An open book and a jug are standing upon a table, covered with a rich Turkey mat. Signed with the monogram of the painter.

On wood, 15½ in. *h.* by 12½ in. *w.*

No. **159.** THE DUTCH HOUSEWIFE. A girl scraping parsnips, with a child by her side watching her. On the other side is the Flemish kruik or beer-jug, so often introduced into the pictures of this master. Signed, and dated 1655.

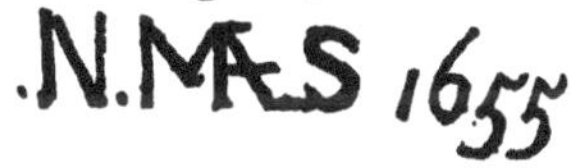

On wood, 13½ in. *h.* by 11½ in. *w.*

Both pictures were bequeathed to the National Gallery, in 1838, by Lord Farnborough.

No. **207.** THE IDLE SERVANT. A kitchen-maid has fallen asleep over her work; before her on the floor are strewed various kitchen utensils; and on a cupboard behind her a cat is in the act of stealing a duckling ready trussed for cooking. Another servant standing by her side, with a beer-jug in her hand, is laughing at the disorder around. In an inner apartment in the back-ground, the family is seen at dinner. Signed, and dated 1655.

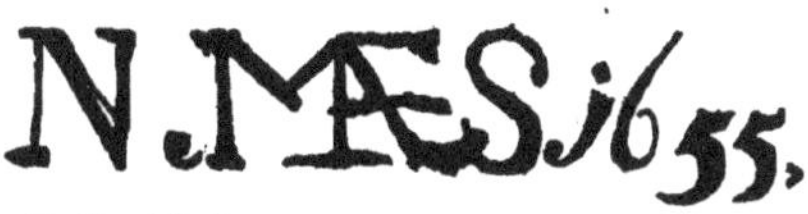

On wood, 2 ft. 3½ in. *h.* by 1 ft. 9½ in. *w.*

Bequeathed to the National Gallery, in 1846, by Mr. Richard Simmons.

MABUSE.

JAN GOSSAERT, commonly called JAN DE MABUSE, from his birthplace, now Maubeuge, and within the French frontier, was born about 1470: he sometimes signed him-

---

* Both pronounced broad, like the a in *Mars*; the former is now the common Dutch form, though the painter signed his name Maes.

† Houbraken, *Groote Schouburg*, &c.; Bartsch, *Le Peintre-Graveur.*

self JOANNES MALBODIUS. Mabuse visited Italy, and he resided some time in this country, when he was employed by Henry VII. At Castle Howard, the seat of the Earl of Carlisle, is one of the master-pieces of Mabuse, representing the "Adoration of the Kings:" it is one of the most elaborate and admirable works of the Flemish school. He died at Antwerp Oct. 1, 1532.*

No. **656.** PORTRAIT OF A MAN DRESSED IN BLACK, with fur over his shoulders. He has a rosary in his hand and appears to be standing in a church. Architectural background. Half-length, small life size.

On wood, 2 ft. 3 in. *h.* by 1 ft. 7 in. *w.*
Purchased at Paris, from M. Edmond Beaucousin, in 1860.

MANTEGNA.

ANDRÉA MANTEGNA, *Cavaliere,* was born of an obscure family, in the neighbourhood of Padua, in 1431; the exact locality is not known; his father's Christian name was Biagio or Blaise.† The youth of Mantegna is said to have resembled that of Giotto; according to Vasari he was a shepherd boy; and having early displayed great aptitude for drawing, he was placed with the celebrated Squarcione of Padua, who was so struck with his ability that he adopted him, and entered his name, in 1441, in the register of painters as follows: *Andrea fiuolo de M. Francesco Squarzon depentore.* It was Squarcione's intention to make him his heir; but Mantegna is said to have forfeited the friendship of his patron, by marrying Nicolosia, the daughter of Jacopo Bellini, Squarcione's rival. This story is doubtful: his wife appears to have been of the Mantua family of the Nuvolosi.‡

In 1468, Mantegna entered the service of Lodovico Gonzaga, Marquis of Mantua, with an allowance of 75 *lire* per month, about 30*l.* a year, at that time a considerable salary. At a later period the Marquis presented him with

---

* Van Mander, *Het Leven der schilders,* &c.

† The date of Mantegna's birth is ascertained from the following inscription on a picture now lost, formerly in the church of Santa Sofia in Padua:—*Andreas Mantinea Patavinus ann. septem et decem natus sua manu pinxit* MCCCCXLVIII. It is preserved in Scardeone's *Antiquities of Padua.* Moschini, *Della Origine, &c. Della Pittura in Padova,* p. 35, Padua, 1826.

‡ Coddè, *Pittori Mantovani,* &c., Mantua, 1837.

a small piece of land near the church of San Sebastiano, upon which, in 1476, Mantegna built himself a house. This house is said by Ridolfi to have been decorated with frescoes by Mantegna himself; but these and other of the painter's more important works in the Castle of Mantua greatly suffered in the pillage of the city by the Imperial troops in 1630, during the war of the disputed succession to the dukedom. The collections of the earlier Gonzagas were dispersed on this occasion; many works were carried to Prague, and many passed into the possession of Christina, Queen of Sweden; the latter eventually formed part of the Orleans collection. It was this dispersion of the art treasures of Mantua that enabled Charles I. of England to become the possessor of the celebrated series at Hampton Court, the nine tempera pictures on cloth of the "Triumph of Julius Cæsar," completed in 1492, for the palace of San Sebastiano at Mantua. Vasari notices this "Triumph" as Mantegna's best work.*

Mantegna was invited by Innocent VIII. to Rome, and in 1488-90† he executed some frescoes there in the chapel of that Pope on the Belvedere of the Vatican; this chapel was afterwards destroyed by Pius VI. to enable him to carry out certain alterations. Mantegna's works of every kind are now scarce, but he is fairly represented in this country. The Marquis Selvatico has enumerated, independently of frescoes, only thirty-three certain pictures by this painter, including the Hampton Court "Triumph." Several of them are in tempera and on cloth.

Mantegna died at Mantua September 13, 1506,‡ and was buried in his own chapel of St. John the Baptist, in the church of Sant' Andrea. He was painter, engraver, sculptor, poet, and architect. His engravings, among the earliest Italian examples of the art, resemble those of Marcantonio. Nearly sixty prints altogether are attributed

* "La miglior cosa che lavorasse mai." *Vite*, vol. v. p. 170. Ed. Le Monnier, Florence, 1846, *et seq.* It was engraved in wood by Andrea Andreani in 1599; in copper by R. Van Audenaert in 1692; and again by S. Clarke in 1712.

† Mantegna visited Rome in the summer of 1488. A letter from Francesco Gonzaga, introducing him to the Pope, is dated June the 10th of that year. See Gaye, *Carteggio Inedito*, &c. III. p. 561. He returned to Mantua, September the 6th, 1490. Moschini, *Della Origine*, *&c.* p. 43.

‡ Mantegna's death was announced to the Marquis Francesco Gonzaga by his son Francesco on the 15th of that month as having taken place on the preceding Sunday, this was the 13th. The letter was published by Zani, *Materiali per servire alla Storia dell' Incisione*, &c., Parma, 1802.

to him, but not half that number with certainty. The works of this great master are imbued with the highest grandeur of feeling; his manner is hard and severe, but his drawing is correct, his modelling fine, and his execution of the utmost vigour and finish. His colouring, in his best specimens, is also powerful and harmonious. His draperies are particularly well elaborated. Like his master Squarcione he was a diligent student of the antique; and in his accessories he displays unusual care and power.

He left by his wife Nicolosia two sons and a daughter. He was aided in some of his works by his second son Francesco, by a favorite scholar known as Carlo del Mantegna,* and by Giovanni Francesco Carotto.†

No. **274.** THE VIRGIN AND CHILD ENTHRONED; ST. JOHN THE BAPTIST AND THE MAGDALEN. The Virgin is seated, with the Child standing on her knee, on a low throne surmounted by a canopy. On the right of the Virgin is St. John the Baptist, on her left the Magdalen, both standing. The back-ground consists chiefly of orange and citron trees. On a scroll attached to the cross held by St. John is written *Ecce agnus Dei, ecce qui tollit peccata mundi;*‡ and on the inner side of the scroll above is the painter's signature—*Andreas Mantinia C P.F.* (Civis Patavinus fecit).

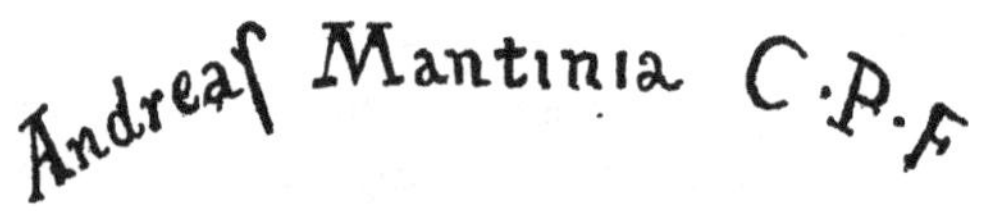

Engraved in Aliprandi's *Private Gallerie Milanesi.*§ In tempera, on canvas, 4 ft. 6½ in. *h.* by 8 ft. 9½ in. *w.*

This picture is described and extolled by various Italian writers on art, including the authors of several guide-books of Milan.‖

---

* See the *Commentary* of the Marquis Selvatico in the edition of Vasari's *Lives* published by Le Monnier, Florence, 1846 *et seq.*, vol. v.

† Vasari, Vita di Fra Giocondo, &c.

‡ "Behold the Lamb of God, which taketh away the sin of the world."—John i. 29.

§ *Raccolta delle Migliori Dipinture che si conservano nelle private Gallerie Milanesi.* Milan, 1813.

‖ *Le Vite, &c.,* di Giorgio Vasari. Firenze, le Monnier, vol. v. 1849, p. 188. The passage referred to is in the commentary, by Selvatico, on the life of Mantegna, with a list of his works.

Storia della Pittura Italiana, &c., da Giovanni Rosini. Pisa, vol. 3, 1841, p. 262.

Milano Nuovamente Descritta del Pittore Franceseo Pirovano. Milano, 1822, p. 256.

Il Forestiere in Milano, de Bartolommeo Borroni. 1808, vol. 1, p. 49.

Nuova Guida di Milano. Milano, 1796, 2da edizione, p. 119.

It is stated by Borroni to have formed part of the collection of the Cardinal Cesare Monti, who was Archbishop of Milan from 1632 to 1650. The principal part of that collection was bequeathed by him to his successors in office, and a considerable portion is now deposited in the Brera Gallery; but the picture in question remained with the Monti family, having been placed by the same prelate—as early, according to tradition, as 1610—in the private chapel of the Palazzo Monti. After the extinction of the Monti family, in the last century, the mansion, and the Mantegna with it, became the property of the Andreani family, when the picture was removed from the chapel to one of the apartments. The families of Mellerio and Somaglia succeeded as proprietors. From the representative of the last-named house the picture, having been first bought by Signor Baslini, passed into the possession of Signor Roverselli, from whom, in the autumn of 1855, it was purchased for the National Collection.

MANTEGNA, FRANCESCO.

FRANCESCO MANTEGNA, the second son of Andrea, was born at Mantua about 1470. He was the pupil and assistant of his father, and completed some works left unfinished by him. Francesco was still living in 1517.* Andrea Mantegna, son of Lodovico, and grandson of the painter, placed a monument, in 1560, in the family chapel in Sant' Andrea, at Mantua, to his father, his grandfather, and his uncle, Francesco, with the following inscription:—OSSA ANDREAE MANTINEAE FAMOSISSIMI PICTORIS CUM DUOBUS FILIIS IN HOC SEPULCRO PER ANDREAM MANTINIAM NEPOTEM EX FILIO CONSTRUCTO REPOSITA MDLX.†

No. 639. CHRIST AND MARY MAGDALEN IN THE GARDEN, called a "Noli me tangere,"—touch me not. *John* xx. 17. A vine of purple grapes hanging over the figure of Christ, is supported on a dead tree; on the other side a bird is seen defending its nest against a snake which has crept up the tree; on the left is a bee-hive.

On wood, 16¾ in. *h.* by 12 in. *w.*

Formerly in the Duroveray Collection. Purchased at Paris, from M. Edmond Beaucousin, in 1860.

---

* Moschini, *Della origine della Pittura in Padova*, &c.

† Coddè, *Pittori*, &c., *Mantovani*.

MARATTI.

Carlo Maratti, *Cavaliere*, was born at Camurano, between Loreto and Ancona, May 15th, 1625. He went early to Rome, where he entered the school of Andrea Sacchi. He soon became the most distinguished pupil of that master; and after the deaths of Pietro da Cortona and Sacchi, he was for nearly half a century the most eminent painter in Rome. He was honoured with the favour of six successive popes—Clements IX and X., Innocent XI., Alexander VIII., Innocent XII., and Clement XI. He was appointed superintendent of the Vatican Chambers by Innocent XI.; and in the years 1702 and 3, he restored with the sanction of Clement XI. (Albani) the frescoes of Raphael there, which had been suffered to fall into a state of decay and imminent ruin. He died in Rome Dec. 15th, 1713, at the advanced age of eighty-eight.*

Maratti was considered by Mengs to have arrested at Rome the general decline of painting which prevailed at the close of the seventeenth century.† He was an ardent admirer of Raphael, whose style, though weakened in his hands by the eclecticism of the Carracci, he endeavoured to uphold, in opposition to the then prevailing school of Cortona, and the *macchinisti* generally. Maratti painted little in fresco; his chief works, which are very numerous, are easel pictures in oil. A "Baptism of Christ" by him, now in the church of Santa Maria degli Angeli at Rome, has been executed in mosaic for the altar of one of the chapels of St. Peter's. From his frequent pictures of the Virgin, he acquired the name of Carlo delle Madonne. His pictures are distinguished for their academic precision of design, but are more conspicuous for the general absence of defects, than for any particular excellence. There are several etchings by this painter.

No. **174.** Portrait of Cardinal Cerri, seated. Half-length, of the natural size.

On canvas, 3 ft. 11 in. *h.* by 3 ft. 2 in. *w.*

Presented to the National Gallery, in 1839, by Mr. Henry Gally Knight.

---

* Lioni, *Ritratti di alcuni celebri Pittori del secolo XVII.*, &c., Roma, 1731, which contains Maratti's life, by Bellori; Pascoli, *Vite de' Pittori*, &c.

† Lanzi, *Storia Pittorica*, &c.; Mengs, *Hinterlassne Werke*, vol. i. p. 304.

MARGARITONE.

MARGARITONE DI MAGNANO,* of Arezzo, painter, sculptor, and architect, was a distinguished master in his time. He was born at Arezzo in 1236, and, as appears evidently from his works, was a student of the Byzantine school of painting. Being an older painter than Cimabue, he was uninfluenced by the innovations of that great master upon the traditionary practice of the time.

Vasari describes many works by Margaritone, at Arezzo and elsewhere, but most of them have long since perished. He was employed at Rome by Pope Urban IV. to decorate the portico of the old Basilica of St. Peter; this Pope died in 1265.

The best of all Margaritone's works, says Vasari, is the monument in marble of Pope Gregory X., executed shortly after 1276, in the episcopal palace at Arezzo. This monument contains a likeness of the Pope from the life, which is still in a good state of preservation.

In the convent De' Zoccoli at Sargiano, there is still a picture of St. Francis of Assisi, signed MARGARIT DE ARITIO PINGEBAT.†

He died at Arezzo in 1313, aged seventy-seven, and weary of life, says Vasari, having quite outlived the art and taste of his own time, which had then been completely superseded by the school of Giotto.‡

No. **564.** THE VIRGIN AND CHILD, WITH SCENES FROM THE LIVES OF THE SAINTS. The Virgin is seated in the centre with the Child in her lap, and surrounded by the *Ichthus* or *Vesica Piscis* glory,§ within which are also two

---

* In the only document known concerning this painter, bearing the date 1262, are the words, *in claustro Sancti Michaelis* (in Arezzo) *coram Margarito pictore, filio quondam Magnani.* Vasari, Ed. Le Monnier, vol. 1, p. 302, note.

† This picture is said by Vasari to be *ritratto di naturale*, an expression often used by him, meaning that the likeness was authentic, not, in every case, that it was taken directly from nature. St. Francis died in 1226. The picture referred to is engraved in the *Etruria Pittrice*. As an architect Margaritone superintended the works of the episcopal palace of Arezzo, and carried out some buildings at Ancona.

‡ Vasari, *Vite, &c.*, Ed. Le Monnier, Flor. 1846, *et seq.*

§ This glory or aureole represents the acrostic symbol the fish, derived from the circumstance of the common Greek word for fish, ἰχθὺς (*ichthus*), containing the initials of the following sentence:—Ἰησοῦς Χριστὸς, Θεοῦ Υἱὸς, Σωτὴρ, Jesus Christ, the Son of God, the Saviour. This glory, which is given only to Christ, or to the Virgin holding the infant Christ, is called by Italian writers on art, including Vasari, the *Mandola* or *Mandorla* from its *almond* shape.

angels, and around the glory outside are the four symbolic images of the four Evangelists—the angel, the ox, the lion, and the eagle. The hand of the infant Christ is in the act of blessing according to the Greek rite.*

Eight small pictures are arranged, four on each side of the *vesica:* the Nativity and Annunciation to the Shepherds; St. John the Evangelist liberated from the cauldron of boiling oil; St. John resuscitating Drusiana; St. Benedict rolling himself among thorns, to resist the temptations of the evil spirit; the martyrdom, and burial of St. Catherine on Mount Sinai; St. Nicholas of Bari exhorting the sailors to throw into the sea the vase given them by the Devil; the same Saint liberating the condemned; and St. Margaret in prison swallowed and disgorged again by the Dragon unhurt. The picture is signed, *Margarit de Aritio me fecit.*† The annotators of the recent (Le Monnier) edition of Vasari express the opinion that "among the few paintings by Margaritone which now remain, this is, on every account, the most characteristic and important."

In tempera, on linen cloth attached to wood, 2 ft. 9 in. *h.* by 5 ft. 9 in. *w.*

An altar front, formerly in the church of Santa Margherita at Arezzo. Purchased at Florence from the Lombardi-Baldi collection in 1857.

MARGARIT DEARITIO ME FECIT

MASACCIO.

TOMMASO GUIDI, commonly called MASACCIO from the slovenliness of his habits—the consequence of an absorbing attention to his studies—was born at Castel San Giovanni in the upper Valdarno in 1402,‡ and was the son of Ser

* See No. 594, Emmanuel, note, p. 86, where this form is explained.

† The small pictures have their subjects inscribed over them, but two of these inscriptions are nearly illegible. They appear to be as follows:— 1. De Partu Virginis Marie et Adnuntiatione Pastorum. 2. Hic Beat. Johẽs Evḡ. a fervore olei liberatur. 3. Hi Scš Johes Ev̄g. suscitat Drusianam. 4 His. Bñedict. jecit se ĩ spinas fugiens Diaboli tẽtatiõem. 5. Hi Sca Cattarina suscepit martyrium et in montem Siny ab angelis *evecta?* 6. Hi Scš Nicolaus precepit Nautis ut vas oblatum a Diabolo ĩ mari jicerent. 7. Hi Sc̃s Nicolaus liberat condemnatos. 8. Hi Sca Margarita ingurgitatur a Dracone et ruptis visceribus exit illesa.

‡ The earliest authorities state that Masaccio died at the age of twenty-six. Accordingly, later writers, having assumed that 1443 was the year of his death, placed his birth in 1417. The publication by Gaye (*Carteggio d'Artisti.* Firenze, 1839, tom. i. p. 115) of a document proving that in 1427 Masaccio

Giovanni di Simone Guidi. He is supposed to have been the pupil of Masolino da Panicale who was about his own age. Masaccio continued the series of frescoes commenced by that painter in the Brancacci chapel in the church of the Carmine at Florence: he appears to have been employed in the church and its convent from 1425 till his departure for Rome in 1427.

The frescoes assigned to Masaccio in the Brancacci chapel are—the Expulsion from Paradise; the Tribute Money; St. Peter baptizing; the Apostles restoring the Youth to life (completed by Filippino Lippi); and the Infirm cured by the Shadow of St. Peter.* Another interesting work of the master, the subject called the Italian Trinity, with the Madonna, St. John, and the portraits of the donors, was brought to light in the church of Santa Maria Novella in 1857.† The principal portions are well preserved, and by means of this fresco—the only undoubted production of the painter besides the works in the Brancacci chapel—the latter can be more accurately distinguished. The frescoes ascribed to Masaccio in the church of San Clemente in Rome—a Crucifixion, and a series relating to

---

was twenty-five years of age, necessarily fixed the date of his birth in 1402; but the impossibility of reconciling the pre-arranged chronology of certain works of art with the inference that Masaccio died in 1428, led historians to treat as erroneous the limitation of his life to twenty-six years. His existence was therefore prolonged to the age of forty-one; the old date of of 1443 being retained as the year of his death. A diligent investigator of the archives of Tuscany has recently published some documents relating to various Florentine painters, which set this question at rest. From those extracts it appears that Masaccio died in Rome in 1428 or at latest in 1429; that is, when about the age of twenty-six. It further appears that Masolino da Panicale, who painted in the Brancacci chapel previously to Masaccio, may have begun that work in 1423-1424; that he quitted it, in consequence of having received an offer of employment in Hungary, about 1425; that Masaccio continued the Brancacci frescoes till 1427, when he repaired to Rome where he shortly afterwards died. Milanesi, in the *Giornale Storico degli Archivi Toscani*; anno iv. Luglio—Settembre, 1860.

* The number of frescoes above allotted to Masaccio (and some writers include more) may require re-consideration, when it is remembered that his whole labour in the chapel must be restricted to two years. The frescoes ascribed to Masolino are three only; yet in his case it is not absolutely impossible that he may have worked in the chapel again at a later period. He appears to have returned to Italy, from Hungary, in 1427. He painted some frescoes, partly similar in treatment to those in the Carmine, in the neighbourhood of Como, in 1435, and is supposed to have died in 1440. See the documents before noticed, published by Milanesi.

† Vasari describes this work carefully and correctly, but, strange to say, within two years after the (second) publication of his biographies, it was covered by a gigantic mannered picture of his own. The fresco has been removed, on a solid portion of the wall itself, to another part of the church, where it can now be well seen. *Deutsches Kunstblatt*, 1858, p. 293.

the history of St. Catherine, with other wall paintings—are in an earlier and drier manner than his Florentine works and inferior to them in all respects. If the statement of Vasari with regard to the San Clemente series is to be admitted in any sense, it may be understood to refer to some designs furnished by Masaccio, but executed by a far inferior hand. The shortness of his residence in Rome before his death tends to confirm this view. The tempera picture representing the Madonna and Child with St. Anne, now in the gallery of the academy in Florence, though mentioned by Vasari, cannot in its present state be regarded as an unquestionable specimen of the master.*

The impulse given by Donatello to sculpture was accomplished in painting by Masaccio, who forsook traditionary art for the study of nature; he gave individuality of character to his heads, and great natural ease to his figures and draperies. These qualities are, at the same time accompanied in his works by a breadth of treatment which, were his date unknown, might be judged to belong to a much later period. The certainty now established, that those works were produced from 1425 to 1427 must increase the admiration connected with his name, and confirm the praises which, according to Vasari, were bestowed on his productions by the best painters of the fifteenth century. Though much in the Brancacci series of frescoes has by modern criticism been justly assigned to Filippino Lippi, who completed the chapel more than half a century after the death of Masaccio, enough remains to the latter, even without reference to the recently discovered fresco in Santa Maria Novella, to entitle him to the eloquent encomium of Sir Joshua Reynolds, that "he appears to be the first who discovered the path that leads to every excellence to which the art afterwards arrived, and may, therefore, be justly considered one of the great fathers of modern art."†

Masaccio died in Rome in 1428 or 1429.‡

---

* Engraved in the Galleria dell' Accademia Delle Belle Arti, Firenze 1845.

† Discourse XII.

‡ See the documents before referred to in the *Giornale Storico degli Archivi Toscani*, &c., Vasari, *Vite*, &c., and the commentary on his life of Masaccio in the Le Monnier edition, vol. iii. p. 165. The Brancacci frescoes are engraved by Lasinio; and some of the heads by Thomas Patch; *Masaccio, sua Vita e collezione di 24 teste*; parts are also given in the *Etruria Pittrice*.

No. **626.** HIS OWN PORTRAIT, a head, front view.*
On wood, 14 in. *h.* by 11 in. *w.*
Purchased at the sale of the Northwick pictures in 1859.

MATSYS.

QUINTIN MATSYS, known also as the Smith of Antwerp, was born at Louvain† about 1460; he was brought up as a blacksmith, and was distinguished for his skill in ornamental ironwork. At Louvain and its neighbourhood, and in Antwerp, where he eventually settled, there are still shown several good specimens of his skill in wrought iron. He was admitted a member of the Academy of Antwerp in 1491-2.

In Antwerp, as it is popularly recorded, Quintin fell in love with a painter's daughter, and to obtain her hand he forsook the anvil for the palette: he not only gained his suit, but became the most distinguished painter of the city, raising the school of Antwerp to a celebrity equal to that of Bruges. His masterpiece, "The Taking down from the Cross," painted in 1508, for the altar of the chapel of the Joiners' Company, in the cathedral, is now one of the principal treasures of the Antwerp Museum. It was purchased by the city in 1577 for fifteen hundred florins. Quintin had received for it only the moderate sum of 300 florins, about 25*l.* sterling.

This picture, like all the other works of the painter, is distinguished for careful execution, which he elaborated to a perfection in some instances rivalling that of John Van Eyck.

Rathgeber‡ has enumerated 78 works by, or ascribed to, Quintin Matsys in various European collections; they are chiefly of religious subjects, but he painted some portraits, and the so-called "Misers," (of which a fine example is in the Royal collection at Windsor) he repeated with variations, several times. Portraits of himself and of his second wife

* The traditional designations of works of art are sometimes, for various reasons, retained, when sound criticism might suggest their alteration. The portrait still called that of Masaccio in the gallery of the Uffizj at Florence, is now generally admitted to be the work of Filippino Lippi, and probably his own portrait. The portrait above described, whoever it may represent, also appears to be the work of Filippino. The opinion here expressed may however require the confirmation of time.

† L. Guicciardini, *La Description des Pays-Bas*, 1569, p. 131.

‡ *Annalen der Niederländischen Malerei, &c.*, pp. 205-437.

are in the gallery of the Uffizj, at Florence.* His wife's is dated 1520, the year in which he was visited at Antwerp by Albert Durer. He was twice married.

Quintin died in 1530–31, it is said of the *suette* in the Carthusian convent at Antwerp.† He rarely placed his signature on his pictures; and when it does occur, his name is variously written. A "Holy Family," in the church of St. Pierre at Louvain, is signed *Quintē Metsys*, screef dit. 1509; and a "St. Jerome" in the Lichtenstein Gallery at Vienna, has the signature *Quintin Masys*, f. 1513. The fine picture of the "Banker and his Wife," in the gallery of the Louvre, is signed *Quintin Matsyss schildt*, 1518, T. Quintin left a son, JAN MATSYS, by whom there are several pictures extant: in the Vienna Gallery is a panel signed *Joannes Masiis faciebat*, 1564.‡

No. **295.** SALVATOR MUNDI, AND THE VIRGIN MARY. The Saviour holds in his left hand a crystal globe surmounted by a golden cross; with his right he is blessing. The Virgin has her hands joined in adoration. Bust figures, small life size, on a gold ground.

On wood, with circular tops, each panel, 1 ft. 11 in. *h.* by 1 ft. 1 in. *w.*

There are two similar pictures to the above, but showing less of the figures and slightly varying in the action and accessories, in the Museum at Antwerp. Copies of the Antwerp pictures, once in the possession of Erasmus, are now at Heidelberg. A third pair, also resembling the Antwerp pictures, is in the gallery of the Academy at Turin. The pictures above described were formerly in Madrid, whence they were brought back to the Netherlands in 1816§ and subsequently formed part of the King of Holland's gallery at the Hague, where they were purchased, in 1857, from the Commissioners appointed to dispose of the remainder of that collection.

---

* *Reale Galleria di Firenze.* S. III. vol. i. p. 27, engraved by G. Rossi.

† Quintin Matsys was originally buried in the cemetery of the Carthusians; but Cornelis Van der Ghest removed his remains a century afterwards, and had them reburied in front of the Cathedral. The spot is marked by the simple memorial M.Q.M. obiit 1529; and in the wall of the Cathedral is a slab with the inscription "Quintino Matsys, Incomparabilis artis pictori, admiratrix grataque Posteritas anno post obitum Sæculari cio.ioc.xxix. posuit.—Connubialis amor de Mulcibre fecit Apellem." Quintin, though still living in July 1530, was already dead on the 12th October 1531. See *Catalogue du Musée d'Anvers*, 1857.

‡ Van Mander, *Het Leven der Schilders*, &c., Ed. 1764; Von Mechel, *Catalogue de la Galerie de Vienne;* Schnaase, *Niederländische Briefe*, 1834; Michiels, *Histoire de la Peinture Flamande, &c.;* Nieuwenhuys, *Description de la Galerie, &c., de S.M. le Roi des Pays-Bas*, 1843.

§ Nieuwenhuys, *Catalogue, &c.*, p. 61.

MAZZOLI'NI.

LODOVI'CO MAZZOLI'NI, sometimes called Mazzolini da Ferrara, and Lodovico Ferrarese, was born at Ferrara about 1481. He was the scholar of Lorenzo Costa; and after Garofalo, whom he somewhat resembles in style, may perhaps be considered the most distinguished of the Ferrarese painters. He died at Ferrara in 1530.* His pictures are remarkable for the architectural back-grounds which he frequently introduced into them. His masterpiece is probably the large picture of Christ disputing with the Doctors, in the Gallery of Berlin; it was painted in 1524.

No. **82.** THE HOLY FAMILY, with Saint Francis adoring the infant Christ; behind, are Elizabeth and Saint John. The little Saint John is protecting a lamb from a monkey which appears to menace it. The back-ground is an architectural elevation, adorned with bassi-rilievi.

Engraved in Jones's *National Gallery*. On wood, 1 ft. 9 in. *h.* by 1 ft. $8\frac{1}{2}$ in. *w.*

Formerly in the Durazzo Palace at Genoa. Bequeathed to the National Gallery, in 1831, by the Rev. W. H. Carr.

No. **169.** THE HOLY FAMILY, with St. Nicholas of Tolentino adoring the infant Saviour; St. Joseph is presenting him with cherries. Immediately above the Virgin is the Dove in a glory of light, the symbol of the Holy Ghost, and in the upper part of the picture is a vision of the Father surrounded by a choir of angels.

The whole is symmetrically arranged; the back-ground of the composition is an architectural elevation, enriched with bassi-rilievi.

On wood, 2 ft. $\frac{1}{4}$ in. *h.* by 1 ft. $6\frac{3}{4}$ in. *w.*

Formerly in the Lercari Palace at Genoa: brought to England by Mr. A. Wilson in 1806. Purchased for the National Gallery from Mr. Beckford, in 1839.

No. **641.** THE WOMAN TAKEN IN ADULTERY. The scene represents the interior of the Temple, in which are many people on the floor and in the galleries. Christ has just

---

* The works of this painter are frequently attributed to other masters, his own name being, through Vasari's omission of him, comparatively unknown. He is only slightly noticed by Vasari under the name of Malini, whence, says Lanzi, he has been divided into two—Malini and Mazzolini. His name is also sometimes confounded with that of Mazzolino, a name given by Lomazzo to Parmigiano—Mazzuoli, of which Mazzolino is a diminutive, or what the Italians call a *vezzeggiativo*. A picture in the Costabili collection at Ferrara is signed *Lodovico Mazzolii*, 15 1. Laderchi, *Descrizione della Galleria Costabili*. Ferrara, 1838, p. 45.

completed the writing on the pavement, "He that is without sin among you, let him cast first a stone at her," and the guilty Scribes and Pharisees are self-convicted, and about to turn away from him. *John*, ch. viii.

On wood, 18 in. *h.* by 12 in. *w.*

Formerly in the collection at Fonthill. Purchased at Paris, from M. Edmond Beaucousin, in 1860.

MEMLING.

HANS OR JOHN MEMLING, called also HEMLING, was one of the ablest of the early Flemish masters; the circumstances of his life are as yet little known, but one account assumes, from an old chronicle, that he was born at Constanz, in 1439; and he is supposed to have been the scholar of Roger Vander Weyden. Memling was, however, already, in 1479, living at Bruges, in his own house, in the Rue St. George, as an established painter; and he was then a citizen of property and consideration, and was one of those who in 1480 contributed to the city loan towards defraying the expenses of the war between the Emperor Maximilian and France.

His picture of the "Adoration of the Magi," in the Hospital of St. John at Bruges, is dated 1479; that known as the *Sibyl Lambertha* in the same collection was painted in the following year; and the admirable triptych, by him, in the Academy of Bruges is dated 1484. In 1487 he lost his wife, Anne, by whom he had two sons and a daughter; and on the 10th of December 1495 he himself also was dead, his children being then still minors.*

The Hospital of St. John at Bruges possesses, besides the "Adoration" referred to above, two other of Memling's best works, — the fine altar-piece of the "Marriage of St. Catherine," and the celebrated "Châsse of St. Ursula," with the history of the martyrdom of that saint and her companions. The comparatively large picture of "The Joys and Sorrows of the Virgin," with the journey of the three Kings from the East, in the gallery at Munich, is also one of Memling's most remarkable productions; it is a work of

---

* Weale, *Journal des Beaux-Arts*, 3rd year, p. 21, &c., and *Catalogue du Musée de l'Academie de Bruges*, 8vo., 1861.

extraordinary labour and finish. Rathgeber enumerates about a hundred works attributed to this painter.*

No. 686. THE VIRGIN AND INFANT CHRIST, ENTHRONED, IN A GARDEN. On her right, an angel playing on a guitar; on her left, St. George with the dragon at his feet. In front, the donor is kneeling before the Divine Infant, who, while listening to the music of the angel, is with his left hand turning over the leaves of a book held before him by his mother. In the distance is a view of the sea, with shipping.

On wood, 21¼ in. *h.* by 14¾ in. *w.*

Purchased at Cologne, at the sale of the pictures of Mr. J. P. Weyer, in 1862.

ANTONELLO DA MESSINA.

ANTONELLO DEGLI ANTONJ, commonly called ANTONELLO DA MESSINA, is distinguished among the painters of the 15th century chiefly as having been the means of introducing into Italy the Flemish system of oil painting. Various writers, on both sides of the Alps, have had no difficulty in proving that the mere use of oil in painting was known at an earlier period in Italy as well as in the north. It is, however, no less certain that the earlier, partial practice of oil painting had so far failed to recommend it that even after superior examples of the Flemish method, by Van Eyck and Roger Vander Weyden the elder, had been seen and admired in Italy,† the Italian painters generally still continued for many years to work in tempera.

Vasari's account is the chief source of the history of Antonello. That narrative requires frequent correction in dates; but the leading statements, except where they are irreconcileable with ascertained facts, have been generally adopted.

Antonello was born about the year 1414, and according to the best authorities, at Messina, where his father

* Passavant, *Kunstreise durch England und Belgien*, 1835; Rathgeber, *Annalen der Niederländischen Malerei*; Michiels, *Histoire de la Peinture Flamande, &c.* See also note to Claude, No. 30 in this catalogue.

† Facius, *De Viris Illustribus*, pp. 46, 48. This work, published in the last century, was written in 1456.

Salvadore and even some among his ancestors, the Antonj, it is said, had practised painting.* After studying in Italy, and probably in Rome, he returned to Messina, but was soon afterwards attracted to Naples by the fame of a picture by John Van Eyck, painted, as Vasari states, for Alphonso, king of Naples. The impression produced by this work on Antonello was such that, "putting aside every other avocation and thought," he at once undertook the journey to Flanders in order to see and ingratiate himself with the painter.†

Alphonso having only begun to reign in 1442, after Van Eyck's death, it may be assumed that it was King Réné of Anjou (supplanted by Alphonso) whom the biographer meant. It is indeed probable, on many accounts, that Réné may have recommended Antonello to the Flemish master.‡ The biographer tells us that Antonello, "arrived in Flanders, assiduously cultivated the friendship of Giovanni" (John Van Eyck). The result was that the latter communicated to him the method of painting in oil.

John Van Eyck died in July 1440. Granting Antonello a year to win the favour of the Flemish master and learn his process, he must have been about twenty-five when he reached Bruges. After Van Eyck's death he is supposed to have remained in Flanders, gradually mastering the new art, for some years. In, or soon after, 1451 he may have met Domenico Veneziano in Venice,§ and to him he communicated the Flemish process of oil painting:

---

* *Memorie de Pittori Messinesi*, in Messina, 1821.

† Vasari, *Vita di Antonello da Messina.*

‡ *Kunstblatt*, 1826, No. 84. Puccini, *Memorie Istorico-Critiche di Antonello degli Antonj*, Firenze, 1809, p. 87. Lanzi, *Storia Pittorica* (Firenze, 1822) tom. ii., p. 245. Facius (p. 26) describes a triptych by Van Eyck in the possession of King Alphonso. This was probably the picture which Antonello saw; but whether it was originally painted for Réné or for Alphonso (before the latter acquired the sovereignty of Naples) can only be matter of conjecture.

§ The dates in Domenico's life which affect his relations with Antonello may be here recorded. In 1439 he was painting the principal chapel (of Sant' Egidio) in the church attached to the hospital of Santa Maria Nuova in Florence, with Pietro della Francesca as his assistant. (See an original document quoted by Harzen, *Archiv für den ZeichnendenKünste*, 1856, p. 232.) In 1441 he was again at work in the same chapel with Bicci di Lorenzo. (See the document quoted by Milanesi in the *Giornale Storico degli Archivi Toscani*, Luglio—Settembre 1860.) He was subsequently employed together with Pietro della Francesca at Loreto; they both quitted Loreto on account of the plague (Vasari, *Vita di Pietro della Francesca*, consequently about 1450. Pietro went to Rimini where he painted a fresco dated 1451; Domenico

Vasari tells us that Domenico was afterwards invited to Florence on account of his newly acquired art, and was employed by the Portinari to paint in oil one side of the principal chapel in Santa Maria Nuova.*

Meanwhile, Antonello appears to have established himself at Milan. The statement of an early writer, that he acquired great reputation there, indicates a stay of some years.† His return to his native Messina may not have been uninfluenced by the news of the untimely death of his friend Dominico. The assassination in Florence of that painter, by his rival Andrea dal Castagno, appears to have happened in 1463.‡ The following year may be considered the commencement of Antonello's second residence in Messina. The picture by him about to be described (which, coming from Naples, may be supposed to be of Sicilian origin) is dated 1465.§ The latest of the various works

---

appears to have re-visited his native Venice. If, therefore, he made the acquaintance of Antonello in Venice, as Vasari states, no more probable time can be assigned for their intercourse than between 1451 and 1455; indeed, as Domenico is named as a referee in a contract dated Perugia, December 1454, he may have been then in Florence.

* That is to say, the same chapel of Sant' Egidio in Santa Maria Nuova, where, as we have seen, Domenico had been employed for at least two years at an earlier period. The conclusion is, that his previous works there (which must have been either in fresco or in tempera) were destroyed. Future researches among contemporary documents may explain this; there can, however, be no doubt that the later wall paintings of Domenico in that chapel were in oil. Vasari, *Vita di Andrea dal Castagno e Dom. Veneziano*, not only states this distinctly, but says, as if from his own comparison of the works, that Andrea showed no less skill than Domenico in the management of oil colours. The remaining side of the chapel was allotted, according to the biographer, to Alessio Baldovinetti, who practised a method allied to oil painting.

† "Mediolani quoque fuit percelebris." These words, ascribed to Maurolyco (Lanzi, tom. ii. p. 242), are quoted by that writer from an earlier authority. (See *Memorie de' Pittori Messinesi*, p. 7, note 1.)

‡ In the contract before referred to (Mariotti, *Lettere Perugine*, Perugia, 1788, p. 132), dated Perugia, 1454, three referees are named, one of whom was to be consulted;—either Fra Filippo Lippi, or Domenico Veneziano, or Fra Angelico da Fiesole. The fact that Fra Filippo visited Perugia in September 1461 (not in 1464, as misprinted in the Le Monnier, Vasari, vol. iv. p. 149, note 1,) to determine the doubtful question, may be explained by his being the first named; it is not necessary to infer that Domenico (like Fra Angelico) was then deceased. The architect Filarete, whose MS. preserved in Florence belongs to a period between 1460 and 1464 (Gaye, *Carteggio d'Artisti*, Firenze, 1839, tom. i. p. 205,) states in that work that Domenico Veneziano was "recently deceased." Sandrart (*Acad. Pict.* p. 106) informs us that Domenico was assassinated when Antonello was 49 years of age; consequently, if the date of Antonello's birth has been rightly guessed, in 1463.

§ But a few years since it was remarked, with reference to the chronological order of Antonello's works. "Between the years 1445 and 1474 a gap occurs, and we possess no pictures; the first in the order of dates being one mentioned by Lanzi, dated 1474." Crowe and Cavalcaselle, *The early Flemish Painters, &c.*, London, 1857, p. 217.

painted by him in Messina seems to be that which was a few years since, and probably still is, in the church of San Gregorio in that city: it bears the date 1473.* Antonello must have returned to Venice in that year. A Venetian writer, without any reference to this question, states that the earliest known oil picture in Venice is that by Bartolommeo Vivarini, in the church of SS. Giovanni e Paolo, dated 1473.† A portrait by Antonello now in the possession of the Duke of Hamilton, and which was formerly in Venice, is dated 1474. The celebrated portrait which also came from Venice in the Pourtalès collection bears the date 1475. The Rinuccini (now Trivulzi) portrait, that of 1476. Another, noticed by Zanetti, 1478.‡ Vasari refers to various pictures by Antonello, including the often described altar-piece of San Cassianc, now lost, and speaks of a work allotted to him in the Ducal Palace of Venice, which considered in connexion with other circumstances, supposes Antonello to have been still practising his art in 1493.§ His death may have taken place a few years later.‖

---

* *Memorie de' Pittori Messinesi*, p. 15. The author gives the inscription entire. *Guida per la Città di Messina*, Siracusa, 1826, p. 20.

† Zanetti, *Della Pittura Veneziana*, in Venezia 1771, p. 24.

‡ Zanetti, p. 21.

§ Puccini, *Memorie, &c.*, p. 55.

‖ In reviewing the less questionable particulars of Antonello's history, the following circumstances may be noticed:—His early oil pictures with dates are extremely rare. With the exception of a portrait in the gallery at Berlin, dated 1445, and possibly the Antwerp Crucifixion (the date of which is variously read 1475, 1445), no certain specimen before his return to Messina is at present known. Yet he painted in oil for more than twenty years before that period, in Flanders, in Venice, and in Milan. The probability, therefore, is that he was not then in the habit of signing his pictures, and that many really by him are ascribed, in collections, to other painters. In his latest works also, even when his signature appears, the date is omitted. As yet, no specimen is known with a later date than 1478. The author of the *Memorie de' Pittori Messinesi*, p. 19, cites indeed, on hearsay, a picture in the Riformati at Catania with a much later date, but he appears to have been misinformed. Another remarkable circumstance is that Antonello's works in oil painted in the north of Italy during the period referred to, had not the effect of exciting any Italian painter, Domenico Veneziano excepted, to adopt the Flemish method. This is hardly to be explained by the jealousy with which that method may have been kept secret, as the result in pictures might have been imitated to some extent by ardent admirers. It is rather to be ascribed to the reluctance of the tempera painters generally to abandon their traditional process. The change was, however, effected by time; Antonello, on his re-appearance in Venice found willing converts. Ridolfi, *Le Maraviglie dell' Arte*, Ven. 1648, i. p. 49,) even relates that Giovanni Bellini, the better to observe the Sicilian painter's process, sat to him for a portrait, in the disguise of a Venetian senator. The story is improbable, but there seems no reason to doubt that Antonello's influence greatly accelerated the introduction of oil painting into Venice towards the close of the century.

673. CHRIST AS THE SAVIOUR "SALVATOR MUNDI." The right hand is raised in the act of blessing; the fingers of the left rest on the edge of a parapet. The inner dress is a dark crimson tunic; a portion of blue drapery crosses the left shoulder. Bust figure, seen in front, small life-size. In the lower part of the neck is seen what is called a *pentimento* or correction. The right hand and part of the tunic were originally higher, and their forms, obliterated by the painter, have partly re-appeared.

On wood, 1 ft. $4\frac{3}{4}$ in. *h.* by 1 ft. $\frac{3}{4}$ in. *w.* including a black border about an inch wide.

With a *cartellino*, inscribed as follows:—

The year 1465 corresponds not with the eighth but with the thirteenth indiction. It is therefore supposed either that the painter was misinformed as to the year of the indiction, or, which is more probable, that the freely written V. was originally crossed so as to form X.*

Purchased in September 1861 from the Cavaliere Isola, Genoa.

MICHELANGELO.

MICHELANGELO BUONARRO'TI was born at Castel Caprese, in the diocese of Arezzo in Tuscany, March 6, 1475 :† his father Lodovico Buonarroti was governor of the castles Caprese and Chiusi. On the 1st of April 1488, he was apprenticed by his father to the celebrated painter Domenico Ghirlandajo, for three years, during which period Michelangelo was to receive 24 florins for his services, an unusual arrangement.

* See p. 160, note, an instance of similar ambiguity in a memorandum by a Ferrarese painter, L'Ortolano.

† This date is commonly given as 1474, because the Florentines commenced their year at that time with the 25th of March, the Annunciation day. This practice was introduced by the Florentines about the tenth century. See *L'Art de Vérifier les Dates.*

Michelangelo soon distinguished himself from the other pupils of Ghirlandajo, and evinced such superior ability in his drawings and models, made in the garden, or so-called academy, of Lorenzo de' Medici, near the church of San Marco, that that eminent patron of the arts took him under his especial protection, and employed Michelangelo to execute several pieces of sculpture: Michelangelo devoted his attention for many years from this time chiefly to sculpture. After the death of Lorenzo in 1492, to avoid the disturbances which ensued upon the accession of his son Pietro to the government of Florence, Michelangelo removed for a short time to Bologna; he returned however to Florence in the following year, in 1494. Very shortly after this period, in consequence of the remarkable excellence of a "Sleeping Cupid" which he produced after his return to Florence, and which was sold at Rome as a veritable *antique*, he was persuaded to try his fortunes in the papal capital: and it was during this first visit to Rome that he produced his celebrated *Pietà*,* or group of the dead Christ on the knees of the Virgin, which is now in the Church of St. Peter.

He returned again to Florence about the year 1501, and there executed his colossal statue of "David," now in the Piazza del Granduca. About 1503 he received a commission from Soderini, then Gonfaloniere of Florence, to decorate one end of the Council Hall; the opposite wall being intrusted to Leonardo da Vinci.† Leonardo began but did not complete his picture. Michelangelo's does not appear to have been commenced; but his cartoon, well known as the "Cartoon of Pisa," was finished about the year 1506: it represented some Pisan soldiers, while bathing in the Arno, surprised by Florentines. Both designs presented so many various and masterly views of the human figure, that they became, to use the words of Benvenuto Cellini, "The School of the World."‡ During the progress of this cartoon, Michelangelo paid a second visit to Rome by the invitation of Julius II., recently elected to the papal chair, who commissioned him to make a design for a

---

* The representation of the Virgin Mary weeping over the dead Christ was called a *Pietà*, as that of the enthroned Saviour or enthroned Virgin was called a *Maestà*.

† See the notice of Da Vinci in this catalogue.

‡ *Vita di Benvenuto Cellini*, Milan, 1806, p. 31. Gaye, *Carteggio, &c.*, v. ii. p. 90. Vasari, *Life of Michelangelo.*

mausoleum which that Pope intended to erect for himself in the church of St. Peter. Michelangelo, however, returned again to Florence in 1505, having taken offence at certain treatment from one of the Pope's servants; but he was reconciled to the Pope at the close of the following year, at Bologna; he there made the well-known statue of Julius II., which was afterwards destroyed, then cast as a cannon, and used against the Pope by the Bolognese. In 1508 Michelangelo returned to Rome.

In this year he was commissioned by Julius to paint the ceiling of the Sistine Chapel. He commenced this task very reluctantly, and adverted to Raphael, whose fame was already great, and who was then about to commence his series of frescoes in the Vatican Stanze, as a more fit person to execute the work. Michelangelo commenced his designs in 1508, and the ceiling was finished on All Saints' Day (Nov. 1), 1512.* The painting, says Vasari, was executed by Michelangelo alone, in the short space of twenty months: but it need not be assumed that these were consecutive months, especially as a writer quoted by Fea speaks of the ceiling as already begun in 1509.† In any view of the question, the greater part of the time above specified must have been employed on the designs and cartoons. The frescoes represent the creation of the world and of Man; his Fall; and the early history of the world, with reference to Man's final redemption and salvation.‡

These extensive frescoes necessarily caused Michelangelo to suspend his labours for the mausoleum of Julius; and as the Pope died shortly after their completion, in 1513, the monument was never finished.

During the whole pontificate of Leo X., the successor of Julius II. (nearly nine years), Michelangelo was employed in the unworthy occupation of procuring marble from the

---

* There is a document in the possession of the Buonarroti family at Florence which purports to be an original contract made by Michelangelo with the Pope, respecting the commencement of his designs for this ceiling; it is dated May 10, 1508. The whole work, therefore, occupied Michelangelo about four years, for his scaffolding was still not removed from the chapel by Christmas-day, 1512, as noticed in the *Diary of Paris de Grassis*, quoted by Pungileoni, *Elogio Storico*, &c. p. 131; and by Passavant, *Rafael von Urbino*, i. p. 167. See also the *Kunstblatt*, No. 105, 1844.

† Franc. de Albertinis, *Mirab. Romæ*, lib. iii. Fea, *Notizie*, &c. p. 27.

‡ There is an outline of this ceiling in the English translation of Kugler's *Handbook of Painting*, Italy, vol. i. See the Editor's notes on the subjects of the frescoes, pp. 203, 206, 216.

quarries of Pietra Santa, for the façade of the church of San Lorenzo at Florence. During the pontificate of Leo's successor, Adrian VI., and part of that of Clement VII., he was employed on the works of the Medici Chapel in the Church of San Lorenzo at Florence: in the tenth year, however, of Clement's pontificate, 1533, thirteen years after the death of Raphael, he commenced his cartoons for the celebrated fresco of the Last Judgment, on the altar wall of the Sistine Chapel. It was continued during the pontificate of Paul III., and was finished in 1541.* Michelangelo did little more in painting from this period; the frescoes of the Cappella Paolina, built for Paul III., were his last works of the kind: they were finished in 1549, when he was seventy-four years of age. He had been appointed, in 1547, to succeed Antonio da San Gallo, as architect of St. Peter's, which, though the first stone had been laid by Julius II. in 1506, was still very little advanced: the original architect was Bramante. Michelangelo undertook the responsibility without salary. He continued architect throughout the pontificates of Paul III., Julius III., Marcellus II., Paul IV., and Pius IV., until his death; he carried the building to the base of the cupola.

Michelangelo died at Rome, February 17, 1564;† his body was taken to Florence, and, on the 14th of March following, was buried in a vault in the church of Santa Croce.

The opinions concerning Michelangelo are so uniform in their expressions of praise, and so well known, that to quote them would be superfluous; that of Raphael, however, may be here recorded: this prince of painters is said to have

---

* This great fresco measures 47 feet in height by 43 in width. The Cappella Sistina, or Sistine Chapel, was built by Baccio Pintelli, for Sixtus IV. in 1473, whence its name of Sistine. There are a ground plan and sections of the chapel in Appendix XIV. to the Third Report of the Commissioners on the Fine Arts. The chapel is of an oblong shape, with a vaulted roof; is 133 feet long, 43 wide, and 58 high. It is reserved for the especial use of the Popes: the church ceremonies of the first Sunday in Advent and of the Holy Week take place in it. The scrutiny also of the votes for the papal dignity takes place in this chapel, when the cardinals hold their conclave in the Vatican.

† He lived 88 years 11 months and 15 days, whence he must have been born in 1475, for Vasari expressly states that he died February 17, according to the Florentine mode of reckoning in 1563, but, according to the Roman, in 1564. *Vita di Michelangelo, Vite*, pt. iii. The Romans appear to have always commenced their year with January. See the ***Kalendarium Gregorianum Perpetuum***, Rome, 1582.

often exclaimed, that he thanked God he was born in the days of Michelangelo.*

To his acquirements already noticed, Michelangelo added the cultivation of poetry.† As a painter he is almost exclusively known by his productions in fresco: he executed a few works in distemper, one of which, a Holy Family in the gallery of Florence, painted for Angelo Doni, is well authenticated.‡

No. 8. A DREAM OF HUMAN LIFE. A naked figure, seated, is reclining against a globe; he appears to be roused by the sound of a trumpet which an angel is blowing immediately above him. Beneath his seat is a collection of masks illustrating the insincerity or duplicity of human dealings, and around him are visions of the many vices and depravities of mankind.

Engraved by J. Bonasone, the contemporary of Michelangelo; also by others; and recently in Jones's *National Gallery*. On wood, 2 ft. 1 in. *h.* by 1 ft. 9 in. *w.*

This picture, of which there are several repetitions, was painted from a design by Michelangelo, by one of his scholars, and was formerly in the Barberini Palace at Rome. It was bequeathed to the National Gallery, in 1831, by the Rev. W. H. Carr.

---

* Condivi, *Vita di Michelangelo Buonarroti*, &c. § lvii. Flor. 1746 (Ed. Prin. Rome, 1553). Duppa, *Life of Michelangelo*, London, 1816. Sir Joshua Reynolds' last discourse, the Fifteenth, consists chiefly of a recommendation to study the works of Michelangelo. The following are the concluding words of this discourse, and the last uttered by Sir Joshua in the Academy:—"If the high esteem and veneration in which Michelangelo has been held by all nations and in all ages should be put to the account of prejudice, it must still be granted that those prejudices could not have been entertained without a cause: the ground of our prejudice then becomes the source of our admiration. But, from whatever it proceeds, or whatever it is called, it will not, I hope, be thought presumptuous in me to appear in the train, I cannot say of his imitators, but of his admirers. I have taken another course, one more suited to my abilities, and to the taste of the times in which I live. Yet, however unequal I feel myself to that attempt, were I now to begin the world again, I would tread in the steps of that great master; to kiss the hem of his garment, to catch the slightest of his perfections, would be glory and distinction enough for an ambitious man.

"I feel a self-congratulation in knowing myself capable of such sensations as he intended to excite. I reflect, not without vanity, that these discourses bear testimony of my admiration of that truly divine man; and I should desire, that the last words which I should pronounce in this academy, and from this place, might be the name of Michelangelo."

† His poems, chiefly sonnets, were first published by his great-nephew Michelangelo Buonarroti, at Florence, in 1623, and again by Bottari in 1726 Select specimens have been translated into English by Mr. J. E. Taylor, *Michelangelo considered as a philosophic Poet; with translations, &c.*; 8vo., London, 1840. A *Life* of Michelangelo by Mr. J. S. Harford was published in 1856. London, 2 vols. 8vo., with a folio of plates.

‡ Lanzi, *Storia Pittorica, &c.*

MOLA.

PIETRO FRANCESCO MOLA was born in or near Milan,* in 1612. He went very early with his father, Gio. Battista Mola, an architect, to Rome, where he studied painting under the Cavaliere d'Arpino. He removed while still young to Venice, where he dwelt some time; but he afterwards returned to Rome, and then visited Milan, and subsequently Bologna, where he adopted the style of the Bolognese painters, imitating especially Albani, whose landscape pieces embellished with figures were particularly suited to the taste of Mola. He settled finally in Rome in the latter part of the pontificate of Innocent X., and died there in 1668.† He had held the office of President of the Academy of St. Luke, and he had been invited to settle in Paris as Court-painter to Louis XIV. Mola painted large and small figures, and excelled in landscape: in light and shade he was much influenced by the style of Guercino. He etched a few plates.

No. **69.** ST. JOHN PREACHING IN THE WILDERNESS; the Saviour is seen approaching in the distance:—

"The next day John seeth Jesus coming unto him, and saith, Behold the Lamb of God, which taketh away the sin of the world. This is he of whom I said, After me cometh a man which is preferred before me, for he was before me."—*John* i. 29, 30.

Landscape, with five small figures.

On canvas, 1 ft. 8½ in. *h.* by 2 ft. 2 in. *w.*

Formerly in the Robit‡ collection at Paris: bequeathed to the National Gallery, in 1831, by the Rev. W. H. Carr.

No. **160.** THE REPOSE; landscape with small figures. The "Holy Family," during the flight into Egypt, is reposing under the shade of some trees; three angels are hovering over the sleeping infant, who is watched by its mother: in the distance is a shepherd tending his flock. This subject, which is often treated by the Italian painters, is commonly called the Riposo.

---

* Lanzi says Como; in Goethe's *Winkelmann und sein Jahrhundert*, it is stated that he was born at Coldre, in Italian Switzerland.

† Passeri, *Vite de' Pittori*, &c. Pascoli, a more modern writer, says 1666; but Passeri, Mola's contemporary, is the better authority.

‡ Mr. Buchanan's *Memoirs of Painting* contains a catalogue of this and of many other valuable collections, which were dispersed at the period of the French Revolution.

Engraved by J. Cœlemans. On canvas, 1 ft. *h.* by 1 ft. 6 in. *w.* Formerly in the Orleans collection; bequeathed to the National Gallery, in 1838, by Lord Farnborough.

IL MORETTO.

ALESSANDRO BONVICINO, commonly called Il Moretto da Brescia, where he was born about the year 1490, was one of the greatest painters of the sixteenth century. He first studied under Fioravante Ferramola, a painter of Brescia, and afterwards with Titian at Venice. In the earlier period of his career, Moretto was an imitator of Titian, and was likewise an admirable portrait painter; but later in life he became an enthusiastic admirer of the works of Raphael, though it is not known that he ever visited Rome, and he endeavoured to paint in the style of the great Roman master. The works of Moretto range from 1524 until 1556.* The year of his death as well as that of his birth, is unknown, but he died probably about 1560.

Lanzi remarks that Moretto was better as an oil than as a fresco painter. He has left great works in both departments of the art; as the series of frescoes in the Villa Martinengo at Novarino, near Brescia, and several altar-pieces still preserved in the principal churches of Brescia, besides others in some of the public galleries in Europe. The following are the most celebrated of his works at Brescia. The "Five Virgin Martyrs," and the "Ascension of the Virgin," in San Clemente; the "Coronation of the Virgin," in SS. Nazaro e Celso; "St. Joseph," in the church of the Madonna delle Grazie; and "St. Nicholas of Bari," in Santa Maria de' Miracoli. In the Gallery of Vienna is a "Sta. Justina," formerly attributed to Pordenone.† The Galleries also of Berlin and Frankfort possess fine examples of this painter. In Santa Maria della Pietà at Venice, is a picture by Moretto, signed *Alex. Morettus Brix. F.* M.D.XLVIIII. He was the master of the celebrated portrait painter Moroni.‡

* Brognoli, *Nuova Guida per la Città di Brescia*, 1826, p. 228.

† Engraved as such by Rahl.

‡ Ridolfi, *Vite, &c.* Baron von Ransonnet, *Zeitschrift für Oestreichische Literatur und Kunst*; and the *Kunstblatt*, 1844, p. 160.

No. **299.** PORTRAIT OF AN ITALIAN NOBLEMAN, Count Sciarra Martinengo Cesaresco, of Brescia, seated, leaning his head upon his right hand. Half length, life-size. On the cap is a label, inscribed ΤΟΥ ΑΙΑΝ ΠΟΘΩ—" By the desire of the extreme," referring to his anxiety to avenge the death of his father, who was assassinated. Count Sciarra was killed in France in the Huguenot campaign which closed with the battle of Moncontour, Oct. 3rd, 1569.*

On canvas, 3 ft. 8½ in. *h.* by 3 ft. 1 in. *w.*

Formerly in the collection of Count Lechi, at Brescia, from which it passed into the possession of Mr. Henfrey, at Turin, from whom it was purchased for the National Gallery in 1858. When in the Lechi gallery it was attributed to Moretto's scholar, Moroni.

No. **625.** ST. BERNARDINO, of SIENA, with St. Jerome St. Joseph, St. Francis, and St. Nicholas of Bari; the Virgin and Child, with St. Catherine and St. Clara, appearing in the clouds above. St. Bernardino is holding up in his right hand a circle containing the monogram of Christ, I.H.S.,† in his left an open book, with the words "Pater manifestavi nomen tuum hominibus (Father I have manifested thy name to men);" at his feet are three mitres, inscribed with the names of the three cities of which he is said to have refused the bishoprics—Urbino, Siena, and Ferrara. He was canonized in 1458.

On canvas, 11 ft. 7. in. *h.* by 7 ft. 6 in. *w.*

Formerly in the possession of Dr. Faccioli at Verona, from whom it passed in 1852 into the collection of Lord Northwick, at Cheltenham. Bought at the sale of the Northwick pictures in 1859.

MORO.

ANTONIJ MORO, commonly called in this country Sir Antonio More (though it is not known when or where he was knighted), was born at Utrecht in 1525, and was the scholar of Jan Schoorel. He studied also in Italy, and he became eventually the most distinguished of the Dutch and Flemish portrait painters of his time. Moro was when still young taken into the service of the Emperor Charles V., for whom, in 1552, he visited in his capacity as portrait painter Madrid and Lisbon, and also England early in the

* Rossi, *Elogi Historici di Bresciani Illustri*, Brescia, 1620.

† Interpreted both as Jesus (ΙΗΣΟΥΣ), and as Jesus Hominum Salvator: See the inscription on the picture by Segna di Buonaventura, p. 216, where they signify *Jesus*.

reign of Queen Mary, who appointed him her painter. After the Queen's death in 1558, Moro remained in the service of her husband Philip II. of Spain, and visited Madrid a second time: besides portraits, he executed some copies of Titian for that monarch.

Having made himself obnoxious to the Inquisition, Moro was compelled to leave Madrid. He finally established himself at Brussels, where he had secured the protection of the Duke of Alva; and though invited back to Madrid by Philip, he did not venture to return to Spain.

Moro was also an historical painter. Van Mander mentions an unfinished picture of th "Circumcision of Christ" by him, for the Cathedral of Antwerp, as one of his most successful works. He died rich at Antwerp in 1581. The prices Moro received for his portraits were very large, varying from one hundred to two hundred ducats, in Portugal, and one hundred pounds in England, where he was very much employed as a portrait painter in the reign of Queen Mary.* His own portrait is in the Painters' Gallery at Florence.†

No. **184**. PORTRAIT OF JEANNE D'ARCHEL, of the House of Egmont, in her eighteenth year, dressed in red, with a gold chain on her neck. Count Egmont was beheaded by the Duke of Alva in 1568.‡ Three-quarter length, life size.

On canvas, 2 ft. 5 in. *h.* by 2 ft. 1½ in. *w.*

Dated 1561. Formerly in the collection of Mr. Beckford in Fonthill Abbey, from which it passed in 1823 into the possession of Colonel Hugh Baillie. Purchased for the National Gallery from M. C. J. Nieuwenhuys in 1858.

MURILLO.

BARTHOLOMÉ ESTÉBAN MURILLO was born at Seville, and baptized on January 1, 1618. After receiving some

---

* Moro, says Walpole, "remained in England during the reign of Mary, and was much employed; but having neglected, as is frequent, to write the names on the portraits he drew, most of them have lost part of their value, by our ignorance of the persons represented. The poorest performers have it in their power to add so much merit to their works as can be conferred by identifying the subjects, which would be a little reparation to the curious world, though some families should miss imaginary ancestors."—*Anecdotes of Painting*, p. 141, Ed. 1849.

† Van Mander, *Het Leven der Schilders*; Amsterdam, 1764, vol. 1, p. 172. Walpole; *Anecdotes of Painting*, &c.

‡ Clouet, *Eloge historique du Comte d'Egmont*; Brussels, 1825.

education, he was placed with Juan del Castillo, a relation, to learn painting, for which he had shown a decided ability. In 1641, in his twenty-fourth year, having acquired a little money by painting heads of Saints and sacred pictures for South America, he was induced by Pedro de Moya, a former fellow student, who had studied in England under Vandyck, to proceed to Madrid, with the intention, as some writers state, of going on to England and to Italy. Arrived at Madrid he was kindly treated by Velazquez, his *paisano*, or fellow townsman; soon the death of Vandyck, his own limited resources, and the counsels of Velazquez, induced him to remain at Madrid, where every facility to finish his studies was procured for him by Velazquez, which the high position of that master, as painter to the king, enabled him to offer.

In the year 1644, Murillo had made such progress that Velazquez recommended him then to prosecute his journey to Rome, and offered him letters of recommendation from the King; Murillo, however, now felt no desire to go to Italy, and he returned in the following year, 1645, to Seville. His first works in Seville were a series of pictures illustrating the life of St. Francis, in the Franciscan convent of that city; and, though unknown in his native place up to this time, he thenceforth became the *caposcuola*, or head of the school of Seville; his principal rivals being Francisco de Herrera the younger, and Juan de Valdes Leal. In 1648 he married a lady of fortune of Pilas, and from this time his house became a favourite resort of people of taste and fashion. In 1660 he established the Academy of Seville, of which he was in that year president, but he never filled the office after the first year.

Among Murillo's principal works were eight large pictures, painted for the Hospital of St. George, called La Caridad, and which he completed in 1674: they represent Moses striking the rock; the miracle of the loaves and fishes; the Return of the Prodigal Son; Abraham visited by the Angels;* Christ healing the Sick of the Palsy (commonly called the Pool of Bethesda);† the Angel liberating St. Peter from Prison; and the two following illustrating charity,—San Juan de Dios bearing a poor man upon his back; and Santa Isabel, Queen of Hungary, healing the sick poor; the last picture

* These two pictures are now in the possession of the Duke of Sutherland.
† Now in the possession of Mr. George Tomline.

went by the name of El Tiñoso, from the diseased head of the principal figure. Many of these pictures are now dispersed: some of them formed part of the acquisitions of Marshal Soult during the Peninsular war; the Tiñoso is at Madrid.

Murillo's last work was the large altar-piece of St. Catherine, painted at Cadiz for the church of the Capuchins there: this picture he never completed; owing to a fall which he had from the scaffolding while engaged upon it, he was forced to return to Seville, and died there not long afterwards, April 3, 1682. Two sons and a daughter survived him; his daughter had taken the veil eight years before his death.

Murillo, in the latter part of his life, changed both his style and his subjects. His earlier pictures, which are painted in a forcible manner, are chiefly illustrative of humble life; his latter works, with equal truth, are in a more elevated and chaste style, and are almost exclusively scriptural or religious in their subjects. He occasionally painted landscapes. His favourite masters were Spagnoletto, Vandyck, and Velazquez.*

No. **13.** THE HOLY FAMILY. The youthful Saviour, with the Virgin seated on the right, and Joseph kneeling on the left, is represented standing on the base of a ruined column: the Holy Spirit is descending upon him from above, where the Father is represented supported by angels.

Engraved by A. Bridoux. On canvas, 9 ft. 6 in. *h.* by 6 ft. 10 in. *w.*

This picture, which is one of Murillo's last works, was painted at Cadiz when he was probably about sixty years of age. It belonged to the family of the Marquis del Pedroso until 1810, during the French occupation of Spain, when it was sold and brought to this country: and, after passing through various hands, was in 1837 purchased from Mr. T. B. Bulkeley Owen for the National Gallery. It is sometimes called the Pedroso Murillo: it is mentioned by Palomino, and by Cean Bermudez.

No. **74.** A SPANISH PEASANT BOY. A laughing boy, with one shoulder exposed, is leaning on his elbows, and appears to be looking out at a window.

---

* Cean Bermudez, *Diccionario Historico de los mas Ilustres Profesores da las Bellas Artes en Espana*, Madrid, 1800; and the Letter of the same author on the *School of Seville*, Cadiz, 1806; translated in Davies's *Life of Murillo*, London, 1819.

Engraved by J. Rogers, for Jones's *National Gallery;* and by W. Humphrys, for the *Associated Engravers.* On canvas, 1 ft. 9 in. *h.* by 1 ft. 3 in. *w.*

Formerly in the collection of the Marquis of Lansdowne; presented to the National Gallery in 1826 by Mr. M. M. Zachary.

No. **176.** St. John and the Lamb. An image of the divine mission of the Baptist. St. John, a child, embraces the lamb, and with his left hand points towards heaven: an illustration of the words,—"Behold the Lamb of God," *John* i. 29. The standard of the Lamb is lying upon the ground: a dark rocky landscape forms the back-ground.

Engraved by V. Green, F. Bacon, and others. On canvas, 5 ft. 5 in. *h.* by 3 ft. 7 in. *w.*

Formerly in the collection of M. Robit, from which it passed into the possession of Sir Simon Clarke, at the sale of whose pictures, in 1840, it was purchased for the National Gallery.

ORCAGNA.

Andrea di Cione Arcagnuolo, commonly called Orcagna, one of the most distinguished of the early Florentine artists, as painter, sculptor, and architect, was born in Florence about 1315. Having acquired the rudiments of his art from his father, who was a goldsmith, he became the pupil of Andrea Pisano.

When still young he was engaged with his brother Bernardo in Santa Maria Novella. The Heaven and Hell, painted by the two brothers, from Dante in the Strozzi chapel in that church, are still preserved. They executed similar subjects in the Campo Santo at Pisa; Andrea painting "the Triumph of Death," and "the Last Judgment;" he afterwards repeated the same subjects in Santa Croce at Florence, but these have long since perished. Besides these considerable works in fresco, Orcagna painted several altar-pieces in tempera; one for the Strozzi chapel in Santa Maria Novella, signed and dated 1357, which is still preserved, and is one of his best works; he executed about the same time the great example in this collection.

As an architect, Orcagna constructed the church of Or San Michele, and its Tabernacle in 1359; he also designed the celebrated "Loggia de' Lanzi" in the Piazza del Granduca at Florence, which, though decided upon by the authorities in 1356, was not actually commenced until twenty years later;* Orcagna died before it was completed. The accounts of him do not reach later than 1376; and in that year he was dead.† According to Vasari, he died aged only sixty.

Orcagna was in the habit of signing his name differently on his sculpture and in his pictures; on the former he wrote *Fece Andrea di Cione, Pittore,* and on the latter *Fece Andrea di Cione Scultore.* Francia adopted a similar practice. The principal scholar of Andrea was Francesco Traini: his brothers Bernardo and Jacopo, who survived him, completed his unfinished works; Bernardo the pictures, and Jacopo the sculpture.

No. **569.** The Coronation of the Virgin, Angels and Saints in Adoration. A large altar-piece in three divisions. In the centre, Christ crowning the Virgin, with two Angels standing on each side of the throne, and ten others below, eight of them kneeling, some playing various musical instruments—a keyed organ, harp, lute, viol, guitar, and bag-pipes.

In each of the side pictures are twenty-four Saints, kneeling in rows around the throne in adoration. On the spectator's left is St. Peter, supporting on his knee the model of the church of San Pietro Maggiore in Florence, for which the picture was painted.‡

---

* It was begun September 22nd, 1376, and finished June 5, 1377. Gaye, *Carteggio, &c.*, vol. i. pp. 526-8.

† Bonaini, *Memorie inediti*, p. 105. Vasari, Ed. Le Monnier, vol. ii. p. 134.

‡ As many of the Saints here represented are without their characteristic emblems, it is difficult to identify them all. They appear to be, however, as nearly as can be ascertained the following:—

On the spectator's left,—

1. St. Peter.
2. St. Bartholomew.
3. St. Stephen.
4. St. John the Evangelist.
5. An Apostle.
6. St. Sigismond.
7. St. Ambrose.
8. St. Francis.
9. Mary Magdalen.
10. St. Philip.
11. St. Cosmas?
12. St. Blaise.
13. St. Gregory the Great.
14. St. Benedict.
15. St. Lucy.
16. An Apostle.
17. St. Luke.
18. St. Clement?
19. A Bishop.
20. Eastern King, Balthasar.
21. St. Elizabeth of Hungary
22. Eastern King, Caspar.
23. Eastern King, Melchior.
24. St. Euphemia?

In tempera, on wood, the centre picture, 6 ft. 9½ in *h.* to the point of the arch, by 3 ft. 9½ in. *w.*; the side pictures, 5 ft. 6½ in. *h.* by 3 ft. 8½ in *w.*; the Gothic frame, 9 ft. 7 in. *h.* by 13 ft. 1 in *w.*

Originally painted for the church of San Pietro Maggiore in Florence, where it was placed over the high altar; in 1677 it had been removed to the Della Rena chapel.* It was inherited from the Della Rena family by the Marchese Roberto Pucci, from whom it passed into the possession of the late proprietors in 1846. Purchased at Florence from the Lombardi-Baldi collection in 1857.

The following nine pictures also were portions of this altarpiece, being originally placed over the three principal pictures described above.

No. **570.** THE TRINITY. The Holy Spirit, in the form of a dove, is descending upon a crucifix, which is supported by the Almighty.

Nos. **571, 572.** ANGELS ADORING, constituting the sides of No. 570.

In tempera, on wood, 2 ft. 10 in. *h.* by 1 ft. 3 in. *w.*

No. **573.** THE NATIVITY, and the Annunciation to the Shepherds. The child is lying in the manger, over which is hovering a choir of Angels.

No. **574.** THE ADORATION OF THE KINGS OF THE EAST, camels and attendants in the background. St. Joseph is receiving a golden vessel, one of the presents, from the hand of the child. Immediately over the stable is a star.

No. **575.** THE RESURRECTION OF CHRIST, who is ascending with a standard marked with a red cross, in his hand; below, the Roman guards are asleep around the tomb.

No. **576.** THE "THREE MARIES" AT THE SEPULCHRE, Mark xvi. 1. Mary Magdalene, Mary the mother of James, and Salome, are standing with vases of sweet spices in their

---

On the spectator's right,—

1. St. Paul.
2. St. Matthew.
3. St. Lawrence.
4. St. John the Baptist.
5. St. Damianus ?
6. A youth with sword.
7. St. Nicholas of Bari.
8. St. Dominic.
9. St. Catherine of Alexandria.
10. St. James the Greater.
11. An Apostle.
12. A Monk with purple scull cap.
13. St. Bernard.
14. St. Antony Abbot.
15. St. Agnes.
16. An Apostle.
17. St. Mark.
18. St. Marcellinus ?
19. St. Augustine.
20. St. Jerome.
21. St. Scholastica.
22. St. Zenobius.
23. A youth with sword.
24. St. Reparata ?

* Cinelli, *Bellezze della Città di Firenze, &c.*, p. 354.

hands, by the side of the vacant tomb; on the opposite side are two angels.

No. **577.** THE ASCENSION OF CHRIST, the Virgin and Apostles grouped in a circle below regarding the ascending Saviour.

No. **578.** THE DESCENT OF THE HOLY SPIRIT.

"And suddenly there came a sound from Heaven as of a rushing mighty wind, and it filled all the house where they were sitting. And there appeared unto them cloven tongues like as of fire, and it sat upon each of them. And they were all filled with the Holy Ghost, and began to speak with other tongues as the spirit gave them utterance."

"Now, when this was noised abroad the multitude came together, and were confounded, because that every man heard them speak in his own language." —Acts ii. 2.

The composition is in two divisions, the descent of the Holy Spirit being represented above, and below, the multitude confounded, every man hearing his own language.

In tempera, on wood, each 3 ft. ½ in. *h.* by 1 ft. 7 in. *w.*

Portions of No. 569. Purchased at Florence from the Lombardi-Baldi collection in 1857.

ORLEY.

BERNARD VAN ORLEY, called also Bernard van Brussel, was born at Brussels, 1470-1, and studied under Raphael, in Rome; he and Michael Cocxie had the superintendence of the manufacture of the tapestries of the Vatican made from Raphael's cartoons for Leo X. Van Orley died at Brussels, January 6th, 1541. He painted in oil, and in *tempera*, and for glass. Some of the windows of St. Gudule, at Brussels, are from Van Orley's cartoons. The brilliancy of his colour in some of his oil pictures is attributed to their being painted upon a gilt ground. He was in the service of Margaret, Regent of the Netherlands, and had also the title of court painter to the Emperor Charles V., and he is said to have visited England. There are a few engravings by his hand. His pictures are scarce.*

No. **655.** THE MAGDALEN, READING. She is dressed in crimson velvet, and looking into an illuminated book;

* *Het Leven*, &c.; Michiels, *La Peinture Flamande*, &c., vol. iii.; Walpole, *Anecdotes*, &c.

on the table before her is a vase. Half-figure, small life size.

On wood, 16¼ in. *h.* by 14½ in. *w.*
Purchased at Paris, from M. Edmond Beaucousin, in 1860.

L'ORTOLANO.

Giovanni Battista Benvenuti, of Ferrara, called L'Ortolano, from his father's occupation, who was a gardener, is said to have studied the works of Raphael and Bagnacavallo at Bologna about 1512–13.* The circumstances of his life are, however, very little known, his works and his biography being confounded with that of Garofalo. He is supposed to have died about 1525, but he must have been still young at that date.

No. **669.** St. Sebastian, St. Rock, and St. Demetrius. St. Sebastian is in the centre of the picture, tied to a tree and pierced with arrows; in the foreground is lying a cross-bow. On his right is St. Rock as a pilgrim, and on his left St. Demetrius, in armour. The background is a landscape; on the left are seen some horsemen near a village, and in the distance is a walled town. Entire figures, life-size.

On wood, 7 ft. 7 in. *h.* by 5 ft. 1½ in. *w.*
Originally, and as lately as 1844, the altar-piece of the parochial church of Bondeno, near Ferrara, where it was generally considered the painter's masterpiece. Purchased in 1861 of Mr. Alexander Barker, who procured the picture from Sig. Ubaldo Sgherbi, and brought it to England.

PACCHIAROTTO.

Jacopo Pacchiarotto, the son of Bartolommeo, was born at Siena in 1474. His career was troubled and unfortunate; in 1525 he pleaded a numerous family, and great poverty, as a justification of his receiving alms from the authorities of the city; he had then six daughters: in 1526 he received an aid of twelve scudi from the municipality.

---

* Or 1507–8. This fact is ascertained from the title of a book of sketches noticed by Baruffaldi—"Studio di me Zoane Bapta d. Benvegnù fatto in Bologna suxo le dipinture del Bagnac° e del Sangio da Urbino, a li anni MD.VII. et MD.VIII." These dates are otherwise read as MDXII., MDXIII. See Lanzi, *Storia Pittorica, &c.*, vol. v. p. 202; Baruffaldi, *Vite de' Pittori, &c.*, vol. i. p. 168; and Laderchi, *Pittura Ferrarese*, p. 93.

Pacchiarotto executed considerable works at Siena; but as he is omitted by Vasari, he has been neglected and forgotten also by posterity, and his best works have been attributed to Pietro Perugino.

His troubles seem to have continued: in 1535 he was involved in a conspiracy against the authorities, by which he endangered his life, and he is said to have fled from Siena to France, where he was protected by Il Rosso, who employed him on the extensive works which Francis I. was then carrying out at Fontainebleau: he was again in Siena in 1536. In 1539, however, he was banished and outlawed by the Government, but through the intercession of his wife, Girolama, he was pardoned and restored to his family August 17, 1540: from this date nothing further is known of him.

Pacchiarotto's principal work is the fresco in the church of Santa Caterina of Siena, of that saint visiting the body of Saint Agnes, of Montepulciano, which, says Speth, can be compared only with Raphael; and he adds, that to describe Pacchiarotto as of the school of Perugino is only magnifying the injustice he has already undergone in having had some of his best works attributed to that master. His forms are fuller than Perugino's, and though his taste is that of the *quattrocento*, some of his heads have great beauty of feature, and sweetness of expression; his colouring has very considerable force. He is distinct from the Girolamo di Pacchia slightly noticed by Vasari in the "Life" of Il Sodoma.*

No. **246.** MADONNA AND CHILD. The Virgin, in a blue hood and mantle, seated, with the Child on her knees; landscape back-ground. Half-length, small life-size.

On wood, in oil, 2 ft. 5 in. *h.* by 2 ft. *w.* Purchased for the National Gallery at the sale of M. Joly De Bammeville's collection, iu 1854.

PADOVANI'NO.

ALESSANDRO VAROTA'RI, commonly called PADOVANINO, from his birth-place Padua,† where he was born in 1590, was

---

* Gaye, *Carteggio Inedito d'Artisti*; Lanzi, *Storia Pittorica*, &c.; and Speth, *Kunst in Italien*, vol. II. p. 57. Vasari, *Vite, &c.*, Ed. Flor., 1846 *et seq.* vol. XI.

† In Italian, Padova.

the son of Dario Várotari, a Veronese painter. Alessandro lost his father when very young, and went early to Venice, where he became a diligent student of the pictures of Titian, and he is accounted one of the most successful imitators of that painter. He lived alternately at Venice and Padua, and his pictures are seldom seen out of these places. He died in 1650.

Padovanino excelled in painting children, and often introduced them into his pictures: he was also a good landscape-painter. His masterpiece is the "Marriage at Cana," formerly in the monastery of San Giovanni di Verdara at Padua, now in the Academy at Venice. Like many of the Venetian painters, he was more remarkable for facility of execution and for colouring than for correctness of form.*

No. **70.** CORNELIA AND HER CHILDREN. Cornelia, daughter of the elder Scipio Africanus, and "mother of the Gracchi," when asked by a Campanian lady, who was ostentatious of her jewels, to show her her ornaments, pointed to her two sons, Tiberius and Caius, just then returning from school, and said, "These are my ornaments."† Composition of four figures, of the natural size.

On canvas, 4 ft. 8 in. *h.* by 4 ft. *w.*
Bequeathed to the National Gallery, in 1837, by Lieut. Col. Ollney.

PALMEZZANO.

MARCO PALMEZZANO, one of the principal painters of the Romagna, was born at Forlì in or about the year 1456;‡ he was the scholar of Melozzo da Forlì, and occasionally signed his name *Marchus de Melotius*, as in a picture in the Church del Carmine at Forlì, and in another in the Church of San Francesco dei Zoccolanti at Matelica; the latter example is dated 1501. His ordinary signature was

---

* Ridolfi, *Le Maraviglie dell' Arte, &c.*; Orlandi, *Abecedario Pittorico*, Bologna, 1719; Lanzi, *Storia Pittorica, &c.*

† See Plutarch's lives of the Gracchi; the anecdote is told by Valerius Maximus.

‡ The Palmezzani family at Forli is in possession of a portrait of this painter, on the frame of which is inscribed—MARCUS PALMESANUS NOB. FOROL. SEMETIPSUM PINXIT OCTAVA—ÆTATIS SUÆ 1536. Memorie intorno a Marco Palmezani da Forli e ad alcuni suoi dipinti Forli 1844. See also Vasari, Ed. Le Monnier, *Commentario alla Vita dei Genga*, vol. xi. p. 108.

Marcus Palmezanus Pictor Foroliviensis faciebat. He was still living in 1537; a picture signed by him and bearing that date was formerly in the Ercolani Gallery at Bologna.

His works are generally characterized by the prevailing hardness of style of the fifteenth century, but are not deficient in feeling or expression.

No. **596.** The Deposition in the Tomb. The dead Christ is being placed in the tomb by the Virgin, Mary Magdalen, and St. John the Evangelist; the Virgin, on the right, is supporting the body in a sitting posture, while the Magdalen, on the same side, is kneeling, holding the left arm of Christ, and compassionately regarding the wounded hand. On the other side is St. John, clasping his hands in sorrow. To the spectator's right is standing San Mercuriale, first bishop of Forlì, holding the Guelphic banner of the Church, a red cross on a white flag: on the extreme left is San Valeriano with the standard of Forlì, a white flag striped with blue. In the foreground is a green cloth, hanging on the side of the tomb in front. Half figures life-size.*

On wood, 3 ft. 3 in. *h.* by 5 ft. $5\frac{1}{2}$ in. *w.*

Originally of a semicircular shape, but subsequently shortened and piecened so as to form a quadrangular picture.

This picture was the lunette of an altar-piece, representing "Christ administering the sacrament to the Apostles," now in the gallery at Forlì, and which was placed in the Cathedral of Forlì in 1506. Purchased in Rome from Signor Gismondi in 1858.†

PANNI'NI.

Giova'nni Pa'olo Pannini, *Cavaliere,* was born at Piacenza in 1691, but lived chiefly at Rome, where he attained a great reputation by his views of ruins and other architectural pictures. He died at Rome in 1764.‡ His shadows are considered generally too dark and too brown for exteriors.

---

* See a detailed description of this picture in Reggiani's *Alcune Memorie intorno il Pittore Marco Melozzo da Forlì,* p. 16, Forlì, 1834, where it is erroneously attributed to Melozzo da Forlì.

† Though the principal picture, which is engraved in Rosini's *Storia della Pittura Italiana,* pl. 141, is signed *Marcus Palmezanus faciebat,* it is described by Vasari, ed. Le Monnier, vol. xi. p. 93, together with the *lunette* and *predella,* as the work of Rondinello of Ravenna. Vasari's error was corrected by Scannelli as early as 1657. See *Il Microcosmo della Pittura,* p. 281.

‡ Lanzi, *Storia Pittorica, &c.*

No. **138.** ANCIENT RUINS, WITH FIGURES. The pyramid of Cestius in the middle-ground. A composition.

On canvas, 1 ft. 7½ in. *h.* by 2 ft. 1 in. *w.*

Bequeathed to the National Gallery, in 1837, by Lieut.-Col. Ollney.

PARMIGIA'NO.

GIRO'LAMO FRANCESCO MARIA MAZZO'LA, commonly called PARMIGIA'NO, and sometimes PARMIGIANI'NO, from his birth-place Parma, was born Jan. 11, 1503.* In consequence of the death of his father, Filippo Mazzola, when he was still very young, he was brought up by his uncles Michele and Pietro Ilario, who, as well as his father, were both painters, and Parmigiano was determined to follow the same profession. When Correggio visited Parma in 1519, Parmigiano was much struck with the works of that great master, and he became a successful imitator of his style. After acquiring considerable distinction in Parma, he went in 1523 to Rome, where he was well received by Clement VII. He was at Rome during the memorable sack of the city by the soldiers of Charles V. under Bourbon, in 1527; and the picture of St. Jerome in this collection was painted there at that period.

Parmigiano left Rome shortly after this event, and resided some time at Bologna. In 1531 he returned to Parma, and was engaged to execute some extensive frescoes in the choir of the church of Santa Maria della Steccata, to be completed by the 10th of November 1532, Parmigiano having received half payment (200 gold scudi) in advance; but, owing to his repeated delays, having scarcely commenced the frescoes after a lapse of five or six years from the time of the original agreement, he was thrown into prison by the authorities of the church for breach of contract. Instead of prosecuting the work after his release from prison, according to his promise, he fled to Casal Maggiore, in the territory of Cremona, where he died very soon afterwards, August 24, 1540, in the thirty-seventh year of his age.

The well-known figure of "Moses breaking the Tables of the Law," is a part of the unfinished frescoes of the Steccata.

---

* According to the Register, or 1504 according to the present mode of reckoning; 1504 is the year given by Vasari.

Sir Joshua Reynolds* says of this figure,—" We are at a loss which to admire most, the correctness of the drawing or the grandeur of the conception." The most celebrated of Parmigiano's altar-pieces is the Santa Margherita in the academy at Bologna: it was preferred by Guido to the St. Cecilia of Raphael. Of the easel-pictures of this master, the most admired is the "Cupid making a Bow," painted about 1536 for Francesco Boiardi, and now in the gallery at Vienna: it is well known in prints and copies, and was commonly attributed to Correggio. Parmigiano etched a few plates, and is said also to have executed several wood-cuts. His drawings are celebrated.†

No. **33.** THE VISION OF ST. JEROME. Such is the title given to this picture by Vasari. John the Baptist, kneeling on one knee on the ground, is pointing upwards to a vision of the Virgin with the infant Saviour; in the middle-ground is St. Jerome lying on his back, asleep; his figure is much foreshortened. Composition of four figures, somewhat larger than the life.

Engraved by J. Bonasone, the painter's contemporary; and by W. T. Fry, in Jones's *National Gallery*. On wood, 11 ft. 6 in. *h.* by 5 ft. *w.*

This picture was painted at Rome, in 1527, in Parmigiano's twenty-fourth year, for Maria Buffalina, to be placed in her family chapel, in the church of San Salvatore di Lauro, at Città di Castello: he was in the act of completing the work when the city was stormed by the Imperialists under the Constable Bourbon.‡ It remained in Città di Castello until 1780, when the church of

---

* Discourse XV.

† Vasari, *Vite de' Pittori, &c.*; Affò, *Vita del Graziosissimo Pittore, Francesco Mazzola, detto il Parmigianino*, Parma, 1784; *Sketches of the Lives of Correggio and Parmigiano*, London, 1823.

‡ The anecdote related by the Padre Affò is a modern counterpart to more than one classic story of the kind, resembling more particularly that of the painter Protogenes, who, we are told, pursued his occupation in tranquillity while Rhodes was stormed by Demetrius Poliorcetes. "Parmigiano was earnestly engaged in giving the last touches to the picture for La Buffalina, when the walls of Rome having been scaled and the city itself taken by the invaders, the wild soldiery ran from house to house intent on spoil. The painter absorbed in his occupation, paid no attention to the roar of the artillery, the tumult of the people, or the shouts of the military, till some of the enemy rushing into the very house and searching every corner, suddenly entered the room where the artist was at work. The amazement of the soldiers on seeing him thus quietly pursuing his labours was greater than his own on finding himself surrounded by lawless and hostile men. Fortunately the leader of the band, who had meanwhile taken possession of the house, happened to be an amateur of painting. He felt an interest for the artist, and contented himself by only requiring him to execute a good number of drawings."—Affò, *Vita, &c.*, p. 60.

San Salvatore was ruined by an earthquake, and the picture was purchased by an English collector, and brought to this country. After passing through different hands, it was finally purchased by the Governors of the British Institution, at the sale of Mr. G. Watson Taylor's pictures, in 1826, and by them presented to the National Gallery. There are several old copies of the picture extant.

PERUGI'NO.

PIETRO VANNU'CCI, commonly called IL PERUGINO, was born at Città della Pieve about 1446: he was established in the neighbouring city of Perugia, where he had the right of citizenship, whence his surname of Perugino.* His first master is unknown; but Vasari states that when in Florence he studied under Andrea Verocchio: this is confirmed by various circumstances. Perugino's first works of note were painted in Florence; he afterwards distinguished himself by his works at Siena, Vallombrosa, the Certosa di Pavia, Naples, Borgo San Sepolcro, Bologna, and Rome. He executed several works for Pope Sixtus IV. in the newly-built Cappella Sistina, and in the Stanze of the Vatican. He began his frescoes in Rome about 1480, four years before the demise of Sixtus, and appears to have been employed there altogether about ten years. In 1495, after having executed some works in Florence, he was again engaged in Perugia, and it was then that Raphael, a boy of twelve years of age, was placed by his uncles with the great painter; for Pietro was now the most celebrated of all the Umbrian masters.

After this period, Perugino executed several works for Florence, and other places; but the great *cinquecénto* style, which was now rapidly superseding that of the earlier schools, began to obscure the reputation of the older painters; and when Pietro saw the Cartoons of Michelangelo and Leonardo Da Vinci at Florence, in 1506, he felt that his own star was declining, and accordingly set himself against the innovation. He made no secret of his distaste for the new style, and having unreservedly expressed his opinions in the presence of Michelangelo, the imperious *innovator* called him a *dunce*† in art; Pietro took him before a magistrate for the affront, but,

---

* He is sometimes called Petrus de Castro Plebis, and Civis Perusinus. Mariotti, *Lettere Pittoriche Perugine.*

† Goffo nell' arte: literally, inexpert. Vasari, *Vite de' Pittori, &c.*

according to Vasari, the dispute ended with little honour to the complainant.

Perugino returned to Perugia, where he married a young wife; and after executing several works there and in the neighbourhood, he died, possessed of considerable property, at Castello di Fontignano, in 1524, at the advanced age of seventy-eight.*

Perugino was one of the principal *quattrocento* masters. As an oil-painter his example was important. Vasari, in the *Proemio* or Introduction to the third part of his *Lives of the Painters,* speaks of the great sensation produced on the artists of the time by the rich and forcible colouring of Perugino and Francia, an excellence then, in a great measure, new; since those masters were among the first Italian oil-painters. The scholars of Perugino were numerous, and no pupils probably have been more faithful to the style of their master: with the single exception of Raphael, they all persevered in the *quattrocentismo,* or that peculiarity of taste in design which had prevailed from the time of Masaccio to that of Michelangelo and Raphael; but as regards colouring most of his imitators were inferior to him.

No. **181.** THE VIRGIN AND INFANT CHRIST, WITH ST. JOHN. Landscape back-ground. Three small figures; the Virgin and St. John half-length.

On wood, 2 ft. 2½ in. *h.* by 1 ft. 5½ in. *w.*

This picture, which is painted in tempera, was obtained by the late Mr. Beckford at Perugia, and was purchased of him for the National Gallery, in 1841. It has been attributed to Lo Spagna, a fellow-scholar of Raphael with Perugino. Petrus Peruginus is inscribed in gold on the hem of the mantle of the Virgin.

* The memoirs of Perugino are numerous; besides the notice of Vasari there are—a notice in the *Vite de' Pittori Perugini,* by Pascoli, 1732; Mariotti, *Lettere Pittoriche Perugine,* 1788; Orsini, *Vita, Elogio e Memorie dell' Egregio Pittore Pietro Perugino e degli Scolari di esso,* Perugia, 1804; and Mezzanotte, *Della Vita e delle Opere di Pietro Vanuucci da Castello della Pieve, Commentario Istorico,* Perugia, 1836.

No. **288.** The Virgin adoring the Infant Christ. Three principal portions of an altar-piece. The centre picture represents the Virgin adoring the Infant, who is presented to her by an angel; three distant angels, standing on clouds and singing, appear above. The compartment on the left of the spectator represents the Archangel Michael; that on the right, the Archangel Raphael with the young Tobias.

On wood, each compartment 4 ft. 2 in. *h.*; the centre compartment 2 ft. 1½ in. *w.*; the side pictures each 1 ft. 10½ in. *w.*

This picture was painted by Perugino, as recorded by Vasari, for the Certosa, or Carthusian convent near Pavia. The entire altar-piece consisted of six compartments. Above the three portions already described were—in the centre, a figure of the Almighty, which is still in its original place in the Certosa; on the sides, the subject of the Annunciation, the Angel on the left of the spectator, the Virgin on the right; all these were half figures. The two last-named have disappeared; but their places, as well as the places of the three portions now in this collection, have long been supplied by copies. The three principal pictures above described were purchased from the Certosa at Pavia by one of the Melzi family in 1786, and were bought for the National Gallery of Duke Melzi of Milan in 1856.*

The left compartment is inscribed below:—

PETRVS PERVSINVS

PINXIT

---

* Some connoisseurs have assumed that Raphael assisted his master in this work. Rumohr has stated various reasons for concluding that Raphael aided in its execution. "To me," he observes, "it appeared throughout Raphaelized; in the general treatment as in the parts, altogether re-cast." He speaks of the improved action of the St. Michael, as compared with that of the same saint in an altar-piece of Vallombrosa, painted by Perugino in 1500; and remarks that "the hand on the shield is very happily drawn from nature, not in the customary manner of Perugino, but true and graceful." *Italienische Forschungen*, Dritter Theil, 1831, p. 27.

Passavant (*Rafael von Urbino, &c.* i. p. 59), speaks of the picture as follows: "The truly Raphaelesque feeling which pervades every part; the more accurate study of nature (as compared with Perugino's manner), which is especially remarkable in the hands, have often given rise to the opinion that Raphael must have assisted his master to a considerable extent in this work. This opinion receives an additional confirmation from a drawing from nature as a study for the Archangel Raphael with the young Tobias, formerly in the Lawrence Collection, and which appears to be by Raphael. From the great merits of the picture it must be assumed that if Raphael really assisted in its production its date could not be earlier than 1503." At that date Raphael was twenty years of age.

The drawing in question is now in the Randolph Gallery at Oxford; it is thus described by Dr. Waagen:—"No. 75, Tobias and the Angel, on tinted paper, with silver point. Study for that part of Perugino's altar-piece for the Certosa, at Pavia, which Raphael executed, and which is now in the possession

PERUZZI.

Baldassa're Peruzzi, sometimes called Baldassare da Siena, was born at Accajano, near Siena, in the beginning of the year 1481. His master is not known. His first work of merit was executed at Volterra; and he distinguished himself at Rome, in the beginning of the pontificate of Julius II. (1503-13). At Rome, having attracted the notice of Agostino Chigi, of Siena, he turned his attention to the study of perspective and architecture, in which he obtained no less distinction than in painting. For Agostino Chigi he built a villa—the well-known Farnesina—on the western bank of the Tiber. From this period his time was chiefly devoted to architecture. He was appointed by Leo X., in 1520, the successor to Raphael as architect of St. Peter's; the salary, however, of this post was only 250 scudi per annum. At the sack of Rome, in 1527, he was plundered of all he possessed by the Imperial soldiers, and was forced to paint a picture of their general, the Constable Bourbon, who had been killed in the first assault of the city.* After the completion of this picture, he escaped to Siena, where he was well received by his fellow-citizens. He was made city architect, was employed in the superintendence of the fortifications, and received a pension from the authorities. After a few years he returned again to Rome, and died there in his fifty-sixth year, at the close of 1536, not without suspicion of having been poisoned. He was buried in the Pantheon, near the tomb of Raphael. Antonio da San Gallo succeeded him as architect of St. Peter's.†

Though Peruzzi excelled in drawing, his occupations were too various to admit of his acquiring the reputation of a great painter; but as an architect, he ranks with the artists of the highest class.

---

of Duke Melzi of Milan. Of delicate feeling for nature, and most elevated in the expression of melancholy in the head of the angel. About 1501."—*Treasures of Art in Great Britain, &c.* Murray, 1854, vol. ii. p. 56.

The glowing colouring of this work characterizes the best period of Perugino. The art of oil painting was, even at this date, not universally adopted in Central Italy, but in the hands of Perugino and Francia the gradation and fusion of tints which were the result, according to Vasari, attracted universal admiration.—Vasari, *Le Vite, &c., Proemio alla terza parte*; see also the "*Introduzione,*" c. 21.

* Benvenuto Cellini claims the merit of having killed this general. See his autobiography.

† Vasari, *Vite de' Pittori, &c.*; Della Valle, *Lettere Sanesi*; Milizia, *Memorie degli Architetti Antichi e Moderni*; Lanzi, *Storia Pittorica, &c.*; Platner and Bunsen, *Beschreibung der Stadt Rom, &c.*; Gaye, *Carteggio Inedito d'Artisti.*

No. **167.** The Adoration of the Kings. The Magi, or Kings, are approaching with their presents, and their retinues, from both sides of the picture. In the centre, near a picturesque ruin, of which a great arch is the principal feature, is seated the Holy Family, attended by the adoring shepherds. The Father appears above the infant Redeemer, surrounded by a glory of angels. The back-ground is an extensive rocky landscape. A drawing in chiaroscuro.

Engraved nearly the same size, in several sheets, by Agostino Carracci, in 1579. On paper, 3 ft. 8 in. *h.* by 3 ft. 6 in. *w.*

This drawing was made at Bologna, in 1521, for Count Giovanni Battista Bentivogli. Girolamo da Trevigi painted an excellent picture from it for the same nobleman. The drawing was presented to the National Gallery, with a print from the plate engraved from it by Agostino Carracci, by Lord Vernon, in 1839.

No. **218.** The Adoration of the Magi. See above, No. 167.

Engraved by Agostino Carracci, in 1579. On wood, 4 ft. 8½ in. *h.* by 4 ft. 1½ in. *w.*

This may possibly be the picture painted by Girolamo da Trevigi, in the year 1521, from Baldassare Peruzzi's drawing for the Count G. B. Bentivogli, unless the report be true that Girolamo's picture was lost at sea: it appears, however, to have been copied several times; a copy was made from it by Bartolomeo Cesi, which was formerly in the possession of the Rizzardi family at Bologna.* The Three Magi are portraits of Titian, Raphael, and Michelangelo. Presented in 1849 by Mr. Edmund Higginson: it was formerly in the Lapeyrière and Gray Collections.

POLLAJUO'LO.

Antonio Pollajuo'lo, painter, sculptor, goldsmith, and engraver, was born in Florence about 1430; the exact date is uncertain.† He was placed by his father, says Vasari, with the goldsmith Bartoluccio,‡ the stepfather of Lorenzo Ghiberti; and Lorenzo having discovered the ability of Antonio, employed him as one of his assistants in modelling the ornaments of the architrave of the central gates of the

---

* Lanzi, *Storia Pittorica, &c.*, vol. i.

† The dates vary from 1426 to 1433. According to Vasari, who has preserved the inscription formerly on Antonio's tomb, in the Church of San Pietro in Vinculis at Rome, he was born in 1426; according to an assessment return made in the year 1457 by Antonio's father Jacopo del Pollajuolo, 1433 was the year of his birth; and according to a similar return made by Antonio himself in 1480, he was born in 1431. See Gaye, *Carteggio Inedito d'Artisti.* 1. 265.

‡ This can scarcely have been before 1445, when Bartoluccio, if living, must have been upwards of eighty years of age.

baptistery of Florence, completed in 1452. Shortly after this time Antonio Pollajuolo worked on his own account as a goldsmith.

He became a celebrated sculptor in bronze, was distinguished for his modelling, and is said by Vasari to have been the first artist who had recourse to dissection of the dead subject for the purposes of art. Latterly Pollajuolo turned his attention to painting, and in this art also he became one of the ablest masters of the fifteenth century. He executed several celebrated works conjointly with his brother Piero, ten years the junior of Antonio, and who had studied painting under Andrea del Castagno.

In 1484 Antonio was invited to Rome by Pope Innocent VIII., and after executing some important monumental works in St. Peter's, he died there in the beginning of the year 1498, and was buried in the church of San Pietro in Vinculis. By his will, dated November 4th, 1496, he left to each of his two daughters the handsome fortune of 5,000 golden ducats.*

No. **292.** The Martyrdom of St. Sebastian. The saint is seen in the middle of the picture, bound to the trunk of a tree, and already pierced with arrows. In the fore-ground are four of his executioners, two in the act of shooting with bows, and two stooping and charging their cross-bows. Behind the saint are two others in the act of shooting, and several horsemen and foot soldiers are seen in the distance. The back-ground is an extensive landscape. Composition of seven principal figures, nearly life size.†

On wood, 9 ft. 6 in. *h.* by 6 ft. 7½ in. *w.* Engraved in the *Etruria Pittrice*, and in Rosini's *Storia della Pittura Italiana*, Vol. III.

This picture, mentioned by Vasari as the principal of Antonio's works in painting, was finished in the year 1475 (the year in which Michelangelo was born), for the altar of the Pucci chapel, in the church of San Sebastiano de' Servi at Florence. Purchased at Florence of the Marchese Pucci in 1857.

---

* Vasari, *Vite, &c.* Ed. Le Monnier, vol. v. Gaye, *Carteggio Inedito d'Artisti.*

† The saint is said to be a portrait (Rittratto dal vivo) of Gino Capponi, who, however, was dead before the painter was born; if a portrait, therefore, it must have been copied from an earlier work.

PONTORMO.

JACOPO CARUCCI, commonly known as JACOPO DA PONTORMO, where he was born in 1493, was the scholar of Andrea del Sarto, and became eventually an imitator of the style of Michelangelo: he was also an excellent portrait painter. He died at Florence in 1558. Pontormo executed some extensive frescoes in the church of San Lorenzo in Florence, representing the "Deluge" and the "Last Judgment." They occupied him eleven years; but they were in the style of the mannered imitators of Michelangelo, and they have been long since whitewashed over. This mannerism, belonging more particularly to his later years, did not extend to Pontormo's portraits, which are powerfully painted, warm in colour, animated, and yet admirably finished: he painted some of the Medici family. He was the master of Angelo Bronzino.*

No. **649.** PORTRAIT OF A BOY, in a crimson and black dress, holding in his left hand the hilt of his sword. Standing, full-length, life-size.

On wood, 4 ft. 2½ in *h.* by 2 ft. *w.*
Formerly in the collection of the Duke of Brunswick. Purchased at Paris from M. Edmond Beaucousin, in 1860.

No. **670.** A KNIGHT OF MALTA, in his robes, and with the red cross on his breast. Full length life-size, standing; his right hand holding a book and resting on a table, richly carved in the taste of the sixteenth century in Italy (*cinquecento*).

On wood, 6 ft. 9½ in. *h.* by 3 ft. 10½ in. *w.*
Presented in 1861 by Mr. George Frederick Watts.

PORDENO'NE.

GIOVANNI ANTONIO LICINIO, *Cavaliere*, commonly called, from his birth-place in the Friuli, IL PORDENO'NE, was born in 1483. He is called also Cuticelli, the name of his mother, and De Regillo. He died at Ferrara in 1539. The works of Pordenone are scarce. He was the scholar of Pellegrino da San Daniele, but was influenced by the example of Giorgione; and, both as a fresco painter and oil painter,

---

* Vasari, *Vite*, &c.

became one of the most distinguished masters of the Venetian school; having been for a time a powerful rival of Titian. Two fine pictures at Burghley House,—"The Finding of Moses," and "The Adoration of the Kings,"—attributed respectively to Titian and Bassan, are, according to Dr. Waagen, works of Pordenone. Bernardino Licinio, Giovanni Maria Calderari, and Pomponeo Amalteo, Pordenone's son-in-law, were scholars and imitators of this painter. He signed his name ANTONIUS PORTUNAENSIS and DE PORTUNAONIS.*

No. **272.** AN APOSTLE. A portion of a colossal figure, seated over an arch.

On canvas, 4 ft. 11 in. *h.* by 3 ft. 9 in. *w.*

Said to have been formerly in a church near Venice. Presented to the National Gallery by the Cavaliero Vallati of Rome, in 1855.

POUSSIN, GASPAR.

GASPARD, or GASPAR DUGHET, commonly called after his brother-in-law, POUSSIN, was born of French parents at Rome, in 1613. He is called by the Italians *Gasparo Duche*, and he has inscribed his name thus on his etchings. He is called Gaspre Poussin by the French. He was the pupil of Nicolas Poussin, who afterwards married his sister, He died at Rome in 1675.

The works of this celebrated landscape-painter are very uniform in character. Ramdohr observes, that they impel the mind to reflection, and convey impressions of solemnity and melancholy. Owing to his habit of painting upon dark grounds, his pictures have become low in tone, and have, perhaps, thus acquired a greater character of gloom than was originally intended. He etched a few plates.†

No. **31.** A LANDSCAPE, WITH FIGURES, representing Abraham and Isaac going to the Sacrifice. In the elevated fore-ground is a broad rocky and woody glen, overhung by

---

* Ridolfi, *Le Maraviglie dell' Arte, &c.*; Lanzi, *Storia Pittorica, &c.*; Maniago, *Storia delle Belle Arti Friulane*, 4to, Venice, 1819.

† Pascoli, *Vite de' Pittori, &c.*; Ramdohr, *Malerei und Bildhauerarbeit in Rom, &c.*; Robert Dumesnil, *Peintre-Graveur Français.*

large forest-trees on each side; an extensive country, bounded by the sea, appears in the distance, with mountains on the extreme left. Abraham and Isaac are seen on the right ascending the mount to the sacrifice; Isaac bears the wood, his father follows with a lighted torch. In the middle-distance below, the two servants of Abraham are awaiting his return.

Engraved by Giuseppe Cunego; by P. Parboni; by J. Pye; and by W. Radclyffe, for Jones's *National Gallery*. On canvas, 5 ft. 3 in. *h*. by 6 ft. 6 in. *w*.

This picture, by some considered the painter's masterpiece, remained in the Colonna Palace, at Rome, to the period of the French Revolution, when it was brought to this country by Mr. Day. It was subsequently in the Lansdowne Collection, from which it passed to that of Mr. Angerstein, and was purchased with the rest of the Angerstein pictures, in 1824.

No. **36.** A LAND STORM. Mountain scenery; shepherds seeking refuge for their flocks. A winding road at the outskirts of a forest occupies the fore-ground; an oak in the middle of this part of the picture has just been snapped asunder by the storm, and lies prostrate on the ground. The effect of the strong wind is forcibly expressed throughout the whole scene. In the middle-distance, a lone building, very beautifully lighted from the bright streaks of sky in the horizon, is effectively relieved by the more distant mountain behind it. The partial light of the distance contrasts powerfully with the dark driven clouds above, and with the general gloom which pervades the picture elsewhere.

Engraved on a large scale by Vivares; and small by S. Lacy, for Jones's *National Gallery*. On canvas, 4 ft. 11 in. *h*. by 6 ft. *w*.

Purchased at Rome by Mr. Irvine for Mr. Buchanan in 1803. Subsequently in the Delmé and Lansdowne collections, afterwards in that of Mr. Angerstein, with which it was purchased for the nation in 1824.

No. **68.** A WOODY LANDSCAPE, EVENING. A view near Albano. In the fore-ground a shepherd boy is leading home his flock: on the right is a thick forest of oaks; on the left a steep bank, under the shade of which two figures are reposing.

Engraved by J. B. Allen for Jones's *National Gallery*. On canvas, 1 ft. 7 in. *h*. by 2 ft. 2 in. *w*.

Formerly in the Corsini Palace at Rome: subsequently in Mr. Ottley's collection, sold in 1801. Bequeathed in 1831 by the Rev. W. H. Carr.

No. **95.** Landscape, with Dido and Æneas taking shelter from the Storm. Virgil, *Æneis*, iv. 119.

> A pitchy cloud shall cover all the plain
> With hail and thunder and tempestuous rain;
> The fearful train shall take their speedy flight,
> Dispersed and all involved in gloomy night;
> One cave a grateful shelter shall afford
> To the fair princess and the Trojan lord.—*Dryden.*

This is the moment represented in the picture:—Æneas and Dido are just visible at the entrance of the cave, above which are two hovering Cupids; a third, at a little distance before it, is holding the bridle of the "lofty courser" of the queen. In the clouds is the goddess Juno, accompanied by Venus and Hymen, promoters of the storm.

Engraved by J. C. Varrall, for Jones's *National Gallery*. On canvas, 4 ft. 10 in. *h.* by 7 ft. 4 in. *w.*

Formerly in the Falconieri Palace at Rome. Bequeathed to the National Gallery, in 1831, by the Rev. W. H. Carr.

No. **98.** View of La Riccia. A small town, situated on a rock, fourteen miles south-east of Rome. Horace spent the first night at this place on his journey from Rome to Brundusium: it still preserves its ancient name, Aricia. The view is from the south: the little town and its picturesque rock occupy a large portion of the picture. Three figures and a dog are seen on the winding road in the fore-ground, and in the distance is a view of the Roman Campagna, bounded by the Apennines. A solitary tree in the fore-ground to the right gives expanse to the scene.

Engraved by A. Smith, for Jones's *National Gallery*. On canvas, 1 ft. 7 in. *h.* by 2 ft. 2 in. *w.*

Companion to No. 68.

Formerly in the Corsini Palace at Rome: subsequently in the Ottley collection. Bequeathed to the National Gallery, in 1831, by the Rev. W. H. Carr.

No. **161.** An Italian Landscape. Mountain scenery, with the view of a town on the slope of a hill, and a cascade in the middle-ground; snow is visible on the distant mountains. Some figures and a couple of dogs are seen in the fore-ground, to the left of which is a rocky bank covered with trees.

On canvas, 2 ft. 8 in. *h.* by 5 ft. 5 in. *w.*

Formerly in the Colonna Palace at Rome. Bequeathed by Lord Farnborough, in 1838.

POUSSIN, NICOLAS.

NICOLAS POUSSIN was born at Andely in Normandy, about June 19, 1594, of a noble family of Soissons. He learnt painting under Quintin Varin at Andely. At the age of eighteen he visited Paris, where he prosecuted his studies for a short time under some other masters, and greatly improved himself by drawing from casts and copying prints after Raphael and Giulio Romano. After various vicissitudes, he at length visited Rome in 1624, in his thirtieth year. He lived in the same house with Du Quesnoy, afterwards celebrated under the name of Il Fiammingo: they were of mutual aid to one another in their studies. It was probably owing to his intimacy with Du Quesnoy, that Poussin paid so much attention to the ancient bassi-rilievi: he modelled some of those works. He also devoted some time to practical anatomy, and he attended the Academy of Domenichino, whom he considered the first master in Rome. He had, however, to contend against poverty for a considerable period, until the return to Rome of Cardinal Barberini from his embassy in France and Spain: Poussin had been introduced to him, before his departure from Rome, by the poet Marino, who died shortly afterwards at Naples. This cardinal, soon after his return, commissioned Poussin to paint two pictures—the "Death of Germanicus" and the "Capture of Jerusalem:" the latter subject he painted twice. From this period he acquired rapidly both fame and fortune. The above pictures were followed by the "Martyrdom of St. Erasmus;" the "Plague of Ashdod;" the "Seven Sacraments;" and others. The last-named works were painted for the Commendatore Del Pozzo, and were, a few years afterwards, repeated by Poussin for M. de Chantelou at Paris.*

Poussin, after an absence of sixteen years, returned with M. de Chantelou to Paris in 1640, when he was introduced by Cardinal Richelieu to Louis XIII., who wished to retain him in his service: he gave him apartments in the Tuilleries, and appointed him his painter in ordinary, with a salary of 120*l.* a year. Poussin, however, wishing to have his wife with him in Paris (he married in 1629), departed in 1642, with permission, for Rome; but as Louis XIII. died shortly

* Both sets are now in England, the former in the collection of the Duke of Rutland at Belvoir Castle, the other in that of the Earl of Ellesmere, in London, known as the Bridgewater Gallery. They are engraved by Pesne.

afterwards, he never returned to his native country. He continued to increase in wealth and reputation during twenty-three years from this time: he died at Rome, on the 19th of November, 1665, in his seventy-second year, and was buried in the church of San Lorenzo in Lucina.* "No works of any modern," says Sir Joshua Reynolds,† "have so much of the air of antique painting as those of Poussin. His best performances have a remarkable dryness of manner, which, though by no means to be recommended for imitation, yet seems perfectly correspondent to that ancient simplicity which distinguishes his style. Like Polidoro, he studied the ancients so much that he acquired a habit of thinking in their way, and seemed to know perfectly the actions and gestures they would use on every occasion."

Poussin excelled as a landscape as well as a figure painter. His works are very numerous: the prints that have been engraved after his principal pictures amount to upwards of two hundred.

No. **39.** The Nursing of Bacchus. Landscape, with nymphs and fauns tending the infant Bacchus, who is eagerly imbibing the juice of the grape, which a Satyr is squeezing into a bowl. A goat occupies a prominent place in the picture, Composition of six small figures.

Engraved by M. Pool. On canvas, 2 ft. 6½ in. *h.* by 3 ft. 1 in. *w.* Bequeathed to the National Gallery by Mr. G. J. Cholmondeley, in 1831.

No. **40.** Landscape, with Figures; Phocion. A wooded spot in the neighbourhood of a city, which is seen at the base of a range of mountains in the distance. In the foreground to the left is a man in a plain, undyed robe, supposed to represent Phocion;‡ he is washing his feet at a public fountain, as if to indicate the purity and simplicity of his life.

On the opposite side is a monument, near which are two figures, seated, in conversation: a third party is passing by

---

* Bellori, Vita di Nicoló Pussino in the *Vite de' Pittori, &c.*, Rome, 1672; Felibien, *Entretiens sur les Vies et sur les Ouvrages des plus excellens Peintres, Anciens et Modernes*, Paris, 1685. Gault de St. Germain published a life of Poussin in 1806, and a *Collection de Lettres de Poussin* was published at Paris in 1824.

† Discourse V.

‡ Phocion, the contemporary of Philip and Alexander the Great, was a favourite Athenian general and statesman; he, however, died by poison, by the decree of the Athenian people themselves. See Plutarch's *Life of Phocion*.

behind them. Towards the middle of the picture, another figure is reclining at full length at the foot of a large tree, on the stem of which are hanging some votive offerings. A small stream flows through this part of the picture.

Engraved by E. Baudet; and by W. Radclyffe, for Jones's *National Gallery*. On canvas, 2 ft. 6 in. *h.* by 3 ft. 7 in. *w.*

Presented to the nation by Sir George Beaumont, Bart., in 1826.

No. **42.** A BACCHANALIAN FESTIVAL. A landscape with satyrs, fauns, centaurs, and animals, in wild revelry. To the left, the drunken Silenus is being placed under a temporary canopy by two fauns, one of whom is about to crown him with a wreath of flowers. On the opposite side, a female satyr is supported by a faun, upon the back of a goat which is attempting to throw her off. In the centre is a kneeling satyr on the verge of intoxication, still drinking from a bowl, into which a faun is pouring wine; and the various phases of intemperance, boisterous mirth, contention, and insensibility, are forcibly pictured in the groups behind him.

Engraved by T. Phillibrown, for Jones's *National Gallery*. On canvas, 4 ft. 8 in. *h.* by 3 ft. 1 in. *w.*

This is one of a series of three pictures said to have been painted for the Duke de Montmorenci; the other two were formerly in the possession of the Earl of Ashburnham. Bellori notices four "Bacchanals" by Poussin, which were painted at Paris in 1641, 42, for Cardinal Richelieu. Formerly in the Barberini Palace, and subsequently in the Angerstein collection, with which it was purchased for the nation, in 1824.

No. **62.** A BACCHANALIAN DANCE. Landscape, with a group of fauns and bacchanalian nymphs, or bacchantes, dancing in a ring, interrupted in their merriment by a satyr, who has thrown one of the nymphs on the ground, for which another nymph is striking him on the head with a cantharus: behind this group, near a thick cluster of trees, is a terminal figure of Pan decorated with flowers. Still further to the right on this side, an infant bacchanal is bending over and drinking from a large vase on the ground; two other infant bacchanals are contending for the juice one of the bacchantes is squeezing from a bunch of grapes which she holds above their heads; a fourth is sleeping on the ground behind them.

Engraved by G. T. Doo, R.A., for the *Associated Engravers*; by Van Merlen; by R. Cooper; and by S. S. Smith, for Jones's *National Gallery*. On canvas, 3 ft. 3 in. *h.* by 4 ft. 8 in. *w.*

This picture, one of the painter's master-pieces, is probably one of the four painted for Cardinal Richelieu: it formed part of the collection of M. de Calonne, by whom it was brought to this country;* it passed subsequently into the possession of Mr. Hamlet, of whom it was purchased for the National Gallery, in 1826.

No. **65.** CEPHALUS AND AURORA. Cephalus, before whom a little cupid holds up the portrait of his wife Procris, is endeavouring to free himself from the arms of Aurora: behind is the winged Pegasus. The elevated scene of the drama is indicated by the presence of a river god, probably Ilissus, as that river rises in Mount Hymettus, from which Cephalus was carried off.† In the back-ground is a naiad or some mountain nymph; and Phœbus, in his chariot, is seen in the heavens just above the horizon: all indicating the early morning.

Engraved by W. Holl, for Jones's *National Gallery*. On canvas, 3 ft. 2 in. *h.* by 4 ft. 3 in. *w.*

Bequeathed to the National Gallery, in 1831, by Mr. G. J. Cholmondeley.

No. **91.** VENUS SLEEPING, SURPRISED BY SATYRS. While one of the satyrs lifts up the drapery of the goddess, another rouses Cupid who has been sleeping by her side. Composition of four small figures.

Engraved by M. Pool; by J. Daullé; and by W. T. Fry, for Jones's *National Gallery*. On canvas, 2 ft. 2 in. *h.* by 1 ft. 8 in. *w.*

Formerly in the collection of M. de Calonne, at Paris. Bequeathed to the National Gallery, in 1831, by the Rev. W. H. Carr.

No. **165.** THE PLAGUE AMONG THE PHILISTINES AT ASHDOD. The Philistines, having overcome the Israelites, removed the Ark of the Lord to Ashdod, and placed it in the Temple of Dagon; on the next morning they found their idol fallen, and the city was afflicted with a loathsome plague.

"And the head of Dagon and both the palms of his hands were cut off upon the threshold of the door."—1 *Samuel*, v. 4.

The broken Dagon is seen before the Ark in the temple to the right, with a crowd of the citizens in consternation before it. In the fore-ground are the bodies of a woman and her child; a second child is approaching the breast of its dead mother, while a man stoops down and gently averts it from the infectious corpse.‡ Various groups of dead and dying are

* See Buchanan's *Memoirs of Painting*.

† Ovid, *Met.* vii. 701. See No. 147, p. 46, No. 2, p. 59, and No. 55, p. 63, of this catalogue.

‡ A somewhat similar group to this, but much less gross in its details, was in the celebrated picture by the Greek painter Artistides, which Alexander the Great, at the sack of Thebes, claimed for himself, and sent to his palace at

dispersed over the picture: the scene is a handsome street in Ashdod, with noble piles of architecture on each side, viewed in perspective.

Engraved by E. Picart; by J. Baron; and by C. Niquet. On canvas, 4 ft. 3 in. *h.* by 6 ft. 8 in. *w.*

This is a repetition of a picture which was painted by Poussin at Rome in 1630, and for which he received, says Bellori, only sixty scudi, about twelve guineas; it came afterwards into the possession of Cardinal Richelieu, who paid 1,000 scudi for it; it is now in the gallery of the Louvre at Paris. The picture above described was formerly in the Colonna Palace at Rome, from which it was purchased by Mr. Irvine for Mr. Buchanan: * it was presented to the National Gallery by the Duke of Northumberland in 1838.

RAPHAEL

Raphael, or Raffaello † Santi, or Sanzio, as the modern Italians write his name, was born at Urbino in the Contrada del Monte, April 6,‡ 1483. He was first instructed in painting by his father Giovanni Santi, who was a good painter for his period.§ After the death of his father in 1494, (his mother died three years before,) Raphael was placed by his uncles, Simone Ciarla and Bartolomeo Santi, with Pietro Perugino, the most celebrated painter at that time in Umbria, and then engaged on the frescoes of the Sala del Cambio (Exchange) at Perugia. He remained with Perugino several years, visiting various places during that period.

In October 1504, Raphael paid his first visit to Florence, carrying with him a letter of introduction to the Gonfaloniere Soderini from Johanna della Rovere, Duchess of Sora, and sister of the reigning Duke of Urbino. He appears to have made Florence his chief place of residence from this time until 1508, when he proceeded to Rome. With the exception

---

Pella. See the Author's *Epochs of Painting.* There is also a very similar group in a design by Raphael, *Il Morbetto,* known from the print of it by Marcantonio. See the remarks of Fuseli, on the comparative merits of these groups, in his first lecture.

* See Ramdohr, *Ueber Malerei, &c.,* vol. ii. p. 106.

† There are copies of three letters of Raphael extant; one only is a fac-simile, and in it the writer has signed himself Raphaello. The English form Raphael, therefore, is nearer to this name than any of the modern Italian forms. Vasari wrote Raffaello. See the works of Longhena and Passavant, quoted in note, p. 184.

‡ See note, p. 183.

§ Pungileoni, *Elogio Storico di Giovanni Santi, Pittore e Poeta, padre del gran Raffaello da Urbino.* Urb. 1822.

of a few months passed at Perugia in 1505, and a short interval at Bologna and Urbino in 1506, the whole period was spent in Florence. He became acquainted with Francia during his visit to Bologna, and ten years afterwards Raphael consigned to Francia's charge the well-known picture of St. Cecilia, which he painted at Rome for one of the churches of Bologna.* Among the pictures painted by Raphael, previous to his visit to Florence in 1504, may be mentioned the "Coronation of the Virgin,"† now in the Vatican; and the celebrated "Spozalizio,"‡ or "Marriage of the Virgin," in the Gallery of the Brera at Milan. The small picture No. 213, in this collection, belongs to the same period. The works executed at this time are said to be in his first or Peruginesque manner; those produced between 1504 and 1508, (when he settled in Rome,) are said to be in his Florentine manner. Among the works of this latter period may be mentioned the "St. Catherine" in this collection; the "Entombment of Christ"§ in the Borghese Gallery at Rome; "La Belle Jardinière"‖ in the Louvre; and the "Madonna del Baldachino"¶ in the Pitti Palace at Florence. The celebrated picture at Blenheim, painted in 1505, holds a middle place between the two styles.**

Raphael had every opportunity of improving himself while at Florence: he was intimate with Fra Bartolommeo di San Marco, distinguished for his effective treatment of light and shade, and for his colouring; and the rival cartoons of Leonardo da Vinci and Michelangelo were at that time the common models in design of all the Florentine painters. He was at length, through the recommendation of his countryman, Bramante, invited by Pope Julius II. to Rome, where he arrived about the middle of the year 1508. From his arrival until the death of Julius in 1513, he was almost constantly employed by that Pope. It was by the order of Julius that Raphael commenced the frescoes of the so-called Stanze of Raphael, in the Vatican. The first of these works was the "Theology," commonly called the Dispute on the Sacrament; it was probably finished in the year 1509, and is painted in Raphael's second or Florentine

* See the notice of FRANCIA in this catalogue.

† Engraved by E. Stöbzel.

‡ Engraved by Giuseppe Longhi.

§ Engraved by Volpato; and by S. Amsler, in 1832.

‖ Engraved by N. Poilli.

¶ Engraved by F. A. Lorenzini.

** Engraved by L. Gruner.

manner. In the same apartment, called the Stanza della Segnatura, are also the frescoes of "Poetry," or Mount Parnassus; "Philosophy," or the School of Athens; and "Jurisprudence." These were all finished in or before 1511. In the second chamber, known as the Stanza dell' Eliodoro, are the "Expulsion of Heliodorus from the Temple of Jerusalem,"* the "Mass of Bolsena," the "Attila," and "St. Peter delivered from Prison." The two former were painted in 1512, during the lifetime of Julius;† the two latter in 1513 and 1514, during the pontificate of Leo X. The third chamber, called the Stanza dell' Incendio, was painted almost wholly by Raphael's scholars; and the fourth, the Sala di Costantino, was completed from the designs of Raphael after his death, under the direction of Giulio Romano.

The slow progress of the Vatican frescoes, after the painting of the Stanza dell' Eliodoro, was owing to the numerous commissions with which Raphael was almost overwhelmed, from Leo X. and other Roman patrons, and from numerous admirers of his works in distant parts. He executed in the meanwhile, besides many designs, portraits,

---

* Maccabees II. ch. ii. v. 25.

† Thus the principal frescoes of Raphael in the Vatican were executed at least as soon as those of Michelangelo on the ceiling of the Sistine Chapel. (See the notice of Michelangelo in this catalogue.) Raphael, however, saw the grand works of his rival in progress, as they were uncovered before the whole ceiling was completed, and enlarged his style in consequence. That this was the common opinion in Rome at the time, appears not only from Vasari's general statement, but also from the following interesting passage in a letter from Sebastiano del Piombo to Michelangelo himself, written apparently just after the completion of the ceiling of the Sistine Chapel, for the letter is dated October 15, 1512, and Michelangelo was then in Florence: the observation is attributed to Pope Julius. "Look at the works of Raphael, who, when he had seen the works of Michelangelo, suddenly forsook the manner of Perugino, and approached as near as he could to that of Michelangelo; but he is terrible, as you see; one can do nothing with him;" (ma è terribile, come tu vedi, non si pol pratichar con lui). These words refer to the character, not the style, of Michelangelo. Gaye, *Carteggio Inedito d'Artisti*, Ap. vol. ii. p. 489.

The style of Michelangelo cannot have been new to Raphael when in Rome, as he must have been well acquainted with the "Cartoon of Pisa;" but the great change in his own taste (though without a direct imitation of Michelangelo) is most visible on comparing the fresco of the "Theology" with his other works in the same apartment: the remark of Julius is borne out and exemplified by that change. Vasari instances Raphael's Isaiah, in Sant' Agostino, executed later, and his Sibyls in the Chiesa della Pace, painted in 1514, as exhibiting direct evidence of an emulation of Michelangelo. But Vasari was perhaps influenced by the coincidence of the subjects with some of those on the ceiling of the Sistine Chapel: as regards the style of the works in question, his observation is only just in reference to the Isaiah: on the whole, the judgment of the Pope may be considered as better founded, and it confirms the received opinion.

Holy Families, Madonnas, and Saints, the "St. Cecilia," at Bologna; the "Madonna di San Sisto," at Dresden; the "Spasimo," at Madrid; the Cartoons, at Hampton Court; and the "Transfiguration,"—his last production, now in the Vatican. In addition to all these occupations, he had the superintendence, as architect, of the building of St. Peter's, in which office he succeeded Bramante.

The whole of these works, including all the Vatican frescoes, except the "Theology," are painted in what is termed Raphael's third manner, or in that style which peculiarly characterises him, and constitutes the Roman school in its highest development; it is distinguished for its dramatic composition and expression, for its correct and vigorous design, and, at least in the frescoes, for a grand and appropriate tone of colouring.

Raphael died at Rome on his birthday,* April 6, 1520, aged exactly 37 years; and, after lying in state, was buried with great pomp in the church of Santa Maria ad Martyres, or the Rotonda, the ancient Pantheon.†

Raphael was of a sallow complexion, with brown eyes, slight in form, and about 5 ft. 8 in. high. He was never married, but is said to have been engaged to Maria Bibiena, the niece of Cardinal Bibiena: she preceded him to the grave. He was said to have left property to the value of 16,000 ducats: he bequeathed all his painting materials and works of art to his favourite scholars, Gianfrancesco Penni and Giulio Romano, with the condition that they should complete his unfinished works in the Vatican. The numerous school of painters, formed by Raphael at Rome, was dispersed at the sack of that city in 1527, but the

---

* The inscription by Cardinal Bembo on Raphael's tomb in the Pantheon is perfectly clear on this point. The concluding lines are:—

Vixit An. XXXVII., Integer Integros.
Quo die natus est, eo esse Desiit
VIII. Id. Aprilis, MDXX.

That is, he lived *exactly* 37 years; he died on the same day (of the year) on which he was born, April 6. From the circumstance that April 6, 1520, was Good Friday, Vasari, and others after him, were led into the erroneous notion that Raphael, as he died on Good Friday, was also born on Good Friday, overlooking the fact of this day being a moveable feast. Schorn and others, following the vague assertion of Vasari, have inferred an error in the very particular inscription of the Cardinal, who was the painter's intimate friend, and, doubtless, well aware of the real facts of the case. See a communication on this subject, by Mr. J. Dennistoun, in the *Art-Union Journal* of January 1842.

† His tomb was opened in 1833, and the skeleton, with all the teeth, found entire: a mould was taken from the skull.

elements of that school were spread over Italy; his most distinguished followers, besides those already mentioned, were Pierino del Vaga, Polidoro da Caravaggio, and Garofalo.*

No. **213.** THE VISION OF A KNIGHT. In the foreground a young knight in armour is sleeping upon his shield at the foot of a laurel tree: on the left is a female figure holding a sword and a book; on the opposite side is another younger female, holding a sprig of myrtle in bloom. The back-ground is a varied landscape. Immediately below the picture is the original pen-and-ink drawing from which it was traced.

Engraved by L. Gruner. On wood, 7 in. square.

This picture belongs to Raphael's first period, probably to the time when he was with Pietro Perugino. It was formerly in the Borghese Gallery at Rome, whence it was procured at the end of the last century, by Mr. W. Y. Ottley; it passed subsequently into the possession of Sir Thomas Lawrence, and afterwards became successively the property of Lady Sykes, and of the Rev. Thomas Egerton, from whom it was purchased for the National Gallery, in 1847.

No. **168.** ST. CATHERINE of Alexandria. St. Catherine, a princess of Alexandria, a Christian, was, about the year 311, condemned by the Emperor Maxentius to be crushed with wheels; the apparatus, however, was broken to pieces by an angel, and the saint was afterwards beheaded.† She is represented in the picture looking upwards, with an expression full of resignation, and is leaning with her left arm on the wheel, the intended instrument of her martyrdom; the back-ground is a landscape. Small figure, three-quarter length.

Engraved by A. Desnoyers in 1824. On wood, 2 ft. 4 in. *h.* by 1 ft. 9½ in. *w.*

---

* The accounts of Raphael are very numerous: among the most prominent are:—Vasari, *Vite de' Pittori, &c.*; Bellori, *Descrizione delle Immagini depinte da Raffaello da Urbino, nel Palazzo Vaticano, &c.*; Duppa, *Life of Raffaello Sanzio*, London, 1816; Rehberg, *Rafael Sanzio aus Urbino*, München, 1824; Quatremène de Quincy, *Histoire de la Vie et des Ouvrages de Raphael*, Paris, 1824; Longhena, *Istoria della Vita e delle Opere di Raffaello Sanzio da Urbino, del Sig. Quatremère de Quincy, &c.*, Milan, 1829; Pungileoni, *Elogio Storico di Raffaello Santi da Urbino*, Urbino, 1829–31; Platner and Bunsen, *Beschreibung der Stadt Rom*, vol. ii. 1832; and especially J. D. Passavant, *Rafael von Urbino und sein Vater Giovanni Santi*, Leipzig, 1839, which contains an accurate account of all Raphael's works.

† See the story of St. Catherine, from Peter de Natalibus, in Lord Lindsay's *Sketches of the History of Christian Art*, vol. i.

This picture was painted about the year 1507, and is in Raphael's second style. It was formerly in the Aldobrandini collection in the Borghese Palace at Rome, from which it was procured by Mr. Day at the close of the last century; it passed into the possession of Lord Northwick, who subsequently sold it to Mr. Beckford, from whom it was purchased in 1839. An original drawing by Raphael of this picture is in the possession of the Duke of Devonshire, and there is a finished cartoon of it in the Collection of Drawings in the Louvre at Paris.

No. **27.** PORTRAIT OF JULIUS II., seated in a chair Pope Julius II., previously known as the Cardinal della Rovere, was elected to the papal chair in 1503, and died in 1513; he commenced the present church of St. Peter at Rome. Three-quarter length, of the natural size.

Engraved by A. Chataigner; by E. Morace; and by R. Page, for Jones's *National Gallery*. On wood, 3 ft. 6 in. *h.* by 2 ft. 8 in. *w.*

This portrait was repeated several times by Raphael, or his scholars. The original and the finest is in the Pitti Palace. Passavant enumerates *nine* repetitions, including the picture now referred to, besides three of the head only. The Pitti portrait was taken probably in 1511 or 1512, before Raphael executed the fresco of "Heliodorus," in which Julius is introduced in much the same attitude as in this portrait. The original cartoon is in the Corsini collection at Florence.* This picture was formerly in the Falconieri Palace at Rome; and subsequently in the possession of Mr. Angerstein, with whose collection it was purchased in 1824.

No. **661.** THE MADONNA DI SAN SISTO. A tracing by Jacob Schlesinger made in 1822 from the celebrated picture by Raphael in the Dresden Gallery. In the centre, the Madonna and Child in the clouds; on her right is kneeling St. Sixtus, Pope; on her left St. Barbara; two angels below. Six figures, life-size.

Mounted on thick paper attached to canvas, 8 ft. 5 in. *h.* by 6 ft. 7 in. *w.*

Presented in 1860 by Messrs. P. and D. Colnaghi, Scott, and Co.

REMBRANDT.†

REMBRANDT HERMANSZOON (son of Herman) VAN

---

* Passavant, *Rafael von Urbino*, ii. 119, 489.

† The half fabulous statements of Houbraken and Weyerman respecting Rembrandt's life and character had been universally adopted by biographers till within the last ten years. For the rectification of these errors by a careful investigation of original documents, the public is chiefly indebted to M. Scheltema, Keeper of the Archives of North Holland. In May 1852, preparatory to the ceremony of placing the statue of Rembrandt in Amsterdam, M. Schel-

RYN* was born at Leyden, July 15, 1606, or according to his own statement at his marraige in 1608.† His parents sent him to the Latin School at Leyden, with a view to his subsequently studying jurisprudence in the University of that city; but his inclination for the art in which he was destined to excel soon manifested itself so strongly that he was placed with the painter Jacob Van Swanenburg, with whom he remained three years; he studied also for a short time under Pieter Lastman, at Amsterdam, and under Jacob Pinas at Haarlem. He returned home after an absence of about four years, and became from that time a diligent and exclusive student of nature. He appears to have met with very early success: in 1630, at the age of twenty-two, he settled in Amsterdam, where he remained till his death. He there married, June 22, 1634, Saskia Uilenburg a lady of good family, and possessed of some fortune. She died in 1642; at a later period of his life he married again; in what year is uncertain. In 1653 Rembrandt incurred considerable debts; his difficulties went on increasing, and in 1656 he was publicly declared insolvent. This disaster has been commonly explained by the impoverished condition of Holland — the consequence of more than one war — at the period referred to, when, as some writers state, upwards of two thousand houses

---

tema embodied in a discourse the result of his laborious researches. That discourse was shortly afterwards published (*Redevoering over het Leven en de Verdiensten van Rembrand van Rÿn*, Amsterdam, 1853), and was commented on in some of the leading European periodicals connected with art. It was not, however, till 1859 that the pamphlet was translated into French, with an introduction and notes by W. Burger, a name well known by many valuable works on the Galleries of Europe. The dates and other circumstances in the above short account of Rembrandt are in accordance with the well authenticated statements of Scheltema: a few only of his conclusions being modified by the observations of his accurate editor, Burger. See *Rembrandt, Discours sur sa Vie et son Génie par le Dr. P. Scheltema. Traduit par A. Willems. Revu et annoté par W. Burger.* Bruxelles, 1859.

* The name of Rembrandt's father was Hermann Gerritszoon (son of Gerrit) van Rÿn; that of his grandfather being Gerrit Roelofszoon (son of Roelof) van Rÿn. The name of Gerrit seems to have been erroneously transferred by some writers to the great painter himself. A half length portrait by Rembrandt of Dr. Matthÿs Kalkoen, dated 1632, has the inscription Rt. H. (Rembrandt Hermanszoon) van Rÿn. See a note by Burger in the translation of Scheltema's pamphlet, above quoted, p. 73. See also the monograms in Immerzeel, *De Levens en Werken der Hollandsche en Vlaamsche Kunstschilders*, &c., 1842. It may be observed that the form *Rembrand* adopted by some writers, though possibly more correct, is not warranted by the artist's signatures.

† Orlers, *Description de la Ville de Leyden*, and other contemporary writers give 1606 as the date.

in Amsterdam were untenanted, and distress was general. Rembrandt's embarassments are, however, partly to be accounted for by the fact, that in his passion for collecting works of art he was sometimes utterly regardless of their cost.* This, at the same time, is in itself a sufficient answer to the absurd but often repeated stories, respecting his supposed miserly habits. His misfortune appears to have had no effect on his professional energies, his works produced during and immediately after the period when it occurred exhibit all his wonted powers.†

The earliest pictures by Rembrandt, with dates, are, the "Presentation in the Temple," in the Gallery in the Hague, and a portrait of a young man, contributed from the royal collection at Windsor, to the Manchester Exhibition, both are dated 1631.‡ The "Anatomical Lecture," painted in 1632, is also at the Hague. Of his maturer time, the "Night Watch," as it is called, now in the gallery at Amsterdam, dated 1642, is regarded as the prominent example; while the portraits of the "Syndics," in the same gallery, painted in 1661, is sometimes selected as the type of his

---

* Instances of the large prices he sometimes paid for such works are not wanting. See Waagen, *Handbook of Painting, the German, Flemish, and Dutch schools*; London, Murray, 1860; Part ii. p. 338.

One of the liabilities which must have pressed heavily on Rembrandt is not to be overlooked. By the will of his first wife, the bulk of her fortune was bequeathed to Rembrandt during his life, or till his second marriage, and then to their only surviving son Titus. Scheltema, after speaking of the debts above referred to, connects Rembrandt's actual insolvency with his second marriage, which involved the necessity of paying his son Titus the amount of Saskia's bequest. As already shown, the great painter's embarrassed circumstances may perhaps be traced to other sufficient causes, and the date of his second marriage is uncertain. The sale of his property and valuable collection of works of art, including numerous pictures by various masters, and more than sixty by his own hand, besides his drawings and etchings, produced, in consequence of the depressed state of the coutry, less than 5,000 guilden. The inventory of his collection, first published in English by C. J. Nieuwenhuys, in his instructive work, *A Review of the Lives and Works of some of the most eminent Painters*, London, 1834, shows that however decided Rembrandt's own taste and practice were, he was capable, as a collector, of taking an interest in fine examples of his art of whatever school. Waagen, *Handbook* &c., Part ii. p. 338.

† Josi, in his *Beredeneerde Catalogus der Werken van Rembrandt van Rhyn en van Zijne Leerlingen en Navolgeren, &c.*, Amsterdam, 1810, preface p. 11, indicates the fine etchings executed in the year of Rembrandt's disaster.

‡ Among the fac-similes of monograms before referred to in Immerzeel's Dictionary, the date 1630 occurs, followed in one instance by the word *pinxit*, but without reference to any particular work. In Kugler's *Hundbuch der Kunstgeschichte*, 1861, vol. ii. p. 468, note, a picture by Rembrandt is mentioned with the date 1627.

later manner. The last work of the artist is supposed to be the "Betrothèd Jewess," in the Van der Hoop gallery at Amsterdam; the date now effaced, is believed to have been 1669.*

Rembrandt was equally distinguished as an etcher and a painter. "He was," says Fuseli, "a genius of the first class, in whatever relates not to form. In spite of the most portentous deformity, and without considering the spell of his chiaroscuro, such were his powers of nature, such the grandeur, pathos, or simplicity of his composition, from the most elevated or extensive arrangement to the meanest or most homely, that the best cultivated eye, the purest sensibility, and the most refined taste, dwell on them equally enthralled."†

Rembrandt died at Amsterdam in 1669, and was buried there (in the Wester Kerk) on the 8th of October of that year.‡ He had two children by his first wife; one of them died young; the other, Titus, was brought up as a painter, but he possessed little ability and died before his father. The name of Rembrandt's second wife has not been preserved; of two children by her nothing is known, except that they survived him. Among his numerous scholars, Gerbrand Van den Eeckhout was his best imitator in Biblical subjects; Ferdinand Bol and Govert Flinck were his rivals in portraiture; and Bernard Fabritius sometimes closely followed the bolder manner of the master.§ Rembrandt's pictures are numerous; his etchings, which amount to nearly four hundred, are dated from 1628 to 1661.‖

---

* Burger, *Musées de la Hollande*, Paris 1860, p. ii.

† Lecture II.

‡ The original entry is "*Deynsdach*, 8 *October* 1669. *Rembrandt van Rijn, Schilder, op de Roosegraft, teghenover het Doolhof. Laet na* 2 *Kynders.*" That is, Tuesday, 8th Oct., 1669, Rembrandt van Rhyn, Painter, on the Rosecanal opposite the Labyrinth. Leaves behind two children. Scheltema, *Redevoering, &c.*, p. 86.

§ Burger, *Musées de la Hollande*, ii. p. 170.

‖ Bartsch's *Peintre-Graveur*, Smith's *Catalogue Raisonné of the Works of Dutch and Flemish Painters*, Rathgeber's *Annalen der Niederländischen Malerei, &c.*, and Nagler's *Künstler-Lexicon*, contain more or less complete lists of the works of Rembrandt. In addition to the writers already referred to, the following may be consulted. Van Eÿnden en Van der Willigen, *Geschiedenis der Vaderlandsche Schilderkunst*, &c. 1842; Immerzeel *Aanteekeningen op de Lofrede op Rembrandt*, 1841; Burnet, *Rembrandt and his Works*, 1848. See also the list of authorities quoted by Waagen, *Handbook*, &c., 1860, Part ii. p. 336, note.

No. **43.** CHRIST TAKEN DOWN FROM THE CROSS. The dead Christ is on the knees of the Virgin, who is sinking back in a swoon: to the left is Joseph of Arimathea, and beyond him are the three crosses, two bearing the thieves who were crucified with Christ. In the back-ground is a view of Jerusalem. A sketch in light and shade; numerous small figures.

Etched by Rembrandt himself; engraved by Picart; by J. B. Jackson; by J. Burnet, for the *Associated Engravers;* and by Freeman, in Jones's *National Gallery.* On wood, 13 in. *h.* by 11 in. *w.*

Formerly in the Collection of M. J. De Barry, at Amsterdam, subsequently in the possession of Sir Joshua Reynolds; at the sale of whose effects in 1795, it was purchased by Sir George Beaumont, and by him presented to the nation in 1826. There is an original drawing by Rembrandt of this composition in the British Museum.

No. **45.** THE WOMAN TAKEN IN ADULTERY. The woman, surrounded by her accusers, is kneeling before Christ, on the floor of the temple, at the foot of a broad flight of steps which lead to the great altar. The principal light of the picture is concentrated around the figure of the woman; the rest of the picture, except immediately before the altar, is enveloped in deep obscurity. See *John,* ch. viii.

Engraved by G. H. Phillips; by J. Burnet; and by W. T. Fry, in Jones's *National Gallery.* On wood, 2 ft. 9 in. *h.* by 2 ft. 3 in. *w.*

This picture was painted for Jan Six, Heer van Vromade, the well-known patron of Rembrandt, and came afterwards into the possession of the Burgomaster, Willem Six. It was sold by auction by the descendants of the Burgomaster in 1734, and passed eventually into the possession of Mr. Angerstein, with the rest of whose collection it was purchased for the nation, in 1824. Signed and dated—

Rembrandt. f. 1644.

No. **47.** THE ADORATION OF THE SHEPHERDS. The scene is a dark stable, or cattle-shed; the illumination of the picture proceeding, almost entirely, as in the "Notte" of Correggio, from the Infant Saviour. The effect of this supernatural light is much enhanced by the comparative faintness of the rays from the lantern in the hands of one of the shepherds, and the principal group is forcibly relieved by the deep shadow of the kneeling figure in the foreground; a second group is just entering the shed on the right; the remotest figure bearing another lantern. Composition of eleven principal figures.

Engraved by S. Bernard; by R. W. Sievier; by J. Burnet, for the *Associated Engravers*; and by H. C. Shenton, for Jones's *National Gallery*. On canvas, 2 ft. 1 in. *h.* by 1 ft. 10 in. *w.*

Formerly in the Angerstein collection, with which it was purchased for the nation, in 1824. Signed—

No. **51.** Portrait of a Jew Merchant, seated, resting his hands upon a stick; on his head is a turban. Half-length, of the natural size.

Engraved by J. Burnet, for the *Associated Engravers*; by G. Shenton; by J. Rogers, for Jones's *National Gallery*; and printed in colours in the Supplement to the *Pictorial Gallery of Arts*. On canvas, 4 ft. 5 in. *h.* by 3 ft. 5 in. *w.*

Presented to the nation, in 1826, by Sir George Beaumont, Bart.

No. **54.** A Woman Bathing. A woman, holding up her dress, is standing in a brook or pool of clear water; part of her clothes are lying on the bank behind her.

Engraved by P. Lightfoot, for Jones's *National Gallery*. On wood, 2 ft. *h.* by 1 ft. 6¼ in. *w.* Signed *Rembrandt f.* 1654.

It was formerly in the collection of Lord Gwydyr, at the sale of whose pictures it passed into the possession of the Rev. W. H. Carr, by whom it was bequeathed to the National Gallery, in 1831. Signed—

No. **72.** Landscape, with figures representing the story of Tobias and the Angel.* The two figures which give a title to this landscape are near the middle of the picture, at the edge of the river (the Euphrates); in the middle-ground to the right is a dark clump of foliage, behind which are light clouds; some hilly broken ground occupies the left of the picture.

---

* See No. 48, p. 77.

Engraved by J. Appleton for Jones's *National Gallery*. On wood, 1 ft. 10 in. *h.* by 2 ft. 10 in. *w.*
Bequeathed to the National Gallery by the Rev. W. H. Carr, in 1831.

No. **166.** PORTRAIT OF A CAPUCHIN FRIAR. Bust, life-size.

On canvas, 2 ft. 10½ in. *h.* by 2 ft. 1½ in. *w.*
Presented to the National Gallery by the Duke of Northumberland in 1838.

No. **190.** A JEWISH RABBI. Bust, life-size.

On canvas, 2 ft. 6 in. *h.* by 2 ft. 2 in. *w.*
Formerly in the possession of the Duke of Argyll, and subsequently in Mr. Harman's collection, at the sale of whose pictures in 1844, it was bought by Mr. Farrer, of whom it was purchased for the National Gallery.

No. **221.** THE PAINTER'S OWN PORTRAIT, at an advanced age. He is in a brown cloak, with a brown cap on his head; his hands are clasped. Bust.

On canvas, 2 ft. 9 in. *h.* by 2 ft. 3½ in. *w.*
Purchased for the National Gallery at the sale of the collection of Viscount Midleton, Pepper-harrow, in 1851.

No. **237.** PORTRAIT OF A WOMAN. In a high dark dress, a white bodice underneath, long pearl ear-rings; her hands crossed, resting on a book; in her right a white hankerchief. Life-size, short half-length.

On canvas, 2 ft. 2¼ in. *h.* by 1 ft. 11¼ in. *w.*
This picture is signed "*Rembrandt, f.* 1666," and is accordingly one of the latest of the painter's works. Bequeathed to the National Gallery by Lord Colborne, in 1854.

No. **243.** A MAN'S PORTRAIT. A stout elderly man, with gray hair and a red cap on his head, seated at a table; his hands clasped before him. Half-length, life-size.

On canvas, 3 ft. 3 in. *h.* by 2 ft. 8$\frac{3}{4}$ *w.*

Signed and dated 1659. Bequeathed to the National Gallery by Lord Colborne, in 1854.

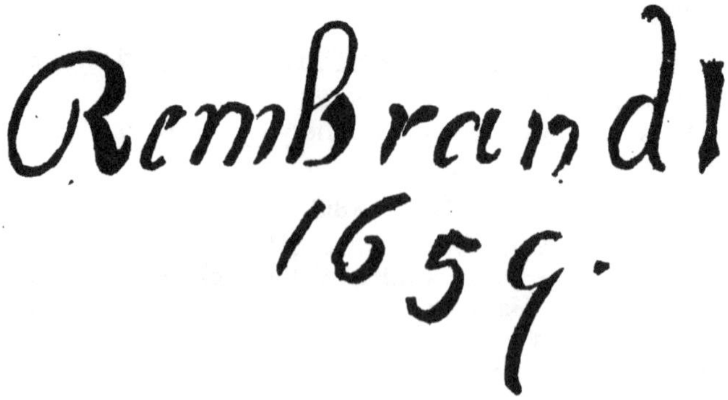

No. **289.** THE AMSTERDAM MUSKETEERS, commonly called the NIGHT WATCH. The picture represents an interior with a company of the Burgher guard of Amsterdam apparently just returned from a shooting match. One of the company, in the background, has created some alarm by discharging his piece in the hall. The principal figures are all portraits:* the two last to the spectator's left are not now in the large picture at Amsterdam, but they are in the print of it by Frey.

On wood, 2 ft. 2 in. *h.* by 2 ft. 9 in. *w.*

This is a small copy of the large picture of this subject in the museum at Amsterdam, though it differs from it in some slight details. That picture has become so exceedingly dark and obscured through time, that, although it represents a daylight scene, it has acquired the popular designation of the *Night Watch*. This example was formerly in the collection of Randon de Boisset, from which, in 1777, it passed into that of M. Lafitte, the banker in Paris. It was subsequently imported into this country, and purchased by Mr. Gillow. It was bequeathed to the nation as a work of Rembrandt, by the Rev. Thomas Halford, in 1857.

No. **672.** HIS OWN PORTRAIT when aged about 32, the picture is signed and dated.† He is dressed in a dark cap and over-coat, the latter edged with fur on the

---

* On the back of the picture is pasted a list of the persons represented, with their names in full, said to be written by the hand of Van Coppenol, the writing master and friend of Rembrandt. The following are the names of the officers: —Frans Banning Cock, *captain;* Willem van Ruytenburg, *lieutenant;* Jan Visscher, *ensign;* Rombout Kempen and Reynier Engel, *sergeants;* and Jan van Kampoort, *drummer.*

† The word *conterfeyct* is an old Dutch term for portrait; it was used also by the Germans. Sandrart calls a portrait a *contrafaet.*

shoulders, and is resting on his right arm, looking at the spectator. Half-length, three-quarter face, life-size.

On canvas, 3 ft. 3 in. *h.* by 2 ft. 7½ in. *w.*

Formerly in the collection of General Dupont, at Paris; purchased from his heirs, MM. De Richemont, in 1861.

ROMANINO.

GIROLAMO ROMANI, called IL ROMANINO, was born at Brescia about 1480, and was the scholar of Stefano Rizzi; he was an established painter in 1502, and was still painting in Brescia in June 1541. The first date is found on the frame of an altar-piece by him in San Francesco, one of the painter's masterpieces; the second is the date of a payment for painting the organ doors of the cathedral at Brescia. Romanino appears to have been an imitator of Giorgione and Titian in his more mature works, as in the example in this collection, one of his most celebrated productions. He was the contemporary and rival of Moretto in Brescia, and is considered superior to that painter in some respects, though inferior to him in the choice and finish of his forms. He died at an advanced age, about 1560. An "Ecce Homo" by him in the cathedral at Cremona is signed HIER. RUMAN. BRIX.,* that is, *Hieronymus Rumanus Brixianus.*

No. **297.** THE NATIVITY. In the centre the Virgin and St. Joseph, adoring the infant Christ, with a choir of angels above; on the sides, in separate compartments, St. Filippo Benizio above, and St. Alessandro in armour on the left, below; on the right, St. Gaudioso, bishop of Brescia, above, and St. Jerome in the desert, below.† Figures nearly life-size.

---

* Ridolfi, *Le Maraviglie dell' Arte, &c.*; Brognoli, *Nuova Guida per la Città di Brescia*, pp. 160, 299.

† Chizzola, *Pitture e Sculture di Brescia, &c.*, 1760, p. 120; Brognoli, *Nuova Guida, &c.*, p. 201, expressly notices the figure of St. Alessandro as one of Romanino's capital works, *capi d'opera.*

On wood, the central picture, 8 ft. 7 in. *h.* by 8 ft. 9¼ in. *w.*; the upper side compartments, 2 ft. 5½ in. *h.* by 2 ft. 1½ in. *w.*; the lower compartments, 5 ft. 8 in. *h.* by 2 ft. 1¼ in. *w.*

Painted in 1525,* for the high altar of the church of Sant' Alessandro at Brescia, where it remained until 1785, when it passed into the possession of Count Avveroldi. Purchased at Brescia from the Counts Angelo and Ettore Avveroldi in 1857.

ROMANO, GIULIO.

GIULIO PIPPI, or rather DE' GIANNUZZI,† commonly called Giulio Romano, was born at Rome in 1492, according to Vasari, but according to a document discovered at Mantua, in 1498. He became early the pupil of Raphael, who employed him on some important works in the Vatican, during the pontificate of Leo X. After the death of Raphael in 1520, Giulio and his fellow-pupil, Gianfrancesco Penni, to whom Raphael had bequeathed conjointly his implements and works of art, were entrusted with the completion of the frescoes of the Sala di Costantino, in the Vatican, comprising the "Battle of Constantine," the "Apparition of the Cross," the "Baptism of Constantine," and the "Presentation of Rome to the Pope."

These works were completed in 1523, and in the latter part of the following year‡ Giulio Romano entered the service of Federigo Gonzaga, Duke of Mantua. He introduced the style of Raphael into Mantua, and established a considerable school of art there: Primaticcio was one of his pupils. His greatest works are the "Fall of the Giants," the "Story of Cupid and Psyche," and the other frescoes in the Palazzo del Tè, at Mantua;§ the palace itself was rebuilt by Giulio. The frescoes, however, appear to have been executed chiefly by his pupils from his cartoons: of these pupils, the principal were Benedetto Pagni, Rinaldo

---

* Cozzando, *Istoria Bresciana*, 1694, p. 120.

† Giulio's father was Pietro Pippi de' Giannuzzi, which in full is Pietro di Pippo (or Filippo) de' Giannuzzi—Peter the son of Philip Giannuzzi. It was very common in former times for a son to add his father's Christian name to his own, as in this case, and thus the surname was often lost. Carlo D'Arco, *Istoria della Vita e delle Opere di Giulio Pippi Romano*. Folio. Mantua, 1838. And *Kunstblatt*, No. 31, 1847.

‡ Gaye, *Carteggio Inedito d'Artisti*, ii. 102.

§ Bottani, *Descrizione Storica delle Pitture del Regio-Ducale Palazzo del Tè, fuori della Porta di Mantova detto Pusterla*. Mantua, 1783. Some of these frescoes are engraved by P. S. Bartoli; by Diana Ghisi; by Antonio Veneziano; and in Carlo d'Arco's *Vita di Giulio Romano*.

Mantuano, and Primaticcio, who remained with Giulio Romano six years.

Giulio Romano was not less distinguished as a painter in oil colours than as a fresco painter, and he was equally celebrated as architect and painter. Among his most celebrated oil-pictures may be mentioned, the Martyrdom of St. Stephen, in the church of that saint at Genoa; and a domestic "Holy Family," known as "La Sainte Famille au Basin," in the gallery at Dresden. Giulio is generally considered to have been the most able of Raphael's scholars. He died at Mantua, November 1, 1546, leaving a wife and two children. His son Raphael died young; his daughter Virginia was married to Ercole Malatesta, and survived her father many years.*

No. **225.** THE BEATIFIC VISION OF THE MAGDALENE. Mary Magdalene borne upwards by angels to witness the joys of the blessed; in accordance with the legend from which painters of various schools have borrowed subjects relating to her supposed history.† Seven figures.

Fresco, of semicircular form, 5 ft. 5 in. *h.* by 7 ft. 8 in. *w.*

Formerly in the church of the Trinità de' Monti, Rome. According to Titi,‡ Giulio Romano was aided by Gianfrancesco Penni in the frescoes he executed in this church. Formerly in the possession of M. Joly de Bammeville. Presented to the National Gallery, by Lord Overstone, in 1852.

No. **624.** THE INFANCY OF JUPITER. A cradle containing a sleeping infant attended by three women, on a small verdant island, on the further side of which are two

---

* Vasari, *Vite de' Pittori, &c.*

In the Archivio della Sanità of Mantua is the following entry against Nov. 1, 1546:—"Sig. Giulio Romano, Superintendent of all the ducal buildings, after fifteen days' illness, died of fever, aged forty-seven." According to which, he was born in 1498 or 1499; but in this case he must have been but a boy when he was first employed by Raphael in the Vatican. See Gaye, *Carteggio Inedito d'Artisti*, and the *Kunstblatt*, No. 71, 1838, and No. 31, 1847.

† "Every day during the last years of her penance, the angels came down from heaven and carried her up in their arms into regions where she beheld the glory and the joy prepared for the sinner that repenteth." Provençal legend, quoted by Mrs. Jameson, *Sacred and Legendary Art*, vol. i. p. 337. See also Peter de Natalibus, L. vi. c. cxxiiii. For a list of painters who have treated this subject see the first-mentioned work, p. 364, &c. This subject is sometimes called the Assumption of the Magdalene; but "The Assumption" is strictly appropriated to the subject of the Madonna taken up to heaven. The Magdalene, according to the legend, was favoured with visions of heaven while in the body: the Assumption of the Virgin took place according to the same authority after her burial.

‡ *Nuovo Studio di Pittura, Scoltura, ed Architettura, nelle Chiese di Roma, &c.*

groups of figures playing musical instruments. The landscape is possibly by Giambattista Dossi.

This is an illustration of the classic myth relating to the infancy of Jupiter, the youngest son of Saturn and Rhea; he was born in Crete and secreted by his mother, and nursed by the Melian nymphs to save him from his father, who used to devour his sons as soon as they were born, from the fear of the fulfilment of the prophecy that one of them would dethrone him, as he had dethroned his father. The figures in the background are the Curetes, making a noise with horns and by the clashing of cymbals, lest Saturn should hear the cries of the infant, and thus discover the trick that had been imposed upon him; he had swallowed a stone instead of the young Jupiter.

Engraved by J. B. Patas for the *Orleans Gallery*. On wood, 3 ft. 5½ in. *h.* by 5 ft. 9 in. *w.*

Formerly in the Orleans Gallery, subsequently in that of Lord Northwick at Cheltenham, from which it was purchased in 1859.

No. **643.** THE CAPTURE OF CARTHAGENA; AND THE CONTINENCE OF PUBLIUS CORNELIUS SCIPIO. New Carthage was taken by Scipio in 210, and he distinguished himself by the generosity with which he treated the Spanish hostages kept there by the Carthaginians.

Engraved by Nicolas Tardieu, and by Couchè and Michel.

No. **644.** THE ABDUCTION OF THE SABINE WOMEN; AND THE RECONCILIATION BETWEEN THE ROMANS AND THE SABINES. *See* No. **38.**

Engraved by Philippe Simoneau, and by Couchè fils, and J. B. Racine.

On canvas from wood, each picture 14 in. *h.* by 5 ft. *w.*

Formerly in the Orleans Collection. Purchased at Paris from Mr. Edmond Beaucousin, in 1860.

ROSA.

SALVATOR ROSA was born at Renella, in the neighbourhood of Naples, July 21, 1615. He adopted painting contrary to the desires of his father, who was an architect: his first instructor in the art which he preferred was Ciccio Fracanzano, a relation. Salvator's favourite subjects were landscapes, selected chiefly from wild and romantic scenery; and he was so much encouraged by Lanfranco, who purchased some of his pictures at Naples, that he was induced, in 1635, to try his fortunes in Rome. Here he found a patron in the Neapolitan Cardinal

Brancacci, bishop of Viterbo. Salvator accompanied the Cardinal to Viterbo, and painted several pictures for him there. He returned to Naples, but owing to the great applause with which his picture of "Tityus torn by the Vulture" was received by the connoisseurs of Rome, he finally settled in that capital of the arts in 1638. He died at Rome, March 15, 1673: his wife and one of two sons survived him. "What is most to be admired in the works of Salvator Rosa," says Sir Joshua Reynolds, "is the perfect correspondence which he observed between the subjects which he chose and his manner of treating them. Everything is of a piece: his rocks, trees, sky, even to his handling, have the same rude and wild character which animates his figures."* The energetic language of Fuseli is well suited to the character of Salvator's landscapes. "He delights," says that writer, "in ideas of desolation, solitude, and danger; impenetrable forests, rocky or storm-lashed shores; in lonely dells leading to dens and caverns of banditti, alpine ridges, trees blasted by lightning or sapped by time, or stretching their extravagant arms athwart a murky sky, lowering or thundering clouds, and suns shorn of their beams. His figures are wandering shepherds, forlorn travellers, wrecked mariners, banditti lurking for their prey or dividing their spoils."† Many of Salvator's best pictures are in this country. He executed several etchings.‡

No. 84. LANDSCAPE, WITH MERCURY AND THE DISHONEST WOODMAN, from the fable of Æsop. Mercury stands in a stream§ in the fore-ground, which is shaded by a dark cluster

---

* Discourse V. There are many accounts of Salvator which contain much that is improbable and fictitious: the whole has been collected and dwelt upon at length, by Lady Morgan, in her well-known romance, called "The Life of Salvator Rosa." In the above brief notice the account of Salvator's friend Passeri has been followed, *Vite de' Pittori, &c.* See also Salvini, *Satire e Vita di Salvator Rosa, &c.* 8vo., Flor. 1833.

† *Note in Pilkington's Dictionary of Painters.* 1810.

‡ See Bartsch, *Peintre-Graveur.*

§ A woodman lost his axe in a stream sacred to Mercury, and while he was weeping on the bank, the god appeared with a golden axe in his hand, and asked him whether it was the one he had lost? "No," said the woodman; on his disclaiming also a silver one, Mercury at last produced his own, and presented him with the other two for his honesty. A fellow-labourer hearing the story from the woodman, threw his own axe into the water, hoping for the same good fortune as his companion; but having claimed the golden axe immediately on seeing it, the god rebuked him for his impudence, and left him unaided, to repent of his folly.

of overhanging trees to the right: an open hilly country is seen on the left.

Engraved by P. Parboni. On canvas, 4 ft. 1½ in. *h.* by 6 ft. 7½ in. *w.*

Formerly in the Colonna Palace at Rome, and brought to England at the close of the last century by Mr. Ottley, who sold it to Sir Mark Sykes. It came subsequently into the possession of Mr. Byng, of whom it was purchased for the National Gallery, in 1887.

ROSSELLI.

COSIMO, the son of Lorenzo ROSSELLI, a Florentine mason, was born at Florence in 1439;* he was taught painting by Neri di Bicci, under whose charge he was placed when 14 years of age; he remained with him three years, until 1456.

Cosimo early distinguished himself by some works for the church of Sant' Ambrogio at Florence, especially in a fresco, still in good preservation, representing the "Removal of a miracle-working Chalice from the Church to the Episcopal Palace," in which are introduced a religious procession and a crowd of spectators.† He was one of those invited, about 1480, by Pope Sixtus IV. to decorate his new chapel in the Vatican—the now celebrated Sistine Chapel.‡ The Pope had offered a prize to the most successful, and Vasari relates that Cosimo Rosselli, conscious of his inability to rival his more able competitors, among whom were Domenico Ghirlandajo, Luca Signorelli, and Pietro Perugino, and being equally doubtful of the judgment of the Pope, loaded his figures with ultramarine and gold, by which artifice he gained the Pope's admiration and obtained the prize. These frescoes, representing scenes from the Old and New Testaments, are still preserved.§

Rumohr observes that Cosimo in the commencement of his career followed the paths which were opened out by Fra Giovanni da Fiesole and Masaccio, but that after a few

---

* Gaye, *Carteggio Inedito d'Artisti*, 11. 457, note.

† Described by Richa, *Chiese di Firenze*, vol. ii., p. 244, engraved by Lasinio and in part in the *Etruria Pittrice* of Lastri.

‡ See the article on Botticelli in this catalogue.

§ Vasari, *Vite, &c.*, Ed. Le Monnier, vol. v., p. 30. Platner and Bunsen, *Beschreibung der Stadt Rom.*, vol. ii. pt. 1.

brilliant examples of his ability he forsook the study of those masters and of nature, to follow a lifeless and repulsive mannerism.*

Cosimo Rosselli was still living in November 1506. He was the master of Fra Bartolomeo; and the eccentric Piero di Cosimo was his constant assistant.

No. 227. St. Jerome in the Desert kneeling before a Crucifix, in a distinct compartment of the picture; standing at the sides, on the spectator's left, are Saints Damasus and Eusebius, on the right Saints Paola and her daughter Eustochia; kneeling below are Girolamo Rucellai and his son; and on each side above are three angels. In the *predella* beneath the principal pictures are, in four compartments, incidents from the lives of the saints represented above, who were the contemporaries of St. Jerome, with the arms of the Rucellai at each end. On a plinth below the central compartment is inscribed —S. Dammasus, S. Eusebius, S. Jeronimus, S. Paula, S. Eustocium.— Five principal figures, half-life scale.

In tempera, on wood; the principal picture 5 ft. *h.* by 5 ft. 8 in. *w.*; the predella 6½ in. *h.* by 7 ft. 4 in. *w.* It is in its original frame.

Formerly an altar-piece in the Ruccellai chapel in the church of the Eremiti di San Girolamo at Fiesole. This order was suppressed by Clement IX. in 1668: the church and convent are now within the precincts of the Villa Ricasoli. In the Fiesole Guide this picture is described as being "*di buona antica maniera.*" † It was purchased for the national collection of the Conte Ricasoli at Florence in 1855.

ROTTENHAMMER.

Johann Rottenhammer was born at Munich in 1564, and was the pupil of an obscure painter of the name of Donauer; he studied also in Rome, and in Venice, where he executed two large altar-pieces, imitating Tintoretto, then still living. Jan Breughel and Paul Brill frequently painted the landscapes of his pictures. Rottenhammer lived latterly at Augsburg, and died there in 1623.

---

* *Italienische Forschungen*, ii. 265.

† Moreni, *Notizie Istoriche dei contorni di Firenze.* Flor. 1792, pt. iii. p. 153. Can. A. M. Bandini, *Lettere xii. nelle quali si ricerca e s'illustra l'antica e moderna situazione della città di Fiesole, &c.* Siena, 1800, p. 139. Del Rosso, *Guida di Fiesole*, 1846, p. 52.

He was much patronized by the Emperor Rudolph II., and made a considerable fortune, but squandered it away, and died poor. His small pictures are the most appreciated of his works; they are generally executed on copper.*

No. **659.** PAN AND SYRINX. The nymph Syrinx, one of the naiads, is pursued by Pan, and takes refuge among some bulrushes; the god thinking to grasp the nymph finds only reeds in his hands, these he constructed into a rude instrument, hence the name of Syrinx given to the Pan-pipes.

On copper, 9½ in. *h.* by 7½ in. *w.*

The background of this picture appears to be by the hand of Jan or Velvet Breughel, of Antwerp (1568—1625). Purchased at Paris from M. Edmond Beaucousin, in 1860.

RUBENS.

PETER PAUL RUBENS was born at Siegen, in Westphalia, on the day of St. Peter and St. Paul, June 29, 1577. His parents, John Rubens and Mary Pypeling, were natives of Antwerp, but they had emigrated in 1568 on account of the religious disturbances which prevailed in the Netherlands at that period. In 1578 they settled in Cologne, where Rubens remained until 1587, when his father died, and his mother returned with her family to Antwerp.

Rubens was destined by his mother to follow the law, the profession of his father; but he had such a decided taste for the fine arts that he persuaded her to allow him to be a painter. Accordingly, after he had received some instruction from Tobias Verhaagt and Adam Van Noort, he was placed with Otto Van Veen (Otho Venius), the most celebrated painter of his time at Antwerp. After studying for four years with Van Veen he went in the spring of 1600 to Italy; there he entered the service of Vincenzio Gonzaga, Duke of Mantua, but much of his time was spent at Venice and Rome, where he copied several pictures for the Duke. In 1605 he was sent on a mission by the Duke to Philip III. of Spain, and while at Madrid he painted several portraits of the Spanish nobility. Rubens returned to Antwerp, from Genoa, in the autumn of

---

* Nagler, *Künstler Lexicon*; Sandrart, *Accademia Todesca*, &c.

1608, after an absence from home of eight years and a half. His return home was hastened by the illness of his mother, but he did not arrive until after her death.

It was the intention of Rubens to return to Mantua, but he was induced to remain in Antwerp by the Archduke Albert, then Governor of the Netherlands; and he was appointed court painter to Albert and Isabella in 1609. In October of that year he married his first wife, Isabella Brant; and in 1610 he built himself a magnificent house at Antwerp. In 1620 he visited Paris by the invitation of Maria de' Medici, and there received the commission for his celebrated series* of pictures for the new palace of the Luxembourg, commemorating the marriage of that princess with Henry IV. of France: the pictures were completed in 1625. In 1628 Rubens was sent by the Infanta Isabella, widow of the Archduke Albert, on a diplomatic mission to Philip IV. of Spain: and in the following year he was sent on a similar mission to Charles I. of England, by whom he was knighted in 1630. He was knighted in the same year by Philip IV. of Spain. In this year he married his second wife, Helena Fourment, a beautiful girl, in her sixteenth year only: his first wife, by whom he had two sons, died in 1626. Rubens himself died, possessed of immense wealth, at Antwerp, on the 30th of May 1640, and was buried with extraordinary pomp in the church of St. Jacques. He had five children by his second wife, who was afterwards married to Baron J. B. Broechoven, a Flemish nobleman in the Spanish service in the Netherlands.†

Rubens's pictures are extremely numerous, amounting, it is said, to several thousands, but many of them were painted from his sketches by his scholars; of whom the most celebrated are Vandyck, A. Van Diepenbeck, J. Van Hoeck, T. Van Thulden, G. Zegers, Jordaens, Snyders, and Erasmus Quellinus. Rubens executed a few etchings, but there are altogether about 1,200 prints, engraved by various masters, after his works.

---

* These pictures, twenty-one in number, are now in the Louvre at Paris. Most of the Sketches, which were painted by Rubens himself, are now in the Pinacothek at Munich. See *La Gallerie du Palais du Luxembourg, peinte par Rubens; dessineé par les Sieurs Nattier et gravée par les plus illustres graveurs &c.* Folio, Paris, 1710.

† A portion only of Rubens' collections produced by private sale upwards of 20,000*l.* sterling. See the list printed by Dawson Turner. *Catalogue of the Works of Art in the Possession of Sir P. P. Rubens, &c.* 8vo. Yarmouth.

"Rubens," says Sir Joshua Reynolds,* "was, perhaps, the greatest master in the mechanical part of the art, the best workman with his tools, that ever exercised a pencil."

"This power, which Rubens possessed in the highest degree, enabled him to represent whatever he undertook better than any other painter. His animals, particularly lions and horses, are so admirable, that it may be said they were never properly represented but by him. His portraits rank with the best works of the painters who have made that branch of the art the sole business of their lives; and of those he has left a great variety of specimens. The same may be said of his landscapes."

Fuseli observes†—"What has been said of Michael Angelo in FORM may be said of Rubens in COLOUR: they had but one. As the one came to nature and moulded her to his generic form, the other came to nature and tinged her with his colour—the colour of gay magnificence. He levelled his subject to his style, but seldom, if ever, his style with his subject."

Rubens's masterpiece is generally considered "The Descent from the Cross," at Antwerp; painted a few years after his return from Italy. He is still seen to great advantage at Antwerp; but probably the best idea of his great and versatile powers is conveyed by the collection in the Pinacothek at Munich, in which alone are disposed 95 of his works, several of them his masterpieces.‡

---

* *Journey to Flanders and Holland.*—Character of Rubens.

† Lecture IX.

‡ The accounts of Rubens, both early and recent, from Sandrart downwards, are numerous; among the most valuable are the following:—*Lettres Inédites de P. P. Rubens, publiées par Emile Gachet,* Bruxelles, 1840. These letters are written chiefly in Italian, the language which Rubens seems to have preferred after his residence in Italy; he generally signed his name *Pietro Paolo.*—*Historische Levensbeschrijving van P. P. Rubens, Ridder, &c.,* by Victor C. van Grimbergen, Antwerp and Rotterdam, 1840, originally published in 1774; it is referred to by Immerzeel in his *Levens en Werken der Hollandsche en Vlaamsche Kunstschilders, &c.,* Amsterdam, 1843. A biography of Rubens appeared also in Raumer's *Historisches Taschenbuch,* Berlin, 1833, by Dr. Waagen; it was translated into English by R. R. Noel, and edited by Mrs. Jameson, under the title *Peter Paul Rubens, his Life and Genius,* London, 1840. Another Life by M. Michiels has appeared in Paris—*Rubens et l'Ecole d'Anvers,* 8vo., 1854, and "*Original unpublished Papers illustrative of the life of Sir P. P. Rubens, as an artist and a diplomatist, &c.*" has been lately published by W. Noel Sainsbury, 8vo. London, 1859. Sir Joshua Reynolds's *Journey to Flanders and Holland* contains some excellent remarks on the style and works of Rubens.

No. **38.** The Abduction of the Sabine Women. A tumultuous throng of men and women in violent struggle. To the right, seated on a throne, is Romulus, directing the sudden assault on his unsuspecting guests, whom he had invited from the surrounding neighbourhood to witness some games in honour of the god Consus. At an appointed signal, during the celebration of these games, the Romans carried off by force all the unmarried women.* Composition of many small figures, some on horseback.

Engraved by P. F. Martinasie; by J. Stewart, for the *Associated Engravers;* and by J. Outrim, for Jones's *National Gallery.* On wood, 5 ft. 7 in. *h.* by 7 ft. 9 in. *w.*

Formerly in the possession of Madame Boschaert at Antwerp; it formed subsequently part of the Angerstein collection, with which it was purchased for the National Gallery, in 1824.

No. **46.** Peace and War; or Peace and Plenty: an allegory. Peace, nourishing her children from her bosom, is surrounded by Abundance, Wealth, and Happiness; while War, with its attendants, Pestilence and Famine, are repelled by Wisdom. Composition of fifteen figures, of the natural size.

Engraved by C. Heath; by W. Greatbach, for the *Associated Engravers;* and by T. Garner, for Jones's *National Gallery.* On wood, 6 ft. 6 in. *h.* by 9 ft. 9 in. *w.*

Presented to Charles I. by Rubens when in England in 1630. After the death of Charles it passed into the possession of the Doria family at Genoa, where it was known as the "Family of Rubens."† It was purchased, in 1802, by Mr. Irvine for Mr. Buchanan, and subsequently obtained by the Marquis of Stafford, first Duke of Sutherland, who presented it to the National Gallery, in 1828.

No. **57.** The Conversion of St. Bavon.‡ The saint, about to enter the monastic life, is met on the steps of the church of his convent by St. Amand, Bishop of Maestricht. On the right is the worldly retinue of the noble penitent; to the left, his property is being distributed among the poor: in a more elevated part of the picture, on this side, is a group of ladies of the family of St. Bavon, returning thanks for the mercy accorded him by his conversion. Composition of many small figures.

Engraved by P. Lightfoot, for Jones's *National Gallery.* On wood, 3 ft. 5½ in. *h.* by 5 ft. 5¾ in. *w.*

---

* See Plutarch's *Life of Romulus.*

† Vanderdoort, *A Catalogue and Description of King Charles the First's Capital Collection of Pictures, &c.* London, 1757 Buchanan, *Memoirs of Painting,* vol. ii. p. 108.

‡ A Brabant noble of the seventh century. *Acta Sanctorum,* vol. 2.

Formerly in the Carrega Palace at Genoa, from which it was purchased for Mr. Buchanan by Mr. Irvine in 1805. Bequeathed to the National Gallery by the Rev. W. H. Carr in 1831. There is a large picture of this subject, by Rubens, in the Church of St. Bavon at Ghent. It is engraved by F. Pilsen.

No. **59.** THE BRAZEN SERPENT.

"And the Lord sent fiery serpents among the people, and they bit the people; and much people of Israel died.

"And the Lord said unto Moses, Make thee a fiery serpent, and set it upon a pole: and it shall come to pass, that every one that is bitten, when he looketh upon it, shall live. And Moses made a serpent of brass, and put it upon a pole, and it came to pass, that if a serpent had bitten any man, when he beheld the serpent of brass, he lived."—*Numbers* xxi. 6—9.

On the left are Moses and Eleazar, by the brazen serpent; before them, on the right, are the Jewish people, men, women, and children, prostrated by the plague of serpents. Composition of many figures, of the natural size.

Engraved by Bolswert; by F. Ragot; by C. Galle; and others. On canvas, 6 ft. 2 in. *h.* by 8 ft. 9 in. *w.*

Formerly in the Marana Palace at Genoa: brought to England by Mr. A. Wilson in 1806. Purchased for the National Gallery, of Mr. T. B. Bulkeley Owen, in 1837. There is another picture by Rubens of this subject in the gallery at Madrid.

No. **66.** A LANDSCAPE, AUTUMN, WITH A VIEW OF THE CHATEAU DE STEIN, the residence of Rubens, near Mechlin. To the left is the château, surrounded by picturesque foliage; in the fore-ground below it, a two-horse waggon, carrying a calf, is fording a brook. To the right is an extensive open country, with the view of a town in the distance: in the immediate fore-ground is a sportsman, with his dog and gun, creeping up to a covey of birds. The time is morning.

Engraved by G. Cooke; and by G. B. Allen, for Jones's *National Gallery.* On wood, 4 ft. 5 in. *h.* by 7 ft. 9 in. *w.*

Formerly in the Balbi Palace at Genoa, from which it was purchased by Mr. Irvine for Mr. Buchanan in 1802. Presented to the National Gallery by Sir George Beaumont, in 1826.

No. **67.** A HOLY FAMILY, with Saint George, and other saints. The figures are said to be portraits of Rubens and his family. The group on the right, of children playing with the lamb, has been introduced into several designs by Rubens: the whole portion of this composition to the right of the columns was cut on a very large scale, in wood, by Christopher Jegher, from a drawing on the block by Rubens himself. Composition of nine small figures.

Engraved by P. Lightfoot, for Jones's *National Gallery.* On canvas, 4 ft. 1 in. *h.* by 5 ft. 4 in. *w.*

Formerly in the Angerstein collection, with which it was purchased by Parliament for the National Gallery, in 1824.

No. **157.** A LANDSCAPE; SUNSET. A flat country, with the view of a farm-house, and a village church in the distance.

Engraved by Bolswert. On wood, 1 ft. 7 in. *h.* by 2 ft. 9 in. *w.*

Bequeathed to the National Gallery by Lord Farnborough, in 1838.

No. **187.** THE APOTHEOSIS OF WILLIAM THE TACITURN, of Holland. A sketch of a picture in the possession of the Earl of Jersey, at Osterley Park.

On wood, of a circular form, 2 ft. 1 in. in diameter.

Formerly in the possession of Sir David Wilkie, when it was known as the Apotheosis of James I. Purchased in 1843.

No. **194.** THE JUDGMENT OF PARIS. At the nuptials of Thetis and Peleus, an apple was thrown amongst the guests by Discord, to be given to the most beautiful: Juno, Minerva, and Venus, were competitors for the prize, and Paris, the son of Priam, was ordered by Jupiter to decide the contest. The Trojan shepherd, seated with Mercury by his side, on the right, is on the point of awarding the apple to Venus, who stands between her rivals; on her right is Juno, indicated by the peacock at her feet; on her left is Minerva, whose sacred bird, the owl, is perched on a tree behind her; the shield and arms of the goddess are seen below. The decision of Paris was the cause of all the subsequent misfortunes of Troy: Discord is seen already hovering in the clouds above, spreading fire and pestilence around.

Engraved by J. Couché and Dambrun for the *Galerie du Palais Royal.* On wood, 4 ft. 9 in. *h.* by 6 ft. 3 in. *w.*

Formerly in the Orleans collection. Purchased for the National Gallery, at the sale of Mr. Penrice's collection, in 1844. There is a small copy of this picture in the Louvre.

No. **278.** THE TRIUMPH OF JULIUS CÆSAR. A procession; to the left, dancing girls with flowers, and other figures leading animals for the sacrifice; on the right elephants bearing fruit, and lighted candelabra; and wild beasts for the shows. In the back ground a hill surmounted by a temple, with crowds of spectators.

On canvas, attached to wood, 2 ft. 11½ in. *h.* by 5 ft. 5 in. *w.*

This sketch was made from a portion of the same subject by Andrea Mantegna, now at Hampton Court. It was in Rubens' possession at his death, and is thus noticed in the English catalogue of his effects:*—"*Three cloathes pasted uppon bord, beinge the Triumph of Julius Cesar, after Andrew Mantegna, not full*

---

* Privately printed by Dawson Turner, Esq. *Catalogue of the Works of Art in the possession of Sir Peter Paul Rubens at the Time of his Decease, &c.* 2d Ed. 8vo. 1839.

made." It was subsequently in the Balbi Palace, Genoa; in 1802 it was bought by Mr. Irvine, and became the property of Mr. Champernowne, from whose collection it passed to that of Mr. Rogers, and at the sale of his pictures in 1856 it was purchased for the National Gallery.

No. **279.** THE HORRORS OF WAR. Mars leaving the temple of Janus open, is held back by Venus, while Europe bewails the inevitable miseries of war; but he is drawn on by the Fury Alecto, who is preceded by Plague and Famine: the figure on the ground with the broken lute represents Concord overthrown.* Mars and the two female figures behind him are said to be the portraits of Rubens and his two wives. A sketch.

On paper attached to canvas, 1 ft. 7½ in. *h.* by 2 ft. 6¼ in. *w.*

This sketch of the large picture painted in 1637 for his friend Sustermans, and now in the Pitti Palace at Florence, was formerly in the Balbi Palace at Genoa, from which it was purchased by Mr. Irvine in 1803; it was subsequently in the collection of Mr. Champernowne, from which it passed to that of Mr. Rogers, and at the sale of his pictures in 1856 it was purchased for the National Collection.

RUYSDAEL.

JACOB RUYSDAEL, or RUISDAAL, the younger brother of Solomon Ruysdael, was born at Haarlem about 1625. His father, who was an ebony-frame maker, gave Jacob a good education, and intended him for the medical profession: he was formerly styled *Doctor*, sometimes. Ruysdael removed early to Amsterdam where he is supposed to have received some instruction in painting from Berchem. The figures in his pictures are said to have been inserted generally by Adrian Vandevelde, Ph. Wouvverman, or Lingelbach. He died at Haerlem, and was buried there November 16th 1681.

The landscapes of Ruysdael are generally simple natural views, well selected, and somewhat resemble those of Van Everdingen and Hobbema in style: his favourite subjects were woody scenes and waterfalls. His touch is exceedingly spirited and crisp, but his colours appear to have darkened through time. The views chosen are generally of a northern character, and some are assumed to be Nor-

* See the letter of Rubens, published in the account of Sustermans by Baldincuci, in the *Notizie dei Professori del Disegno*, Dec. III. Sec. V.

wegian, though it is not known that Ruysdael ever visited Norway. He sometimes painted marine pieces: there are also a few etchings by his hand. Hobbema is supposed to have been the scholar of Jacob Ruysdael; Jan Van Kessel and Jan Renier de Vries were his imitators.*

No. **627.** LANDSCAPE WITH WATERFALL. The whole fore-ground is occupied by the waterfall, a wooden bridge and a cottage are in the middle distance, the cottage is partly concealed by trees. Signed *J. Ruÿsdael f.*

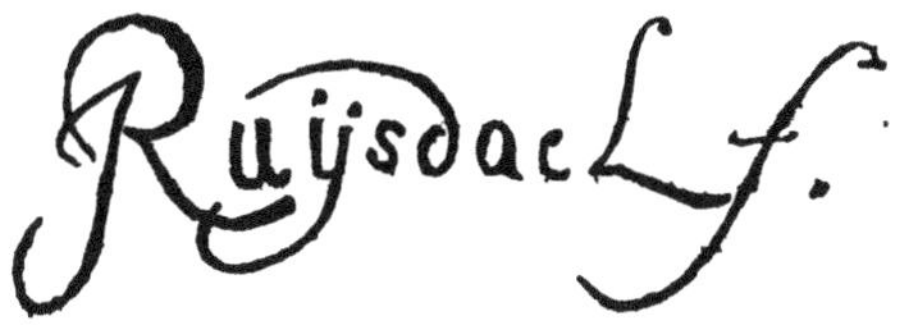

No. **628.** LANDSCAPE WITH WATERFALL. In the middle distance a wooden bridge; in the fore-ground a dead tree lying in the water. Signed as above.

On canvas, each picture 8 ft. 4½ in. *h.* by 2 ft. 10 in. *w.* Engraved, on a large scale, in mezzotint by J. G. Prestel.

Formerly in the collection belonging to Count Stolberg, at Söder, near Hildesheim; purchased at the sale of that collection, at Hanover, in 1859.

SALVIATI.

FRANCESCO ROSSI, called del SALVIATI, from his patron the Cardinal of that name, was born at Florence in 1510. He studied under Andrea del Sarto and other masters; was an imitator of Michelangelo, and the intimate friend of Vasari. In 1540 he was in Venice, and there painted a portrait of Pietro Aretino, which the poet sent to Francis I. Salviati visited France in 1554, in the reign of Henry II., but returned dissatisfied the next year. He painted much in Rome, where he completed the Chigi altar-piece in Santa Maria del Popolo left unfinished by Sebastiano del Piombo.† He had settled in Rome in 1548, and he died there, November 11, 1563.

---

* Houbraken, *Groote Schouburg*, &c.; Immerzeel, *De Levens en Werken*, &c., Rathgeber, *Annalen der Niederländischen Malerei*, &c, 1844. 333 works attributed to Ruysdael are described in Smith's *Catalogue Raisonné*, pt. vi.

† *Vite*, Vasari, &c., vol. xii.

No. **652.** CHARITY. A woman seated, offering her breast to a child who has turned away, and is caressing another child; on her right is a third boy standing near a brazier with live coal in it. Small figures.

On wood, 9¾ in. *h.* by 7 in. *w.*
Purchased at Paris from M. Edmond Beaucousin, in 1860.

SAN SEVERI'NO.

LORENZO DI SAN SEVERI'NO, with his brother Jacopo, were painting in Urbino in the early part of the fifteenth century. In the Oratory of San Giovanni Battista are still preserved some frescoes by these painters of the early date of 1416, representing passages from the life of the Baptist, and also the Crucifixion of Christ. The paintings bear the following inscription:—ANNO. DOMINI. MCCCCXVI. DE.XVIII. JULII. LAURENTIUS. DE. SANTO. SEVERINO. ET. JACOBUS. FRATER. EJUS. HOC. OPUS. FECERUNT.

Lanzi remarks, that these painters, though they lived in the fifteenth century, painted like the Florentines of the fourteenth; and he adds, that we have works by them as late as 1470. The frescoes are hard and positive in colour; but, if Lorenzo and his brother were established painters in 1416, it is, though possible, hardly probable, that they were still painting in 1470.

The picture by Lorenzo lately added to this collection appears certainly to belong to the later date, both from its subject, the Marriage of St. Catherine, and from its execution; the signature also, LAURENTIUS I.I. SEVERINAS PĪSIT, seems to indicate a *second* Lorenzo di San Severino, Laurentius II. (secundus), who may have been the son of the first Lorenzo, the painter of the Urbino frescoes, and a better known master.

No. **249.** THE MARRIAGE OF ST. CATHERINE. The Virgin and Child enthroned, surrounded by four saints, with a choir of angels above. On the right of the Virgin is St. Dominick, on the left St. Augustine; before the throne are kneeling on the left St. Demetrius of Spoleto, and on the right St. Catherine of Siena, on whose finger the infant Christ is in the act of placing the ring. St. Catherine wears her monastic dress, and in the gold nimbus, or glory, around her head is written, SANTA KTRINA DE SENA, allowing of no question as to her identity: in the nimbus of Christ are the words, SUM LUX; in that of the Virgin, AVE GRATIA PLENA DOMI. On the step of the throne are a fig or cucumber and an apple; and in a cartouche on the front of the step is the signature given above. Gold ground, figures small life-size.

On wood, 4 ft. 9 in. *h.* by 4 ft. 9 in. *w.*

Formerly in the sacristy of the church of Santa Lucia at Fabriano.* Purchased for the National Gallery at the sale of M. E. J. De Bammeville's collection, in 1854.†

SANTACROCE.

GIROLAMO DA SANTACROCE, a scholar of Giovanni Bellini, was painting at Venice between 1520 and 1548. He at

* Passavant describes it as there, in his life of Raphael—*Rafael von Urbino*, &c., 1839, vol. i. p. 428.

† There are two St. Catherines: the earlier, a young queen of Alexandria, according to the legend, belongs to the fourth century. She was at first a pagan, but, on being baptized, was espoused to the infant Christ. Her subsequent history will be found in the description of Raphael's picture of St. Catherine, p. 184. The later St. Catherine was born at Siena in 1347; she became a Dominican nun, and ended a short life of extraordinary piety and zeal in Rome, in 1380. The legend of the mystic marriage, as exemplified in the picture above described, also belongs to her; and it would not be easy to determine, without a careful comparison of the dates of the mediæval legends, which saint had the distinction ascribed to her first. The attribute of the wheel belongs, however, exclusively to St. Catherine of Alexandria.

The Sienese saint was canonized by Pope Pius II. in 1461. The ceremony is the subject of Pinturicchio's ninth fresco in the library of Siena, which bears the inscription:—"*Pius Pontifex Maximus Catherinam Senen. ob innumera ejus miracula inter Divas retulit.*" The date of the canonization, 1461, would at first appear to limit the date of Lorenzo di S. Severino's altar-piece, by precluding the possibility of its having been executed before that year; but the popular voice has constantly anticipated the formal recognition of the Church, which necessarily, in many instances, only confirms the voice of the people. It might not be difficult to find instances of saints represented as such before their canonization. A case in point occurs in Siena, in the church of St. Catherine, where she is represented by Pacchiarotto visiting the body of St. Agnes of Montepulciano, almost a century before the solemn recognition of St. Agnes by the Church. The fact, therefore, that Catherine is here represented as a saint is not absolute evidence of the corresponding later date of the picture; and the Laurentius II. Severinas of this work may still be the Laurentius de Santo Severino who executed the frescoes of 1416 at Urbino.

first followed his master in style, but afterwards became an imitator of Giorgione and Titian.*

No. **632.** A SAINT, reading. Full length, small life size.

No. **633.** A SAINT, holding a white standard with a red cross in one hand, and in the other a Monastery or Fortress. Full length, small life size.

On wood, each picture, 3 ft. 11 in. *h.* by 1 ft. 7 in. *w.*
Formerly the doors of an altar-piece. Purchased from M. Edmond Beaucousin, at Paris, 1860.

A. DEL SARTO.

ANDRE'A VANNU'CCHI, commonly called Andrea del Sarto, from the occupation of his father, who was a tailor, was born at Florence in 1488, and became the pupil of Piero di Cosimo. After the exhibition of Michelangelo's celebrated "Cartoon of Pisa," in 1506, he became a decided imitator of that painter in design: in colour, and light and shade, Fra Bartolommeo appears to have been his model. Having earned a great reputation by his works in Florence, both in oil and in fresco, he was invited by Francis I. to France. He arrived in Paris in 1518, and was well received by the King, but owing to the importunities of his wife, whom he had left behind, he returned to Florence in the following year, and having squandered away some money with which Francis had entrusted him to purchase works of art, Andrea never ventured to return to France. He died at Florence of the plague in 1530, aged only forty-two.†

Andrea del Sarto was one of the most distinguished painters of the sixteenth century. He is best known by his Holy Families, in oil; but he painted also many extensive works in fresco; the most celebrated are those of the convent of the Santissima Annunziata at Florence:‡ from the excellence of these frescoes he was called—*Andrea Senza Errori* (Andrea without faults). Of his easel pictures, the Madonna di San Francesco, now in the Tribune at Florence, is considered his masterpiece.§ Vasari, Jacopo da Pontormo,

* Zanetti, *Della Pittura Veneziana*, &c.

† Vasari, *Vite de' Pittori, &c.*; Lanzi, *Storia Pittorica, &c.*; Biadi, *Notizie Inedite della Vita d' Andrea del Sarto, raccolte da Manoscritti Documenti autentici.* Florence, 1830.

‡ Engraved by Alchiari, 1832–33.

§ Engraved by P. Lasinio; by Lorenzini; and by J. Felsing.

Franciabigio, and Domenico Puligo, were all scholars of Andrea del Sarto.

No. **17.** THE HOLY FAMILY. The Virgin with the infant Christ on her knees, and Elizabeth with the little St. John, seated on her right hand.

Engraved by P. W. Tomkins; and by S. Freeman, for Jones's *National Gallery*. On wood, 3 ft. 6 in. *h.* by 2 ft. 8 in. *w.*

Formerly in the Aldobrandini Villa at Rome, from which it was purchased for Mr. Buchanan by Mr. Irvine in 1805. Bequeathed to the National Gallery, in 1831, by the Rev. W. H. Carr.

No. **690.** HIS OWN PORTRAIT. Bust, life size. Signed with the painter's monogram, A.V.,—Andrea Vannucchi.

On canvas, 2 ft. 4 in. *h.* by 1 ft. 10 in. *w.*

Purchased at Florence from the effects of Nicolo Puccini in 1862.

SASSOFERRATO.

GIOVANNI BATTISTA SALVI, commonly called, after his birthplace, Sassoferrato, was born July 11, 1605. He was the pupil of his father Tarquinio Salvi; and belongs to the so-called *Carracceschi*, or followers and imitators of the Carracci and their scholars. In style and subject, though not in elaborate finish, his works bear considerable resemblance to those of Carlo Dolci. Sassoferrato died at Rome, August 8, 1685.*

No. **200.** THE MADONNA IN PRAYER. Half length.

On canvas, 2 ft. 5 in. *h.* by 1 ft. 11 in. *w.*

Bequeathed to the National Gallery, in 1846, by Mr. Richard Simmons.

SCHALCKEN.

GODFRIED SCHALCKEN, a distinguished Dutch *genre*-painter, was born at Dort in 1643; his father was rector of the Latin school there. He studied painting first under I. van Hoogstraten, from whom he went to Gerard Dow. Schalcken is chiefly distinguished for his pictures of candle-

* Lanzi, *Storia Pittorica*, &c.

light; and he rivals his celebrated master in finish. He died at the Hague in 1706.*

No. **199.** LESBIA WEIGHING JEWELS AGAINST HER SPARROW.†

On wood, 6½ in. *h.* by 5 in. *w.*

Bequeathed to the National Gallery, in 1846, by Mr. R. Simmons.

SCHIAVONE.

GREGORIO SCHIAVONE was a native of Dalmatia, and studied painting in the celebrated school of Squarcione, at Padua, where, about 1450, he was the fellow pupil of Andrea Mantegna.

Schiavone, like Crivelli, was fond of decorating his pictures with festoons and fruit; but his works are less advanced than those of Crivelli. He painted about 1470. He appears to have had an affection for his master Squarcione as he added his name to his own in his signatures of his works.‡

No. **630.** THE MADONNA AND CHILD ENTHRONED, with various Saints. The Madonna and Child in the centre; the dead Christ above; Saints Bernard, John the Baptist, Anthony of Padua, and Peter Martire at the sides; Anthony Abbot, Catherine, Sebastian, and Cecilia, below. Small figures. Signed, OPUS. SCLAVONI. DISIPULI. SQUARCIONI. S.

In tempera, on wood, in ten compartments. Centre picture, 3 ft. ½ in. *h.* by 13¾ in *w.*; upper picture, 15 in. *h.* by 10¼ in. *w.*; side pictures, 2 ft. 2 in. *h.* by 9 in. *w.*; lower pictures, 12 in. *h.* by 9 in. *w.*

Formerly in the Dennistoun collection. Purchased at Paris from M. Edmond Beaucousin, in 1860.

* Houbraken, *Groote Schouburg, &c.*; Immerzeel, *Levens en Werken, &c.*

† Catullus, *Carmen* iii.

‡ Ridolfi, *Le Maraviglie*, &c., *Art.* Squarcione.

SCHOEN.

MARTIN SCHOEN, or SCHONGAUER, was born at Ulm, about 1420; he was an established artist there in 1441. His father, Barthel, was also an artist and probably originally from Augsburg. Martin was apparently first an engraver, but he studied painting at Antwerp under the elder Roger Vander Weyden, called Roger of Bruges, and carried the Flemish taste and method of colouring to Germany. Martin was in Ulm in 1461, but settled shortly after that date at Colmar, where he established a celebrated school, and where he died February 2, 1488. He is known as Bel Martino and Martino D'Anversa by the Italians. Lambert Lombardus speaks of his merits and influence in a letter to Vasari, dated Liege, April 27, 1565.* His engravings, though crude in light and shade, are among the best of the early productions of this class. His pictures are conspicuous for their rich colouring.

No. **658.** THE DEATH OF THE VIRGIN. The Virgin, having received the last offices of the Church, is lying in a bed, surrounded by the twelve Apostles attending on her; above is the Deity supported by angels, about to receive her soul. A composition of many small figures in a chamber with a window looking out upon a square.

On wood, 15 in. *h.* by 13½ in. *w.* Engraved by L. Fleming in the *Gazette des Beaux Arts*, 1859.

Formerly in the collection of the King of Holland. Purchased at Paris from M. Edmond Beaucousin, in 1860.

SEBASTIA'NO DEL PIO'MBO.

SEBASTIANO LUCIA'NI, commonly called Fra Sebastiano del Piombo, from his office of keeper of the Leaden Seals, was born at Venice in 1485. He was originally, says Vasari, a musician, but having a decided taste for painting, he became the pupil of Giovanni Bellini; he studied also for some time under Giorgione. He was invited, about 1512, to Rome, by Agostino Ghigi, for whom he executed some

---

* Gaye, Carteggio Inedito d' Artisti, iii. 177. The dates of Passavant, *Beiträge zur Kenntniss der alten Malerschulen Deutschlands*, Kunstblatt, 1846, have been here followed; but Dr. Waagen, in his *Handbuch der Deutschen und Neiderländischen Malerschulen*, vol. i., Stuttgart, 1862, has adopted 1440–92 as the probable dates of the birth and death of this painter.

frescoes in the Farnesina. He at the same time contracted a friendship with Michelangelo, who employed him to paint some of his designs. Sebastiano obtained so great a distinction through his own powerful colouring and Michelangelo's assistance, that, as a painter of altar-pieces, he was enabled to contend for the palm even with Raphael. He was very successful as a portrait-painter; Vasari particularly notices his great skill in painting a head and hands. He was appointed Frate del Piombo by Clement VII.; an office which he held also under Clement's successor, Paul III., until his death. He died at Rome, in 1547, in the sixty-second year of his age.*

Sebastiano's masterpiece is generally considered the "Raising of Lazarus" in this collection. Of his portraits, that of Andrea Doria, in the Doria Palace at Rome, is the most celebrated.

No. 1. · The Resurrection of Lazarus.

"And when he had thus spoken, he cried with a loud voice, Lazarus, come forth.

"And he that was dead came forth, bound hand and foot with grave-clothes: and his face was bound about with a napkin. Jesus saith unto them, Loose him, and let him go."—*John* xi. 43, 44.

Christ is in the middle of the picture uttering the words, "Loose him, and let him go;" Lazarus, on the point of being freed from his grave-clothes, occupies the right of the composition: on all sides is a dense throng of curious spectators, with astonishment and conviction depicted on their countenances. In the middle-distance to the left is seen a group of Pharisees in eager discussion; beyond them to the right is a bridge conducting to a city, in the extreme distance. Composition of many figures, of the natural size. On a slab of stone beneath the feet of Christ is written—*Sebastianus Venetus Faciebat.*

·SEBASTIANVS·VENETVS·FACIE
BAT·

Engraved by Delaunay; by Vendramini; and by R. W. Lightfoot, for Jones's *National Gallery*. Transferred in 1771 from wood to canvas, 12 ft. 6 in. *h.* by 9 ft. 5 in. *w.*

Painted at Rome, in 1519, for Giulio de' Medici, bishop of Narbonne, afterwards Pope Clement VII. The Transfiguration

---

* Vasari, *Vite de' Pittori, &c.*; Biagi, *Sopra la Vita ed i Dipinti di Fra Seb. Luciani sopranominato del Piombo* in the *Atti del Ateneo di Venezia*, vol. i., 1827.

by Raphael and this picture were painted for this prelate, to be placed in the Cathedral of Narbonne in France. Both works were publicly exhibited together in Rome, and there were not wanting those who preferred the work of Sebastiano to that of Raphael. According to Vasari, Sebastiano was assisted by Michelangelo in the design of parts of this picture. It was sent to the Cathedral of Narbonne, where it remained until it was purchased by the Duke of Orleans early in the eighteenth century. It was brought to England in 1792, with the rest of the Orleans gallery, and came into the possession of Mr. Angerstein, with whose pictures it was purchased for the nation, in 1824.*

No. **20.** PORTRAITS OF SEBASTIANO DEL PIOMBO AND THE CARDINAL IPPOLITO DE' MEDICI. The Cardinal is seated at a table with pen and papers before him; the painter is standing opposite to him with his seal of office in his hand. Half-length figures, of the natural size.

Engraved by W. T. Fry, for Jones's *National Gallery*. On wood, 4 ft. 6 in. *h.* by 3 ft. 8 in. *w.*

Formerly in the Borghese Gallery at Rome, where it was sometimes called Borgia and Macchiavelli, and was attributed to Raphael. Ramdohr,† in his account of the works of art in Rome, in 1784, notices this picture as only probably by Sebastiano del Piombo. Bequeathed to the National Gallery, in 1831, by the Rev. W. H. Carr.

No. **24.** PORTRAIT OF A LADY, as ST. AGATHA; formerly supposed to be Giulia Gonzaga, a lady of the ruling family of Mantua, distinguished for her beauty and accomplishments. The nimbus, or glory, around the head indicates the Saint, and the pincers at the side, St. Agatha. Half-length, rather above the natural size.

Engraved by L. Stocks, R.A., for Jones's *National Gallery*. On canvas, 3 ft. *h.* by 2 ft. 6 in. *w.*

The portrait of Giulia Gonzaga, "a divine picture," as Vasari terms it, was painted at Fondi for the Cardinal Ippolito de' Medici, and by him presented to Francis I., of France, who placed it in his gallery at Fontainebleau, from which it was some time afterwards lost. This picture, said to be the portrait in question was painted in Rome; it is signed F. SEBASTIANUS, VEN. FACIEBAT, ROMÆ, was formerly in the Borghese Gallery at Rome, and

* Sir Thomas Lawrence was in possession of several drawings of parts of this composition, by Michelangelo, including two sketches of the figure of Lazarus: they were subsequently in the collection of the late King of Holland at the Hague.

† *Ueber Malerei und Bildhauerarbeit in Rom, &c.,* i. 289.

bequeathed to the National Gallery, in 1831, by the Rev. W. H. Carr.

·F· SEBASTIANVS
· VEN ·
· FACIEBAT ·
· ROMÆ ·

SEGNA.

SEGNA DI BUONAVENTURA, the pupil of Duccio di Buoninsegna, painted at Siena between the years 1305 and 1319.* His works are exceedingly rare; in the Gallery at Siena is a portion of an altar-piece, containing the Virgin and three Saints, in which *Segna me fecit* is inscribed on the sword of St. Paul, one of the Saints represented.†

No. **567.** CHRIST ON THE CROSS, with the Virgin and St. John at the extremities of the side limbs of the cross. A crucifix, with a projecting nimbus around the head of Christ; inscribed above, IHS. NAZARENUS REX JUDEORUM.

In tempera, on wood, 7 ft. 1 in. *h.*, by 6 ft. *w.*

Formerly in the Vanni Collection at Siena. Purchased at Florence, from the Lombardi-Baldi Collection, in 1857.

LO SPAGNA.

GIOVANNI DI PIETRO, called LO SPAGNA and LO SPAGNOLO (the Spaniard), was, after Raphael, the most distinguished of the scholars of Pietro Perugino. Few of the circumstances of his life are known: he was an established painter in Italy probably in 1503, and certainly in 1507. In 1516 he was made a citizen of Spoleto, and in the following year he was elected head of the Society of Painters there—*Capitano dell' Arte dei Pittori*: he was still living in 1530.

* Vasari, *Vite de' Pittori*, &c. Ed. Le Monnier. Flor. 1846.

† Engraved in Rosini's *Storia della Pittura Italiana, &c.*, vol. ii. p. 165. 2nd Ed. vol. ii. p. 4.

In his latest works Lo Spagna was an imitator of Raphael's third or Roman style; his best performances are considered those executed in the taste of his master Pietro Perugino. The Madonna Enthroned, painted in 1516, and now in the chapel of San Stefano, in the lower church of San Francesco at Assisi, is accounted by Rumohr this painter's masterpiece.*

No. **282.** The Glorification of the Virgin. The Virgin, holding in her left hand a lily, is seated in clouds, with the Child standing upon her knee: she is surrounded by cherubim, two of which are supporting a crown above her head; two others are holding lighted candles. On a marble platform below are two infant angels, seated; one playing on a viol, the other blowing a flageolet. In the landscape back-ground are seen a church, and distant mountains.

On wood, 5 ft. 10 in. *h.* by 2 ft. 7½ in. *w.*, circular top.

Formerly in the Ercolani Collection at Bologna. Purchased for the National Gallery at the sale of the Earl of Orford's pictures, in 1856.

SPAGNOLETTO.

Giusep'pe Ribe'ra, commonly called Lo Spagnoletto (the little Spaniard), was born in Spain, at Xativa, near Valencia, January 12, 1588. He was destined by his parents, says Cean Bermudez, for the pursuit of letters, but his passion for the arts induced him to prefer the school of Francisco Ribalta to the University. He went, when still a youth, to Italy, and, in spite of extreme poverty, prosecuted his studies as a painter with untiring energy, though sometimes depending entirely for support on the precarious charity of his fellow-students, in Rome. He was at first engrossed by the works of Raphael and Annibale Carracci, but eventually adopted the forcible and attractive style of Michelangelo da Caravaggio.

He studied also the works of Correggio at Parma; but on his return to Rome, finding that he could not agree with his old companions, Ribera determined to try his fortunes in Naples, where he married the daughter of a rich picture-

---

* Marriotti, *Lettere Pittoriche Perugine*, p. 95; Vassari, *Vite de' Pittori*, &c.; Life of Pietro Perugino, ed. Le Monnier, vol. vi. p. 54; Rumohr, *Italienische Forschungen*, vol. ii. p. 349.

dealer, and from this time entered upon a more important professional career, being employed, through the interest of his patron, the then Spanish Viceroy the Count de Monterey, on many commissions for Philip IV. of Spain. In 1630 he was elected a member of the Academy of St. Luke, at Rome, and in this year he entertained Velazquez at Naples; in 1644 he was decorated by the Pope with the insignia of the Order of the "Abito di Cristo." Cean Bermudez, following the account of Palomino, says that he died in Naples, honoured and rich, in 1656; but Dominici, the Italian historian of the painters of Naples, states that Spagnoletto disappeared from the city in 1648, and was not again heard of: this writer also claims him as an Italian, as a native of Gallipoli, in the Neapolitan province of Lecce, though of Spanish descent, an account contradicted by the Spanish historian, who quotes the register of Ribera's baptism at Xativa.

Ribera was perhaps the most able of all the so-called *naturalist* painters; he displays a remarkable power and facility even in his most unpretending works: they are correct in form, though it is of the most ordinary character; and, notwithstanding his excessive love of strong shadows, his pictures are rich in colour. He had many imitators; his influence was felt throughout Italy and Spain, but more especially at Naples; and though he cannot dispute the first place, in his style of art, with Caravaggio, the popularity of that peculiar class of painters known as the *Tenebrosi* and *Naturalisti* depended as much on the example of Ribera as of Caravaggio.

Belisario Corenzio, a Greek, Giambattista Caracciolo, a Neapolitan, and Ribera, formed a memorable cabal at Naples, the object of which was, by intimidation or otherwise, to banish all competing talent, whether native or foreign, and to monopolize the chief patronage of the city for themselves,—a conspiracy in which they succeeded too well for many years, until the death of Caracciolo in 1641. Domenichino, Annibale Carracci, the *Cavaliere* D'Arpino, and Guido, were all more or less victims of this cabal; Domenichino may be said to have died from the vexations it brought upon him. Luca Giordano and Salvator Rosa were the most eminent of Ribera's pupils.*

* Cean Bermudez, *Diccionario Historico de los mas ilustres profesores de las Bellas Artes en España*; Dominici, *Vite de' Pittori, &c. Napolitani*, Naples, 4 vols. 8vo. 1840–46.

No. **235.** The Dead Christ; or the subject termed a *Pietà* by the Italians—the Virgin weeping over the dead body of Christ; in this instance she is accompanied by St. John and Mary Magdalen. Four figures, of life size.

On canvas, 4 ft. 2 in. *h.* by 5 ft. 10 in. *w.*
Presented to the National Gallery, in 1853, by David Barclay, Esq.

No. **244.** Shepherd with a Lamb. Seated under a tree; in his left hand the crook. Full-length life size. Probably a portrait.

On canvas, 4 ft. 4¾ in. *h.* by 3 ft. 6¼ in. *w.*
Bequeathed to the National Gallery by Lord Colborne, in 1854.

SPINELLO ARETINO.

Spinello di Luca Spinelli, commonly called Spinello Aretino, was born at Arezzo about 1330. He became the pupil, before his twentieth year, of Jacopo di Casentino, while that painter was engaged at Arezzo.

After having executed several works at Arezzo, which have nearly all perished, Spinello in 1361 was employed by the Monks of Camaldoli, in the Casentino, to paint the principal altar-piece of their church; it remained in the church until 1539, when it was removed to give place to an altar-piece by Vasari.

He then painted some scenes from the life of St. Benedict in the sacristy of the Monastery of San Miniato al Monte, near Florence, which works are still in good preservation. An Annunciation and some other subjects still exist also in the Convent degl' Innocenti at Arezzo; one of which bears the inscription—*Hoc opus fecit fieri Clemens Pucci, &c. Anno Domini* 1377, *die* 15 *mensis Martii.*

In 1384 Spinello completed an altar-piece for the Convent of Monte Oliveto near Florence, on which were inscribed the names of Simone Cini, the carver, and Gabriello Saracini, the gilder, of the frame, as conspicuously as that of Spinello, the painter of the picture.*

From this time, owing to political disturbances at Arezzo, Spinello resided in Florence, until about 1387–8, when he

* A part of this altar-piece is now in the Gallery of Siena. Vasari, Ed. Le Monnier, vol. ii. p. 194, note.

was invited to Pisa to execute some frescoes in the Campo Santo there. These works, subjects from the lives of Saints Efeso and Potito, are by Vasari considered his masterpieces.* He remained in Pisa until the murder of Pietro Gambacorti, in 1392, when the disturbances arising from it compelled him to leave Pisa and return to Florence;† and after a year's sojourn in Florence, says Vasari, Spinello returned to his native place. This would be about 1394, and Spinello was still in the vigour of life. He executed several works at Arezzo after his return, of which the most remarkable was the "Fall of the Angels," in the church of Santa Maria degli Angeli, preserved till very recently.‡ There is also a "Coronation of the Virgin," in the Academy at Florence, which was painted in 1401;§ and in 1404–5, he painted the frescoes of the Church of San Niccolo at Arezzo.

In 1405 Spinello was in Siena; and on the 18th of June of 1407 he contracted for himself and his son (Parri Spinelli) to paint the series of frescoes still preserved in the Sala dei Priori, in the Palazzo Pubblico there, illustrating the struggle for supremacy between Pope Alexander III. and the Emperor Frederick II., at the monthly pay of 15 golden ‖ florins for the two, besides maintenance. A payment was made on the 4th of April 1408, but Spinello's name does not occur in the accounts after the 11th of July of that year.¶ He died at a very advanced age at Arezzo; the exact date is not

---

* These frescoes of the Campo Santo were paid for in 1392. Spinello received 150 gold florins (not 30*l.*) for three pictures. See Förster, *Beiträge zur neueren Kunstgeschichte*, 1835, p. 118.

† Vasari, *Vite, &c.* Ed. Le Monnier, vol. ii. p. 196. Professor Tomei of Lucca is in possession of a picture of the Virgin with Saints, signed: HOC OPUS PINXIT SPINELLUS LUCE DE ARITIO in A. 1391.

‡ A fragment of this wall-painting, transferred to cloth, and containing part of the St. Michael, the principal figure, is now in the possession of H. A. Layard, Esq. Engraved by Carlo Lasinio in 1821. It forms plate XXVI. of the *Affreschi Celebri del XIV. e XV. Secolo*. 1841.

§ Engraved in the *Galleria del I. e Reale Accademia delle Belle Arti di Firenze, &c.* 1846.

‖ The value of the gold florin varied at different times and in different places; but the modern Scudo or Francescone, about four shillings English, is sufficiently near to it to give an adequate idea of a sum computed in gold florins. The pay alone of Spinello on this occasion was nearly double that received by Duccio for his altar-piece (without maintenance) just one hundred years before. In the fourteenth century money had about twenty times its present value. The gold florin was worth between three and four shillings.

¶ Rumohr, *Italienische Forschungen*, vol ii. Milanesi, *Documenti per la Storia dell' Arte Senese*, vol. i. p 43, and vol. ii. p. 32, 1854.

known. Vasari remarks that his drawings or sketches were superior to his paintings. His execution is slight, but his colouring is good, and his draperies are managed with great skill.

No. **581.** St. John the Baptist with St. John the Evangelist and St. James the Greater. St. John the Baptist holds a scroll inscribed *Ego vos clamante in deserto, Parate via.** Three figures, small-life size.

In tempera, on wood. The entire picture 6 ft. 2 in. *h.*, by 5 ft. 1 in. *w.* The separate compartments each 4 ft. 6 in. *h.* by 1 ft. 7 in. *w.*

Formerly in the Hospital Church of Santi Giovanni e Niccolo, near Florence. Purchased at Florence from the Lombardi-Baldi Collection, in 1857.

TACCONI.

Francesco Tacconi, a distinguished painter of Cremona in the fifteenth century, of whom very few works now remain. Francesco and his brother Filippo Tacconi were in 1464 honoured by their fellow citizens with an exemption from personal taxes, on account of a Loggia painted by them in the Palazzo Pubblico of Cremona. In 1490 Francesco Tacconi was employed in the Church of St. Mark at Venice, for which he painted the doors of the organ then in use—on the outsides the Adoration of the Kings and of the Shepherds; on the insides, the Resurrection of Christ. These doors are still preserved, but the paintings are injured. The recorded inscription, O. Francisci Tachoni Cremon. Pictoris 1490 Maii 24, is no longer preserved.†

No. **286.** The Virgin enthroned; holding the Child upon her right knee, the right foot being raised on a foot-stool: in the background a green curtain. Inscribed on a plinth below, Op. Francisi Tachoni, 1489. Octu. Figures half-life scale.

On wood, 3 ft. 3 in. *h.* by 1 ft. 8½ in. *w.*

---

* Vox clamantis in deserto: Parate viam Domini. Matth. iii. 3.

† Moschini, *Guida per la Città di Venezia*, Ven. 1815, vol. i. p. 287. See also the Dictionary of Grasselli, *Abecedario Biografico*, Milan, 1827, in which the picture in this collection is mentioned. It is noticed likewise in the dictionaries of the Abate de Boni, Ticozzi, and Nagler.

Formerly in the Casa Savorgnan; purchased, for the National Gallery, at Venice, of the Baron Galvagna in 1855.

·OP·FRANCISI·
·TACHONI·1489·
·OCTV·

TENIERS.

DAVID TENIERS, the younger, was born at Antwerp in 1610. He was taught painting by his father, the elder Teniers, whose style he adopted; he received also some instruction from Adrian Brouwer. Teniers' success was commensurate with his abilities: his works were in universal request; the Archduke Leopold William, governor of the Spanish Netherlands, appointed him his court painter and one of his chamberlains; and he bought himself a country seat at Perth, a village between Antwerp and Mechlin, which became a constant resort of the Spanish and Flemish nobility: he gave Don Juan, of Austria, lessons in painting. This prince painted the portrait of Teniers' son, and presented it to the painter as a token of his regard. Teniers died at Brussels in 1694, and was buried at Perck. He was twice married: his first wife was the daughter of Velvet Breughel.*

Teniers, though a Fleming by birth, belongs rather to the Dutch school in style: he is one of the principal of the Dutch and Flemish *genre*-painters; his works, however, vary very much, both in subject and in execution. Some of his pictures are solidly executed, while others are painted so thinly that the ground of the painting is in many parts barely covered: he is said to have often commenced and finished pictures of the latter class at a single sitting. His general subjects are—fairs, markets, merry-makings, guard-rooms, beer-houses, and other interiors: he painted also landscapes. Sir Joshua Reynolds particularly directs the attention of the painter, who wishes to excel in execution, to the works of Teniers. "His manner of touching," he says, "or what we

* Houbraken, *Groote Schouburg, &c.;* Immerzeel, *Levens en Werken der Hollandsche Kunstschilders, &c.*

call handling, has, perhaps, never been equalled; there is in his pictures that exact mixture of softness and sharpness which is difficult to execute."* The prints after this painter are very numerous; there are also several etchings by his own hand. Many of his best pictures are in this country.

No. **154.** A Music Party; a woman, accompanied by a man with a guitar, is entertaining some peasants with a song. An interior; seven small figures.

Engraved by W. Pether.

D · TENIERS · F.

No. **158.** Boors Regaling; a man, expressing somewhat boisterous merriment in his attitude, is holding out a glass of ale at arm's-length; by his side is an old woman filling her pipe: a third figure is standing behind them. An interior; companion piece to the above.

On wood, both pictures, 10 in. *h.* by 14 in. *w.*
Bequeathed to the National Gallery, in 1838, by Lord Farnborough.

D · TENIERS . F.

No. **155.** The Misers, or Money-changers. A man and his wife counting their money; they are seated at a table covered with gold and silver coin, loose and in bags; some of the accessories seem to indicate considerable business transactions.

Engraved by C. W. Sharpe. On canvas, 2 ft. ½ in. *h.* by 2 ft. 9 in. *w.*
Bequeathed to the National Gallery, in 1838, by Lord Farnborough.

DAVID · TENIERS

No. **242.** Players at Tric-trac, or Backgammon. A Dutch interior, with eight small figures.

On wood, 1 ft. 2½ in. *h.* by 1 ft. 9 in. *w.*
Bequeathed to the National Gallery by Lord Colborne, in 1854.

· D · TENIERS . F.

---

* *Journey to Flanders and Holland.*

TINTORETTO.

JA'COPO ROBUSTI, commonly called Tintoretto, from the trade of his father, who was a dyer (Tintore), was born at Venice in 1512. He may be said to be self-taught, for the few days which he attended the studio of Titian can scarcely be said to constitute a pupilage under that great painter. Titian dismissed Tintoretto without assigning any cause for his disgrace.* This extraordinary rebuff appears to have added vigour to the young painter's energies: he commenced a course of indefatigable application, depending henceforth entirely upon his own resources. He bought casts from the antique and from the works of Michelangelo; he devoted the day to painting, and in the night he made drawings from his casts; he professed openly to draw like Michelangelo and to colour like Titian, and wrote the following line on the wall of his studio—

"Il disegno di Michelangelo ed il colorito di Tiziano."

He undertook every commission which offered itself, and frequently executed large works for the mere price of the materials. Such persevering labour did not fail eventually to procure him a high position among the painters of Venice; and, before he was forty years of age, he became the acknowledged rival of Titian himself. The Miracle of St. Mark, known as the "Miracolo dello Schiavo,"† Tintoretto's masterpiece, was painted when he was thirty-seven years of age: it is now in the Academy of Venice. This picture was painted for the Scuola di San Marco, with three others, which are also among Tintoretto's best works. —The "Exhumation of the body of Saint Mark at Alexandria;" the "Transport of the body to the ship;" and the "Miraculous preservation of a Saracen sailor, at sea, by the Saint." These pictures are still in the Scuola di San Marco; and Pietro da Cartona is reported to have said that, if he lived at Venice, he would never pass a holiday without going to see them.

Tintoretto painted other equally celebrated pictures for the Scuola di San Rocco; among them is the Crucifixion,

---

* Titian's attention being attracted by some very spirited drawings which he saw in his studio, he inquired who made them; and upon learning that they were Tintoretto's, who had been with him only ten days, he ordered one of his scholars to conduct the boy home.—Ridolfi.

† Engraved by J. Matham.

which was engraved by Agostino Carracci in 1589. The "Miracolo dello Schiavo," this "Crucifixion," and the "Marriage at Cana,"* painted for the Padri Crociferi, but now in the church of Santa Maria della Salute, are the only pictures to which Tintoretto put his name. He died at Venice in 1594, aged eighty-two. He left a son, Domenico, who died in 1637; his daughter, Marietta, an excellent portrait-painter, died before her father, in 1590, aged only thirty.

Tintoretto, from the rapidity of his execution, received the nickname of *il Furioso:* Sebastiano del Piombo said that Tintoretto could paint as much in two days as would occupy him two years. He was very unequal in his execution; the Venetians used to say that he had three pencils: one of gold, one of silver, and a third of iron. Annibale Carracci well expressed his inequality in the following words—"if he was sometimes equal to Titian, he was often inferior to Tintoretto."†

No. **16.** St. George destroying the Dragon. The Saint, mounted on his charger, is in the act of spearing the dragon, on the brink of the lake: on the ground before the knight is the dead body of a man: the exposed princess, for whom the knight ventured on his perilous exploit, is kneeling in the fore-ground.‡

Engraved by G. Corbould, for Jones's *National Gallery.* On canvas, 5 ft. 2 in. *h.* by 3 ft. 3 in. *w.*

Bequeathed to the National Gallery, in 1831, by the Rev. W. H. Carr.

TITIAN.

Tizia'no Vece'llio, commonly called Titian, was born in 1477, at Capo del Cadore, a small town on the river Piave, in the territory of Venice. He was placed, about the age of ten, with Sebastiano Zuccati, to learn painting. He quitted Zuccati for Gentile Bellini, but he left this painter also shortly afterwards to study under his more eminent brother Giovanni Bellini, with whom Giorgione, his future rival, was his fellow-pupil. Titian first appeared as a great

---

* Engraved by Volpato, and by Fialletti.

† Ridolfi, *Le Maraviglie dell' Arte, ovvero le Vite degli illustri Pittori Veneti, &c.;* Zanetti, *Della Pittura Veneziana, e delle opere pubbliche de' Veneziani Maestri;* Lanzi, *Storia Pittorica, &c.*

‡ See No. 75, p. 77, note.

painter, in 1514, at the court of Alfonso I., Duke of Ferrara, for whom he executed several celebrated works; among them, the "Bacchus and Ariadne," in this collection. It was during this visit to Ferrara that he painted the portrait of Ariosto, who thus commemorates the painter in his "Orlando Furioso:"—

> Bastiano, Rafael, Tizian ch' onora
> Non men Cadore, che quei Venezia e Urbino.*

After the death or owing to the great age of Giovanni Bellini, Titian was employed to finish the works which that painter had left incomplete in the Sala del Gran Consiglio, in Venice, and the Senate was so well satisfied with the manner in which he performed this task, that he was rewarded with the office of *La Senseria*, with a salary of 300 crowns per annum, by which he was obliged to paint, for eight crowns, the portrait of every Doge who might be created in his time.† Titian now produced a succession of celebrated works. In 1516 he painted his magnificent picture of the "Assumption of the Virgin," for the great altar of the church of Santa Maria de' Frari—it is now in the Academy at Venice; and in 1528 he added still more to his reputation by the celebrated picture of "St. Peter Martyr," for the chapel of that saint in the church of SS. Giovanni e Paolo. In 1530 he was invited to Bologna, by the Emperor Charles V., who sat to him for his portrait: from Bologna he went to Mantua, with the Duke Federigo Gonzaga, for whom he executed several commissions. In 1532 he returned to Bologna, and painted there a second portrait of the emperor, whom he is supposed to have accompanied into Spain. Madrid still possesses some of Titian's master-pieces, which may have been painted there during this visit. Cean Bermudez assumes that Titian took leave of the emperor at Barcelona, in 1535, when the latter went on his expedition to Africa. The emperor created Titian a Count Palatine of the Empire, and a Knight of the order of St. Iago: the patent of nobility was dated at Barcelona, in 1535.‡ The whole

---

* Sebastiano (del Piombo), Raphael, and Titian who honours not less Cadore than they Venice and Urbino. Cant. xxxiii. st. 2.

† Titian painted, by virtue of this office, the portraits of Pietro Lando, Francesco Donato, Marcantonio Trevisano, and the Venieri; the last two doges of his time he was unable to paint on account of the infirmities of age.

‡ Ridolfi says 1553; but Cean Bermudez, in his *Diccionario, &c.*, has shown that this is scarcely possible, and has conjectured that the date 1553 is an error of the copyist for 1535.

story of the visit to Spain is, however, doubted by Italian writers. In 1543, when Pope Paul III. was at Bologna, he invited Titian to that place to paint his portrait. Titian painted Paul III. a second time, two years afterwards, at Rome, during the painter's only visit to the great capital of the arts; but in this second picture, one of the most celebrated of his portrait-pieces, he introduced the Cardinal, and the Duke Octavio, Farnese, the pope's relatives. According to Vasari, the pope offered Titian the place of Sebastiano del Piombo, who died in 1547; but if the biographer is correct, that offer must have been made after Titian's return to Venice. He appears to have left Rome in May 1546. The offer was declined.

During Titian's stay in Rome, Michelangelo visited him, in company with Vasari, in the Belvedere, where he was engaged on a picture of Jupiter and Danäe. Vasari states that Michelangelo praised the picture very much when in Titian's presence, and that he spoke highly of the colouring and execution afterwards. but at the same time he expressed his regret to Vasari that the Venetian painters had not a better method of study, and were not early initiated in sound principles of drawing; adding—"if Titian had been as much assisted by art as he is by nature, nothing could surpass him."

After the abdication of Charles V., Titian found as great a patron in his son Philip II., and when, in 1554, the painter complained to Philip of the irregularity with which a pension of 400 crowns granted to him by the emperor was paid to him, the king wrote an order for the payment to the governor of Milan, concluding with the following words: "You know how I am interested in this order, as it affects Titian: comply with it therefore in such a manner as to give me no occasion to repeat it."

Vasari paid Titian a second visit in 1566, but this time in Venice, and although he was then nearly ninety years of age, Vasari found him with his pencil in his hand, and states that he derived great pleasure from his conversation. This great painter died at Venice, of the plague, in 1576, having attained the unusual age of ninety-nine years.

To be enabled to appreciate fully the extraordinary powers of Titian, it is necessary to examine his works at Venice; after Venice he is seen to most advantage at Madrid. His scholars were not numerous; the most distinguished are Paris Bordone, Bonifazio Veneziano, Girolamo di Tiziano, and his own son Orazio Vecellio. Titian is said to have engraved on copper and on wood.*

No. **3.** A Concert, or a Maestro di Cappella giving a Music Lesson. Five figures, half-length, of the natural size.

Engraved by H. Danckerts; by J. Groenswelt; and by J. Garner, for Jones's *National Gallery.* On canvas, 3 ft. 2 in. *h.* by 4 ft. 1 in. *w.*

Part of the Mantua Collection, purchased by Charles I., in 1630. It is mentioned in Vanderdoort's Catalogue as a "Music Party." Formerly in the Angerstein collection, with which it was purchased by Parliament for the nation in 1824.

No. **4.** A Holy Family; a Shepherd adoring: landscape, back-ground. Composition of four small figures.

Engraved by J. Rolls, for Jones's *National Gallery.* On canvas, 3 ft. 5½ in. *h.* by 4 ft. 8 in. *w.*

Formerly in the Borghese Palace at Rome. Bequeathed to the National Gallery, in 1831, by the Rev. W. H. Carr.

No. **32.** The Rape of Ganymede. Ganymede, son of Tros, one of the early kings of Troy, was carried off by an eagle to Olympus to be the cup-bearer of Jupiter. The beautiful youth, represented naked, with a bow in his hand, is being carried upwards by the eagle: a flowing red-coloured scarf gives effect and lightness to the composition. Figure of the natural size.

Engraved by G. Audran; by D. Cunego, for the *Schola Italica, &c.*; and by J. Outrim, for Jones's *National Gallery.* On canvas, an octagon, 5 ft. 8 in. each way.

Painted for a compartment of a ceiling; it corresponds with the description of the picture mentioned by Ridolfi originally in the Casa Sonica at Padua, painted by Damiano Mazza, a scholar of Titian's. That picture was generally reported to be by Titian, and was sent elsewhere as such. The picture above described was formerly in the Colonna Palace; the back-ground is a restoration by Carlo Maratta.† It was brought to England in 1800 by Mr. Day, and subsequently formed part of the Angerstein collection, with which it was purchased for the nation, in 1842.

---

* Vasari, *Vite de' Pittori, &c.*; Ridolfi, *Le Maraviglie dell' Arte, &c.*; Zanetti, *Della Pittura Veneziana, &c.*; Cadorin, *Dello Amore di Veneziani di Tiziano Vecellio*; Cean Bermudez, *Diccionario Historico, &c.*; Northcote, *The Life of Titian, with Anecdotes of the distinguished persons of his time*, London, 1830.

† Ridolfi, *Maraviglie*, &c. i. 290. Moschini, *Della Pittura in Padova*, p. 69. Ramdohr, *Ueber Malerei, &c., in Rom*, ii. 72.

No. **34.** Venus and Adonis; sometimes described as Cephalus and Procris: it was known under this title when in the Colonna Palace at Rome.* Venus withholds Adonis from the chase, while the young huntsman, holding his hounds in a leash with one hand and his spear with the other, is making an effort to free himself from the embrace of the enamoured goddess: Cupid is seen asleep in the back-ground.

Engraved on a large scale by Jul. Sanuto, the painter's contemporary; in small, by R. Sadeler, sen.; by Sir R. Strange; and by W. Holl, for Jones's *National Gallery*. On canvas, 5 ft. 9 in. *h.* by 6 ft. 2 in. *w.*

Formerly in the Colonna Palace at Rome. Imported by Mr. Day in 1800, subsequently in the collection of Mr. Angerstein, with the rest of whose pictures it was purchased for the nation, in 1824. Titian painted several repetitions of this picture, with slight variations.

No. **35.** Bacchus and Ariadne. Ariadne, daughter of Minos, king of Crete, deserted by Theseus, on the island of Naxos, is discovered by Bacchus, when returning with a train of nymphs, fauns, and satyrs from a sacrifice. The god no sooner sees the hapless princess than he becomes enamoured of her. Ariadne is on the left; Bacchus is represented in the centre of the picture leaping from his chariot to approach her: to the right, in the boisterous train of the god, is seen the drunken Silenus riding on an ass. Above Ariadne is the constellation of the golden crown with which Bacchus presented her, on her becoming his bride.† The back-ground is a glowing landscape, with a view of the sea, on which the departing ship of Theseus is seen in the distance. Composition of ten figures.

Etched by G. A. Podesta; and by J. Juster in 1691; and engraved in small in Jones's *National Gallery*. On canvas, 5 ft. 9 in. *h.* by 6 ft. 3 in. *w.*

Painted in 1514, at Ferrara, for the Duke Alfonso I. It was subsequently in the possession of the Barberini family, and afterwards in the Villa Aldobrandini at Rome, from which it was purchased by Mr. Irvine for Mr. Buchanan in 1806, and brought

---

* Ramdohr, *Ueber Malerei, &c., in Rom*, ii. 72.

† For the story of Bacchus and Ariadne, see Keightley's *Mythology*. This composition appears to be taken from Catullus, car. lxiv. 251. See Notts' Translation.

to England. It passed into the possession of Mr. Hamlet, of whom it was purchased for the National Gallery, in 1826.

TICIANVS. F.

No. **224.** The Tribute Money.

"Tell us therefore, what thinkest thou? Is it lawful to give tribute unto Cæsar or not?"

"And he saith unto them, Whose is this image and superscription? They say unto him, Cæsar's. Then saith he unto them, Render therefore unto Cæsar the things which are Cæsar's; and unto God the things that are God's."—*Matthew* xxii. 17—21.

Three figures, half-length.

Engraved by Martin Rota. On canvas, 4 ft. *h.* by 3 ft. 4½ in. *w.*

Purchased at the sale of Marshal Soult's collection, for the National Gallery, in 1852.

No. **270.** Christ appearing to Mary Magdalen after his Resurrection, commonly called "Noli me tangere," from the words of the Latin Vulgate.

"Then saith Jesus unto her, Touch me not; for I am not yet ascended to my Father."—*John* xx. 17.

The Magdalen is represented kneeling before Christ, who is partially clad in white drapery, and with a hoe in his hand. The scene is a landscape, in which a solitary tree in the middle ground is a conspicuous object; in the background, on a hill to the spectator's right, are some prominent buildings; on the left is a view of a distant country.

Engraved by Nicolas Tardieu. On canvas, 3 ft. 6½ in. *h.* by 2 ft. 11½ in. *w.*

From an autograph note to Mr. Rogers's catalogue, it appears that this picture was formerly in the cabinet of the Muselli family, at Verona; it was afterwards in the Orleans collection, whence it passed into the possession of Mr. Champernowne; at his sale, in 1820, it was purchased by Mr. Rogers, who bequeathed it in 1855 to the National Gallery.

No. **635.** The Madonna and Child with St. John the Baptist and St. Catherine embracing the Divine

Infant. A hilly landscape, evening; the Angel appearing to the Shepherds in the distance. Signed TICIAN. Small figures.

On canvas, 8 ft. 3½ in. *h.* by 4 ft. 7½ in. *w.* Engraved badly by Charles Andrau.

Formerly in the Sacristy of the Escurial, in Spain, where it was possibly painted; it has the Escurial mark N°. 78 Di. Titi°. Subsequently in the Coesvelt Collection. Purchased at Paris from M. Edmund Beaucousin, in 1860.

TICIAN

No. 636. PORTRAIT OF ARIOSTO, in a low crimson and purple dress, showing his neck and shirt; with a gold chain on his neck, and fur hanging over his shoulders, and holding in his left hand, which rests on a book, a rosary. In the background a laurel bush. Ariosto, the author of *Orlando Furioso*, and the friend of Titian, who painted him more than once,* was born on the 8th of September 1474; he died June 6th, 1533. Half-length, full size.

Transferred from wood to canvas, 2 ft. 3½ in. *h.* by 2 ft. *w.*

Apparently the portrait described by Ridolfi as then in the possession of Niccolo Renieri. Transferred to canvas by Paul Kiewert at Paris, in 1857. Formerly in the possession of Mr. Tomline. Purchased at Paris from M. Edmond Beaucousin, in 1860.

TREVISO, G. DA.

GIROLAMO DA TREVISO, the son and pupil of Piermaria Pennacchi, was born at Treviso in 1497. He painted chiefly in Bologna, Venice and Genoa; was an imitator of Raphael, and was a good portrait painter. He left Genoa on account of the too powerful rivalry of Perino del Vaga, and finally came to England, where he entered the service of Henry VIII., as architect and engineer. There are a few works by Girolamo still preserved at Bologna, but his pictures are very scarce. The "Adoration of the Kings," painted by him from the drawing of that subject by Baldassare Peruzzi, No. 167, which was presented to the Gallery by Lord Vernon, is probably the picture from that drawing, No. 218, in this collection. Girolamo was killed by a cannon ball in 1544, near Boulogne, while acting as an

* The woodcut profile of Ariosto in the edition of the *Orlando Furioso* of 1532, copied in the edition of Mr. Panizzi of 1834, was from a drawing by Titian.

engineer in the service of Henry VIII., when in his 47th year only.*

No. 623. THE MADONNA AND CHILD ENTHRONED, under a canopy, with Saints Joseph, James, and Paul; the last is presenting the donor, the patron of the Boccaferri chapel, to the infant Christ; behind the throne are some angels playing musical instruments. The view of a town in the background.

On wood, 7 ft. 5½ in. *h.* by 4 ft. 10 in. *w.* Engraved on wood by Gmo. Gandini.

Signed *Ieronimus Trevisius P.*, and mentioned by Vasari as the best of the painter's works—"*la migliore delle cose sue,*" (vol. iv. p. 52, ed. Le Monnier). It was formerly the altar-piece of the Boccaferri chapel in San Domenico in Bologna, from which it was sold and removed to Imola between 1706 and 1733.† It passed subsequently into the Solly collection. Purchased at Cheltenham, at the sale of the Northwick pictures, in 1859.

IERONIMVS·TREVISIVS ·P·

TURA.

COSIMO TURA, called COSMÈ, was born in Ferrara about 1418,‡ and was the pupil of Galasso Galassi, whom he surpassed in drawing, invention, and vivacity, but he did not emancipate himself from the dryness of manner of his master. He is called the Mantegna of Ferrara.

Cosimo succeeded Piero della Francesca as painter to the Duke of Ferrara, and he executed the fresco decorations of the new palace of Schifanoja, or Scandiana,§ for the Duke Ercole. The works executed by Piero were destroyed with the old palace in 1469. The decorations of Cosimo, commenced about 1471, were in twelve divisions, illustrating the achievements of Ercole's brother, the Duke Borso; they were long neglected, but seven of them were recovered from whitewash and oblivion in 1840, by Sig. Al. Cam-

---

* Vasari, *Vite, &c.* Federici, *Memorie Trevigiane su le opere di Disegno, &c.*, 1803, professes to correct Ridolfi who gives 1508 as the year of Girolamo's birth.

† Zanotti, *Le Pitture di Bologna*, ed. 1706, p. 241, where this picture is described; in the edition of 1733 the notice of it is omitted.

‡ Assuming that he did not exceed the age of 63. See Baruffaldi, *Vite, &c.* vol. i. p. 83 *n.*

§ Near Sant' Andrea, now a tobacco manufactory.

pagnoni.* Many of Cosimo's pictures also are preserved at Ferrara in the Costabili collection, in which are the two organ doors of the Cathedral, representing St. George and the Annunciation, painted in 1469, and reputed by some to be the painter's masterpieces. In the Strozzi Palace, at Ferrara, is a portrait of Tito Strozzi, the poet, by Cosimo. Cosimo Tura was still living on the 8th of February, 1481, the date of a contract entered into by him; he was buried in San Giorgio, in Ferrara, at the entrance of the Campanile, but the date of his death is not known.†

No. **590.** CHRIST PLACED IN THE TOMB, by St. John the Baptist and Joseph of Arimathea. Three small half-figures.

In tempera, on wood, $10\frac{1}{2}$ in. *h.* by 8 in. *w.*

Formerly in the possession of Professor Rosini, at Pisa. Purchased at Florence, from the Lombardi-Baldi Collection in 1857.

TURNER.

JOSEPH MALLORD WILLIAM TURNER was born in the spring of 1775, in Maiden-lane, Covent Garden, where his father carried on the business of a hair-dresser; he was christened in St. Paul's, Covent Garden, in May of that year. The friendship of Girtin, the water-colour painter, and the privilege of copying a collection of drawings in the possession of Dr. Monro, of the Adelphi, gave facilities for the development of the young painter's talent at an early age. Turner entered as a student of the Royal Academy in 1789, and he exhibited a drawing the following year; in 1799 he was elected an associate, and in April 1802 he became a member of the Academy. In this year he visited France and Switzerland. In 1807 he was elected Professor of Perspective in the Royal Academy, in which office he succeeded Edwards. In 1807 he commenced to publish his "*Liber Studiorum*," or book of sketches in imitation of Claude's "*Liber Veritatis*:" and for a few years during

---

* Il Conte Laderchi, *Descrizione dei dipinti di Schivanoja*, Ferrara, 1836, and Baruffaldi, vol. i. p. 84, 1844.

† Baruffaldi, *Vite de' Pittori e Scultori Ferraresi*, vol. i., Ferrara, 1844. Il Conte Laderchi, *La Pittura Ferrarese*, Ferrara, 1857.

this period of his life he painted in emulation of the style of Claude. In 1812 he built a house in Queen Anne Street West, No. 47, which he retained until his death, and in which he had a gallery where he for many years exhibited some of his pictures. Turner visited Italy three times:—in 1819, in 1829, and about 1840.

After a life of almost unrivalled success, and an industry unsurpassed, this great landscape-painter died, unmarried, and under an assumed name, at an obscure lodging at Chelsea, December 19th, 1851. He was buried by the side of Sir Joshua Reynolds, in the crypt of St. Paul's Cathedral. His large fortune, both in pictures and in funded property, he bequeathed to his country;—his finished pictures to the nation, on condition that the Government should provide suitable accommodation for them within ten years; and his funded property towards the establishment of an institution for the benefit of decayed artists.*

Turner's career comprehends, independently of his imitations of Claude, three distinct styles, in the first of which, previously to 1802, he was more remarkable as a water-colour painter; his early drawings are conspicuous for their careful completion, subdued colour, and effective light and shade; his earliest oil pictures resemble those of Wilson in style. In middle life, from about 1802 until about 1830, or his second visit to Rome, he was as distinguished for a masterly and vigorous execution and an unrivalled brilliancy of colouring; the majority of his greatest works belong to this time, from his "Calais Pier," 1803, to the "Ulysses deriding Polyphemus," 1829. During the last twenty years of his life, light, with all its prismatic varieties, seems to have chiefly engrossed his attention, yet some few of his finest works belong to this period, as his "Childe Harold's Pilgrimage," exhibited in 1832, and the "Temeraire," exhibited in 1839. His later pictures are painted on a white ground. Specimens of all his styles are numerous,

* The will was disputed, but in accordance with a compromise between the parties in litigation, it was decided by an order of the Court of Chancery, dated March 19th, 1856, that all pictures, drawings, sketches, finished or unfinished, by the hand of Turner, should belong to the nation, and that all engravings should belong to the next of kin. The finished pictures thus acquired for the National Gallery amount to about one hundred in number.

independent of book illustrations and other small water-colour drawings, for Turner was a large contributor to the annual exhibitions of the Royal Academy, having exhibited nearly 300 drawings and pictures on its walls.*

No. **479.** THE SUN RISING IN A MIST, fishing-boats arriving and unloading, fishermen cleaning and selling fish; guard-ship in the distance: tide low.

On canvas, 4 ft. 4 in. *h.* by 5ft. 10 in. *w.*
Engraved by J. C. Armytage, for the "Turner Gallery."

No. **498.** DIDO BUILDING CARTHAGE. A river scene with the sun in the centre of the picture; a bridge in front, and piles of classic architecture, completed and in progress, on either side; high banks and rocks in the back ground. Dido, Queen of Carthage, is seen surrounded by her people on the left.

On canvas, 5 ft. ½ in. *h.* by 7 ft. 5½ in. *w.*
Engraved by J. A. Prior and by E. Goodall, for the "Turner Gallery."

These pictures were considered by Turner two of his best works, and were bequeathed by him to the National Gallery, on condition that they should be hung between two Claudes, now placed by their side. "The Sun Rising in a Mist" was exchanged for the "Shipwreck," painted in 1805, and purchased by Sir John F. Leicester, afterwards Lord De Tabley, and at the sale of the De Tabley pictures, in 1827, it was repurchased by Turner. "The Sun Rise" was exhibited in 1807, the "Carthage" in 1815, and both belong to the painter's most vigorous period. They were placed in the gallery in 1853. On the extreme left of the Dido is inscribed, with Turner's name and the date of the picture, "Dido Building Carthage, or the Rise of the Carthaginian Empire."

UCCELLO.

PAOLO DI DONO, commonly called, from his love of painting birds, PAOLO UCCELLO,† was born at Florence in 1396–7,‡ and was originally brought up as a goldsmith. He was one of the assistants of Lorenzo Ghiberti in

---

* The Royal Acadamy Catalogues; *Art Journal*, Jan. 1852 and Jan. 1857; *Athenæum*, Dec. 1851, Jan. 1852; also *Turner and his Works; illustrated with examples from his pictures and Critical Remarks on his Principles of Painting.* By John Burnet. The Memoir by Peter Cunningham. 1852. "*The Turner Gallery, a series of sixty engravings from the principal works of J. M. W. Turner. With a Memoir and illustrative text by Ralph Nicholson Wornum, &c.*" Folio, London. 1861.

† Vasari, *Vite, &c.*, Ed. Le Monnier, vol. iii. p. 91.

‡ Gaye, *Carteggio Inedito d'Artisti*, vol. i. p. 146.

preparing the first pair of the celebrated gates made by Lorenzo for the Baptistery of Florence.

The majority of Paolo's works have perished. He painted the stories of Adam and Eve, and of Noah, in one of the cloisters of Santa Maria Novella, in Florence, of which traces still remain. And in the Cathedral of Florence there is still a colossal equestrian figure of John Hawkwood, an English adventurer and soldier of reputation, who died in the Florentine service in 1393. It is a chiaroscuro in *terra verde*: on the pedestal of the horse is written PAULI UCCELLI OPUS.* He painted some giants in the same method in the Casa de' Vitali in Padua, which, says Vasari, were greatly admired by Andrea Mantegna.†

In the gallery of the Louvre is a panel by Paolo Uccello, containing the heads, life-size, of Giotto, Donatello, Brunelleschi, Giovanni Manetti, and himself, representing painting, sculpture, architecture, mathematics, and perspective.

Paolo read geometry with Manetti, and was passionately devoted to the study of perspective, over which, says Vasari, he wasted so much of his time, that he became "more needy than famous."‡ He does not, however, appear to have been very poor, as he lived in his own house, which he bought, in 1434, for 100 florins. He died at Florence, aged eighty-three, in 1479.§

No. **583.** THE BATTLE OF SANT' EGIDIO, July 7, 1416, in which Carlo Malatesta, Lord of Rimini, and his nephew Galeazzo, were taken prisoners by Braccio di Montone.‖

---

* In 1842, about four centuries after it was painted, this picture was transferred from the wall to canvas, and is now placed over the door of one of the aisles, in the Cathedral.

† Each giant was painted in a single day, and at the price of a ducat, very high pay for a day's work, compared with the general accounts of the time. Morelli, *Notizia d'opere di Disegno, &c.*, 1800, p. 23.

‡ His wife complained to her friends that he sat up the whole night studying the rules of his favourite science, and that the only answer she got to her remonstrances was, *Oh! che dolce cosa è questa prospettiva*,—"What a delightful thing is this perspective." —Vasari, *Vite, &c.*, vol. iii., p. 99.

§ Gaye, *Carteggio Inedito, &c.* Vasari, *Vite, &c.*

‖ This battle took place on a plain between Sant' Egidio and the Tiber, on the road to Assisi, and Malatesta was captured during a repose in the fight, when his men went down to the river to drink.—Campanus *in Vita Brachii Perusini.* See Muratori, *Rerum Italicarum Scriptores*, vol. 19, p. 529. and in the *Chronicon Foroliviense*, p. 883; also in the *Cronaca Riminese*, vol. 15, p. 927. See also the *Annali* of Muratori, vol. 13, p. 149.

From the fragments of arms, &c., strewed upon the ground, the battle has been already fought; and the incident represented appears to be an attempt at rescue; which supposition is strengthened by the fact that Malatesta is marching under a strange standard. Of the many armed knights on horseback represented, only four are engaged, but all except Malatesta and his nephew have their faces concealed by their visors. The young Galeazzo, not yet a knight, carries his bassinet in his hand. The figure lying on the ground to the left is an illustration of the painter's love of foreshortening. In the background is a hedge of roses mixed with pomegranate and orange trees, and some hilly ground behind.

In tempera, on wood, 6 ft. *h.* by 10 ft. 5 in. *w.*

One of four battle pieces originally painted for the Bartolini family in Gualfonda;* subsequently the property of the Giraldi family in Florence, from whom it was obtained in 1844 by the late proprietors. Purchased at Florence from the Lombardi-Baldi Collection in 1857.

VANDER HELST.

BARTHOLOMEUS VANDER HELST, one of the most distinguished of the Dutch portrait-painters, was born at Haarlem in 1613. His masterpiece, the *Schuttersmaaltyd,* in the Museum at Amsterdam, is one of the most remarkable productions of the Dutch School of Painters. It contains thirty-five portraits of the natural size, twenty-four of which are named on the picture, and represents a banquet given by a company of the civil-guard of Amsterdam, in commemoration of the Peace of Münster, in 1648: the Spanish Ambassador is present at the feast. Sir Joshua Reynolds observes of this work—"This is, perhaps, the first picture of portraits in the world, comprehending more of those qualities which make a perfect portrait than any other I have ever seen."† Vander Helst died at Amsterdam in 1670.‡

No. **140.** PORTRAIT OF A LADY, standing; half-length.

On wood, 2 ft. 9½ in. *h.* by 2 ft. 2½ in. *w.*

Dated 1647. Bequeathed to the National Gallery, in 1837, by Lieut. Col. Ollney.

---

* Vasari, *Vite, &c.,* vol. iii., p. 96, note 2. The annotators notice the excellent state of preservation of this picture.

† *Journey to Flanders and Holland.*

‡ Houbraken, *Groote Schouburg, &c.;* Immerzeel, *Levens en Werken, &c.*

VANDER MEIRE.

GERARD VANDER MEIRE, born probably at Ghent not earlier than 1410, is said to have been the scholar of Hubert Van Eyck. His name occurs in the list of the corporation of Painters of Ghent first in 1452; and in 1474 he was elected one of the two *sworn members* of the corporation for that year. The earliest picture by him recorded is the portrait of a nun of St. Clara, Collette, who died at Ghent in 1447: he also painted a picture of the Virgin for the church of St. John at Ghent. The chief of his remaining works is the altar-piece of St. Bavon, representing, in the centre, Christ on the cross between the two thieves, a composition of many figures; on the right, the brazen serpent, on the left, Moses striking the rock.

Vander Meire is considered to approach nearer to the execution of the Van Eycks, or rather of Hubert, than any of the school; there is the same laborious elaboration of costume, but his forms are considered elongated, his light and shade weaker in effect, and his colouring inferior to that of the Van Eycks. The landscape was an important accessory in his works. He is probably the Gerard van Ghent who contributed, with Memling, to the miniatures of the celebrated Missal in the Library of St. Mark at Venice The majority of his pictures were destroyed by the iconoclasts of the 16th century, during the religious disturbances in the Netherlands.

Gerard had a brother, Jan Vander Meire, who died at Nevers in 1471.*

No. **264.** A COUNT OF HENEGAU WITH HIS PATRON SAINT, AMBROSE. The count is represented as a Carmelite monk praying, in bishop's robes, with the crosier on his arm, and a richly ornamented mitre by his side. On the front of the mitre is embroidered the Crucifixion, with the Virgin and St. John by the side of the cross. Behind the kneeling figure is the Saint, in a richly-embroidered stole, and wearing the bishop's mitre, holding a cross in his left hand, and a scourge in his right. The execution of the costume, jewellery, &c., is extremely elaborate. Small figures, half-length.

---

* Busscher, *Notice sur l'Ancienne Corporation des Peintres et Sculpteurs a Gand*, 8vo, Brussels, 1853; Passavant, *Kunstreise durch England und Belgien, &c.*; Rathgeber, *Annalen der Niederländischen Malerei*; Michiels, *Histoire de la Peinture Flamande et Hollandaise.*

On wood, 2 ft. 4½ in. *h.* by 9 in. *w.*
Purchased for the National Gallery with other pictures in the Collection from Herr Krüger of Minden, in 1854.

VANDER NEER, A.

Aart or Arthur Vander Neer was born probably at Gorinchem, about 1613 or 1619: the exact date is not known; nor is it known under what painter or painters he studied. He lived chiefly at Amsterdam; but at the close of his life he appears to have resided at Rotterdam, where he was still living in 1691.*

Aart Vander Neer excelled in moonlight scenes. He was the father of Eglon Vander Neer.

No. **152.** A Landscape, with Figures and Cattle; Evening. A country-house is seen in the middle-ground; beyond it to the right is a view of a town: shipping in the distance. The figures were painted by Cuyp, whose name is inscribed on the pail.

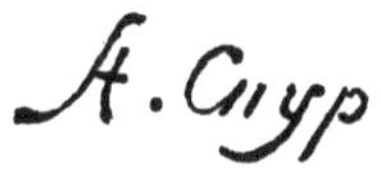

Engraved in the *Galerie de Lucien Bonaparte.* On canvas, 3 ft. 11 in. *h.* by 6 ft. 3½ in. *w.*
Formerly in the collections of M. Erard, and Lucien Buonaparte. Bequeathed to the National Gallery by Lord Farnborough, in 1838. Signed with the painter's monogram, A. V. D. N.

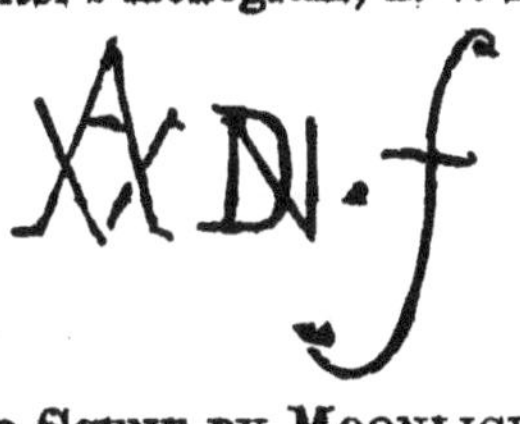

No. **239.** River Scene by Moonlight, with Shipping. On the left a town; the moon rising in the middle-distance. Low-water.

On wood, 1 ft. *h.* by 1 ft. 6½ in *w.* Formerly in the collection of R. Heathcote, Esq., sold in 1805. Bequeathed to the National Gallery, in 1854, by Lord Colborne. Signed with the painter's monogram.

---

* Van Eynden and Vander Willigen, *Geschiedenis der Vaderlandsche Schilderkunst, &c.*; Immerzeel, *Levens en Werken, &c.*

VANDER WEYDEN.

ROGER VANDER WEYDEN the elder, called by Vasari *Ruggieri da Bruggia,* and *Rogerius Gallicus* by Facius,* was a native of Brussels, where he was born at the close of the fourteenth century: he was already a painter of reputation as early as 1430. Roger is considered the most able of the scholars of the Van Eycks, whose style he carried to Brussels and even to Italy; he was appointed painter to the city of Brussels in 1436, and in 1449 he visited Italy, and was present at Rome at the celebration of the jubilee in 1450. He died at Brussels, June 16th, 1464, aged upwards of sixty, and was buried in the church of Saint Gudule.

Vander Weyden, says Van Mander, greatly reformed the Flemish style of design; he was a great master of expression, and though his outline is generally harder than John Van Eyck's, his heads are often much softer in their character. He painted in distemper and in oil, and was the first to paint on fixed canvases for the decoration of rooms, and appears also to have been the first to prefer linen cloth to wood, to paint upon.†

No. **664.** THE DEPOSITION IN THE TOMB: Joseph of Arimathæa, St. John, the Virgin Mary, &c. Composition of eight small figures in a landscape; woody distance.

In *tempera* on linen, 2 ft. 10 in. *h.* by 2 ft. 4 in. *w.*

Purchased in Milan from the representatives of the Guicciardi family, in 1860.

VANDER WEYDEN.

ROGER VANDER WEYDEN the younger, probably the son or grandson of the elder painter of that name, was born at Brussels about 1450, and died of the *Suette* at Antwerp in 1529. He was a member of the Academy

---

* *De viris illustribus,* &c., Flor. 1745, p. 48. Facius notices (1456) some pictures by Roger, in the possession of Alphonso, King of Naples, on *linen,*—"nobiles in linteis picturæ," such probably as the present example is painted on.

† Van Mander, *Het Schilder Boek,* &c.; Passavant, *Kunstblatt,* 1843; Michiels, *Les Peintres Brugeois,* 1846; Waagen, *Handbook of Painting,* 1860.

of Antwerp, but the circumstances of his life are not known.*

No. **653.** Portraits of himself and Wife; the painter wearing a red turban, his wife with a white cloth on her head. Busts, life size.

On wood, each panel 16 in. *h.* by 11 in. *w.*

No. **654.** The Magdalen, in a green dress, and gold brocaded petticoat, seated, reading a book; before her on the floor is a small vase. Entire small figure.

On wood, 2 ft. *h.* by 1 ft. 8⅛ in. *w.*
Both pictures purchased at Paris from M. Edmond Beaucousin, in 1860.

VANDEVELDE.

William or Willem Vandevelde the younger, a distinguished Dutch marine painter, was the son of the elder William Vandevelde, and was born at Amsterdam in 1633; he was instructed by his father, and by a marine painter of the name of Simon de Vlieger. Both the Vandeveldes were established in England in the service of Charles II. in 1675. They were each granted a pension of 100*l.* per annum by the King; the father "for taking and making draughts of sea-fights," and the son "for putting the said draughts into colours."† These painters lived at Greenwich, where the father died in 1693, aged 83; the son died in London in 1707.

"William Vandevelde, the son," says Walpole,‡ "was the greatest man that has appeared in this branch of painting; the palm is not less disputed with Raphael for history, than with Vandevelde for sea-pieces."

No. **149.** A Calm at Sea.

On wood, 8 in. *h.* by 11 in. *w.* Signed—

W.V.V.

No. **150.** A Fresh Gale at Sea.

On canvas, 9 in. *h.* by 13 in. *w.* Signed—

W.V.V.

Bequeathed to the National Gallery, in 1838, by Lord Farnborough.

* Van Mander, *Het Leven der Schilders*, &c.

† The "Draughts" alluded to, of the elder Vandevelde, were generally drawn on prepared canvas, in pen-and-ink.

‡ *Anecdotes of Painting.*

VANDYCK.

ANTONY VANDYCK was born at Antwerp, March 22, 1599. His father, Frans Vandyck, was a merchant in that city, and Antony was the seventh of a family of twelve; his mother, Maria Cupers, died when he was only eight years old, in 1607. He became the pupil of Hendrik Van Balen so early as 1609; but Vandyck's great instructor was Rubens, with whom he lived about four years. He was still acting as Rubens's assistant in 1620, although he had been admitted a master of the Antwerp Corporation of Painters early in the year 1618, before his twentieth birthday.* Having attained sufficient proficiency as a painter, he, by the advice of Rubens, visited Italy in 1623; he spent about five years in that country, dividing his time between Genoa, Venice, and Rome; he paid also a short visit to Palermo. Shortly after his return to Antwerp, in 1628, he painted a picture of St. Augustin, for the church of the Augustines of that city, which established his celebrity as one of the first masters of his age; this was followed by a still more celebrated work, the Crucifixion, for the church of St. Michael at Ghent; and he soon acquired an unrivalled reputation as a portrait-painter.

About the year 1630–31, Vandyck appears to have visited England, but not meeting with that reception which he had anticipated, he returned after a short time to his own country: he had already visited England before, in 1621, previous to his journey to Italy.† In 1632, however, Charles I., who had seen a portrait of Nicolas Laniere, his chapel-master, by Vandyck, sent an express invitation to the painter to come to England, and, on this occasion, he was most courteously received. He was lodged by the king at Blackfriars, was knighted in the following year, and was granted a pension of 200*l.* per annum for life, with the title of painter to his Majesty. Vandyck settled for the remainder of his life in England, where his very successful career as a portrait-painter enabled him to live in great style. He had a country house at Eltham, in Kent, where he spent a portion of the summer; he kept great state when in town, "he always went magnificently dressed, had a numerous and gallant equipage, and

---

* *Catalogue du Musée d'Anvers*, 1857.

† See W. Carpenter, *Memoir of Sir Anthony Vandyck, &c.* London, 1844.

kept so good a table in his apartment, that few princes were more visited or better served."*

Vandyck died in London, December 9, 1641, in the forty-third year of his age: and was buried in the old church of St. Paul, near the tomb of John of Gaunt. He left a daughter, his only child, by his wife Mary Ruthven, grand-daughter of the unfortunate Lord Ruthven, Earl of Gowrie. Notwithstanding his expensive style of living, Vandyck left property to the value of about 20,000*l.* sterling.† Of the numerous portraits executed by this painter the best are in England; there are also several etchings by his hand.‡

No. 49. THE PORTRAIT OF RUBENS, half-length, standing, his left arm leaning on a table; to the right are parts of two other figures, pointing to a piece of sculpture.

Engraved by J. H. Robinson, for the *Associated Engravers*; and by W. Holl, for Jones's *National Gallery*. On canvas, 3 ft. 9 in. each way.

Formerly in the possession of Sir Joshua Reynolds, by whom the picture was much prized. It passed subsequently into the Angerstein collection, with which it was purchased in 1824.

No. 50. THE EMPEROR THEODOSIUS REFUSED ADMISSION INTO THE CHURCH BY ST. AMBROSE. The Emperor Theodosius, after the massacre of Thessalonica in the year 390, was placed under the ban of the Church, and on his attempting afterwards to enter the Cathedral of Milan he was repulsed at the door by the Archbishop Ambrose.§ Composition of, in all, eleven, but only four principal figures.

Engraved by R. W. Sievier; by J. H. Robinson, for the *Associated Engravers*; and by S. Freeman, for Jones's *National Gallery*. On canvas, 4 ft. 10 in. *h.* by 3 ft. 9 in. *w.*

Copied, with slight alterations, from the original picture by Rubens, in the Imperial Gallery at Vienna, of which there is a large print by J. M. Schmutzer. This picture was formerly in the possession of the Earls of Scarborough, from whom it passed into that of Mr. Angerstein, and was purchased by Parliament for the nation, with the rest of that gentleman's pictures, in 1824.

---

* Graham, *Essay towards an English School*, at the end of the Translation of De Piles. London, 1706.

† Houbraken, *Groote Schouburg, &c.*; Bellori, *Vite de' Pittori, &c.*; Descamps, *La Vie des Peintres Flamands, &c.*; Walpole, *Anecdotes of Painting in England, &c.*; W. Carpenter, *Memoir of Vandyck.*

‡ See the Catalogue in Carpenter's *Memoir, &c.* For a list of his pictures, see Smith's *Catalogue Raisonné, &c.*

§ Gibbon, *Decline and Fall*, c. xxvii.

No. **52.** PORTRAIT OF A GENTLEMAN, commonly called GEVARTIUS. It has been generally supposed to represent Caspar Gevaerts, or Gevartius, the intimate friend of Rubens.* Bust.

Engraved by Sievier; by T. Woolnoth; by G. T. Doo, R.A., for the *Associated Engravers;* and by J. Rogers, for Jones's *National Gallery*. On wood,† 2 ft. 7 in. *h.* by 2 ft. 2 in. *w.*

Formerly in the Angerstein collection. Purchased by Parliament for the nation in 1824.

No. **156.** A STUDY OF HORSES. In the upper part of the picture is the sketch of a zephyr's head. The painter intended to represent in this study the horses of Achilles, Xanthus and Balius, the offspring of Zephyr.‡ *Equi Achillis,* and some other words now illegible, are written on a scroll in the lower corner of the picture to the left.

On wood, 3 ft. 6 in. *h.* by 2 ft. 11 in. *w.*

Formerly in the Delmé collection; afterwards in that of Sir Joshua Reynolds. Bequeathed to the National Gallery, in 1838, by Lord Farnborough.

No. **680.** THE MIRACULOUS DRAUGHT OF FISHES. Composition of eleven small figures, with two boats.

"Cast the net on the right side of the ship, and ye shall find. They cast therefore, and now they were not able to draw it for the multitude of fishes."—*John* xxi. 6.

"And Jesus said unto Simon, Fear not; from henceforth thou shalt catch men."—*Luke* v. 10.

On paper, 1 ft. 9¾ in. *h,* by 2 ft. 9½ in. *w.* Engraved the same size by S. Bolswert.

Painted by Vandyck from the large picture by Rubens at Mechlin, for the engraver Bolswert to work from. Bought from the Cav. Raffaele Carelli at Naples in 1861.

VELA'ZQUEZ.

DON DIEGO VELA'ZQUEZ DE SILVA§ was born at Seville in the spring of 1599, and studied painting first under Fran-

---

* Caspar Gevartius was born in 1593; and if the picture represents this person, it cannot have been painted by Vandyck, as the age of the original when this portrait was taken must have been about sixty. The Canon John Gevartius died in 1623, when Vandyck was quite a young man, and in Italy. See Waagen *Kunstwerke und Künstler in England.* According to some writers, the picture represents Cornelius Vander Geest, an amateur of the arts and intimate friend of Rubens. See Dallaway, vol. ii. p. 186, *note.*

† The head, which is painted upon some other material and fixed upon or in the wood, is supposed by some critics to have been painted by Rubens, and the dress only by Vandyck. See Passavant, *Kunstreise, &c.*, and Waagen, *l. l.*

‡ Homer, *Il.* xvi. 146.

§ Or, as Cean Bermudez says, more correctly, Don Diego Rodriguez de Silva y Velázquez: his father's name was Juan Rodriguez de Silva, his mother's Gerónima Velazquez.

cisco Herrera the elder. He left this master to enter the school of Pacheco, whose daughter he afterwards married.

In 1622, Velazquez paid a visit to Madrid; in the following year he was invited to return to the capital by the Duke of Olivares, who introduced the young painter to Philip IV., and from this time Velazquez was established as a royal favourite: he was appointed court painter to the king. It was in this year, 1623, that he painted a portrait sketch of our Charles I. when Prince of Wales.

In the summer of 1629, Velazquez made his first visit to Italy: he spent a year in Rome, and some time in Naples, where he contracted a friendship with his countryman Spagnoletto: he returned in 1631 to Madrid, and was presented by Philip IV. with a painting-room in the royal palace. At the close of the year 1648, the king sent him again to Italy to purchase works of art for him, and it was on this occasion that Velazquez painted his celebrated portrait of Pope Innocent X., now in the Doria Gallery at Rome. After his return, the King created him his *Aposentador Mayor*,* and decorated him with the Cross of St. Iago. This post rendered it necessary for Velazquez to be a constant attendant on the King's person whenever he left the capital; and the duties of this office were the immediate cause of his death: it was, probably, in consequence of the exertions he made in providing the royal quarters on the occasion of the conference at Irun, in June 1660, which led to the marriage of Louis XIV. with the Infanta Maria Teresa, that he was taken ill a few days after his return to Madrid; he returned July 31, and died on the 7th of August following, in the sixty-second year of his age. He was buried with great pomp in the church of St. Juan, and his wife followed him to the grave seven days afterwards.†

Velazquez, though eminent in history, portrait, and landscape, belonged, like most of the painters of Spain, to the "naturalist" school: the *Aguador*, or water-carrier, is a celebrated picture of his early manner. His style of execution bears much resemblance to that of his countryman Ribera, but he is much more extensive in his range of subjects. His greatest

* It was the duty of the Aposentador Mayor (Quarter-master) to superintend the personal lodgment of the King during excursions.

† Cean Bermudez, *Diccionario Historico de los mas ilustres profesores de las Bellas Artes en España*. There is a critical account of Velazquez in the *Penny Cyclopædia*, by Richard Ford. See also Cumberland's *Anecdotes, &c.*

works are still at Madrid, where alone he can be adequately appreciated. He had such mastery in execution, says Mengs, alluding particularly to his picture of The Women Spinning, *Las Hilanderas*,* that he appears to have painted with his *will* only without the aid of his hand.† The works of Velazquez consist chiefly of portraits, among the most celebrated of which is one of himself painting the Infanta Margarita Maria, afterwards Empress of Germany.‡

No. **197.** PHILIP IV. OF SPAIN HUNTING THE WILD BOAR. The hunt is taking place in an enclosed piece of ground, in the front of which are many spectators; hills and foliage occupy the back-ground. Numerous small figures.

On canvas, 6 ft. 2 in. *h.* by 10 ft. 3 in. *w.*

Formerly in the royal palace at Madrid, until it was presented by Ferdinand VII. to the late Lord Cowley, of whom it was purchased for the National Gallery, in 1846.

No. **232.** The NATIVITY, or ADORATION OF THE SHEPHERDS, commonly called "THE MANGER"—the *Presepio* of the Italians. The Holy Family is in the stall on the left, the infant Christ lying in the manger near the head of the ox; the Virgin is uncovering him; on the right are the adoring shepherds bringing presents according to their means,—lambs, fowls, &c. In the distance is seen the guiding angel as the star of the Epiphany. Nine figures of the natural size.

On canvas, 7 ft. 7 in. *h.* by 5 ft. 6 in. *w.*

This picture was purchased for Louis Philippe, late King of the French, by Baron Taylor, from the Count D'Aguilar, in whose family it had remained from the time of its being painted. It is an early work, in the simple naturalistic manner of the painter, in the style of Spagnoletto. It was purchased for the National Gallery at the sale of Louis Philippe's collection in London, in 1853.

VENEZIA'NO.

BARTOLOMMEO VENEZIA'NO, a Venetian painter of the sixteenth century, by whom three pictures only, at present, are known:—A Virgin and Child, with a land-

---

* Engraved by F. Montañes.

† In his letter to Ponz; it is quoted by Cean Bermudez, *Diccionario, &c.*, v. 177.

‡ This is the picture known, from the exclamation of Luca Giordano, as *La Teologia de la Pintura*: there is a Spanish print of it by D. Francisco de Goya: it is engraved also by P. Audouin.

scape background, in the Villa Lochis,* inscribed *Bartolomæus Venetus* 1505; a female portrait, formerly in the Manfrini Gallery at Venice,† inscribed with the same name, and dated 1530; and the male portrait, now in this collection, also of the year 1530, and inscribed as below.

No. **287.** PORTRAIT OF A YOUNG MAN. Lodovico Martinengo, in a red mantle and cap, the latter with a white ostrich feather in it, the costume of the Compagnia della Calza. The right hand is raised and holding a glove; in the background is a green curtain. The picture is inscribed on a white scroll—LUDOVICUM MARTI. ÆTATIS SUÆ ANNO XXVI. BARTOLOM. VENETUS FACIEBAT MDXXX. XVI. ZUN. Half-figure, life size.

On wood, 3 ft. 5¼ in. *h.* by 2 ft. 4 in. *w.*

Purchased, for the National Gallery, in Venice, of the heir of the Conte Girolamo Martinengo, in 1855.

VERNET.

CLAUDE JOSEPH VERNET, one of the most celebrated of the French landscape and marine painters, was born at Avignon, August 14, 1714. He was instructed by his father Antoine Vernet, and Adrian Manglard, a landscape painter. He went in 1732 to Italy, with a view of improving himself in historical painting; but the beautiful scenery of Genoa and Naples induced him to devote himself entirely to marine landscape. He remained in Italy, altogether, including a short visit to Greece, about twenty years, during a considerable portion of which he was in a state of great poverty; a picture was sold at the sale of M. de Julienne for 5,000 francs,

---

* *La Pinacoteca e la Villa Lochis, &c.* Milano, 1846, p. 59.

† Recently purchased by Mr. Barker, of Piccadilly.

which Vernet had painted for a single suit of clothes. In 1752 he was invited by Louis XV., through M. de Marigny, to Paris: he was elected a member of the French Academy of Arts in the following year. It was in this year also, 1753, that he was commissioned by the French Government to paint his celebrated pictures of the sea-ports of France. He painted in all fifteen views,* which occupied him the greater part of ten years: he received for each picture, including his travelling expenses, only 7,500 francs; the king, however, gave him apartments in the Louvre.

Vernet died at Paris Dec. 3. 1789: he was the grandfather of the eminent painter, M. Horace Vernet.†

No. **236.** Castle of Sant'Angelo, Rome, with the Bridge of Sant'Angelo and neighbouring buildings, and a fête on the Tiber, representing tilting in boats, and other festivities. Numerous small figures.

On canvas, 3 ft. 3 in. *h.* by 4 ft. 7½ in. *w.* Engraved by P. J. Duret.

Painted at Rome in 1750. Formerly in the collection of the Marquis de Villette. Presented to the National Gallery by Lady Simpkinson, in 1853.

Joseph Vernet. f.
· Romæ · 1750 ·

VERONE'SE, PA'OLO.

Pa'olo Caliari, or Ca'gliari, commonly called from his birthplace Paolo Veronese, was born at Verona in 1528,‡ and was taught the rudiments of design by his father, Gabriele Caliari, who was a sculptor; he learnt painting of his uncle, Antonio Badile. After executing several works at Verona, Mantua, and other places in the neighbourhood, by which he acquired considerable reputation, Paolo established himself in Venice, where he ultimately became the rival of Titian, Tintoretto, and other great masters of the Venetian school.

---

* They are engraved by Le Bas, and are now in the Louvre.

† Gault de Saint Germain, *Les trois Siècles de la Peinture en France*, Paris, 1808; *Les Ports de France, peints par Joseph Vernet, &c.*, Paris, 1812; *Biographie Universelle.*

‡ According to Zanetti; Ridolfi says 1532.

After a few years' residence in Venice, he visited Rome about 1563, in the suite of Girolamo Grimani, Venetian ambassador to the papal court. Some time after his return he was invited by Philip II. to Spain to assist in the decorations of the Escurial; but he declined the invitation, on account of his numerous engagements at Venice. This great painter died at Venice, April 20, 1588. He was buried in the church of San Sebastiano, in which he had executed some of his most celebrated works, and a monument was there dedicated to his memory by his two sons, Carlo and Gabriele, and his brother Benedetto: they all followed the profession of Paolo, and, with Battista Zelotti, were his principal scholars and imitators. His brother, Benedetto Caliari, is said to have executed the magnificent architectural back-grounds, for which some of the pictures of this master are so conspicuous. "Paolo Veronese," says Count Algarotti, "was the creator, as it were, of a new manner. Though careless in design, and in costume extremely licentious, he had a most noble fancy, and the utmost fertility of invention. It is difficult to look upon his magnificent pictures without longing to be a party in the scene; and it may justly be said of him, that even his faults are pleasing."* One of the most celebrated works of this painter is the magnificent picture of the "Marriage at Cana," now in the Louvre: this great work contains about 120 figures or heads, comprising portraits of many of the most distinguished persons of the time at Venice, not omitting its most eminent painters.†

No. **26.** THE CONSECRATION OF ST. NICHOLAS, Bishop of Myra, in Syria, in the fourth century. The saint, surrounded by ecclesiastics and other persons, is kneeling before the altar of a church, and is consecrated by a bishop: an angel brings him the mitre and crozier from above. Composition of ten figures of the natural size.

Engraved by R. Golding, for the *Associated Engravers;* and by H. C. Shenton, for Jones's *National Gallery.* On canvas, 9 ft. 5 in. *h.* by 5 ft. 9 in. *w.*

---

* "In quibusdam virtutes non habent gratiam, in quibusdam vitia ipsa delectant." Quintilian, *Inst. Oratur.* xi. 3. Algarotti, *Saggio sopra la Pittura Opere,* Venice, 1791.

† It is engraved by J. B. Vanni. Ridolfi, *Le Maraviglie dell' Arte, &c.* Dal Pozzo, *Vite de' Pittori Veronesi, &c.;* Zanetti, *Della Pittura Veneziana, &c.;* Lanzi, *Storia Pittorica, &c.*

Formerly in the church of San Niccolo de' Frari at Venice. Presented to the National Gallery, in 1826, by the Governors of the British Institution.

No. 97. THE RAPE OF EUROPA. Jupiter, enamoured of Europa, a Phœnician princess, transformed himself into a white bull, and mingled with her father's herds; the princess, struck by the beauty and gentle nature of the beast, ventured to seat herself upon his back, when the animal walked with her to the sea, and plunging in, swam with her to the island of Crete.* Europa has just seated herself upon the bull, who kneels to receive her; her attendant women are arranging her dress. She is again represented in the middle-ground about to enter the sea, and in the extreme distance the bull is swimming with her towards the island.

Engraved by V. Le Febvre; also by De Launay in the *Galerie du Palais Royal*; and by H. Fernell, for Jones's *National Gallery*. On canvas, 1 ft. 11 in. *h*, by 2 ft. 3 in. *w*.

This is the finished study of a large picture now in the Imperial Gallery at Vienna; it is also very similar in composition to the magnificent picture of the same subject by this painter in the ducal palace at Venice. This sketch was formerly in the Orleans collection, and subsequently in that of the Rev. W. H. Carr, who bequeathed it, with the rest of his pictures, to the National Gallery, in 1831.

No. 268. THE ADORATION OF THE MAGI, OR THE WISE MEN'S OFFERING.

"And Joseph also went up from Galilee,"—"to be taxed with Mary, his espoused wife."

"And she brought forth her first-born son, and wrapped him in swaddling clothes, and laid him in a manger; because there was no room for them in the inn."—*Luke* ii. 4, 7.

"Now when Jesus was born in Bethlehem of Judæa, there came Wise Men from the East." "And when they were come into the house they saw the young Child with Mary his mother, and fell down and worshipped him: and when they had opened their treasures they presented unto him gifts; gold, and frankincense, and myrrh."—*Matthew* ii. 1, 11.

The picture represents a ruined building of Roman architecture, with pillars, a portion of which is roofed with thatch, and has served as a stable. Under this roof, on the right of the spectator, is seated the Virgin, somewhat elevated on some loose blocks, and holding in her arms the Infant, who is receiving the adoration of the three Wise Men; the foremost is kneeling; the second is behind him in the same attitude; and on the extreme left of the spectator stands the third. A ray of light, with several winged cherubs hovering along its course, falls upon the Infant;

* See Keightley's *Mythology*.

above is a group of Infant Angels. The retinue of the Magi are behind, some bearing presents, others attending to their horses and camel. Some peasants are looking down from the ruins on the Divine Infant; another figure is seen on the right with some dogs. On the same side are the ox and the ass; some young lambs placed below the Infant appear to be a shepherd's offering. The upper part of the back-ground, on the left, is formed by a stately archway, through which are seen distant mountains. Below, near the right corner, is the date 1573. Composition of sixteen figures, life size.

Engraved by Carlo Sacchi, 1649. On canvas, 11 ft. 7 in. h. by 10 ft. 7 in. w.

Painted in 1573, and originally placed in the church of San Silvestro, in Venice. This church having, about twenty years since, required extensive repairs, the numerous pictures which it contained, comprising works by Tintoret, the Last Supper by Palma Vecchio, and the Adoration of the Magi, above described, were, in 1837, removed from the walls. The intention was to replace these works when the repairs of the building should be completed; but it seems that in the course of restoration the internal design of the church was so much changed that not one of the larger pictures could be fitted to the new altars and compartments. After much delay, a Papal decree, together with an order from the local authorities, was obtained for their sale. In August, 1855, they became the property of Signor Angelo Toffoli, of Venice, from whom, in November, 1855, the Paolo Veronese was purchased for the National Collection. This picture is particularly mentioned in most of the guide books and descriptions of Venice that have been published for the last two centuries. From the following passage in the often reprinted "Forastiero Illuminato della Città di Venezia," it would appear that so lately as 1792 it was the most attractive picture in the church of San Silvestro:—"Many are the pictures (in this church) by Tintoretto, by scholars of Titian, by Palma Vecchio, by Antonio Bellucci, by Carlo Lotto, by Girolamo da Santa Croce, &c. But among them all the famous Adoration of the Magi by Paolo Veronese, which has been engraved by Carlo Sacchi, deserves especial attention." *Giornata quarta*, p. 277. Ed. 1792.* Paolo Veronese often treated this subject; the picture in Santa Corona at Vicenza most resembles the composition above described. A copy of a portion of this composition at Hampton Court, attributed to Carlo Cagliari, was engraved by Gribelin in 1712.

* For other notices of this picture the reader is referred to Ridolfi, *Le Maraviglie dell' Arte*, 1648, p. 302, where it is spoken of in the highest terms; to Sansovino, *Venetia Città Nobilissima*, &c., 1581, p. 65; to Boschini, *Ricche Minere*, p. 253, Ed. 1664, p. 269, Ed. 1733, where it is called the "Famosissimo Quadro;" and to Zanetti, *Della Pittura Veneziana*, 1771, p. 185. In various modern guides it is equally extolled.

No. **294.** The Family of Darius at the Feet of Alexander, after the battle of Issus, B.C. 333. The royal captives having mistaken Hephæstion for Alexander, the queen mother Sisygambis implores pardon of the conqueror, who, pointing to his friend, tells her she has not erred, for that Hephæstion is another Alexander. The elder of the two daughters, Statira, kneeling immediately behind her mother, became the wife of Alexander; she was, however, subsequently put to death by Perdiccas, through the instigation of Roxana, the second Persian wife of Alexander. The captive family, presented to the king by one of the ministers of Darius, is kneeling in the centre of the picture, Alexander and his generals Hephæstion and Parmenio, being on the spectator's right. In the back-ground is a marble arcade, from the top of which many spectators are looking down. The principal figures are portraits of the Pisani family.*

On canvas, 7 ft. 8½ in. *h.* by 15 ft. 6¼ in. *w.*

There is an inferior print by N. R. Cochin in the *Tabellæ selectæ* of C. C. Patina, folio, Padua, 1691; in which work this picture is described as the most celebrated of all the works of Paul Veronese.†

Painted for an ancestor of the Count Pisani. D'Argenville‡ states, on the authority of the Procuratore Pisani of his time, that Paul Veronese, having been detained by some accidental circumstance at the Pisani villa at Este, painted this work there, and leaving it in his room, afterwards informed the family that he had left wherewithal to defray the expense of his entertainment.

Purchased at Venice of the Count Vittore Pisani, in 1857.

VINCI, L. DA.

Leona'rdo da Vinci was born at Vinci, in the Val d'Arno, below Florence, in 1452. His father, Pietro da

* The following description is from the manuscript notes of Rumohr, author of the *Italienische Forschungen*, often quoted in this catalogue:—"The celebrated picture of the wife of Darius mistaking Hephæstion for Alexander. In excellent condition; perhaps the only existing criterion by which to estimate the genuine original colouring of Paul Veronese. It is remarkable how entirely the genius of the painter precludes criticism on the quaintness of the treatment. Both the incident and the personages are, as in a Spanish play, romantically travestied. The princesses with laced boddices and full Venetian gowns, have, nevertheless, a charming and becoming appearance, while the male figures, in their picturesque attire, look chivalrous, refined, and noble. The treatment of colour, especially in the flesh, and the excellence of the execution, are such as to render us almost unjust to other great colourists. In the presence of this work we forget for a time all other productions in painting."

† Inter eximia Pauli Veronensis opera, illud precipue apud venetos Procere Pisanos emicat, in quo Alexander Magnus prostratas matrem uxorem et liberos Darii benignissime excipiens exprimitur.

‡ *Abrégé de la Vie des plus fameux Peintres, &c.* Paris, 1745, vol. 1, p. 182.

Vinci, was a notary, and in 1484 notary to the Signory of Florence. Leonardo was placed early with Andrea Verocchio, a Florentine painter and sculptor, who, finding after a short time that he was surpassed by his pupil in painting, gave up the art in despair, and thenceforth confined himself to sculpture, in which he attained great eminence.

Although Leonardo was completely devoted to painting, his insatiable desire of knowledge led him to the study of many other subjects: he excelled in sculpture, architecture, engineering, and mechanics generally; botany, anatomy, mathematics, and astronomy; he was also a poet, and an admirable extempore performer on the lyre. The letter which he addressed to Lodovico il Moro about the year 1483, offering his services to that prince, gives an extraordinary picture of the acquirements of one man: this memorable letter contains the following passage:—"I will also undertake any work in sculpture; in marble, in bronze, or in terra-cotta: likewise in painting, I can do what can be done, as well as any man, be he who he may." The duke took Leonardo into his service, with a salary of 500 scudi per annum. In 1485 he established an academy of arts at Milan, which eventually had great influence on the development of painting in Lombardy. About ten years afterwards he executed his celebrated picture of the "Last Supper;" it was painted in oil on the wall in the refectory of the Dominican convent of the Madonna delle Grazie, and was generally considered the greatest work that had appeared up to that time in painting; he thus more than warranted the bold assertion in his letter, quoted above.* This was the last work of importance executed by Leonardo at Milan, which he left in 1499, when the Duke Lodovico fled before Charles XII. of France. He returned to Florence, where he was well received by the Gonfaloniere Soderini, who took him into state employ at a fixed salary. He was commissioned by Soderini, in 1503, to paint one of the ends of the council-hall of the Palazzo Vecchio. The celebrated cartoon of "The Battle of the Standard" was the result of this com-

* This great work, owing either to the injudicious selection of materials, or the unfit state of the wall, was already half obliterated within about half a century from the time when it was painted. It has been engraved by Frey, Morghen, Wagner, and A. L. Dick; there are also several copies of it extant, the most valuable is that by Marco d' Oggione, now in the Royal Academy of Arts, in London. See Bossi, *Del Cenacolo di Leonardo da Vinci;* Goethe, *Propylaeen;* and the Author's *Epochs of Painting*, ch. xvi.

mission, but the painting was never completed. The so-called "Cartoon of Pisa," by Michelangelo, was designed for the opposite end of the same apartment.* The subject of Leonardo's cartoon was the defeat of the Milanese under Nicolo Picinino, by the Florentines, at Anghiari, near Borgo San Sepolcro.†

Leonardo, after having visited Milan twice during his second residence in Florence, set out, Sept. 24, 1514, for Rome; he went in the train of Giuliano de' Medici, the brother of Leo X., who introduced the painter to that Pope. His residence in Rome, however, was very short. Leo had commissioned him to execute some work in the Vatican, but finding much apparatus for varnishes, &c., and no sign of commencement, he exclaimed to his attendants—"Ah! this man will never do anything; he thinks of the end before the beginning of his work."‡ This want of courtesy, and likewise a misunderstanding with Michelangelo, appear to have made Rome unpleasant to Leonardo, and he is said to have left it in disgust. He visited Francis I. of France, at Pavia, and entered the service of that monarch with a salary of 700 crowns per annum. He accompanied Francis to France, in Jan. 1517, but his health was now much enfeebled by age, and he executed no new work in France; the King could not even prevail upon him to colour a cartoon of St. Anne and the Virgin, which he had brought with him from Italy.§ He died at Cloux, near Amboise, on the 2d of May 1519, in his 67th year.‖

This great painter had three different styles of execution. His earliest works were painted in the dry manner of the age; his second style is conspicuous for a much greater fulness of

---

* See the notice of Michelangelo in this catalogue.

† There is a print of part of this design by Edelinck. Another, in the *Etruria Pittrice*, professes to be more faithful to Leonardo's design.

‡ "Oimè, costui non è per far nulla, dacchè commincia a pensare alla fine innanzi al principio dell' opera."—Vasari, *Vita di Leonardo.*

§ This drawing is now in the Royal Academy of Arts, in London.

‖ This date is from an old copy of Leonardo's will, once in the possession of the Melzi family, on the back of which was written:—*Morse in Ambosa 2 Mag.* 1519. Le Comte De Laborde, *La Renaissance des Arts à la Cour de France.* Vasari relates that Leonardo da Vinci died in the arms of Francis I., who happened to be with him at the time; but this statement appears to be an error, for the Court was then at St. Germain, and no journey was undertaken on the day in question. Amoretti, *Memorie storiche su la Vita, gli Studj, e le Opere di Leonardo da Vinci*, Milan, 1804; Brown, *The Life of Leonardo da Vinci, with a critical account of his works*, London, 1828; Vasari, *Vite de' Pittori, &c.*; Lomazzo, *Trattato della Pittura*, Milan, 1584; Gaye, *Carteggio Inedito d'Artisti*, Rigollot, *Catalogue de L'Oeuvre de Léonard de Vinci.* Paris, 1849.

form, and for such an original force, and, at the same time, delicacy of light and shade, that he may be almost termed the inventor of *Chiaroscuro;* this is his Milanese style, and it more or less distinguishes the works of the Lombard painters generally: most of the genuine pictures which are attributed to Leonardo belong to this second period. His third or Florentine style differs little from his Milanese, except that, as more mature, it exhibits greater freedom and power. To this period belong his cartoons of "St. Anne," the "Battle of the Standard," his own portrait, now in the gallery at Florence, and the celebrated "Mona Lisa," in the Louvre.

Leonardo's principal work as a sculptor was the model of an equestrian statue of Francesco Sforza, father of the Duke Lodovico il Moro. This model was destroyed by the French, after the departure of Lodovico from Milan, in 1499. Leonardo da Vinci was also the author of numerous treatises, many of which still exist, but very few have been published. The principal of these is the "Treatise on Painting," *Trattato della Pittura,* of which there are several editions in several languages.* His principal scholars were Bernardino Luini, Francesco Melzi, Andrea Salaino, Marco d'Oggione, and

---

* The principal edition of this work is that published at Paris in folio, 1651, by Du Fresne; it is illustrated with drawings by Nicolas Poussin. The best as regards the text, is that of Rome, 1817.

Leonardo's greatest literary distinction however, says Mr. Hallam, is derived "from those short fragments of his unpublished writings that appeared not many years since; and which, according at least to our common estimate of the age in which he lived, are more like revelations of physical truths vouchsafed to a single mind, than the superstructure of its reasoning upon any established basis. The discoveries which made Galileo, and Kepler, and Maestlin, and Maurolicus, and Castelli, and other names, illustrious, the system of Copernicus, the very theories of recent geologers, are anticipated by Da Vinci, within the compass of a few pages, not perhaps in the most precise language, or on the most conclusive reasoning, but so as to strike us with something like the awe of preternatural knowledge. In an age of so much dogmatism, he first laid down the grand principle of Bacon, that experiment and observation must be the guides to just theory in the investigation of nature. If any doubt could be harboured, not as to the right of Leonardo Da Vinci to stand as the first name of the fifteenth century, which is beyond all doubt, but as to his originality in so many discoveries, which probably no one man, especially in such circumstances, has ever made, it must be on an hypothesis, not very untenable, that some parts of physical science had already attained a height which mere books do not record." —*Introduction to the Literature of Europe.* The extracts alluded to were published by Venturi at Paris in 1797, under the following title—"*Essai sur les Ouvrages Physico-Mathématiques de Léonard da Vinci, avec des Fragmens tirés de ses Manuscrits apportés de l'Italie.*" The MSS. in question were taken to France by Napoleon, who is said to have carried these and Petrarch's 'Virgil' to his hotel, himself, not allowing any one else to touch them, exclaiming

others: Gaudenzio Ferrari, though not actually Leonardo's scholar, was one of the principal imitators of his style.

No. 18. CHRIST DISPUTING WITH THE DOCTORS, or Christ arguing with the Pharisees. Composition of five figures, half length, somewhat less than the natural size.

Engraved by D. Cunego, for the *Schola Italica, &c.*; and by W. Radcliffe, for Jones's *National Gallery*. On wood, 2ft. 4½ in. *h.* by 2 ft. 10 in. *w.*

Formerly in the Aldobrandini apartments in the Borghese Palace at Rome. It is mentioned by Ramdhor, who notices the fine expression of the head of Christ, and praises particularly the hands, and the drawing generally. It was imported into this country by Mr. Day in 1800, and was bequeathed to the National Gallery by the Rev. W. H. Carr, in 1831. There are several old copies of it.

VIVARI'NI.

BARTOLOMMEO VIVARI'NI painted at Venice between 1459 and 1498, neither the precise date of his birth or death being known; he was of the family of the Vivarini of Murano in the neighbourhood of Venice. It is recorded of Bartolommeo that he painted the first oil picture that was exhibited in Venice; this was in 1473. This picture is still in the Church of Santi Giovanni e Paolo. The new process of painting was acquired from Antonello da Messina, who, some years before, had learnt the method of the Van Eycks at Bruges.*

Zanetti† praises the colouring of Bartolommeo Vivarini, but remarks, at the same time, on the hard and cutting outline of his forms, both in his earliest and in his latest works, several of which are still to be seen in the Academy and churches of Venice, and in good preservation.

"Questi sono miei" (these are mine). These MSS. were afterwards restored to Milan, where they are still preserved.

An interesting collection of Leonardo's anatomical studies is preserved in the royal library at Windsor. They are small pen-and-ink sketches, made apparently about the year 1490, while attending the demonstrations of Marcantonio della Torre at Pavia. These studies were doubtless made as memoranda for his own use only, in giving his instructions in the Milanese academy. Some portions of the human body, supposed in the history of anatomy not to have been known till a century later, are well defined in Leonardo's drawings; but though careful and minute they are not always correct, and very few could be made serviceable to artists. A few of these sketches were published in a volume by Chamberlain, with other drawings from the same collection, in 1812.

* See the notice of John Van Eyck in this catalogue.

† *Della Pittura Veneziana, &c.* Venice, 1771.

No. 284. The Virgin with the Child in her Arms, the Child sitting upon a cushion. Behind, are standing, one on each side, St. Paul holding a sword, and St. Jerome with a book in his hands. Figures life size, gold ground. Inscribed below—Opus Bartolomei Vivarini de Murano.

In tempera. On wood, 3 ft. 1 in. *h.* by 2 ft. 1 in. *w.*

Originally in the Contarini Gallery.* Purchased at Venice from the Conte Bernardino Corniani degl' Algarotti, in 1855.

OPVS+BARTOMEI+VVARINI+DEMVRANO

WEENIX.

Jan Weenix the younger was born at Amsterdam in 1644, and was the scholar of his father, Jan Baptista Weenix, who, however, died when Jan was only sixteen years old; but even then he had completely acquired his father's style, so that his earlier works cannot be distinguished from those of Jan Baptist Weenix; but he eventually surpassed his father, especially in freedom of execution, and in colouring. He painted a great variety of subjects—figures, animals, birds, landscape, ruins, fruit, and flowers; but his great name was acquired by his pictures of hunts, and dead game. Many excellent examples of his works are in England. He was much employed by John William, Elector of the Palatinate. He died at Amsterdam, September 20, 1719. His pictures have steadily increased in value. Van Gool, writing in 1750, notices 300 florins as a high price to be paid for a picture of dead game by Weenix; Immerzeel, less than a century afterwards, notices much higher sums, up to 1,900 florins, being paid, even in Amsterdam, for a similar piece.†

No. 238. Dead Game, and Dog: landscape back-ground with sportsman in the distance. A couple of hares, a stag, and heron; a fowling-piece, and other implements of the chase, in the fore-ground.

On canvas, 5 ft. $7\frac{1}{2}$ in. *h.* by 5 ft. $1\frac{1}{2}$ in. *w.*

* This picture is fully described in the *Atti dell' Accademia di Venezia*, 1817, p. 43, note, and p. 51, note.

† Van Gool, *Nieuwe Schouburg der Nederlantsche Kunstschilders, &c.*; Immerzeel, *Levens en Werken der Hollandsche en Vlaamsche Kunstschilders, &c.*, 1842.

Signed J. Weenix, f. 1708. Formerly in the Lansdowne Collection which was sold in 1806; bequeathed to the National Gallery by Lord Colborne, in 1854.

WILLIAM OF COLOGNE.

William of Cologne, or Meister Wilhelm, a native of Herle, a village near Cologne, whence he is also named Wilhelmus de Herle, was the earliest distinguished master of the school of the Lower Rhine, and the most renowned painter of his time in the north. This school had attained considerable celebrity at Cologne and Maastricht in the fourteenth century, and even earlier.*

William bought a house at Cologne, and settled there in 1358, with his wife Jutta; 1372 is the last year in which he appears by name in the public accounts of the city, and it was then for the payment of a miniature. In 1378 he died; and his widow was married in the following year to Henry Wynrich, of Wesel, also a painter, settled at Cologne, and apparently Meister Wilhelm's scholar.

Several works are attributed to this old master, at Cologne and elsewhere, wall paintings, and some good *tempera* pictures on panel; the principal of which is the St. Clara altar-piece, now in the Johannis Kapelle, one of the chapels in Cologne cathedral. Meister Stephan or Stephen Lochner, the best master of this school, was the scholar of William of Cologne.†

---

* Wolframb of Eschenbach, writing in the thirteenth century, says in his "Parcival," speaking of the Knight—that no painter of Cologne or Maastricht could have made a better picture than he appeared on horseback. And in an old chronicle of Limburg is written,—"Eodem tempore, 1380, Coloniae erat pictor optimus, cui non fuit similis in arte suâ, dictus fuit Wilhelmus, depingit enim homines quasi viventes." — Fiorillo, *Geschichte der Zeichnenden Künste in Deutschland*, 1815, vol. 1, p. 418; compare Passavant, *Kunstreise, &c.*, p. 403; Schnaase, *Geschichte der Bildenden Kunste, &c.*, vol. vi., p. 423.

† J. J. Merlo, *Nachrichten von dem leben und den Werken Kölnischer Künstler*, Cologne, 1850–52; Schnaase, *Geschichte, &c.*, vol. vi., 1861.

No. **687.** The SANCTA VERONICA, or Holy true Image of our Lord. St. Veronica is represented holding before her the SUDARIUM,* a white cloth containing the miraculous portrait of the Saviour, according to the church legend, with a golden nimbus inscribed Χρς. Ιης. (Christ Jesus). Head, life size.

In tempera,† on wood, 1 ft. 9½ in. *h.* by 1 ft. 1¼ in. *w.*
Formerly in the Lorenz-Kirche at Cologne; purchased at Cologne, at the sale of the pictures of Mr. J. P. Weyer, in 1862.

ZELOTTI.

BATTISTA ZELOTTI was born at Verona about 1532, he was the fellow scholar of Paul Veronese in the school of Badile, and became afterwards the assistant and rival of that great painter: according to Vasari, who mentions him as Battista da Verona, he studied also with Titian. Zelotti worked chiefly in fresco, and as he was much employed in comparatively obscure provincial towns, his works, though excellent, did not obtain him that distinction and competence acquired by his more fortunate rivals, who were employed in capital cities. He died in poor circumstances, aged 60, about 1592. Many of his works have been attributed to his more distinguished rival Paul Veronese.‡

No. **595.** PORTRAIT OF A LADY in a low green dress. Bust, life-size.

On canvas, 2 ft. 4½ in. *h.* by 1 ft. 10 in. *w.*
Purchased at Rome, from Signor Menchetti in 1858.

* The legend of the *Sancta Veronica*, of Edessa, is told by John Damascenus, *De Fide Orthodoxâ*, iv. 16; the miraculous "image" itself is first noticed by Evagrius. Two of these miraculous cloths are mentioned; that carried from Christ by Ananias to Abgarus, King of Edessa, now said to be preserved in the church of San Silvestro in Capite, at Rome; and the other, the handkerchief given by a woman (St. Veronica) to the Saviour to wipe his face with, while carrying his cross in the procession to Calvary, said to be in San Bartolommeo at Genoa. For full details respecting this legend, see the author's "EPOCHS OF PAINTING," p. 143, ed. 1859; consult Gretser, *Syntagma de Imaginibus manu non factis, &c.*, opera, vol. xv., p. 178, *et seq.*

† On the *tempera* employed by the Cologne painters, see Sir Charles Eastlake's "*Materials for a History of Oil Painting*," 1847, p. 101.

‡ Ridolfi, *Maraviglie, &c.*, vol. ii. p. 94, ed. 1835; Dal Pozzo, *Pittori Veronesi, &c.*; Vasari, Ed. Le Monnier, vol. xi. p. 134, where the error of earlier commentators, in assuming Vasari, when speaking of Battista da Verona, to allude to Battista Fontana, is repeated.

ZOPPO.

MARCO ZOPPO, born in Bologna in the earlier half of the fifteenth century, was the fellow pupil of Mantegna in the school of Squarcione at Padua; in the Manfrini gallery at Venice there is or was a Madonna signed *Opera del Zoppo di Squarcione.* But he can scarcely have been, as is affirmed by Malvasia, the pupil of Lippo Dalmasio, of whom the latest known work is of the date 1409. Marco Zoppo was the first distinguished painter of Bologna; his pictures extend from 1471 to 1498; there is a Madonna enthroned, with saints, in the gallery of Berlin, inscribed *Marco Zoppo da Bologna pinxit MCCCCLXXI. in Venexia;* and some fresco decorations of the Casa Colonna at Bologna are dated 1498. He was the master of Francia, and is called sometimes the founder of the school of Bologna: his style is hard and dry, but he bestowed great labour on the finish of the accessories of his pictures.*

No. **597.** ST. DOMINIC, as the Institutor of the Rosary. The saint is standing on a pedestal and pointing with his right hand to a rosary suspended behind him; in his left he holds an open book. Above is Christ in glory, surrounded by angels bearing the instruments of the passion.† Whole length figure, small life-size.

In tempera, on wood, 5 ft. *h.* by 2 ft. 11½ in. *w.*

Formerly in the collection of the Marchese Giovanni Costabili at Ferrara, from which it was purchased for the National Gallery 1858.

ZU'RBARAN.

FRANCISCO ZU'RBARAN was born at Fuente de Cantos, in Estremadura, in the early part of November 1598. His parents belonged to the agricultural labouring class, but discovered early their son's ability, and sent him, when still very young, to the school of Juan de Roélas, at Seville. There he made rapid progress—painting constantly from

---

* Malvasia, *Felsina Pittrice*, i. p. 37, &c., ed. 1841; Vasari, *Vite. &c.*; Waagen, *Verzeichniss der Gemaelde Sammlung zu Berlin, &c.*

† The figure of the saint in this picture, evidently copied from nature, is supposed to be a portrait of Alanus de Rupe, an English Dominican monk who, in 1460, in consequence of a vision, revived the use of the rosary, and the prayers connected with it, as instituted by St. Dominic.—See the "Rosario della glorio ?? Virgine Maria," in Venetia, &c., MDLXIX. folio 10 *b*.

nature, and adopting a forcible natural style which acquired him the name of "the Spanish Caravaggio;" he probably had opportunities of copying some of the works of that master at Seville. Zurbaran's great altar-piece, now in the museum at Seville, the celebrated picture of "St. Thomas Aquinas," painted for the church of the college of that Saint at Seville, was executed before his thirtieth year.

He painted many other celebrated works in the following years at Seville; and subsequently at Madrid, in the Palacio Nuevo, and in the Buenretiro. He was appointed, about the year 1633, painter to Philip III. He was painter also to Philip IV. He died at Madrid in 1662. His principal scholars were—Bernabe de Ayala and the brothers Polanco, distinguished painters of the school of Seville.

Zurbaran's works are uncommon out of Spain; at Seville they are numerous, and the early works from the life of San Pedro Rolasco, at the Merced Calzada, at Seville, are among the best; they exhibit in perfection one of his peculiar excellences,—the skilful management of white draperies. He made great use of the lay figure, and his draperies are generally much studied; the Carthusians were favourite subjects with him. The museum at Seville possesses now the best collection of his works, though not a numerous one: that of the Louvre has been dispersed; it contained, according to the catalogues, ninety-two pictures attributed to Zurbaran; the collection of the Prado at Madrid contains fourteen.* An admirable virgin and child, with the infant St. John, by this painter, is in the collection of the Duke of Sutherland, at Stafford House.

No. **230.** A FRANCISCAN MONK, kneeling in prayer, and holding a skull in his hands. Entire figure of the natural size.

Engraved by Alp. Masson. On canvas, 5 ft. 1 in. *h.* by 3 ft. 3 in. *w.*

This picture formed part of the Spanish Gallery of Louis Philippe in the Louvre, procured for the late King, in Spain, by M. Le Baron Taylor; it was generally considered by connoisseurs one of the best pictures in that gallery;† and at the sale of the collection in London, in 1853, was purchased for the National Gallery.

---

* Cean Bermudez, *Diccionario Historico, &c.*

† See Kolloff, *Königliche Museen, &c. zu Paris*, Paris 1841, who notices this picture as "ein wahres Wunder von Ausdruck," a miracle of expression; and Stirling's *Annals of the Artists of Spain*, London, 1848.

UNKNOWN.

No. **195.** Portrait of a Medical Professor. His left hand rests upon a skull. Half-length.

On wood, 3 ft. 2 in. *h.* by 2 ft. 5¼ in. *w.*

Purchased for the National Gallery, in 1845. This picture was bought as a work of Holbein. It has been attributed, by some eminent connoisseurs, to Nicholas Lucidel, more properly called Neufchatel, a portrait-painter, who resided chiefly at Nuremberg, and who died about the year 1600. Specimens of his works are in the galleries of Munich and Berlin.

Lists of Pictures purchased for, presented and bequeathed to, the National Gallery; arranged according to the order of their acquisition.*

Pictures Purchased.

No.	Subject.	Painter's Name.	When acquired.
1	Raising of Lazarus	Seb. Del Piombo	1824
2	Landscape	Claude	—
3	Concert	Titian	—
5	Sea-port	Claude	—
7	Study of Heads	Correggio	—
12	Landscape	Claude	—
14	Sea-port	——	—
25	St. John	An. Carracci	—
27	Julius II.	Raphael	—
28	Susannah	L. Carracci	—
30	St. Ursula	Claude	—
31	Landscape	G. Poussin	—
32	Rape of Ganymede	Titian	—
34	Venus and Adonis	——	—
36	Land-storm	G. Poussin	—
37	Study of Heads	Correggio	—
38	Rape of the Sabines	Rubens	—
42	Bacchanalian Scene	N. Poussin	—
45	Woman taken in Adultery	Rembrandt	—
47	Adoration of the Shepherds	——	—
49	Portrait of Rubens	Vandyck	—
50	Emperor Theodosius	——	—
52	Gevartius	——	—
53	Landscape	Cuyp	—
67	Holy Family	Rubens	—
76	Christ in the Garden	Correggio	—
88	Erminia and the Shepherds	An. Carracci	—
94	Bacchus and Silenus	——	—
111	Lord Heathfield	Sir J. Reynolds	—
112	Own Portrait	Hogarth	—
113, 114, 115, 116, 117, 118	Marriage "à la Mode"	Hogarth	—
122	Village Festival	Sir D. Wilkie	—
23	Holy Family	Correggio	1825
9	Christ appearing to Peter	An. Carracci	1826
35	Bacchus and Ariadne	Titian	—
62	Bacchanalian Dance	N. Poussin	—
10	Mercury instructing Cupid	Correggio	1834
15	Ecce Homo	——	—
13	Holy Family	Murillo	1837
59	Brazen Serpent	Rubens	—
84	Mercury and Woodman	Salvator Rosa	—

* The collection of Robert Vernon, Esq., of 157 pictures of the British School, presented to the Nation in 1847 is not comprised in these lists.

Pictures Purchased—*continued.*

No.	Subject.	Painter's Name.	When acquired.
168	St. Catherine	Raphael	1839
169	Holy Family	Mazzolini	—
170	Holy Family	Garofalo	—
176	St. John	Murillo	1840
177	Magdalen	Guido	—
179	Holy Family and Saints	Francia	1841
180	Pietà	——	—
181	Holy Family	Pietro Perugino	—
186	Portraits	John Van Eyck	1842
187	Apotheosis of William the Taciturn	Rubens	1843
189	Doge Loredano	Gio. Bellini	1844
190	Jewish Rabbi	Rembrandt	—
191	Christ and St. John	Guido	—
192	Own Portrait	Gerard Dow	—
193	Lot	Guido	—
194	Judgment of Paris	Rubens	—
195	A Medical Professor	Unknown	1845
196	Susannah	Guido	—
197	Boar Hunt	Velazquez	1846
198	St. Antony	An. Carracci	—
213	Vision of a Knight	Raphael	1847
221	Own Portrait	Rembrandt	1851
222	Man's Portrait	J. Van Eyck	—
224	Tribute Money	Titian	1852
230	Franciscan Monk	Zurbaran	1853
232	Adoration of the Shepherds	Velazquez	—
234	Warrior adoring the Infant Christ	School of Gio. Bellini	—
245	Madonna and Child	Pacchiarotto	1854
246	Marriage of St. Catherine	Lorenzo di San Severino	—
247	The Vision of St. Bernard	Fra Filippo Lippi	—
248	Ecce Homo	Niccolo Alunno	—
249	Man's Portrait	Albert Dürer	—
260	Three Saints	The Meister von Liesborn	—
261	Three Saints	——	—
265	Penitent and Saint	Vander Meire	—
266	Pietà	Lambert Lombard	—
226	The Virgin and Child, with angels, &c.	Sandro Botticelli	1855
227	St. Jerome, with Saints	Cosimo Rosselli	—
268	Adoration of the Magi	Paolo Veronese	—
274	The Virgin and Child, enthroned	Mantegna	—
275	The Virgin and Child	Botticelli	—
276	Two Apostles	Giotto	1856
277	The Good Samaritan	Jacopo Bassano	—
278	Triumph of Julius Cæsar	Rubens	—
279	Horrors of War	——	—
280	Madonna and Child	Giovanni Bellini	—
281	St. Jerome Reading	Marco Basaiti	—
282	Glorification of the Virgin	Lo Spagna	—
283	The Virgin and Child, enthroned, surrounded by angels and saints	Benozzo Gozzoli	—
284	The Virgin and Child, St. Paul and St. Jerome	Bart° Vivarini	—
285	Virgin and Child	Girolamo dai Libri	—
286	Virgin and Child, enthroned	Francesco Tacconi	—

Pictures Purchased—*continued.*

No.	Subject.	Painter's Name.	When acquired.
287	Portrait of Lodovico Martinengo	Bart° Veneziano	1856
288	The Virgin adoring the Infant Christ; the Archangel Michael; the Archangel Raphael and Tobias	Pietro Perugino	—
290	A Man's Portrait	J. Van Eyck	1857
291	Portrait of a Lady	Lucas Cranach	—
292	Martyrdom of St. Sebastian	Antonio Pollajuolo	—
293	The Virgin and Child, with saints	Filippino Lippi	—
294	The Family of Darius at the Feet of Alexander	Paul Veronese	—
295	"Salvator Mundi" and the Virgin Mary	Quintin Matsys	—
296	The Virgin adoring the Infant Christ	Domenico Ghirlandajo	—
297	The Nativity, with Saints	G. Romanino	—
298	The Marriage of the two Saints Catherine	Borgognone	—
564	Virgin and Child, with scenes from the lives of the Saints	Margaritone of Arezzo	—
565	The Madonna and Child. Angels adoring	Cimabue	—
566	The Madonna and Child St. Dominic and St. Catherine	Duccio da Siena	—
567	Christ on the Cross	Segna di Buonaventura	—
568	Coronation of the Virgin	School of Giotto	—
569	Coronation of the Virgin, with Angels and Saints	Andrea Orcagna	—
570	The Trinity		
571	Angels Adoring		
572	Angels Adoring		
573	The Nativity		
574	The Adoration of the Kings		
575	The Resurrection of Christ		
576	The Three Maries at the Sepulchre		
577	The Ascension of Christ		
578	The Descent of the Holy Spirit		
579	The Baptism of Christ, and the Birth and Death of St. John the Baptist	Taddeo Gaddi	—
580	St. John the Evangelist lifted up into Heaven	Jacopo di Casentino	—
581	St. John the Baptist, St. John the Evangelist, and St. James the Greater	Spinello Aretino	—
582	The Adoration of the Kings	Fra Giovanni Angelico	—
583	The Battle of Sant' Egidio—1416	Paolo Uccello	—
585	Portrait of Isotta da Rimini	Piero della Francesca	—
586	The Madonna and Child surrounded by Angels and Saints	Fra Filippo Lippi	—
589	The Virgin, an Angel presenting the Child		
590	Christ placed in the tomb	Cosimo Tura	—
591	The Rape of Helen	Benozzo Gozzoli	—
592	The Adoration of the Magi	Filippino Lippi	—
593	The Virgin and Child	Lorenzo di Credi	—

Pictures Purchased—*continued.*

No.	Subject.	Painter's Name.	When acquired.
594	Saints Cosmas and Damianus - -	Emmanuel - - -	1857
184	Portrait of Jeanne d' Archel - -	Antony Moro - -	1858
299	Do. an Italian Nobleman - -	Moretto - - -	—
300	Infant Christ standing on the knees of the Virgin - - - - - - -	Giambattista Cima	—
595	Portrait of a Lady - - - - - -	Battista Zelotti -	—
596	Deposition in the Tomb - - - -	Marco Palmezzano	—
597	St. Dominic - - - - - - - -	Marco Zoppo - -	—
598	St. Francis - - - - - - - -	Filippino Lippi -	—
599	Infant Christ asleep on the lap of the Virgin - - - - - - - -	Marco Basaiti -	—
602	Pietà - - - - - - - - - -	Carlo Crivelli - -	1859
623	Madonna and Child enthroned - -	G. da Treviso - -	—
624	Infancy of Jupiter - - - - - -	Giulio Romano -	—
625	Saint Barnardino of Siena, and other Saints - - - - - - - -	Moretto - - - -	—
626	Head of Masaccio - - - - - -	Masaccio - - -	—
627	Landscape with Waterfall - - -	Ruysdael - - -	—
628	Ditto - - - - - - - - - - -	—	—
629	Madonna and Child enthroned, &c.	Lorenzo Costa -	—
630	Ditto - - - - - - - - - - -	Gregorio Schiavone	1860
631	Portrait of a Lady - - - - - -	F. Bissolo - - -	—
632	Saint, reading - - - - - - -	G. da Santacroce -	—
633	Saint, with Standard - - - - -	—	—
634	Madonna and Infant Christ - - -	Cima da Conegliano	—
635	Madonna and Child, St. John and St. Catherine - - - - - - -	Titian - - - -	—
636	Portrait of Ariosto - - - - - -	—	—
637	Daphnis and Chloe - - - - - -	Paris Bordone -	—
638	Virgin and Child with Saints - -	Francia - - -	—
639	Christ and the Magdalen in the Garden - - - - - - - - -	Francesco Mantegna - - -	—
640	The Adoration of the Magi - - -	Dosso Dossi - -	—
641	The Woman taken in Adultery - -	Mazzolini - - -	—
642	Christ's Agony in the Garden - -	Garofalo - - -	—
643	The Capture of Carthagena; and the Continence of Scipio - - -	Giulio Romano -	—
644	The Rape of the Sabines; and the Reconciliation of the Sabines and Romans - - - - - - - -	—	—
645	The Virgin and Child - - - - -	Albertinelli - -	—
648	The Virgin adoring the Infant Christ - - - - - - - - - -	Lorenzo di Credi -	—
649	Portrait of a Boy - - - - - -	J. da Pontormo -	—
650	Portrait of a Lady - - - - - -	Angelo Bronzino -	—
651	Venus, Cupid, Folly, and Time - -	—	—
652	Charity - - - - - - - - - -	F. del Salviati - -	—
653	Portraits of himself and wife - -	Vander Weyden -	—
654	The Magdalen, reading - - - -	—	—
655	The Magdalen, reading - - - -	Bernard Van Orley	—
656	A Man's Portrait - - - - - - -	Jan de Mabuse -	—
657	Portraits of a Man and his Wife - -	J. Cornelissen - -	—
658	The Death of the Virgin - - - -	Martin Schoen -	—
659	Pan and Syrinx - - - - - - -	Rottenhammer -	—
660	A Man's Portrait - - - - - - -	Fr. Clouet - -	—
663	Christ surrounded by Angels, &c.	Fra Giovanni Angelico -	—

Pictures Purchased—*continued.*

No.	Subject.	Painter's Name.	When acquired
664	The Entombment of Christ - - -	Roger Vander Weyden the elder - -	1860
671	The Madonna and Child enthroned, &c.	Garofalo - - -	—
665	The Baptism of Christ - - - -	Piero della Francesca - -	1861
667	St. John the Baptist and other Saints	Fra Filippo Lippi -	—
668	The Beato Ferretti - - - - - - -	Crivelli - - - -	—
669	St. Sebastian and other Saints - -	L'Ortolano - - -	—
672	His own Portrait - - - - - - -	Rembrandt - - -	—
673	Salvator Mundi - - - - - - - -	Antonello da Messina - - - -	—
674	Portrait of a Lady - - - - - - -	Paris Bordone - -	—
680	Miraculous Draught of Fishes - -	Vandyck - - -	—
685	Landscape - - - - - - - - -	Hobbema - - -	1862
686	Madonna and Child enthroned - -	Memling - - -	—
687	The Sancta Veronica - - - - -	William of Cologne	—
690	His own Portrait - - - - -	Andrea del Sarto -	—

PICTURES PRESENTED.*

No.	Subject.	Painter's Name.	By whom Presented.	When.
19	Landscape - - - - -	Claude - - -	Sir George Beaumont, Bart.	1826
40	Landscape, Phocion - -	N. Poussin - -	——	—
43	Crucifixion - - - - -	Rembrandt - -	——	—
51	Jew Merchant - - - -	——	——	—
55	Landscape - - - - -	Claude - - -	——	—
58	Small Landscape - - -	——	——	—
61	Ditto - - - - - -	——	——	—
64	Return of the Ark - -	S. Bourdon - -	——	—
66	Landscape - - - - -	Rubens - - -	——	—
71	Landscape - - - - -	Both - - - -	——	—
99	Blind Fiddler - - - -	Wilkie - - -	——	—
106	Man's Head - - - -	Reynolds - -	——	—
108	Mæcenas's Villa - - -	Wilson - - -	——	—
110	Niobe - - - - - - -	——	——	—
126	Pylades and Orestes - -	West - - -	——	—
127	View in Venice - - -	Canaletto - -	——	—
74	Spanish Boy - - - -	Murillo - - -	M. M. Zachary, Esq. - - -	—
107	Banished Lord - - -	Reynolds - -	Rev. W. Long -	—
26	St. Nicholas - - - -	P. Veronese -	British Institution	—
33	Vision of St. Jerome - -	Parmigiano - -	——	—
131	Healing the Sick - - -	West - - - -	——	—
109	The Watering Place - -	Gainsborough -	Lord Farnborough	1827
121	Cleombrotus - - - -	West - - - -	W. Wilkins, Esq.	—
46	Peace and War - - -	Rubens - - -	Marq. of Stafford -	1828
105	Landscape - - - - -	Sir G. Beaumont	Lady Beaumont	—
119	Jacques and the Stag -	——	——	—
78	Holy Family - - - -	Reynolds - -	British Institution	—
80	The Market Cart - -	Gainsborough -	——	—
132	The Last Supper - - -	West - - - -	George IV. - -	1829
100	Death of Chatham - -	Copley - - -	Lord Liverpool -	1830
120	Portrait of Nollekens -	Beechey - -	Rev. R. E. Kerrick	1835
143	Lord Ligonier - - - -	Reynolds - -	William IV. -	1836
142	J. Kemble as Hamlet - -	Lawrence - -	——	—
144	Portrait of West - - -	——	——	—
129	Portrait of Mr. Angerstein	——	——	—
147	Cephalus & Aurora - -	Ag. Carracci -	Lord Ellesmere -	1837
148	Galatea - - - - - -	——	——	—
133	Portrait of an Actor - -	Hoppner - -	Mr. Serjt. Taddy	—
136	Portrait of a Lady - -	Lawrence - -	F. Robertson, Esq.	—
130	The Corn Field - - -	Constable - -	Bought by Subscription -	—
165	Plague at Ashdod - -	N. Poussin - -	Duke of Northumberland -	1838
166	Capuchin Friar - - -	Rembrandt - -	——	—
167	Adoration of the Kings -	B. Peruzzi - -	Lord Vernon	1839
171	Portrait of Sir J. Soane -	Jackson - - -	British Institution	—
172	Christ at Emmaus - -	M. da Caravaggio	Lord Vernon -	—
173	Male Portrait - - - -	J. Bassano - -	H. G. Knight, Esq. - - -	—
174	A Cardinal - - - -	C. Maratti - -	——	—
175	Portrait of Milton - -	D. Vander Plaas	C. Lofft, Esq. -	—
178	Sir Calepine - - - -	Hilton - - -	Bought by Subscription -	1841

* The Vernon donation and other recent acquisitions of the British School will be found in the catalogue of that portion of the collection.

Pictures Presented—*continued.*

No.	Subject.	Painter's Name.	By whom Presented.	When.
182	Study of Heads - - -	Reynolds - -	Lady W. Gordon	1841
183	Portrait of Wilkie - -	Phillips - - -	The Painter -	—
185	Portrait of Sir W. Hamilton	Reynolds - -	* - - - - - -	1843
188	Portrait of Mrs. Siddons	Lawrence - -	Mrs. Fitz Hugh	—
215	Saints - - - - - - -	Taddeo Gaddi -	W. Coningham, Esq. - -	1848
216	—	—	—	—
217	Portrait of Wm. Woollett	Gilbert Stuart -	. Farrer, Esq.	1849
218	Adoration of the Magi -	B. Peruzzi - -	E. Higginson, Esq. - -	—
220	Portrait of John Hall -	Gilbert Stuart -	Messrs. Graves and Co. -	1850
225	Assumption of the Magdalen - - - - -	Giulio Romano -	Lord Overstone -	1852
228	Christ driving the Money-changers from the Temple - - -	J. Bassano - -	P. L. Hinds, Esq.	1853
229	Portrait of Benjamin West - - - - -	Gilbert Stuart -	J. H. Anderdon, Esq. - -	—
233	Portrait of William Pitt -	Hoppner - - -	G. Moffatt, Esq.	—
235	Dead Christ - - - - -	Spagnoletto - -	D. Barclay, Esq.	—
236	Castle of St. Angelo -	C. J. Vernet - -	Lady Simpkinson	—
272	An Apostle - - - -	Pordenone - -	Cav. Vallati -	1855
273	Portrait of John Smith -	Sir G. Kneller -	W. Smith, Esq. -	1856
661	Madonna di San Sisto (a tracing) - - -	- - - -	P. & D. Colnaghi, Scott and Co.	1860
666	The Annunciation - -	Fra Filippo Lippi	Sir C. L. Eastlake	1861
670	A Knight of Malta - -	J. da Pontormo	G. F. Watts, Esq.	—
679	An Astronomer - -	F. Bol - - -	Miss E. A. Benett	1862

* Deposited by the Trustees of the British Museum and now temporarily exhibited at South Kensington.

Pictures Bequeathed.*

No.	Subject.	Painter's Name.	By whom Bequeathed.	When.
4	Holy Family - - - -	Titian - - -	Rev. W. H. Carr	1831
6	Landscape - - - - -	Claude - - -	—	—
8	A Dream - - - - -	Michelangelo -	—	—
11	St. Jerome - - - -	Guido - - -	—	—
16	St. George - - - - -	Tintoretto - -	—	—
17	Holy Family - - - -	A. del Sarto -	—	—
18	Christ and the Pharisees	L. Da Vinci -	—	—
20	Ippolito de' Medici and Sebastiano del Piombo	Seb. del Piombo	—	—
21	Portrait of a Lady - -	C. Allori - -	—	—
22	Dead Christ - - - -	Guercino - -	—	—
24	Giulia Gonzaga - - -	S. del Piombo -	—	—
29	Holy Family - - - -	Barocci - - -	—	—
41	Death of Peter Martyr -	Giorgione - -	—	—
48	Tobias and the Angel -	Domenichino -	—	—
54	Woman Bathing - - -	Rembrandt - -	—	—
56	Landscape - - - - -	An. Carracci -	—	—
57	St. Bavon - - - - -	Rubens - - -	—	—
63	Landscape - - - - -	An. Carracci -	—	—
68	Landscape - - - - -	G. Poussin - -	—	—
69	St. John Preaching - -	P. F. Mola - -	—	—
72	Tobias and the Angel -	Rembrandt - -	—	—
73	Conversion of St. Paul -	Ercôle da Ferrara	—	—
75	Landscape - - - - -	Domenichino -	—	—
77	Stoning of Stephen - -	—	—	—
81	Vision of St. Augustin -	Garofalo - - -	—	—
82	Holy Family - - - -	Mazzolini - -	—	—
85	St. Jerome - - - - -	Domenichino -	—	—
91	Sleeping Venus - - -	N. Poussin - -	—	—
93	Silenus - - - - -	An. Carracci -	—	—
95	Landscape - - - - -	G. Poussin - -	—	—
97	Rape of Europa - - -	P. Veronese -	—	—
98	L'Aricia - - - - -	G. Poussin - -	—	—
124	Rev. W. H. Carr - - -	Jackson - - -	—	—
65	Cephalus & Aurora - -	N. Poussin - -	G. J. Cholmondeley, Esq. -	—
39	Nursing of Bacchus - -	—	—	—
128	Portrait of Windham -	Reynolds - -	—	—
139	An Allegory - - - -	A. Kaufmann -	J. Forbes, Esq.	1835
70	Cornelia - - - - -	Padovanino - -	Lt. Col. Ollney	1837
101	Infancy - - - - -	Lancret - - -	—	—
102	Youth - - - - - -	—	—	—
103	Manhood - - - - -	—	—	—
104	Age - - - - - - -	—	—	—
123	Moonlight - - - - -	Williams - -	—	—
138	Ruins and Figures - -	Pannini - - -	—	—
140	Portrait of a Lady - -	Vander Helst -	—	—
79	The Graces - - - -	Reynolds - -	Lord Blessington	—
149	A Calm - - - - -	Vandevelde - -	Lord Farnborough	1838
150	A Gale - - - - - -	—	—	—
151	Leda - - - - - -	P. F. Mola - -	—	—
152	Landscape - - - - -	Vander Neer -	—	—
153	The Cradle - - - -	Maas - - - -	—	—
154	A Music Party - - -	Teniers - - -	—	—
155	The Misers - - - -	—	—	—
156	Study of Horses - - -	Vandyck - -	—	—

The Turner Collection of 105 pictures acquired in 1856, and other recent bequests of pictures of the British School will be found in the British School Catalogue.

Pictures Bequeathed—*continued.*

No.	Subject.	Painter's Name.	By whom Bequeathed.	When.
157	Landscape - - - - -	Rubens - - -	Lord Farnborough	1838
158	Boors Regaling - - -	Teniers - - -	——	—
159	Dutch Housewife - - -	Maas - - - -	——	—
160	Riposo - - - - - - -	P. F. Mola - -	——	—
161	Landscape - - - - -	G. Poussin - -	——	—
162	Infant Samuel - - - -	Reynolds - -	——	—
163	View in Venice - - -	Canaletto - -	——	—
125	Izaak Walton - - - -	Huysman - -	Dr. H. Hawes -	—
199	Lesbia - - - - - - -	Schalcken - -	R. Simmons, Esq.	1846
200	Madonna - - - - - -	Sassoferrato -	——	—
202	Domestic Poultry - -	Hondecoeter -	——	—
204	A Gale - - - - - - -	Bakhuizen - -	——	—
205	Itinerant Musicians - -	Dietrich - - -	——	—
206	Head of a Girl - - -	Greuze - - -	——	—
207	The Idle Servant - - -	Maas - - - -	——	—
209	Landscape with Figures	Both and Poelenburg -	——	—
210	View in Venice - - -	Guardi - - -	——	—
211	A Battle - - - - - -	Huchtenburg -	——	—
212	Merchant and Clerk - -	De Keyser - -	——	—
214	Coronation of the Virgin	Guido - - -	W. Wells, Esq. -	1847
223	A Gale - - - - - - -	Bakhuizen - -	C. L. Bredel, Esq.	1851
479	The Sun rising in Mist -	Turner - - -	The Painter -	1853
498	The Building of Carthage	——	——	—
231	Portrait of Thomas Daniell, R.A. - - -	Wilkie - - -	Miss M. A. Fuller	—
237	Portrait of a Girl - - -	Rembrandt - -	Lord Colborne -	1854
238	Dead Game, &c. - - -	Weeninx - -	——	—
239	Landscape, Moonlight -	Vander Neer -	——	—
240	Crossing the Ford - -	Berchem - -	——	—
241	The Village Beadle - -	Wilkie - - -	——	—
242	Players at Tric-trac - -	Teniers - - -	——	—
243	A Man's Portrait - - -	Rembrandt - -	——	—
244	A Shepherd - - - - -	Spagnoletto - -	——	—
267	Landscape - - - - - -	Wilson - - - -	Richard and Miss C. J. Garnons - -	—
269	A Knight in Armour -	Giorgione - -	Samuel Rogers, Esq. - -	1855
270	'Noli me Tangere' - -	Titian - - -	——	—
271	'Ecce Homo' - - -	Guido - - -	——	—
289	The Night Watch - -	Rembrandt - -	Rev. T. Halford	1857
600	The Blind Beggar - -	Dyckmans - -	Miss Jane Clarke	1859

CPSIA information can be obtained
at www.ICGtesting.com
Printed in the USA
LVHW100445110522
718424LV00003B/238

9 783375 006358